END OF DAYS

Other Books by Dennis Danvers

Circuit of Heaven
Time and Time Again
Wilderness

END
OF
DAYS

Dennis Danvers

AVON · EOS

AVON BOOKS, INC.
1350 Avenue of the Americas
New York, New York 10019

Copyright © 1999 by Dennis Danvers
Interior design by Kellan Peck
ISBN: 0-380-97448-7
Visit our website at **www.avonbooks.com/eos**

Library of Congress Cataloging in Publication Data:
Danvers, Dennis.
    End of days / Dennis Danvers.
        p.   cm.
    I. Title.
PS3554.A5834E53   1999   99-20947
813'.54—dc21   CIP

First Avon Eos Printing: June 1999

AVON EOS TRADEMARK REG. U.S. PAT. OFF. AND IN OTHER COUNTRIES, MARCA REGISTRADA, HECHO EN U.S.A.

Printed in the U.S.A.

FIRST EDITION

QPM   10   9   8   7   6   5   4   3   2   1

For Sarah

There is special providence in the fall of a sparrow. If it be now, 'tis not to come; if it be not to come, it will be now; if it be not now, yet it will come. The readiness is all.

—Shakespeare, *Hamlet*

1

DR. DEATH

DONOVAN CARROLL SAT UNDER THE STRIPED AWNING OF A sidewalk cafe and watched the rain. It drummed the taut canvas overhead, and a fine, cool mist settled on his face and hands. Dangling from the awning, a whirling wind chime emitted a high melodic clatter. He took a deep breath. The rain smell left a tang at the back of his throat and made him feel a little high.

Every year some misguided senator introduced a bill to control the weather, arguing, as required for any innovation, that it was both scientifically possible and socially desirable. Donovan didn't know about the possible part. He was no scientist. But any random occurrence was desirable as far as he was concerned. It was bad enough contemplating eternity without the prospect of an endless succession of sunny days. Apparently, most people agreed with him: The rain was still falling when and where it liked.

Donovan checked his watch. He was waiting to meet Freddie—late as usual, like most people. Donovan's anachronistic devotion to timeliness—including his affectation of carrying a watch, for goodness' sake—was a sure sign of his eccentricity. An image he sometimes cursed and sometimes nurtured. He caught the waiter's attention and pointed at his coffee cup. He watched the waiter pour.

When he was a kid, there hadn't been any waiters. You pushed a button or a glowing icon. The world was a huge

1

free-of-charge vending machine. But these days jobs were making a comeback. Anything to fill the time. With Donovan's coffee poured, the waiter tidied up the other tables, none of which needed any tidying. Then he stood by the door, a towel draped over his arm, a crisp white apron from his waist to his shins, staring past Donovan at the rain-swept streets, looking, Donovan decided, vaguely military.

Donovan wondered how old the waiter might be, wondered whether he'd been a waiter in the real world, whether he'd ever lived in the real world at all, for that matter. Maybe he was a newbie like Donovan himself, a virtual life formed from the dance of his parents' genetic uploads, choreographed by the strictest laws of biological science, pure life without the muss and fuss of flesh and blood.

He wondered all those things, but he couldn't ask the waiter. It was rude to ask questions about life before the Bin, especially if, like Donovan, you didn't have one. "Born in the Bin with no body to burn" was the phrase that Donovan had grown up hearing, just as, he imagined, the young of a couple of centuries earlier had gritted their teeth to "footloose and fancy-free." Both were licenses for a certain eccentricity tinged with misplaced envy.

Donovan was about to turn forty, an age when men used to start feeling old, calculating their lives were half over, lamenting they were halfway to nowhere, crying out, "Is this all there is?" Donovan envied them. It'd taken him only forty years to decide his life was pointless. Now he had eternity to figure out what to do about it.

He sipped on his coffee and opened up the newspaper he'd brought with him. He usually didn't read newspapers, though they were all the rage. A nice fat paper could last you all day. The lead story was about the upcoming centennial of the Bin, still months away. There were numerous expert opinions as to "what this incredible milestone might have to say to the human race." Donovan read that part over. The writer had indeed created a talking milestone. And no matter which expert made it talk, it seemed to say pretty much the same thing as far as Donovan could tell:

It's only been a hundred years, and already immortality is getting old.

Donovan looked down the page at a small story about a bill to implement transporter technology, modeled after the old *Star Trek* TV show. The photo showed a senator from Thailand dressed in the knit pajamas that had once passed for the garb of the future. Donovan skipped the technical debate. Nobody much cared about that part of it anymore. If people wanted an innovation badly enough, they'd convince themselves that anything was possible. If they didn't really want it, they'd say the *wheel* was unproven technology. The transporter didn't stand a chance. Who but a masochist would want a technology that saved time *and* decreased privacy?

Naturally, there was a story about the real world, the tabloids' favorite subject—where people still died every day in any gruesome or touching way a writer might care to imagine. No one could check your facts.

The Bin had been cut off from the real world for seventy years now, after some religious zealots attempted to wipe out the Bin with a virus—and almost succeeded. To ensure the future safety of the Bin, all connection with the real world had been severed, thus duping the fundies into thinking their virus had worked. Every schoolboy heard the story ad nauseam. Newman Rogers, inventor of the Alternative Life Medium Assembly (ALMA, commonly called the Bin) that gave the gift of eternal life to all humankind, outwits Gabriel, the wicked and fanatical leader of the Christian Soldiers. Donovan found the whole business saccharine and tedious. The heroes always a bit too pure and the villains— the scenery-devouring fundies—a bit too thick. But it was the Bin's only fling with cataclysm, and everyone loved to wax nostalgic and philosophical about it.

This article rehearsed the Bin's only "brush with disaster," then investigated the claim that the fundies had not been fooled and were preparing an all-out missile attack. With my luck, Donovan thought, they'll miss. Besides the

Bin had dozens of backups waiting in the wings. It would be like trying to wipe out a swarm of bees with a .22.

Not that he believed any of this babble. The writer of the article had probably made the claim in the first place so that he'd have something to investigate. There were no murders, robberies, wars, plagues, famines, rapes, plane crashes, starving babies. What was a writer to do? Immortality even took the wind out of gossip's sails. It was hard to be impressed by scandalous behavior when you stopped to ask yourself who the hell would care in a few centuries what went on several spouses ago.

Donovan turned to the inside pages, looking for the article that'd prompted him to buy the damn thing in the first place. Against his better judgment, he'd agreed to an interview, and now he wanted to see how badly he'd been misquoted. The interviewer, Fawn Riverside, a perky 150-year-old who'd just Started Over as a journalist, had treated him as if he were an aficionado of Bigfoot or the ghost of Elvis, and he'd thought she was a complete idiot.

He paused over a piece claiming that Newman Rogers, inventor and patron saint of the Bin, was alive somewhere, incognito, running the whole show. Probably lived down the street from Elvis, Donovan thought. There was the familiar photo of Rogers making his last public appearance, dwarfed behind a podium, his long white hair blowing every which way. Donovan smiled at the little man and shook his head, thinking, If he is still alive, he must be crazy as a bedbug by now. He checked the byline on the story against the missile-lobbing fundies piece, and indeed, they were the same: GWENNA R. MORSE. Probably a pal of Fawn's.

Donovan turned the page, and his own dour face stared out at him in black and white—the familiar book jacket photo. The photographer had told him *not* to smile, to look, instead, "authorial." To keep from laughing, Donovan had scrunched his face into an exaggerated frown. "Perfect," the photographer had said.

Donovan winced at the headline above the photo: DR. DEATH MUSES ON MORTALITY. It wasn't just the inevitable alliteration. He'd asked the interviewer not to call him by that ridiculous nickname, first coined by the reviewer in the *Times*, who seemed blissfully ignorant of the fact that it had been taken more than a century earlier. It made him feel silly, not a feeling he enjoyed or sought after. Which, according to Freddie, was precisely his problem. "High silliness, Donnie," Freddie counseled. "Leave high seriousness to the dying."

The article itself wasn't so bad, and she did correctly report the time and location of his lecture tomorrow night. After an insipid opening, Fawn transcribed the interview pretty much verbatim as far as Donovan could remember, even though her questions were idiotic. Still, he knew most people would read it and decide that Donovan, not Fawn, was the idiot.

And maybe he was. He'd been born immortal, had never known anyone who'd died a natural death, and yet he'd studied death since he was a boy, even learning Sanskrit so he could read *The Tibetan Book of the Dead* in the original. His parents had encouraged him. It kept him busy. When he reached maturity, they, like the journalist, had Started Over, divorcing each other (his fifth, her sixth), renouncing their pasts, including Donovan.

Starting Over was said to be a healthy thing, a sure cure for immortality anxiety. Donovan thought of it as the latest wisdom of the Ostrich Academy. Mother lived in a memory hive on the banks of the Yangtze. He saw her every year or so, and she'd get him mixed up with the dozens of other sons she remembered from the other hive moms. She always reminded him, when she spoke at all, that she wasn't his mother anymore. Father had moved to a minimalist community where everything looked like a line drawing, but he hadn't stayed there long, and Donovan didn't know where he'd gone, or who he was this time around. Donovan checked the suicide records every once in a while. So far, his dad's number hadn't come up.

In a sidebar was a piece on the suicide rate. He skimmed the familiar statistics, the most recent and most famous suicides, the predictable analysis. Sure enough, they managed to mention Nicole—"wife of Donovan Carroll, popularly known as 'Dr. Death.'"

Three years after they were married, Nicole jumped from a bridge to her death, after a series of unsuccessful suicide attempts. "Practice runs," she used to call them. He sometimes wondered if that hadn't been the attraction, that if he stuck with her, someday he'd see death close up and learn its secrets. If that was the plan, it hadn't worked. She left him a note that never mentioned death, only the unbearable burden of life.

The death he wanted to understand didn't come invited. It showed up unannounced, ready or not, the sole inevitability, case closed. It wasn't a decision you made because you didn't care enough to live. He folded up the paper and shoved it to one side. The ink came off on his fingertips, and he wiped them on a napkin. He shouldn't read newspapers, he told himself. They always upset him. He lit a cigarette and blew a cloud of smoke into the rain.

As Donovan was finishing his cigarette, he spotted Freddie a couple of blocks away, strolling toward the cafe through the driving rain. He wore peasant clothes, baggy muslin shirt and pants, a broad-brimmed straw hat. He was barefoot, walking in the gutters where the water was deepest. The rain gathered on the brim of his hat and formed a slender waterfall a few inches in front of his face. He was grinning from ear to ear.

He stepped under the awning and took off his hat with a flourish, showering Donovan with water. "I just adore the rain," Freddie announced as he sat down at the table. A pool of water formed at his feet. "Sorry I'm late. I got caught up in the whole Gene Kelly thing." He looked down at himself and said, "Clothing, dry and press."

As Donovan and Freddie watched, Freddie's sodden clothes dried and pressed themselves. "It's those little nano-thingies they introduced a few years back," Freddie said. "I can just imagine all these little machines chugging away to make me warm and toasty."

"It's programming, and you know it," Donovan said. "I take it you want to do the 'Gene Kelly thing,' but you don't want to experience the wet and cold afterward."

Freddie groaned. "Oh, Donnie, you are s-o-o-o serious. There are drugs for all that angst, you know."

Donovan smiled. "So you keep telling me."

The waiter stood dutifully by the table, patiently waiting for a lull in the conversation. "Hot chocolate," Freddie said. "With marshmallows." The waiter walked into the cafe, and Freddie watched him go. "Cute butt, don't you think?"

"If you say so."

Freddie arched a brow. "We each have our areas of expertise."

Donovan laughed. "And yours is programming."

Freddie made a face. "Ugly."

Freddie was one of Donovan's few friends. He'd come up after a lecture about a year ago and introduced himself. They'd ended up talking most of the night about death. At first Donovan thought Freddie might be coming on to him, but that wasn't it. He was more paternal than anything else—a frivolous, brilliant father who made him laugh— absolutely nothing like his real father—what passed for "real" in the Bin, that is. Biologically, he had no father, no mother.

Freddie pointed at the newspaper. "I see you've been reading about yourself. You're getting to be quite the celebrity, Dr. Death." For all his silliness, Freddie was the best programmer in the Bin. He'd worked on the Bin's design with Newman Rogers and had been one of its original inhabitants. Freddie knew quite a bit about being famous.

"Don't start, Freddie. I have no desire to be a celebrity. I just want to make people think."

"Ah, youth!" Freddie sighed. "I can't imagine a more hazardous, more frustrating occupation."

The waiter arrived with hot chocolate. Once again Freddie watched the waiter's retreating butt. "People don't want to think, Donnie. They want to enjoy themselves."

"Mindlessly?"

" 'Mindlessly' can be quite delicious." Freddie scooped up a spoonful of hot chocolate and marshmallow and put it in his mouth, savoring it, pulling the spoon out slowly. "Even intellectual pleasure requires a certain mindlessness, don't you think? Tussling with some novel or neutrino as if it were the only thing in the universe that mattered."

"But if it just goes on and on forever without end, how do we decide that *anything* matters?"

Freddie rolled his eyes and waved his spoon in the air. "If it feels good, Donnie, it matters. If you have to *decide* when something feels good, you have my deepest sympathies."

"Is that why people read my books—to 'feel good'?"

"Of course it is. They read all about death and say, 'Glad it's not *us!*' " Freddie hugged himself and gave a theatrical shudder.

Donovan looked out at the rain. It was finally beginning to slack off. "Maybe you're right."

Freddie scooped up two more marshmallows, admired them, and turned them loose. "And maybe I'm not." He laid his spoon down on his saucer. "You know that little program you wanted? I finished it."

For an upcoming seminar, Donovan had asked Freddie to write a virtual death experience based on hundred-year-old recordings of the dying's last conscious moments. The so-called near-death experience had been discredited as superstitious hokum—the brain's last electrochemical hurrah—but it was still as close to death as anyone in the Bin was likely to come without committing suicide. "Did it work?" Donovan asked.

"It worked all right. But I don't think you can use it. I did what you suggested, found a first-rate upload of a woman's death—the dark tunnel, the blinding light, dead loved ones coming to greet her—a classic. Then I set up a program to patch into a user's memories to give them a virtual near-death experience based on their own personal history. Three people tried it. The first two went fine, but they were newbies like you. The third one . . . Maybe I should just show you."

"Come on, Freddie. What happened?"

Freddie picked up his spoon, scooped up a single marshmallow in a puddle of chocolate. "She died."

"You mean she killed herself?"

Freddie thought about this a moment, rocking his head from side to side. "That, I suppose, is subject to interpretation, but I'd say no. She died." He slid the spoon into his mouth.

DONOVAN WAITED IMPATIENTLY WHILE FREDDIE FINISHED his hot chocolate. He wouldn't tell Donovan what the big mystery was, and Donovan had to admit he was enjoying that rarest of emotions in the Bin: suspense. Someone had died. How could that have happened unless she'd killed herself? It was impossible.

When the last drops of his chocolate were consumed, Freddie chose another walk in the rain, while Donovan insisted on taking the Metro to Freddie's place. Donovan didn't have any "nano-thingies" in his clothes, and Freddie wouldn't answer his questions anyway.

Donovan just missed the train and had to wait five minutes for another. If Freddie didn't spend too much time dancing along the way, he might get there first. Donovan had asked Freddie once if he didn't feel ridiculous acting like a kid when he was 164 years old. Freddie said no. He'd felt ridiculous when he was just a kid in his twenties, when all his friends were dying in the second AIDS epidemic and he was trying to act old and wise and strong for the next poor bastard who was going to die. "*That* was ridiculous," Freddie said. "That was truly ridiculous."

A holo-ad for Depression World was playing in front of the station platform: Black roadsters and tommy guns. Dust Bowl victims. Women in slender lamé gowns and golden bobs. A Wobbly taking a riot stick across the jaw—the police uniforms looking like something from another planet, boxy-shaped and festooned with buttons. It ran through the cycle of images in a minute or so, then the slogan appeared in six-foot letters: LET THE DEPRESSION LIFT YOUR SPIRITS AT DEPRESSION WORLD™.

"I been there," a woman on the platform told him. "Save your money. You want an *experience,* go to Prehistoria. They got this saber-toothed tiger will scare the crap out of you." She boarded the car directly in front of her, and Donovan got into the car behind it and took a seat.

A couple of boys, a tall one and a short one, were decorating the other side of the car with a can of spray paint. Both looked to be about eleven. FUCK, they wrote in block letters as tall as they could make them, taking turns with the letters so it came out FuCk. A couple of seats behind Donovan a proper-looking man in a suit—a lawyer, most likely—watched the boys through narrowed eyes. When they'd completed their one-word sentence, he sat up in his seat and stretched out his hand. "May I borrow that?" he asked.

The kids traded a glance, and the short one shrugged, handing over the can of paint. "Sure, why not?" Apparently, it was his can of paint.

The man stood in the aisle and selected a spot—the map of the Metro system most people had memorized a hundred years ago—a square yard of unobstructed Plexiglas set into the wall. The man crouched before it like some martial-arts master, and what Donovan had always regarded as an unnecessary map became a blank Plexiglas slate. The man depressed the button on the can, moving his hand quickly, with a little flick of the wrist at the end. It only lasted a second. The result looked like a jelly donut trying to form itself into letters. Unlike the kids' FuCk, it was dripless, almost elegant. Donovan peered hard at the intricate shape. Though he knew half a dozen systems of hieroglyphics, he could make no sense of it.

"What's that?" the tall kid asked.

"That's my tag," the man said. "I wondered if I could

still do it. Haven't done it in a hundred and thirty-two years." He tossed the paint can to the short kid, who bobbled but caught it. The boys looked at the tag without comment and set to work painting a giant penis in the aisle. The man slumped back into his seat.

As the train hurtled along, Donovan kept trying to read the tag. This would be his only chance. It'd be wiped clean once no one was looking. Vandalism was automatically erased from the Bin. He heard the doors open and close behind him as the boys moved on to the next car.

The proper-looking man stood up as the train slowed, and Donovan pointed at the tag. "What does it say?"

The man smiled, a broad smile transforming his face completely. "Byte," he said, "with a *y*. My tag was 'Byte.' " He continued to smile as the train came to a stop and the doors slid open. "Thanks for asking," he said, stepping off the train. Donovan looked back as the train pulled out of the station, and the man smiled and waved.

When Donovan turned around, the tag was gone, the FUCK and the penis as well. Donovan tried to picture the brainlike shape of the tag in his mind, and he could almost see how the lines formed a chubby rendering of BYTE.

He looked up and down the spotless car. They could've left the tag, he thought. What on earth would it've hurt?

FREDDIE'S PLACE NEVER SEEMED TO LOOK THE SAME WAY twice. Today he was going for a Mayan temple look. The rain had stopped, and the stones glistened in the sun. Donovan sat on the steps and checked his watch: 11:25, Eastern time. He had to laugh at himself. What did that even mean anymore? He wasn't on the surface of the Earth, much less in a particular swath of the sun. He was an electrical pattern, a string of information inside the Bin, a quasiorganic crystalline structure about the size of three or four football stadiums orbiting the Earth, drawing its sustenance from the sun. For all he knew, the real Eastern time zone and everyone who might conceivably care what time it was were glowing embers.

The one bit of real-world rumor Donovan thought likely was that without heathens to kill, the various permutations of fundies had started blowing each other up. If there was only One Truth, no one could afford to be Wrong. When King on the Mountain was no mere game but a moral imperative, *The meek shall inherit the earth* would quickly devolve into *The meek shall bite the dust.*

Perhaps the true meek live in here, Donovan thought. Meek enough to trade their physical existence for life everlasting, hiding from death under a clever rock. What did the brave inherit, he wondered, when they died in their bodies, when—as the old phrase used to have it—their time ran out?

AS HE WAITED FOR FREDDIE, DONOVAN ENTERTAINED HIM-self by translating the hieroglyphs above the massive stone doorway. It took him awhile to get it right: TOO MUCH OF A GOOD THING CAN BE WONDERFUL. Donovan laughed out loud.

Freddie walked up the steps. "I'm glad you approve," he said. "Mae West said that."

"Who's she?"

"Early-twentieth-century hedonist philosopher and sex goddess. I'll download you the movies. You'll love her."

They went into Freddie's workroom, a windowless space, softly lit, thick carpet on the floor and halfway up the walls— Freddie's own blank slate, where he could make anything happen, or seem to happen. Take your pick.

Freddie sat down at a vintage computer console, his interface of choice. Donovan perched on a hillock of carpet that seemed made for that purpose. As he settled in, it became a tiny hill overlooking a field of some grain or other.

"It's sorghum," Freddie said. He was patching Donovan into whatever he was about to run, and he'd picked up the emerging question. "The woman who died is . . . was . . .

Simone Mirabelli. This whole rural thing was hers. I wrote the program so that you can choose where you're going to die." Freddie shrugged. "I thought it was a nice option. Anyway, Simone was a wee bit of a holdout. She was raised by her grandparents on a farm and lived in the real world with them until their deaths in the late sixties. They raised sorghum.

"I recorded everything, of course. I figured we'd start with her death." Freddie rose from his console and joined Donovan on the hillside. "That is, if you're ready."

"I've got a million questions," Donovan said.

"I take that as a yes. You want first-person perspective or third-?"

Donovan opened and closed his mouth, all worked up over something he couldn't quite place. It was just another virtual, he reminded himself. "Third-," he said.

Freddie addressed his computer, "You heard the man, snookums. Run it."

The ceiling transformed into dark heavy clouds, low and threatening. A strong wind, heavy with the scent of ozone, blew into Donovan's face, forcing him to squint. Down below him, Simone Mirabelli stood naked in the sorghum field, looking off at the dark horizon. The sorghum was flattened to the ground, and Simone's long dark hair streamed out behind her. Her skin gave off a luminous glow. The horizon flickered with lightning, and thunder shook the ground.

"What in the hell is she up to?" Donovan whispered.

"It's how she chose to die," Freddie said in a normal voice. Simone didn't seem to notice. "Not a bad choice, I'd say."

Donovan was about to ask what he meant, when a bolt of lightning came out of the clouds and struck Simone in the chest, knocking her into the air like a rag doll. As she fell to the ground, a glowing version of herself remained erect, as if the lightning had knocked a dark husk off— what? Her soul? The sorghum field was gone. Sky and earth had darkened to complete blackness. The wind died down to a light breeze with a damp yeasty smell. There was a sound hanging in the air like the dying note of an enormous bell, barely audible, but it never quite faded away.

Donovan could tell by the way that Simone was standing—her shoulders back so that her spine made a graceful curve—that she wasn't afraid, far from it. The blackness was pierced by a circle of light that expanded slowly, growing brighter and brighter.

"I've toned down the light," Freddie said softly. "It was too bright to look at." Simone, however, stared into it and began walking toward it.

It was then Donovan realized the light was some distance away, at the end of a long tunnel, like the inside of a cornucopia, or a tornado laid on its side, swirling with images of people and places changing too fast to take in.

As the light grew, Donovan could make out the silhouettes of people standing in the light, perhaps a dozen. Two of them began to grow larger, and he realized they were walking toward Simone. A man and a woman. Old and wrinkled. What would probably be eighty or ninety in a real person. A chill went up Donovan's spine.

The three figures, all aglow, came together maybe ten yards ahead of him, wrapping their arms around one another in a strong embrace. The old woman seemed to say something, but there was no sound.

"Turn it up," Donovan whispered intently.

"It's up all the way," Freddie said. "Watch this part."

The three of them looked back toward Freddie and Donovan as if they could actually see them watching this recording. They were almost as bright as the light behind them now. They gave what could only be described as a smile of sympathy, turned away arm in arm, and took a step toward the light.

The whole thing winked out, and Freddie and Donovan were sitting in an empty room. It was over.

"What happened to the rest of it?" Donovan asked. His heart was racing, and he was having trouble catching his breath. Intensity did not come easily for Donovan. There was only one other thing that even came close to this, and that had been a very long time indeed.

"There is no rest of it. I was accessing her consciousness. She . . . broke the connection."

"What does she say happened?"

"Nothing. I told you. She's dead."

"You didn't restore her? She wasn't backed up?"

Freddie let Donovan's shrillness hang in the air for a moment, let him get a grip. "Of course I did. She was showing no life signs at all, so I restored her. She opened her eyes, said 'Leave me alone,' and promptly died again. Her body's in the next room."

"This isn't funny, Freddie."

"Even I will have to agree with you there."

Donovan followed Freddie into the bedroom where Simone Mirabelli's body lay on the bed. Donovan had never seen a dead person. But he didn't have to touch her, take her pulse, or watch her breathing to know she was dead. There was something missing, an absence he'd never felt before. He looked over his shoulder, as if the tunnel might still be there behind them in the next room.

"You didn't try again?"

"She did ask me not to, but yes, I did. Her file is hopelessly corrupted."

"And you checked the suicide records?"

"Of course."

"Did you check again? Maybe it just hadn't showed up yet."

"All suicides are logged the instant they occur, a matter of instantaneous public record. I should know, I wrote the damn code for all the suicide routines. But yes, I checked again."

"Have you tried to locate her?"

"Of course. She's listed as deceased."

" 'Deceased'? What the hell's going on here, Freddie? Was there a virus in your program?"

"A virus?" Freddie drew himself up. "Not likely."

"Then what happened?"

"I'd say it was ghosts," Freddie said.

"The people in the recording?"

"Her grandparents. I found their last passport photos They're about ten years younger and not nearly so beatific, but it's them, all right. The program was written so that the user would be patched into Carmelita Sanchez's near-death experience, substituting people and places from their own past, but essentially following her experience. Once those two start walking out of the light, however, Simone Mirabelli was on her own."

"Or not."

"Exactly." Freddie clapped a hand on his shoulder. "You want a drink? I do."

FREDDIE GAVE HIM A DRINK, AND DONOVAN DOWNED IT quickly, then asked for another. It was Irish whiskey. "In honor of your heritage," Freddie said.

"I've never set foot in Ireland," Donovan said.

"Well, now it's set foot in you."

They went out into a courtyard, thick with tropical plants, still dripping from the rain. Among the plants were sandstone animals, their features eroded to an almost smooth surface. A waterfall fell from somewhere above the treetops into a rock-rimmed pool. A school of foot-long koi moved slowly beneath the surface. Donovan sat down on a moss-covered stone by the pool, running his fingers over the slightly prickly moss tips. Freddie never seemed intimidated by endless possibilities, constantly reveling in the rich details of life. Why can't I do that? Donovan wondered.

"You like the Bin, don't you, Freddie?"

"What's not to like?"

Freddie pushed up his sleeve and plunged his hand into the pool. The koi wheeled about and came to his hand, sliding the length of their bodies up against it. As they moved through his palm, he squeezed them gently. He was petting his fish. Donovan had seen him do this before.

These weren't just holo-fish but uploads from his real life before the Bin.

"I've had these fine finny fellows for over a hundred years, fed them every day. I love them, and they love me. There're worse places than the Bin, Donnie."

But Donovan kept seeing Simone Mirabelli's face just before she turned away from life into—what? She knew, and he didn't. He couldn't help it. He envied her knowledge. "But after what we just saw happen to that woman—doesn't that prove there's something after death? Something we're denying in here—like children who refuse to grow up?"

Freddie slowly pulled his hand out of the water, scratching the heads of a couple of the more boisterous koi before they sank beneath the surface. He let the water drip off his slender fingers, then shook them dry. "Oh, Donnie, you can do better than that tired old Peter Pan thing again." He gave a little shudder. "I abhor tights. Make me look bony."

"You're missing my point."

"No, I'm not. I'm teasing you. Besides, we didn't prove a thing. What we saw were her *perceptions* of what happened. I don't have to explain the difference to a bright lad like you, do I?"

"But what do you think? Did it happen or not?"

"Oh, I think it happened. So what?"

"What do you mean, 'So what'? That changes everything."

"I think you're more Irish than you admit. Need to drink more, though. You think God or the cosmic design or something or other intended for everyone to die and cozy up with the Big Bright Light, but along came the evil old Bin and ruined everything. Well, gosh, I guess we just outsmarted God, then, huh? P-lease! I'm a great programmer, but I'm not that good. Sorry, Donnie, if things are *meant* to be, the Bin has as much right to meaning as anything else."

"But look around you. People are going crazy with boredom. The only reason they have to live is their fear of death."

Freddie smiled. "Catchy. Wasn't that in your last book? Trust me. It's a bad sign when you start quoting yourself."

Freddie had him. He was particularly fond of that line, used it quite often. "Okay. I'm being a pompous jerk. But, Freddie, you've got to admit—people aren't happy."

"People are the same as they ever were. Happiness is like most religions—more people talk about it than actually practice it. They should stop and pet the fish."

" 'Pet the *fish*'?"

"Don't be snotty. Stick your pompous little digits in there and try it, Dr. Carroll."

Donovan rolled his eyes and stuck his hand in the water, fully expecting the fish to wrap themselves around his hand, as they had with Freddie's. But they only circled cautiously, and in spite of himself, he felt disappointed. Freddie plunged in his hand beside Donovan's, and the fish came to him again. "Go ahead," Freddie said. "Pet them."

Slowly, cautiously, Donovan moved his hand into the school of fish and stroked their sides with his fingers. Freddie withdrew his hand, and the fish let Donovan continue to pet them. Shy at first, they gradually warmed to his attentions and jostled against his hand. He smiled at the sensation. When he pulled his hand out of the water, he was still smiling. Perhaps Freddie had a point.

"Don't be so hard on people, Donnie. Maybe when they get bored enough, they'll finally find something to do with their lives that's truly interesting—something new in the cosmic design."

"Maybe." The fish were weaving back and forth, apparently content with their immortality. "Do you really think those were spirits who came for Simone Mirabelli, not just her memories playing out?"

"I do indeed. I believe they were as real as you or me, which, if you think about it, isn't saying a whole, whole lot." He laughed as if that pleased him.

"What do you think would happen if I ran that program?"

Freddie sighed. "As I told you, it was just a particularly affecting virtual as far as the newbies were concerned. Of course, they didn't share your particular passions. You know the script already."

"Yes, but who'd come to meet me?"

"This whole business is about Nicole, isn't it? Why don't you go meet someone in here first? Have a little fun?"

Donovan stood up. "I already met someone in here, Freddie. She committed suicide. And right now I need to go home and work. I've got a lecture tomorrow night at the Rogers Memorial, and I haven't written a word yet."

"Tell them to pet the fish."

Donovan laughed. "They already think I'm nuts."

"We like nuts in here, even more than we used to. They keep things interesting."

AT HOME DONOVAN COMPILED A GRAM OF HASH AND SMOKED it before the fire. He wrote his lecture on a yellow pad with a fountain pen, downing espresso as he worked. Freddie was right. He was just repeating himself. He tried a new tack, something that might wake a few people up. When it was done, he let his computer translate his cramped writing full of cross-outs and insertions, arrows, and addenda into a neat typescript.

Lately, he'd been reading poetry every night. The dying fire reminded him of Coleridge's *Frost at Midnight,* so he reread it and meditated on the lines. Coleridge is sitting in a country house late at night. Everyone else in the house is asleep, including his "cradled infant" beside him. Outside, it's bitter cold, the world plunged in frost. Inside, the "low-burnt fire . . . fluttered on the grate." Coleridge being Coleridge, this scene prompts him to meditate on his own childhood in the city, contrasting it with the life he envisions for his son in the country, close to nature:

> But thou, my babe! shalt wander like a breeze
> By lakes and sandy shores, beneath the crags
> Of ancient mountain, and beneath the clouds,
> Which image in their bulk both lakes and shores

And mountain crags: so shalt thou see and hear
The lovely shapes and sounds intelligible
Of that eternal language, which thy God
Utters, who from eternity doth teach
Himself in all, and all things in himself.
Great universal Teacher! he shall mould
Thy spirit and by giving make it ask.

Therefore all seasons shall be sweet to thee,
Whether the summer clothe the general earth
With greenness, or the redbreast sit and sing
Betwixt the tufts of snow on the bare branch
Of mossy apple-tree, while the nigh thatch
Smokes in the sun-thaw; whether the eave-drops fall
Heard only in the trances of the blast,
Or if the secret ministry of frost
Shall hang them up in silent icicles,
Quietly shining to the quiet Moon.

Donovan didn't know how things actually turned out for
Coleridge's son. He could look it up—he could look anything up—but what did it matter, anyway? The poem wasn't
really about him, but about Coleridge. Donovan couldn't
help wishing that he had a son asleep beside him, wished
that he could imagine any such time with his own father.

But like most poems, it didn't really work without death.
Where's the poignancy of the father imagining his son's
future if the father never dies? If the son never lives on
without him? If the fire will burn forever if you tell it to?

"Go out, fire," Donovan said, and he was staring at a
cold hearth.

There was a way to die, apparently, for those who'd lived
in the real world. But for newbies like him, it was still life
or suicide. Even after the third generation of newbies, those
who'd once walked the Earth, or even lay in an incubator
there, regarded themselves as more real, more human.
Maybe they were. He couldn't even die properly.

It wasn't death he wanted. He only hoped that if it was

out there, waiting for him, he'd want to live and live well. But maybe that was a foolish hope. Maybe Freddie was right, and it was all about Nicole. Maybe all he really wanted to know was why Nicole wanted death more than she'd wanted anything, more than she'd wanted him.

He fell asleep in front of the hearth and dreamed he died in a sorghum field.

NICOLE IS THERE. SHE SITS IN THE DIRT, HER LEGS AKIMBO, her back to the light, her head down as if she's trying to keep from passing out. He grabs her shoulders and shakes her, and she looks up at him, tears streaming down her face. "Leave me alone," she whispers. The light is bright but not blinding. He wants to walk into it, but he can't leave her sitting there. He pulls her to her feet, but she's like a rag doll, staring at him as if he isn't even there. He feels as substantial as a figure in hangman. He tries to drag her toward the light, but with each step, it shrinks until he's moving through a dark narrow tunnel, dragging something he knows isn't Nicole any longer, but he can't let it go.

HE WOKE AS THE SUN WAS COMING UP, STREAMING INTO THE window. He rolled over on his back, feeling cold and stiff. It was unseasonably cold with frost in the corners of the windowpanes. "Fire," he said, and the flames appeared in the fireplace.

Interesting variation, he thought. But you're not fooling me.

2

THE TROLL IN THE MACHINE

WALTER TILLMAN'S MOTHER ALWAYS TOLD HIM HE WOULD grow. Even when he was just a kid, he knew she meant more than just his height. In her imagination, not only would he grow taller, but his eyes would settle serenely into place instead of bulging out at the world like two bubbles on a scummy pond, his mouth would gather itself together into more than a lipless line above a sloping chin, his nose would rise from the flat pasty plane of his face to give a noble shape to the twin sinkholes of his nostrils. And even when he was a kid, he knew she was lying, that she knew in her heart he could only grow into an ugly little man who'd once been an ugly little boy.

The rest of the world stared or looked away, depending on their fascination with the grotesque. A few took an active role in clueing him into the truth. More specifically, one Larry Winesap, the jester of his class, who conducted a straw poll in fourth grade to determine whether Tillman most closely resembled a frog or a toad. Toad won, but that may have been influenced by the time Larry interrupted Mrs. Ostrum's reading of *The Wind in the Willows* to ask if Mr. Toad's first name was Walter. But as he got older and had a few accomplishments, people didn't say stuff like that to his face. When Tillman was forty-two, a brilliant geneticist of international renown, the several dozen handsome folk who worked under him called him "the troll" only when they thought he wouldn't hear them. Most of them even liked him well enough. Somehow that made it worse.

But that was a *very* long time ago. If his mother could only see him now. At the age of 162, he could look any way he wanted. He'd made himself two hundred feet tall once, strode through town, the world at his feet. But it was like tromping through a model railroad, and he bored of it in a hurry. He'd been an eagle for a while, or at least he'd looked like one. Talk about feeling stupid. He was still the same old Tillman, no matter what he looked like. These days he stuck with "the troll." It was what he was used to, and nobody in here cared.

He—or at least his identity—was trapped inside a house-trailer-sized computer in a research facility a stone's throw away from the old Capitol power plant. He wondered what was going on outside in the real world. He had no way of knowing. There were cameras he could access to show him the dull-looking contraption he called home as well as the featureless room it sat in—dark as a tomb for more than a hundred years.

Whoopee.

He hadn't known that much about the hardware end of the consciousness-transfer project before he came in here. His end was workable wetware: fast-growing human clones to act as hosts. Machines never interested him. He only cared about living things—more specifically, how living things made more of the same and how they were all different and evolved over time. His therapist (handsome fellow, dumb as a post) cautiously suggested that Tillman's choice of career might have been influenced by his concern at being "less than handsome." For this he was paying over two hundred an hour? That was less than a bargain.

But once he found himself inside a machine, he figured he better learn all he could about them if he was ever going to find the can opener and get out.

He'd accessed the extensive help system and the library and discovered he had a knack for programming. He hacked the operating system. It was a lot like DNA, just not so elegant. He took it apart, put it back together, making a few improvements. He probably knew the damn thing better than Newman Rogers (who'd designed it) ever had. If Newman had been stuck in here for 120 years, Tillman thought, he wouldn't have thought it was such a great idea in the first place. Not that it wasn't a great piece of work that performed exactly as advertised. And it was nobody's fault but his own that he was stuck in here.

Now that he knew everything there was to know about his home, the long and short of it was there was no way out unless somebody with a spare body in tow came looking for him. Might as well wait for the tooth fairy, a superstition Tillman's father had never endorsed (*Money for a dead tooth? Give me a break!*).

But something strange was up outside. He'd been on emergency power for the last hundred years. Whoever or whatever cut the power hadn't bothered to look if anyone was living inside, or hadn't cared. But the fail-safe system cared automatically—switching on the emergency power. His home couldn't be shut down when there was someone inside it. Even a single someone.

Like Tillman.

He'd been alone in here for 120 years. For all he knew, he was the last man on Earth. Since he wasn't flesh and blood, there were those who'd deny him that distinction, but if they were all dead, to hell with them.

He assumed, as a working hypothesis—he was still a scientist, after all—that he must be completely bonkers by now. Fortunately, his world was endlessly accommodating and chock-full of data.

He could read any book ever written. If it was in a language he didn't know, he could have it translated or be tutored by a virtual instructor until he could read the work in the original. He didn't even get eyestrain. He could go anywhere, do anything, eat anything. All damn fine simulations.

It was a flipping nightmare. How could he tell if he was crazy when he knew his whole world was one big hallucination? Wouldn't sanity be to doubt his reality? To see right past his perceptions to the electrochemical high jinks of Newman's little machine? How could he believe in that Taj Mahal he could see in the sunset, or that steaming plate of veal piccata that made his mouth water? Truth was, his mouth was long gone. He was like one of those guys who's had his leg amputated, but can still feel it—only Tillman had his whole *body* amputated. It was enough to make your brain hurt. But then his brain was as real as his mouth.

Once, in search of the authentic—reading too much Freud and Jung—he slept for three years. And dreamed. With so much time to work with, the usually tangled filaments of his dream world gradually twisted into strong thread, wove themselves into a tapestry. He knew every warp and woof of the silly thing. It was positively medieval: There was this beautiful woman, and he was a unicorn. The bushes were full of guys with bows and arrows. He didn't need Freud to figure that one out.

So he woke up. What was so damn authentic about a bunch of ripped-off archetypes, anyway? Only appearances mattered. Leave authenticity to Sartre.

In that spirit, he'd tried his hand at creating artificial worlds in which he could fly, or sing like Caruso, or play a mean game of basketball, but he felt ridiculous. For one thing, the other characters were always so flat and dull. Artificial intelligence turned out like a long succession of artificial sweeteners—close, but no cigar. If you wanted a convincing person, you had to have something to build on—some*one* to build on. He was, however, the only one in town.

Then it hit him: He had all his memories, populated with enough people to keep him occupied for a long time. Friends, neighbors, strangers on the street. He could resurrect them all. Excluding Larry Winesap, of course, unless he found himself drawn to torture.

At first he was just trying to have a good time. He threw parties. "Life of the party" took on many new layers of meaning. He seduced every woman he remembered, then they seduced him. This wasn't nearly as much fun as he'd anticipated.

Then he went through what he called his "enlightenment phase"—before he'd figured out he was just plain nuts. Maybe it was reading Boethius that did it: Bad fortune is good; good fortune is bad; philosophy is a woman who visits you in jail. Anyway. He took up a rigorous know-thyself regimen, probably hoping to transcend his ass out of here. He relived every significant moment of his life from the forty-two years before he came in here, trying them out every which way, playing out every alternative that crossed his path, examining the hell out of his life to make it worth living. He was struck by two things: There just weren't that many significant moments, and he wouldn't have done anything much differently.

Except for the last few months of his life—from the time he met Stephanie and fell in love until he got himself stuck in here. He kept thinking he could've done *something* to make it turn out differently. He kept looking for a happy ending, but so far he couldn't find it, not unless he wanted to seriously revise his notions of happiness. What did it matter anyway, how he revised his memory? It happened the way it happened, and nothing he could do in here would ever change that. He was reruns. Bogart never gets on that plane, no matter how many times it flies out of Casablanca.

He lived these days in the White House, or his memory of it. He'd done the tour with his mom when he was ten. His dad hated the President (*If you see the cat, get his autograph*) and went to the Holocaust Museum instead. Mom was determined to drag Tillman to the White House—probably so she could imagine him sleeping there someday. Think about it—his puss on the evening news every night. The sheer impossibility of it seemed to fire his mom up. And though he hadn't wanted to go, by the time he left, he had to admit the place was pretty cool. So when he wanted a new house a few years back, he thought, What the hell, make mom happy. If he couldn't grow up, at least he could be President.

He was finishing up breakfast in the Oval Office as he wrote in his journal, a morning ritual for the last few decades. The tour guide, Sally, cleared his tray.

"I won't be having lunch," he said.

"Are you going to visit Stephanie again today, sir?"

"I was thinking about it. How'd you know?"

"You get a certain look in your eye. May I suggest that the gardens are lovely this time of year?"

He smiled at what passed for her subtlety. She was mostly his alter ego, of course. What could he hope for from his memory as a kid trailing along after her through the White House, checking out her legs, imagining, when she smiled at them all, she was smiling at him? But sometimes she almost seemed real. He looked out the window, and there was the gardener, just as he remembered him. "I'm just a glutton for punishment."

"You asked me to remind you, sir, that it will never end any differently."

"When did I do that?"

"The last time, sir. Nine months ago."

"It's been longer than that, hasn't it?"

"Less actually, sir. Two hundred and sixty-three days."

"Why do you keep calling me 'sir'?"

"You told me to, sir, last night. You'd been drinking. You said you never get any respect around here.'

"Forget I ever said that."

"I remember everything you say."

"Well, stop it anyway. Ignore me when I'm drunk."

She looked out the window, her voice almost wistful. "Sometimes you're quite pleasant when you're drunk."

"Well, so are you."

She turned back to him. "I don't get drunk."

"No. I mean you're quite pleasant when *I'm* drunk. It's all a fucking movie, Sally. You know that. You had great legs. I was starting to notice such things. You made an impression. You're just some kid's fantasy. A ten-year-old, for Christ's sake!"

She looked hurt. Only in here could you hurt an illusion's feelings. "I'm sorry," he said.

"I understand, Tillman."

That was one thing about Sally. She always understood—just as much as he did, which wasn't saying much. Sometimes he wished she'd just tell him off. But of course she wouldn't do that. Unless he told her to.

A flipping nightmare.

HE WENT DOWN TO THE RED ROOM. HE'D PARTICULARLY liked it as a kid. He hadn't figured that there'd be red walls anywhere in the President's house. His mother wouldn't have let him paint his walls red in a million years, much less plaster them with red satin. He'd tested this theory out when he got back home from his D.C. visit by thumbtacking bedsheets to his wall—green, he didn't have any red—and his mother took them down the minute she saw them. "This isn't the White House," she said.

He glanced up at the portrait of Audubon, which was ridiculously high on the wall. The famous naturalist was toting the gun he used to plug his specimens, so he could draw all those pretty bird pictures and have a society named after him. Mr. Nature. Looked like Mr. Human to Tillman: *Let me kill you so I can see what makes you tick.*

That's what he figured happened outside: Humans had finally killed themselves off, leaving only the ticking. They'd probably built the damn thing he'd seen the plans for—the Papa Bear version of the computer he was in. Huge thing out in space. That must be it. Now there was probably *nobody* out there on the planet but a bunch of very relieved animals. He imagined all the animals partying: *Yay! Those fuckers are finally gone!*

That had to be it. With that thing, *anybody* could live forever. He'd seen what a whiff of immortality could do to people back when he was making new bodies for rich old geezers. These guys were ready to fork over damn near everything they had and suck Jack Cornran's dick if he asked them to, all to get a shot at a new life with a new body. The project was ass deep in money. They couldn't spend it fast enough.

Tillman's part of the project—the transfer of human personalities into new cloned bodies—was all set to go when he came in here, so that must've gone off, for sure. Must've caused quite an uproar. But with that huge mother in orbit, who needed clones anymore? Hell, who needed bodies? The whole human race was probably up there by now. Life must be one very long party.

And he was down here—in here—a video game that played with itself.

He often tried to convince himself that he was better off in here than out there in a big empty world. But he didn't buy it. Even if he had his old body back, and he was Wally Tillman, ugliest little fuck on the face of the Earth, with nobody to talk to but the cockroaches, it'd *still* be better than being stuck in here.

Every morning he could wake up with a chance at something he was never going to get in here: A change, a variation, an alteration, an adjustment, an anomaly, a deviation, a modification, a mutation, a permutation, a shift. A goddamn *change*! Anything but reruns of Wally's World over and over again. He was a geneticist, for Christ's sake, had tricked and cajoled the genetic code into cranking out a full-grown human—twenty-five years' worth of changes—in forty days flat. Forty days and forty nights. What the hell could he really change in here? Oh, he could make the sky green and the cows purple if he wanted, but that wasn't change. That was interior decoration.

He settled into an American Empire sofa—red, of course—with gilded bronze doodads stuck all over it—leaves and lion heads (Audubon would approve)—just so you'd know it was elegant. He wasn't feeling particularly elegant this morning. He turned it into his dad's La-Z Boy. He used to sit in it when his dad was at work, picking at the swath of duct tape over the tear in the arm, watching the Sci-Fi Channel. Now, Tillman thought, I *am* the Sci-Fi Channel.

He picked at the frayed edges of the duct tape and asked to see a certain Tuesday morning in the fall of 2030. When he first met Stephanie face-to-face.

HE'S IN HIS LAB, BY HIMSELF. THE REST OF HIS TEAM HAS JUST pulled an all-nighter. They are all home, asleep. That's fine with Tillman. He's checking on the clones back in the nursery. It looks like a minibrewery with six stainless-steel vats, only these have round windows, with murky faces floating in the brew. One of the vats is empty, down for repairs, but it's ready to go as soon as some poor slob forks over a few bags of money. Cornran wants to keep production low at first to keep the price cranked, but Tillman's heard rumors there's a huge facility in an old GM factory in Arlington, Texas, that'll turn out 9,000 a month, and that five more just like it were being built. But he doesn't know whether to believe the rumors or not. What would you *do* with 648,000 clones a year?

He smiles at the faces of his babies. They are splendid specimens—every one. His favorite is Ivan (Subject I-356V)—dark head of curly hair, six-foot-three, great nose. Cloned from a Russian chemist who climbed the Himalayas in his spare time. Tillman's thinking: What if I'd had a body like that? What would my life have been like? He tries to imagine scaling a mountain, but he keeps bouncing off the face of a sheer cliff like a damn paddle ball, unable to get a foothold with his stubby little legs.

Then he hears someone closing the door to the lab out front, a woman's voice calling, "Hello?" He steps out, closing the vaultlike door behind him, and there's Stephanie Sanders, or rather, Stephanie Sanders Cornran, standing six feet away from him.

"Are you Dr. Tillman?" she asks.

He doesn't speak for eight and a half seconds. He's timed it. Jesus Christ in person couldn't have rattled him more.

She endures these seconds—they're nothing new to her. Finally he says, "Just call me Tillman. Everybody does. My first name's Walter, but I hate it. Everybody starts calling me Wally, and I can't stand that. There was this kid in school who called me Walleye and had everybody doing it . . ."

He's babbling, his burbly little laugh erupting every other word, and he can't shut up. I mean, my God, Stephanie Sanders, the most beautiful woman in the world, right there in the flesh, just as he's always imagined her. How many times has he looked at his dozens of pictures of her, hell, talked to them, wooed them, made love to them. What's he supposed to say to her? *I'm thrilled to finally meet you in person. I've masturbated to your image many times.* He feels like some stupid adolescent, only he's forty-two years old and still mooning over pictures of beautiful women. He's never done the bootleg virtuals of her. He thought that was going too far, but still he's filled with shame. He stops in midsentence.

And then *she* blushes.

And it hits him: It isn't any better being so damn beautiful than it is being so damn ugly. All these people staring at you like some exotic animal in a zoo. The ugly species and the beautiful species, not humans at all.

He sees her for the first time now, three-dimensional flesh and blood, all wrapped up in an old trench coat like some kid playing private eye, her hair squashed flat from the hat she's been wearing, a straw thing all scrunched in her hands, squeezing it like she's kneading dough. A real person.

She laughs now too, and it's kind of goofy, with a little croak in it.

He likes her. He gives a little bow. "You're Mrs. Corn-ran," he says, the gentleman troll.

"Stephanie." She holds out her hand, and he shakes it, and there's not that slight recoil he's used to from those who even bother to extend their hands, but the answering pressure of someone who's glad to meet you. He's only felt it before from fellow scientists impressed with his work. He looks into her eyes, and he sees she doesn't care that he's butt ugly. It just doesn't matter to her. She wants to be his friend. Fellow freaks, he thinks.

All this takes a little over a minute.

HE STOPPED THE MEMORY AND PONDERED IT ONCE AGAIN. *That's* when he fell in love with her, he'd say. Right then. His endocrine system dumped a blissful cocktail into his bloodstream, and he looked like Bashful in *Snow White*. Oh, sure, maybe that wasn't really love. What did *he,* after all, have to compare it with? It was unique. Nobody'd ever looked at him like that before. He'd never felt anything close. Until something else more powerful came along, he was willing to call that moment "love." After 120 years, it still shook him, made his chest tingle. Of course that could be a glitch in the code in here, not allowing him to grow and change, to adapt with the passage of time like a normal organism . . .

Horseshit. If it looks like a duck, talks like a duck, and walks like a duck, it's a fucking duck, right? Even old Audubon would agree with that—a dead duck was still a duck: He'd fallen for her, and he'd fallen hard.

But maybe it wasn't such a great thing. Trolls had no business falling in love. What if he *hadn't* fallen in love with her? If he'd just, you know, kept his perspective on things.

Right.

Besides—and he'd thought about this plenty—no matter what happened afterward, he wasn't willing to give up that moment.

Not that one.

He started up the memory again.

SHE SAYS, "I'M SUPPOSED TO MEET MY HUSBAND HERE. HE must be running late. He wants me to give blood?"

He's totally thrown by this. Jack Cornran coming down

to the labs? So his wife can give blood? There's only one reason anyone gives blood in Tillman's lab, and that's to be cloned. He imagines her face floating in one of his vats, and his stomach turns. Jack Cornran wants to clone his own *wife*? Tillman doesn't know what to say. Of course, he never understood why she—supermodel, actress, richer than Solomon—married a snake like Cornran in the first place.

And then the man himself arrives. Jack Cornran, one of the richest men in the world. Tillman's boss. In the ten years Tillman has worked here, this is the second time they've met. His suit costs more than Tillman's car, which isn't saying much, and his hair looks like a taxidermist did it. Tillman wonders if perhaps his bright green eyes aren't made of glass.

"Walter," Cornran says warmly, sticking out his smile and his hand, bending over because Tillman's such a shrimp. Always the sensitive guy, that Jack.

TILLMAN SKIPPED OVER THE NEXT PART. CORNRAN'S FACE HAD been on the cover of *Time* and *Newsweek*. Tillman's looked like it belonged on the *Cur Dog Gazette*. That's pretty much how it went. Big dog, little dog. Smart little dog, you prick. Tillman started it up again where Cornran got down to business.

"MY WIFE WISHES TO DONATE BLOOD FOR OUR RESEARCH here. I'm sure you'll agree she is a perfect subject."

She's standing there, the dutiful wife by all appearances. This can't be her idea, Tillman thinks and wonders why a man would do something like that. His own wife. Tillman smells a very large rat. What's the urgency? They don't make a clone from a subject who's still alive—most people don't want a younger twin running around, and she's—what? Twenty-nine? Thirty?

Cornran leans over again, gets in his face. "Walter?"

Tillman reels himself back in and stands as straight as he can. "Tillman," he says. "I prefer to be called Tillman."

Cornran sniffs, a minimalist snarl. "Dr. Tillman," he says precisely. "Please see to my wife. I have a meeting, and I'm twenty minutes late."

(And here's where Tillman couldn't figure out his own mind. Does he already know somewhere in the back of his mind what he's going to do? Doesn't make sense any other way. He must've been literally crazy about her.)

"Actually, sir," he says, "I'm glad you're here. I've been intending to ask you for a sample of *your* blood. You, like your wife, are a perfect subject." He's got the rig ready by this time, he's offering to help Cornran out of his jacket. "And this way, Mrs. Cornran can see what a simple procedure it is."

There's a little twitch at the corner of Cornran's left eye. A hit. A palpable hit. Cornran glances over at Stephanie, calculating something. He doesn't want to spook her. A lot is riding on getting this blood sample from her.

TILLMAN FROZE THE MEMORY, LET THEM ALL STAND THERE.

Back then, he could only guess what Jack was up to. It wasn't till later that he found out the whole sick story. He came out of the La-Z Boy and walked up to Cornran's frozen image. Even on tiptoe, he couldn't really get in the guy's face. "You motherfucker, you were going to make whores out of your own wife!" He searched Cornran's expression for any sign of guilt, but there wasn't a trace. The man was just making a buck—no big deal—or rather, just another big deal.

Tillman turned away, disgusted. Not just with Cornran, with himself. What did he think his clones would be used for once the line of rich old men had petered out? Something for the rich old men to play with, of course. And that would be the least of it. A race of custom-made slaves. Tillman hadn't seen past the end of his stubby little nose.

He flopped onto the La-Z Boy and watched himself taking Cornran's blood, a little vial, wouldn't fill a shot glass. The image of downing a glass of Cornran's blood flitted through his mind, as it had several times now: Dr. Tillman and Mr. Troll.

CORNRAN ROLLS DOWN HIS SLEEVE AND PUTS HIS JACKET BACK on, a tight little smile on his face, while Tillman's bouncing on the balls of his feet, the vial of Cornran's blood in his chubby little fist, thinking: Now I've got you by the balls.

Cornran speaks to Stephanie without looking at her. "I won't be able to make lunch. Something came up. Sorry. Don't forget dinner tonight. I'll meet you there."

Tillman can see this is an empty ritual. The man's not sorry about anything unless it's a dip in the bottom line or whatever it is that bottom lines do.

Stephanie doesn't bat an eye, seems used to these broken dates, resigned to a little death each day. (*See to my wife. What a prick.*) He wonders why she feels like she deserves it. Cornran gives her a peck on the cheek and leaves. If you run it real slow, you can see that his lips don't even touch her skin. But this is his memory, not what really happened, and maybe that's what he wanted to see. He never wanted this jerk to touch her again.

She signs her consent forms without bothering to read them (you needed a lawyer and a scientist to make heads or tails of them anyway) and gives Tillman a trusting smile.

"Are you sure you want to do this?" he asks. "Do you know what we're doing here?"

"Longevity research, right?"

Jeez, what a euphemism that was. He's not supposed to discuss his work with *anyone*. Even the different departments don't know exactly what the others are doing. But this isn't just anyone. This is Stephanie. His friend Stephanie. He takes a deep breath. "We're making clones, so that we can give old people new bodies. Very old, very rich people, at the moment."

"Clones?"

He gestures toward the nursery. "I'll show you," he says.

She rises from her chair and follows him to the nursery. He shuts off the cameras before they step inside. Her eyes widen, and she draws in a little breath. Tillman's violating security big time by even showing her this room, but she's Cornran's wife, and they're going public in a few weeks. It's obvious Cornran hasn't told her what he's volunteered her for. She's staring at the clones, dumbfounded, but he can see she's turning it all over in her mind, putting the pieces together faster than he did. Course, she knows her husband better than Tillman does. Her beautiful mouth settles into a firm line. Her enormous eyes glisten. She turns on her heel and walks back into the lab. Neither one notices she's dropped her hat. By the time Tillman's closed up the nursery, she's sitting in the chair with her sleeve rolled up.

"Are you sure?" he asks again.

And there are tears in her eyes. "Just do it," she whispers. "Please."

TILLMAN SKIPPED THE DRAWING OF THE BLOOD—THE ONLY time in his life it ever made him sick to his stomach. Must've been all that guilt sitting in his gut.

AS HE'S FINISHING UP, ROSS, ONE OF THE SECURITY GUYS, steps into the lab, breathing heavy—he's run all the way. His hand is on the nasty-looking gun at his side.

He's rattled to see Stephanie there. She may be the boss's wife and one of the most beautiful women in the world, more famous than God, but she still doesn't have high-security clearance. That's the kind of guy Ross is. He crosses the room and turns the security cameras back on.

"Did you turn these cameras off, Dr. Tillman?"

Tillman does his best bumbling professor routine. Gosh—must've hit the wrong switch. There's so many, I just can't keep 'em straight.

Ross looks back and forth between Stephanie and Tillman

like a suspicious parent. He starts to say something but thinks better of it in front of Stephanie.

"Never turn those cameras off, Dr. Tillman. You just set off a high-security alert."

"I'm terribly sorry. I certainly didn't mean to," Tillman says pleasantly.

Ross snatches a walkie-talkie from his belt and snaps into it. "Stand down." Ross gives them each a military nod and departs.

"Prick," Tillman mutters under his breath, but Stephanie hears him and breaks into a smile.

"Tillman," she says. "Would you have lunch with me?"

TILLMAN STOPPED IT, SHUT IT OFF COMPLETELY. HE PACED up and down the room, crying again, like some little kid. "Would I have lunch with you? I'd die for you. Hell, I *did* die for you."

And went to hell for it.

3

THE MOST BEAUTIFUL WOMAN IN THE BUSINESS

STEPHANIE HAD BEEN FAMOUS FOR SO LONG BY THE TIME SHE entered the Bin at sixty, that slinking around in floppy straw hat, sunglasses, and an oversize trench coat had become habit. A hundred years later, she still did it, though no one recognized her much anymore. She'd been famous for being young and beautiful, hardly an accomplishment in here.

Except for the occasional pop-culture freak who even knew what a supermodel was, or a devoted tabloid reader with a long memory, nobody cared. Not that she understood why they ever cared, why an endless stream of strangers professed their love, why her navel had become more famous than most people's faces. (One fellow compared it to the Grand Canyon—"the two most breathtaking crevices in the world.") Everyone just seemed to go crazy for a while, starting with her aunt saying "Steph ought to be a model" and ending when she'd been a recluse for so long it was no longer interesting to anyone, certainly not herself, and she went into the Bin.

For her first shoot in '14—she was fifteen, though the agency thought she was at least twenty—they put her in jeans because she was all legs. But the holo-poster in every adolescent boy's bedroom was the topless one, the jeans unzipped, her arms barely crisscrossing her precocious breasts. That poster made more money than both her parents together had made in their entire lives. Her mom calculated that statistic on a cocktail napkin one night for Stephanie's enlightenment, then rolled it up into a little ball and flicked it with her finger. "Such clever tits," she'd said.

But it didn't stop there. When she was eighteen, she let herself be talked into a virtual scan so that her face and body could be borrowed by an actress for roles that met with Stephanie's approval. Somehow this was supposed to aid her ambition to become an actress herself. She vetoed the piles of adventure-porn scripts, but it didn't make any difference. One of the programmers at the studio pirated her scan, put her in a hard-core interactive, and dumped it on the Web, snarling it for months. She became a world-wide virtual sex toy. It was hard to meet a man who hadn't fucked her. Her manager tried to reassure her that it was okay, that nobody thought it was real, nobody'd *really* fucked anybody. But there was a guilty flicker in his eyes, and when she cornered him, he admitted to fucking her a couple of times himself. She slapped his face—hard. For all of them. Rather than giving her an argument, he coordi-nated the platoon of lawyers it took to have the scan destroyed.

She made several virtuals after that, starring her own acting ability and her clever tits. When the deservedly brutal reviews came out, her manager reassured her: "I don't care what anybody says. You're still the most beautiful woman in the business."

So that was the role she played out for a while: the pro-fessional beauty, a face and body for hire, look but don't touch. She'd lend her beauty to worthy causes and give them money in an attempt to feel she did something mean-ingful and make peace with herself. But later on, when she retired at twenty-nine—when she never posed, never gave interviews, when she just wanted her life back so she could do something with it, maybe have kids, work a real job— the world wouldn't let her quit. No matter what she did or what happened to her, it was *still* about her beauty—the beautiful bride on the evening news, the beautiful widow. The beauty turned activist. The reclusive former beauty.

Now, at last, she was no one. And she wanted, more than anything, to die.

She took off her sunglasses and stuck them in her trench coat pocket. "Are we almost there?" she asked the taxi driver.

He glanced at her in the rearview mirror. "It's getting close." This was Stephanie's first time in one of the new cabs. They were a retrovation in D.C., a bit of nostalgia for the tourists, though the roads were closed long before the Bin went on-line. The new roads were narrow romantic shadows of their former selves, winding through the grassy esplanades like horse trails. The cabs were little things, like the cars in old cartoons. She halfway expected the headlights to wink at her.

The cabbie was still looking at her in the rearview mirror. He was wearing a cap with a visor, like army officers used to wear. It had a silver shield on the front showing one of the little cabs with the Washington Monument jutting up in the background. It read: D.C. CABS.

"Do you work?" he asked.

"I'm an actress." she said.

"Virtuals?"

"Stage."

"No kidding? I didn't know they still did that."

"The audiences are very small."

"Must be interesting."

She specialized in playing women who died: Joan of Arc, Juliet Capulet, Lady Macbeth, Hedda Gabler. Long adaptations of novels were fashionable—anything to pass the time—and she'd played Edna Pointellier and Anna Karenina. She got reviews now that never mentioned a single body part. Her 140 years of acting classes had finally paid off. Dying beautifully had replaced being beautiful in the equation of her life, but it still didn't amount to much.

All she said to the cabbie was: "Not really."

He nodded his head in vigorous agreement. "I know what you mean. Do you ever ask yourself why you're doing what you're doing? I mean, why am I driving a cab? I never even

liked to drive in the old life, and here I am driving a cab."
He pushed his cap back and glanced over his shoulder at
her.

"That's tough," Stephanie said, thinking, Here it comes,
the story of his life. No one had to do anything in the Bin.
There was time for an infinite number of choices. The only
thing left to worry about was what it all *meant*.

"I really thought I wanted to do this," the cabbie went
on. "I really did. But I've been doing it for two weeks now,
and I just can't see keeping it up forever."

Stephanie looked out the window, trying to calculate
where she was. She spotted the Washington Monument
poking up through the trees and oriented herself. "Would
you like me to drive?" she asked.

The cabbie cocked his head to one side, thinking about
it. "You wouldn't mind?"

"No. I always wanted to drive a cab."

"No kidding?"

"Well, actually, kidding. But I'll still drive."

The cabbie pulled over, and they traded places. She ran
her hands over the wheel. She hadn't driven in over fifty
years. The last time was at that amusement park in Chicago
with the huge black cars from the 1930s. What a dopey
place that was. But she'd liked the cars.

Since emission control was not a problem in the Bin, the
cabs had been given the comforting rumble of an internal
combustion engine, like a cat purring. She stepped on the
gas pedal and pulled onto the road. She never drove that
much in the real world, never even got a license. There
were limos to take her anywhere she wanted to go and
bodyguards to handle the disruption once she got there.

She wound through a park, past a little pond dotted with
ancient ducks. Wisteria hung from the trees and filled the
air with scent. A man painted at an easel beside the pond.
She wondered how many times he'd painted this scene. She
had a neighbor who'd been painting their street for twenty
years—different styles, different times of day, different perspectives. He intended to synthesize them all one day into

the perfect painting of that particular place. Maybe this painter followed the same immortal duck around. This being the Bin, it was unlikely he was just painting a scene, enjoying himself. God, she hated this place.

She thought about pressing down hard on the accelerator, driving into one of the huge oaks up ahead, catapulting her lovely face through the windshield. The cabbie would be all right. The operating system saved the innocent, dispassionately measuring one's intentions. No one could be killed, and only those who truly wished to die could kill themselves.

The road curved off to the right, and she followed it. There was no point trying to kill herself again. She'd tried enough times to know her intentions would be found wanting. Apparently, deep down, she didn't want to die. Maybe she didn't think it was enough.

"I've never done this before," the cabbie said from the back.

"Ridden in a cab?"

"No. Ridden in my *own* cab. It's pretty cool, actually." He settled into the seat, spreading his arms out along the back, watching the city pass by through the window—a contented fare.

She orbited a traffic circle. Some famous dead man in bronze stood in the middle of it. She imagined herself planted there instead, clad in bronze jeans, her arms across bronze breasts. That would've been fitting once. But nothing was the same in here—there'd be no pigeon shit on her face, no semen dripping from her bronze thighs.

She headed south from the circle until she reached the Rogers Memorial. She pulled into a tree-lined drive out front. "I hate to break up the party," she said, "but this is my stop." She got out, leaving the door open and the motor running, expecting the cabbie to get behind the wheel.

He rolled down the back window and stuck his head out. "You sure you don't want to drive around some more? I'd pay you."

She pointed a thumb over her shoulder. "I'm going to a lecture in there, and I don't want to be late."

The cabbie made a face. "Skip it is my advice. I used to give lectures. In my old life, I was a college professor, if you can believe it. Talk about pointless. You got to start asking yourself . . ."

Stephanie held up her hands. "I'm really sorry," she said. "I have to go." She backed into a sleek Asian couple standing on the curb and mumbled an apology.

"Is this your cab?" the man asked her. His eyes were turquoise blue, and his smile revealed a gold tooth, an inlaid obsidian character in the middle of it. The woman, in a long black dress, looked like a Beardsley print in sepia. They both looked like they were tripping. The man tended to business, while the woman looked off, waiting for matters to be arranged.

"It's mine," the cabbie said, leaning out the window. "You want to drive?"

"Drive?" The man laughed. "Sure," he said and got behind the wheel. The woman, though she hadn't appeared to be listening, opened the back door and motioned for the cabbie to move over. She slid in beside him and caught Stephanie's eye for only a second before she rolled up the window and they drove away.

Stephanie watched the little car until it disappeared into the trees, wondering where it would end up and who'd be driving. She'd put her money on the woman in the backseat.

AS IT TURNED OUT, STEPHANIE WAS EARLY. THE LECTURE WAS supposed to start at seven, but that meant no sooner than seven-thirty. She didn't want to tour the Memorial again. It always made her miserable. She passed through the great hall with her head down, not looking up at the forty-foot holograph of Newman Rogers giving his last speech at the opening of the Bin in 2050. She'd been there, one of the celebrity guests who wasn't quite ready to abandon the world. She tried to tune out his words. If she'd listened more closely to what he said a hundred years ago, she might not have gone in ten years later, but it was too late now.

After the ceremony, Rogers disappeared. No one could find him, either inside or outside the Bin. Maybe he just ascended into heaven, Stephanie thought bitterly, or went straight to hell.

In the exhibits off the great hall were several pictures of her husband, who, before what was euphemistically called his "untimely death" in 2030, headed the company that developed the Bin. In a couple of the photographs, Stephanie, his trophy wife, was on his arm. But the most painful image was a single photo—the whole research team lined up on the lawn in front of the labs—there, second row, fourth from the left, stood Walter squinting in the sun.

Her lover.

By the time she reached the auditorium doors, she was almost running. She burst in, and a few of the people in the near-empty hall turned around and looked at her. She slipped her sunglasses back on and took a seat near the back. She should've known better than to come here.

A memorial, a repository for memories. You'd think they'd lose their sting after all this time, but they just seemed to burrow deeper, tunnel into every nook and cranny of her mind. Maybe this Dr. Carroll could help her end them. She was 151 years old. She hadn't seen Tillman or her husband in 120 years, and here she was on the verge of tears, her chest aching, unable to forget.

She looked down, away from the prying eyes. She took a newspaper out of her coat pocket and spread it on her lap, reading over the article that had brought her here.

"They call him Dr. Death," it began, but Stephanie— who knew exactly who *they* were and what to think of them—didn't hold that against the man. He managed to make sense even when the writer was a complete moron, steeped in Bin clichés like a worn-out teabag:

Q: Why study death of all things? Death is dead, right?
A: Maybe that's not the wonderful thing we've always assumed it is. Because of death, we used to make something of our lives. "Is *this* what I want my life to be

when I die?" we used to ask ourselves as we got older. This question never meant much to a sixteen-year-old. Now it's meaningless to a *116*-year-old.

Or a 151-year-old, Stephanie thought.

Q: So you're saying we're all just a bunch of kids now?
A: Yes. Most of us.
Q: Youth is a state of mind. But tell me, Doctor, since you're so interested in death, why don't you just commit suicide?

Maybe he can't either, Stephanie thought.

A: Suicide is an act of despair. I want a meaningful death.
Q: And what could possibly make death *meaningful*?
A: A meaningful life.

When Stephanie first read that, a chill went up her spine. That was what she wanted, what the operating system knew about her that she hadn't, the reason she couldn't kill herself: She wanted her death to mean something, since her life never had. Except for Tillman, and he was gone.

Stephanie was pulled out of her reverie by a woman and a young girl coming down the aisle, talking and laughing. They took a pair of seats down in front. The girl must've been the woman's daughter or granddaughter, so strong was the resemblance. Even their laughs sounded the same. Stephanie felt a pang of envy. She'd always wanted a daughter. But, she sneered at herself, what would you teach her—how to turn at the end of a runway? How to lean into a camera?

She folded up the newspaper, creasing it hard. Her hands came away smudged with newsprint. She stuffed the paper into her coat pocket. When she looked up, her eyes went to the girl and the woman, turned in their seats facing each other. The girl was telling a story, her face glowing. She was very pretty, like most everyone in here.

Stephanie knew what she'd tell her daughter if she ever had one. *Beauty isn't Truth,* she'd tell her. *Truth isn't Beauty.*

As the auditorium filled up, Stephanie listened to the conversations around her. Most people were here for the oddity, the thrill of a charismatic crackpot. But underneath their wry denials that they ever took any of this stuff seriously was a persistent note of yearning. Maybe this guy had the answer, they hoped secretly, all the while pretending they could care less whether there were any answers at all. "Deep cool," they called it. Frozen was more like it.

"He's cute, anyway," a woman in front of her said as Dr. Death walked out and took the podium.

At first the lecture covered pretty much the same territory as the interview—how death made life more precious—but Stephanie wasn't here to feel good. Now he was talking about an ancient Christian cult whose members meditated on the details of Jesus' death and on their own future deaths—as a spiritual discipline, as a means of taking stock of their lives. Stephanie was wishing he'd just get to the point, when he did.

"We may think, how quaint—those poor wretches deliberately making themselves miserable, and for what? Sure glad *we* don't die." He gripped the sides of the podium and leaned forward, his voice dropping as if revealing a secret. "But the truth is, we will *all* die." The crowd traded nervous and bemused glances, wondering what brand of Doomsday they were in for.

"Not soon, of course. Everything takes a long time in here. When the Bin was first proposed, there were those who said, 'What if it breaks down? What then?' " He did a high hysterical voice to mock these alarmists, and there was a bit of nervous laughter.

"So, as you know, the Bin was made ridiculously redundant. There are a dozen copies ready to take over should this one be hit by a meteor shower or, as the newspaper suggested yesterday, blown up by a fundie missile attack. Then there are even more self-replicating copies hurtling toward younger stars so that we may live on and on, even after our sun burns up. We, you and I, those of us in the Bin, will outlive what will be the lifetime of the *species* in the real world.

"But, still, *eventually,* in billions and billions and billions of years, when the *last* star winks out, we'll all die." Now there was more laughter. He really had them going there for a minute. Billions of years—that was, well, forever. But he wasn't laughing with them. He wasn't letting it go.

"With that in mind, let's see if it still works. Let's all contemplate our inevitable deaths," he said, and the laughter faded away. "This is 2150, the centennial year. Add, say, seven zeros after that, maybe eight—it's hard to call exactly, and when you get up into the billions, it's hard to even imagine, isn't it? But *whenever* it is, I want you to consider that moment when we all die. Close your eyes and meditate on it. No hurry, of course. You have a long, long time."

He let the silence hang in the air.

Some people got up and left right away. Most everyone else looked too stunned to move. No one was even thinking about laughing now. They were all wondering what in hell they would possibly make of all those zeros. Stephanie decided she liked Dr. Death.

Just when they thought he was done with them, he spoke up again. "But what if you don't want to wait that long?" A man a few rows down, who'd just mounted the energy to stand, sank slowly back into his seat. He'd wait to hear the answer to that question. Stephanie leaned forward to listen.

Dr. Death leaned on the podium, his hands folded, no longer looking at any notes. "What if you want to die sooner? What are your choices? There's suicide, of course. An act of despair. Complete hopelessness. The decision that you can't possibly live another worthwhile moment. That's not the same as wanting not to live forever, to want, some-

day, to reach the end. That's not the same thing at all."
Several people were nodding their heads in agreement.

"So if you reject suicide, word on the street is you can
download into the real world, into a real body." He did a
hammy double take. "Of course, I was forgetting. That's
illegal, isn't it?" Someone laughed behind her, and Stephanie wondered if the stories were true, that you could still
download if you had the connections, even though all interaction with the real world was strictly forbidden. "Even
assuming that the real world is still habitable, what kind of
solution is that? Leave family, friends—your entire world—
to die in a world more than likely overrun by fanatics?"

Stephanie had few friends, had left even fewer to come
in here, and she'd long since spared herself any contact
with her family. She imagined the real world—or the many
variations of it that rumor offered—all of them just another
bad script. Only there, you performed your death only once,
with no applause. As for fanatics, she'd been called one
herself. By Bin standards, she was listening to one now.

"Facing death so that you might value your life shouldn't
be an act of despair, shouldn't require you to abandon your
world. There *is* another choice we can make. We can bring
death to the Bin, to *our* world. We can amend the operating system."

So there it was, the punch line. Stephanie amended her
judgment of Dr. Death to include his being totally out of
touch with reality.

"I don't have to convince you it's possible. It used to be,
after all, the one certainty. As for desirable, I'll let you
ponder that on your own unlimited time. But I say it's
cowardice that makes suicide the only way to die, cowardice
that keeps us alive and alive and alive forever. People say
I'm crazy—that the whole reason for the Bin in the first
place was to end death—and now I want to bring it *back*?

"But sooner or later, don't you think we'll all have had
our fill of immortality? This is our world—programmed as
we choose. The wise folks who gave us immortality set it
up that way. There was only one thing they hadn't counted

on: Without death, we don't really care. Without death, we don't know *what* we want."

AFTER THE LECTURE, HE CALLED FOR QUESTIONS, AND THE crowd was timid at first. They didn't know what he might say next. But once he got past his prepared text, he wasn't nearly so ominous. He was as frightened of death as anyone else, maybe more so. He'd just made something of it, like some beautiful damsel in an ivory tower. And when they saw that, the crowd started poking and prodding with their questions. It reminded Stephanie of her press conference right after her husband's death. The difference was that she'd been lying through her teeth, while this guy was just trying to figure out the truth.

Finally a muscular square-jawed man in the middle of the auditorium rose to his feet and thrust out his chin. "Yeah, I got a question. What the hell does a newbie, if you'll pardon the expression, know about death, anyway? *Some* of us here have seen death face-to-face, and we had enough of it, believe you me . . ."

"Have you?" Dr. Death interrupted. Not hostile, but curious, and that took the wind out of the guy's sails.

"Have I *what*?"

" 'Seen death face-to-face.' "

The questioner sensed a trap and swiveled that chin around the room. "I knew plenty of folks who died. Three of my grandparents . . ."

"I don't mean that. Have you ever seen someone die?"

"Well . . . actually *seen* 'em? No, but . . ."

"But you're sure you know what it is, even though you've never seen it. Long before the Bin, death had become anonymous, unreal—a special effect in a virtual. Doctors saw death first hand, policemen did, but most people died hidden away from the living. Have any of you here actually seen someone you know die?"

Stephanie looked around. Nobody was raising a hand. Surely there must be someone else. But Dr. Death was going on, off on some philosophical tangent, so sure of the answer to his question he'd hardly taken a breath, as oblivious as an adolescent talking about his sweetheart. She lurched to her feet. "I did," she blurted out, and the place fell silent. She wanted to sink through the floor. What was she thinking? She could never explain what happened to her. "I saw my . . . husband die." She remembered his chest erupting, as if the bullets were pebbles tossed into a still pond. The dead eyes staring at her, accusing.

She expected some glib answer, but instead Dr. Death looked stunned. Finally he said, "I'm sorry," and he sounded like he really was. She appreciated that. No one ever had before.

AFTER THE LECTURE, IT WAS FUNNY TO SEE HOW MOST EVERY-one regained their balance. He'd gotten to them—Stephanie had seen that, felt it in the room like an electric charge. But now the lights were up and he was standing down at the bottom of the auditorium signing books and chit-chatting, and life could go on as usual. Forever.

Stephanie got in the book-signing line, though she hadn't bought a book at the little table in the back. She wanted to *do* something, not read about why she should. When she reached the front of the line, he gave her an apologetic smile, then looked confused when she didn't hand him a book.

"Do you just sign books?" she asked. "Or do you ever make things happen? I've tried your first choice, and I don't want to wait for your third. Can you help me download?"

He looked at her for a moment. She thought he was going to send her on her way: *So sorry, just making a buck, no harm done. You don't think I mean any of this, do you?* She didn't judge him for that. Who was she to talk?

"Perhaps I can help," he said. He wrote a number on a slip of paper and handed it to her. "Call me." He smiled at the next woman in line. It was then she realized that almost everyone in the line was a woman. All the men had gone home, or were out getting drunk.

ON HER WAY OUT, SHE FOUND HERSELF IRRESISTIBLY DRAWN into the exhibit off the great hall, like a pilgrim to a shrine. The light was low, except for the displays in the middle of the room, the photographs on the wall, little islands of the past. Everything else was twilight gray. She went to the long rectangular group photo in the middle of the back wall. She reached out and touched Walter's face, no larger than the tip of her finger, and began to cry. How many times could she cry over the same thing? There must be a limit, an end. "I'm sorry," she whispered. "I'm so sorry."

The photo was interactive, and a pleasant female voice said, "Walter Tillman, geneticist, was a pioneer in human-cloning techniques and part of the original research team handpicked by Newman Rogers himself. Unfortunately, Dr. Tillman died in a freak laboratory accident in 2030 before he had the chance to see the fruits of his labors in the first successful identity transfer into a cloned human only a few days later. Press 'Help' for related topics."

STEPHANIE WALKED OUT INTO THE EVENING. AFTER A FEW days of almost balmy weather, it was chilly again. She wrapped the trench coat tightly around her and took another taxi home. This time she rode in silence, even though the cabbie, a little less angst-ridden or more drug-filled than the last one, chattered happily the whole way.

Stephanie went up to her apartment. Like most people, she had a maintenance-free place. The faucets never dripped, the food unit never broke down, the carpets were always clean and plush. She'd had it programmed for real-world maintenance for about twenty years there, thinking that vacuuming the carpet and washing windows would give her something to do. But that soon turned into watching the dirt pile up, the appliances break down, the cobwebs fill up the corners of the ceiling, until she lived in a rounded womb of dust. Then one day she called up the system and changed her program, went for a long walk, and when she got back, everything was as it had been before—neat, spotless, a well-disciplined illusion, not unlike her marriage so many years before.

At least she'd quit blaming herself for that one. It'd been hard to meet guys who weren't completely intimidated by who she was. Those who weren't tended to be arrogant jerks. Jack had fooled her. His arrogance had been on such a grand scale, she couldn't see it for what it was, and while he wasn't a mere jerk, he was truly evil.

She checked her messages. A director she'd worked with before wanted her to play Ophelia in a summer Shakespeare festival. A Gwenna R. Morse wanted to interview her for the newspaper. Stephanie decided to deal with them tomorrow. She didn't want to talk to anyone.

There was no line of men waiting to ask her out. She'd tried. God knows she'd tried. But if it got serious, she always told them about Tillman. She wanted to tell them because Walter had touched her more deeply than anyone else ever had, and she hoped they would see this and perhaps they too might find that place within her seemingly hidden even from herself.

But they all felt the need to trivialize it—*How long did you know this guy? Why do you feel responsible? Sounds like he was asking for it.* Or worse, they'd judge him— *Sounds like he had it coming. He tricked you. He betrayed your trust.* She could never make them understand, and when they saw how important it was to her, she usually didn't have to break things off. They'd do it themselves.

Now her reputation preceded her.

She hauled out a fat script her agent wanted her to read about the last days of Marilyn Monroe. A musical. She poured a glass of wine and opened it in her lap.

She didn't bother eating. Her weight stayed constant in here whether she ate or not. She binged occasionally. But that'd lost its charm. Now about the only time she ate was when she came across a new food or when she went camping.

She smiled to herself, remembering her first date with Walter.

"Where do you usually go for lunch?" she asks him. "I'm still new in the city."

"Zach's Rib Shack," he says.

And she doesn't say, *I can't eat the fat,* but takes his arm and says, "Sounds great."

And it was.

"More sauce," he tells her, squirting it on the rib in her hands. She laughs as she gnaws the bone clean, her sauce-smeared face grinning with sheer pleasure. How does he do that? she asks herself. Make me laugh like this?

She wrenched herself out of the memory, wiping at her tear-streaked face, cursing. She tossed the script aside and went to the phone, calling the number Donovan Carroll had given her. They both had the visuals turned off, but he knew who she was. He remembered the one who wanted to die.

"Will you help me?" she asked.

4

GOD'S HIT MAN

SAM PICKED HIS WAY THROUGH THE RUINS OF WHAT HAD BEEN the sprawl surrounding Washington, D.C., renamed New Jerusalem some seventy years ago by his people, the Christian Soldiers, when they marched in and wiped out the squatters there, making it the Soldiers' holy city. This was only forty days after they had destroyed Satan's minions in the Bin. The initial rejoicing over that victory was soon replaced by lamentation, for still the End of Days had not come as prophesied. And then, in the dark of night, an angel of the Lord visited Gabriel—the anointed one of God—and told him: "Only when the Army of the Lord subdues the wicked will the faithful be taken up to heaven." To this end, the Soldiers took New Jerusalem, slew the unfaithful, and prayed for the Lord's deliverance.

At least that was the official revealed Truth. Sam didn't have to think too hard to figure out the angel's choice of D.C. as the holy city: Beneath its ruins lay the largest concentration of military computers in the world. The Satanic technology that led mankind into the hell of the Bin was soon to be a sword in the hands of an angry God.

When Sam's father was about Sam's age, he'd succeeded in unearthing such a computer and hacking the launch codes for several satellite-based missiles. With a few well-placed strikes, the only significant opposition to the faithful's control of the globe—Muslims in the East, and Christian heretics in California—were struck low in a matter of hours.

Still, the End of Days had not come.

Now the Soldiers sought a way to wipe out the Constructs—cloned human bodies with constructed personalities—who lived with their descendants on the outskirts of New Jerusalem—too close for a missile strike. Satan had cleverly counseled the Constructs to move close to the city the very day the infidels of California and the East were destroyed. Conventional military means proved ineffective against the Constructs, who always seemed to vanish from their settlements before the Soldiers could strike. They were said to communicate with each other telepathically, so even if you managed to sneak up on one of their sentries (who could see for miles even in the dark), all the rest of them were alerted at once.

Sam had followed in his father's footsteps, as if on a leash, and was a lieutenant in the Technological Recovery Unit, TRU, now under his father's command. He was investigating a scout's report that there was an active power link to an orbiting solar power station somewhere in this vicinity. Perhaps this was the laser weapons system which had become the Holy Grail of TRU. From everything Sam had hacked in his years as a Soldier, he seriously doubted the existence of any such system, but he kept his opinions to himself. He kept most all his opinions to himself. If only he could keep them *from* himself, he would be a happier and safer man.

But he couldn't help wondering what was next. After the Constructs, who was left but a few crazies? What would the next angel tell Gabriel? Kill off those faithful who weren't faithful enough? Sam wouldn't mind a visit from an angel himself. He had a few questions.

Jeremiah, the good Soldier who walked alongside Sam, was a different matter. He expressed all his opinions, all of them received opinions, true opinions. You could hear the drone of them anytime you liked. But if they were the truth, Sam wondered, why did they grate on him so? He used to think it was because he lacked faith, but when he prayed, he felt the presence of the Lord welling up within him, and he couldn't doubt the love of God. What he doubted was whether the Soldiers were filled with that love, or something else entirely, whether Gabriel's angels spoke for good or evil. Satan had been an angel, he reminded himself.

Sam tried not to listen to Jeremiah's prattle, but he never shut up. It was his way of telling anyone with influence (as he falsely imagined Sam to be) that he was a good Soldier, worthy of any favors they might wish to grant.

"The Constructs kill and eat each other," he said with practiced righteousness. He surveyed the ruins as he spoke, his weapon at the ready, as if some well-armed rat might try to take him by surprise. "They fill themselves with drugs, then perform these disgusting orgiastic rituals. They're monsters, demons . . ."

"Have you ever seen a Construct, Jeremiah?"

Jeremiah jerked his head around, tilted it proudly. "I patrolled the border for six months."

"So you saw them through field glasses."

"They are hideously ugly."

Sam lowered his eyes to the scanner, not really looking at the display, remembering instead his first encounter with Constructs, shortly after his thirteenth birthday. They'd requested a meeting with the Soldiers to negotiate a peace. His father headed the Soldiers' delegation and took his son along, saying, "You're a man now. You should see the enemy face-to-face." And strange faces they were. Their creators had tampered with their genes so they wouldn't look human. From his clandestine reading since, Sam knew this was to make them more acceptable as slaves to the human race, a role they fulfilled admirably until the human race abandoned them to enter the Bin. Now only the Soldiers remained, and they sought to exterminate the Constructs as the work of Satan.

Sam couldn't help feeling sorry for them, though he tried not to let it show. He stood silently at his father's side in the middle of an overgrown pasture, looking at the Constructs' bizarre faces, one by one, until he came to the one who leaned upon a cane. Even though he was covered with green reptilian scales, Sam could tell he was very old and frail. With a start, he realized the Construct was looking back at him, apparently ignoring his father's recitation of terms, looking into Sam's eyes with a kindness and intelligence Sam had never seen before. And then he smiled, a lipless crescent, and Sam found himself smiling back.

"There was this one," Jeremiah was saying, "who looked like a wildcat, with huge yellow eyes . . ."

"Could you shut up for a minute. I'm trying to get a reading here." They were almost on top of the transmission. The whole area had been razed to the ground when the Bin fell, but it had been strictly mob violence—homemade bombs, plastic explosives. Underneath all this debris, the city was honeycombed with facilities designed to take anything short of a nuclear warhead. Sam turned in a circle until the whining hum he had been straining to hear became a clear sharp tone. And then he saw it—a fat cable running up the side of a chimney, all that remained of the building that had once stood here. Atop the chimney was a black dish about the size of a dinner plate. The whole thing was overgrown with honeysuckle and poison ivy, so that it would go unnoticed by the casual observer. Sam studied the readings. This was one big machine.

Sam climbed over the rubble, sonically probing what lay beneath, tottering back and forth on the uneven planes of brick and concrete. Then he found what he was looking for about twenty yards from the chimney and about four yards down—empty space. He moved around the perimeter of it, an underground room with what looked like a very large rectangular rock in the middle of it. The electrical activity was coming from inside the rock. He'd never seen anything like it.

"There's a stairwell, right here," he told Jeremiah. He positioned himself over the door and eyed the chimney. The power cable was partially shielded from here, and it looked like it would take more than a few bits of flying rock to sever it. He showed the display to Jeremiah. "Plant a charge here—just enough to clear the top of the door— then we'll cut our way in. Try to place it so there's a minimum impact on the power source."

"Why not just blow it door and all—with one big charge?"

"We've got a working system down there, Jeremiah. That door is *why* it's still working. Blow that door, and we dump a ton of bricks on it."

Jeremiah gave him a sullen scowl, but he took off his pack and started to work.

"We'll take cover in that car over there." Sam pointed at a rusted minivan, looking like the husk of a giant cicada, about five yards beyond the chimney. It'd probably been left there by some squatter fleeing when the Soldiers marched into the city. The windows were all gone, but miraculously, it still had all its doors. A sign from God, no doubt.

Sam left Jeremiah to his work and went to crouch in the minivan. All the seats were gone, and weeds were growing up through the floorboard, but the roof seemed sound enough to take a few falling bricks. There was a rotting shoe still on the gas pedal. He imagined the driver frantically trying to navigate streets that hadn't been repaired in years while double-timing Soldiers streamed into the city from all directions, shooting everyone on sight, until he finally leaped from the car, leaving his shoe behind, not knowing there was nowhere to run, nowhere to hide.

Sam shook it off. That was a long time ago. Before he was born. You couldn't change it. You couldn't change anything, except maybe where you were in the whole mess. And Sam was in the thick of it.

He watched Jeremiah working, but he didn't pay too much attention. Jeremiah might be a complete moron, but he knew explosives, even doted on them. Sam had a feeling about this site. It was something special. This wasn't just another weather station or bank system. You didn't go to all this trouble to keep something up and running with a power draw like this unless it was extremely important.

This could be a whole new technology. He'd be decorated for distinguished service in the Army of the Lord. Maybe get that promotion he'd been jockeying for, get out of the field and into some sleepy outpost in one of the provinces, running off the occasional scavenging crazy. No more gung-ho peabrains like Jeremiah to deal with. No more holy city. No more living in his father's probing shadow.

Gabriel often dined at Sam's father's house. Sam could ask the great man personally, a favor to a newly decorated Soldier. Once Gabriel granted a favor, no one, not even Sam's father, dared question it.

Jeremiah climbed into the van, looking around nervously. "This thing's probably crawling with spiders," he said.

"We won't be here long. Blow it." Sam lowered the visor on his helmet.

Jeremiah pushed a button on the detonator, and there was a loud *whoomp*. The van hopped into the air. Rock and dirt rained down on the roof as Jeremiah covered his head, and Sam watched the blast scene, admiring Jeremiah's handiwork, as the bulk of the debris blew away from them. He waited for the dust to settle, his fingers crossed.

IT TOOK THEM A COUPLE OF HOURS TO CLEAR THE TOP OF THE door and cut through the heavy steel. Several times Jeremiah wanted to radio for help, but Sam vetoed him. He didn't want a swarm of Soldiers showing up, all ready to take credit for the find. He could see them in his mind's eye, standing up before the crowd as they were decorated: *The Lord showed me the way, and I followed his guidance . . .*

Jeremiah's torch severed the last bit of steel, and the top of the door fell forward, grazing Jeremiah's shin. He fell back with a scream, blanching with pain.

Sam crouched down beside him and steadied him with a hand on his chest. "Lie back. Let me take a look at it." Sam rolled up Jeremiah's pant leg, and there was a shallow gash about an inch wide and eight inches long. Sam probed around the wound. Nothing broken. The whole thing glistened with beads of blood, but it was only a bad scrape. He wouldn't even need stitches.

Jeremiah glared at the dark square hole where the door had been, as if it were to blame for his wound. "I told you we should've blown it," he said through clenched teeth.

Sam knew he should just break out the first-aid kit, douse the cut with alcohol, and bandage it up. He too glanced into the dark hole. "Maybe you should return to the Temple and have this looked at."

Jeremiah didn't hesitate. He gave a tight-lipped nod and took Sam's offered hand. Sam pulled him to his feet, and Jeremiah took a few steps. He could get around okay. Sam helped him into his backpack and gave him a reassuring pat on the shoulder. "It should be fine. I'll see you when I get back."

"You aren't coming?"

"You seem to be able to walk okay. I'm going to check this out before looters get to it."

"Looters? We eliminated them a long time ago."

"Construct spies, then."

Jeremiah narrowed his eyes, apparently trying to determine whether Sam was mocking him or not. "Our orders are not to enter new sites alone."

Sam smiled pleasantly. "Then I'll stand guard over it until the Commander can send someone to accompany me." Sam knew how long that would take. The chain of command had many links as finely wrought as Jeremiah. But with the mention of the Commander—Sam's father—there'd be no more argument from Jeremiah.

SAM WATCHED JEREMIAH LIMP BRAVELY OFF (HIS LIMP GROWing markedly less pronounced as he got farther away) and waited until he'd been out of sight for five minutes before he shone a light into the room and looked around, but all he could see was the carpeted floor.

He hoisted himself feetfirst through the opening and

landed on well-padded carpet. His impact didn't raise a
cloud of dust in the beam of his flashlight. He pointed it
at the ceiling to make sure the ceiling was sound; at the
floor, to make sure it was all there. No cobwebs or mouse
droppings as with most sites. There didn't seem to be any
dust. Someone had done a very good job on environmen-
tal control.

He played the beam along the wall by the door and found
the light controls. He turned them on, and the place filled
with a warm diffuse light. Sam gaped at the thing that took
up most of the room. It looked like a huge rock—dark
green, almost black—chiseled into a rectangular solid. He
scanned it and could find no seams or variations in its com-
position. It was apparently solid, no moving parts, but the
scanner couldn't seem to decide whether it was a liquid or
a solid. He approached it cautiously and lay his palm on
the surface. It had the soft soapy feel of marble, but it
was warmer.

There was a panel set in the side of it, bristling with
standard interface jacks, a shelf where the monitors and
whatever inputs this thing used had apparently once sat,
but they were all gone now. Someone had cleaned this place
out before he came along—either the techs who used this
thing, or looters during the fall of the Bin. But they couldn't
very well take the computer itself.

Sam plugged his scanner in and set it on line input. The
display lit up with a lovely graphic of a mountain stream.
A pleasant female voice asked him for his password. He
entered GUEST, not really expecting to get in. As he was
watching the flowing waters, wondering what was taking so
long, wondering if the thing had been wiped out except for
the front end, the screen went blank, and a line of text
appeared at the top, letter by letter, as if someone were
entering it somewhere: HELLO. NICE OF YOU TO DROP IN.
WHO ARE YOU?

What was this thing? This was the weirdest interface he'd
ever come across. He looked around. There were security
cameras everywhere. Maybe there was somebody still moni-

toring them. Maybe there was another empty room he'd missed in his scan, somebody holed up in it. But that was ridiculous. Nobody could live down here. It'd been sealed up at least sixty or seventy years.

Another line of text appeared letter by letter on the screen: TALK TO ME.

He entered SAM, deciding to keep it simple.

There was a brief delay, as if the system were deciding what to do about him.

COME ON IN, SAM appeared below his name, and he felt a chill go up his spine. A floor plan of the room appeared on the screen. Where he sat was labeled SAM. To the right of the computer, or whatever it was, a circle pulsed with green light. It was labeled VISITOR INTERFACE MODULE. A message flashed below it: ENTER HERE.

Sam walked around to the side of the machine and found a sarcophagus-shaped thing. It was made of some sort of plastic, hard-wired into the black thing. There were what appeared to be several bullet holes in the door or lid. He pulled it open and stepped inside. On the inside of the door, above the bullet holes, was a display screen. He pulled the door shut, and the screen lit up. CHECK DOOR SEAL, it instructed him. But the door seal wasn't the problem, Sam figured, it was those bullet holes. Whatever this thing did, it wasn't going to work until he plugged those holes.

There were four of them, about half an inch in diameter. The plastic, or whatever it was, was a quarter of an inch thick and hadn't shattered or cracked. The holes almost looked like they'd been drilled. It would be an easy matter to plug them, if he just had some caulk or glue. If he went back to the Temple, he'd have company. He could sneak into his quarters, get some caulk or something, but he'd most likely be seen, and by the time he got back, the place could be swarming with Soldiers.

He stepped out of the thing and emptied his pockets and his pack. He crouched over the pile and considered each item. Nothing. He had the torch. Maybe he could soften the plastic, close the holes that way. Or he might just end up making them larger or catching the thing on fire. He hung his head, staring down at his shoes, and then it came to him. He sat on the floor and took off his left boot. With his knife, he cut off the rubber sole, then cut four strips. He lit the torch and passed it over each rubber strip until it softened, rolling them into cylinders, pushing them into the holes, mashing the soft rubber from both sides. When all four holes were plugged, he stepped inside again and closed the door. The display screen lit up. It read: VISITOR INTERFACE MODULE, with a menu beneath it. Sam let out a yelp of delight. "Thank you, Lord," he said.

He touched the STATUS icon and got the following:

EMERGENCY POWER ON
MAXIMUM OCCUPANCY: TWO
CURRENT OCCUPANTS: ONE
OCCUPANTS:
      WALTER TILLMAN (DOE 12/20/2030)

Occupants. Sam felt a tingling in his chest, and he swallowed hard, fighting the urge to throw open the door and get out of here. He forced himself to concentrate on the display. Think. Date of entry: 2030! That was 120 years ago. Before the Bin, before the Soldiers took the city.

He went back to the main menu. There were only two other choices: UPLOAD and DOWNLOAD.

He hit UPLOAD and got a submenu:

SELECT ENVIRONMENT:
      MUTUAL
      EXCLUSIVE

What could that mean? What sort of environment? What kind of system had occupants anyway? And then he realized. The Bin had occupants, billions of them. This thing could only hold two, but it was the same idea. As he was trying to decide which to choose, the MUTUAL icon, two tiny men shaking hands, began to pulse.

He reached out and touched it, and felt a brief but intense falling sensation, and he almost passed out. When he opened his eyes, the screen was flashing UPLOAD SUCCESSFUL, and then the door popped open by itself.

He was in a large stately room, certainly more elegant than anything in New Jerusalem. A young woman in a skirt much too short for any Soldier to wear stood before him, smiling. "Good morning! Welcome to the White House," she said. "My name is Sally. I'll be your guide today. If you'll just step into the library, we can begin."

Cautiously, he stepped into the room, glancing over his shoulder to make sure the Visitor Interface Module was still there. As he turned back to Sally, she was staring at his unshod foot. "Would you like another shoe?" she asked pleasantly. He looked down at his feet and nodded. Instantly, a shoe appeared on his foot, identical to the one he'd cut up. Must be a holograph, he thought. But he moved his toes around inside. It felt just like his old one, even the frayed inner sole under his big toe. He felt a chill. It was a virtual. The whole thing was.

"Isn't that better?" Sally said brightly.

She didn't wait for his reply but was already headed toward the doorway. His duty was clear—to exit immediately and report his findings. But instead, he crossed the room, noting each sensation, looking for any deviation from his accustomed reality. It was perfect.

On either side of the doorway were two paintings that brought him up short. A man and a woman—very strange-looking. The man's face looked painted, and he had a weird growth coming out of the top of his head. He wondered if they were Constructs, but who would paint portraits of Constructs?

Sally noticed his interest. "They are Native Americans," she told him, as if she knew his question without his even asking. "On the left is Sharitarish, or 'Wicked Chief' of the Pawnee Tribe. On the right is Hayne Hudjihini, or 'Angel of Delight' of the Oto Tribe. They visited the White House in 1822."

He kept thinking: 1822. Over 300 years ago. He followed Sally through the grand house, trying to remember who Native Americans were. They had tribes like the Hebrews. Was there perhaps some sort of connection? But why would a chief of his people be named "wicked"? And what sort of angel brought delight? His mind was in a whirl, trying to figure out too many things at once, trying to keep up with Sally's brisk pace, completely ignoring the voice in his head that kept telling him to get out as quickly as possible. But if he listened to that voice, he would've gone back to the Temple with Jeremiah.

And then Sally stopped before an open door, and he almost ran into her. "Go right in," she said, holding her arm out toward the doorway. He stepped inside, and she gave him a little wave before she closed the door. A short man with a froglike face was standing in the middle of the room. Sam didn't think he was a Construct, in spite of his ugliness. His features weren't extreme enough for that.

"I'm Tillman," the man said and offered his hand.

Sam shook it, mumbling, "Sam," as he eyed the red walls and furniture warily. Who would have such a sumptuous house? But then, he reminded himself, this is all an illusion. He wondered what sort of world he'd choose for himself if he'd been in here for 120 years.

"Sit down," Tillman suggested, motioning toward one of the ancient sofas. He himself sat in a battered recliner that looked out of place in here. Sam sat down carefully. The wood creaked slightly under his weight. He ran his fingertips over the gold threads that formed snowflake shapes on the red fabric.

"So what's the uniform, Sam? You some kind of military or something?"

Sam had a million questions, but he decided to keep them to himself for a while. He figured, if he was going to find out anything from this man, he needed to gain his trust. The only way he knew to do that was to tell him the truth. "I'm a Christian Soldier, a lieutenant in the Army of the Lord."

"The Lord has an army now, does He?" Tillman giggled. "Who's the enemy?"

Sam's father would say that anyone who had to ask that question was clearly not among the faithful. "The unfaithful," Sam said, but the word made him uncomfortable.

"And how do you tell who's 'unfaithful'?"

Sam had asked himself the question before. You couldn't tell, could you, what somebody's relationship with God was? He'd seen people burned at the stake with prayers on their lips. Tillman was looking at him quizzically, waiting for an answer. "They're not Soldiers," Sam said.

Tillman slapped his thighs. "Ah! And all the Soldiers wear uniforms like that one."

"Yes."

Tillman nodded. "Pretty good system. What else do you guys believe in, besides uniforms?"

Sam knew he was being made fun of, that a true Soldier would never tolerate this man's disrespectful tone. "The revealed word of God."

"The Bible."

"Yes."

"Great book." Tillman got up out of his chair and paced, mumbling first to himself and then to a painting of a man holding an old-fashioned rifle. It was hung so high on the wall that the little man was looking almost straight up. He stopped his mumbling and turned around. "Do you know where you are, Soldier Sam?"

"I think so," he said. "It's a computer system that maintains a virtual environment for up to two inhabitants. Probably constructed from your memories of real places. You have been in here . . . for a long time."

"One hundred and twenty years, right?"

"Yes, sir."

Tillman giggled again and wagged his finger at Sam. "That's right, boy. Always respect your elders. How old are you?"

"Twenty-five."

"Sounds like you know a lot about computers. Is that what you do for the Lord?"

"I locate and attempt to restore computer systems that might be useful to God's purpose."

"Like what? Doesn't He already know everything?"

Sam had never spoken with anyone who talked so casually about God. It wasn't irreverent exactly. It was almost friendly. This man's been in here for 120 years, Sam reminded himself, there's no telling what strange ideas he might've developed. "I look primarily for military systems."

Tillman slapped his forehead. "Of course! I get it. I'm a little slow sometimes. It's like Sodom, Gomorrah, the Flood. Sinners in the Hands of an Angry God stuff. Army of the Lord—of course, of course, of course." He tilted his head back and gave Sam an appraising look. "So how's it going? God's purpose, that is."

Sam looked around uncomfortably. What if some other Soldiers had shown up and were tapping into the system, monitoring this conversation? As a lieutenant in the Army of the Lord, he should've shot Tillman for blasphemy by now, though he doubted his weapon would have any effect in here. "The End of Days is at hand," he said piously. Always a safe thing to say.

Tillman continued to study him through narrowed eyes. "How do you know that?"

Sam feared he was giving away too much. He had no idea what power Tillman might wield in here. He remembered his shoe, appearing out of nothing. "We are on the verge of the final battle," he said automatically. "The faithful shall soon triumph over the unfaithful."

"Ever find any 'useful' military systems?"

"Yes, sir."

"Like what?"

"I can't really say, sir."

"Come on. Who can I tell? Nuclear weapons?"

Sam nodded his head, remembering the satellite films he'd seen on many a Sunday of mushroom clouds blossoming over the Middle East as millions died. "Praise God!"

the congregation cried. And while Sam mouthed the words (he dare not do anything else), he could never give voice to them.

"Not too many unfaithful left on this side of the crust, huh? Let me make sure I've got this straight: You guys are God's hit men. When all the unfaithful get theirs, you get heaven."

"I wouldn't put it in those words."

"But I've got the gist, right? Well, I hate to disappoint you and your Lord, but this isn't a military computer. It's my home, such as it is. The ultimate getaway—just me and my memories of forty-two years of life, such as it was. No military potential whatsoever unless you count my dad's insults."

"The young lady who showed me in?"

"Quite fetching, isn't she? Alas, she's not real. Made her from one of my memories. High-tech masturbation, more or less."

Sam felt his face flushing.

"Not much with the girls, huh? Me either, as you would've probably guessed." Tillman returned to his recliner, sitting on the front of it, his feet barely touching the floor. He stared up at the painting again. "How are the animals doing?" he asked wistfully, still looking at the painting.

"The animals?"

He looked back to Sam, a humorless smile on his face. "Never mind. Tell me, Sam, have you ever heard of anything called the Alternative Life Medium Assembly?"

It'd been a long time since Sam had heard it called that. "You mean the Bin?"

" 'The Bin.' How apt. That's what it's called?"

Sam nodded. "It was Satan's snare for the unfaithful. It went on-line in 2050. Most all mankind was seduced by it, so that only the chosen of God remained. It was destroyed by the Soldiers in 2081, infected with a virus and shut down."

"The Soldiers did that, huh? Feisty bastards, aren't you?"

He shook his head. "But I find it hard to believe that a bunch of Bible-pounding psychos, if you'll pardon the expression, could run a virus past Newman Rogers. How do you know it's shut down?"

"The transfer stations are all dead."

"Transfer stations?"

"Those who wanted to enter the Bin went to a transfer station and had themselves uploaded."

"And the body?"

"Cremated."

"Jeez, and I thought I had it bad in here. So why did you guys do that—wipe out all those innocent people?"

Sam licked his lips and looked around the room. He was being tested—by God or by Satan—he didn't know which. "They had already surrendered their souls to Satan. They had to be destroyed to bring about the End of Days."

"But it didn't quite do the trick, right?"

"No, sir."

Tillman leaned forward in his chair and gave Sam a sly look. Maybe I should just get out of here after all, Sam thought, but he didn't move, couldn't move. "How do you know they're not playing possum?" Tillman asked him.

"I beg your pardon?"

"Playing possum? You know, like the animal?"

"I've never heard of them."

Tillman winced as if in pain. "Let's just hope you don't get out much. It's an expression. Means playing dead, faking it, to avoid further attack." He flopped back in the recliner and lay perfectly still for a moment, his jaw slack, not breathing, then he came upright again, letting the momentum carry him to his feet. "Maybe Newman just decided to kiss you crazy fucks good-bye. Lock the door and throw away the key."

Sam supposed he should be angry at Tillman's insults, but as he explained his people's beliefs to this man from another time, Sam had to admit it was pretty crazy—even leaving out the true horrors they'd yielded—even (though he'd never say it) pretty fucking crazy. Sam rubbed his cheek with the back of his hand. He'd said "fuck" twice in his life. The first time his father hadn't heard him. "Why do you keep saying the Soldiers are crazy?" he asked.

Tillman scratched his nose. "Not very politic of me, is it? I think anybody who believes in a God as crazy as the one you guys believe in must be nuts. But I think you halfway agree with me, don't you? Smart kid like you? You don't believe God's purpose is to nuke innocent people, do you?"

Sam didn't say anything. He knew he should, but he couldn't.

"Come on, Sam. Nobody can hear us in here. What are you going to do about me, by the way? Somehow I don't see me fitting into your crowd. They might not mind my looks, but I don't think they'd go for my religion and politics."

Sam knew what would become of Tillman. He'd be picked clean of useful information, then erased from the system without hesitation. According to the Laws of God, he'd already lost his soul 120 years ago when he abandoned his body for this place. He stood up. "I need to get back," he said.

"So are you going to tell on me?"

"No."

Tillman nodded, eyeing Sam carefully. Sam dreaded whatever was going to come next, though he had no idea what it might be.

Finally Tillman spoke: "Look, Sam. I'm kind of in a fix here. I'm trapped in this thing. I can't get out without a body. I gave serious consideration to stealing yours, but it just wouldn't be right, you know? You seem like a nice young kid, your whole life ahead of you. Do you guys ever make clones?"

Sam felt a little dizzy. Of course, Tillman could've just downloaded into his body, and then Sam would be the one trapped in here. Instead, he'd sat down and talked with him. Even now, knowing that Sam could put him in grave danger, he merely asked for his help instead of setting himself free. Why?

Tillman waved a hand in front of Sam's face. "Yoohoo, Sam? Clones. Do you guys do any cloning?"

"Clones are the work of Satan," Sam said automatically.

"I was afraid of that."

Sam had heard that the Constructs still practiced identity transfers, cloning, all the Satanic technologies. Though, officially, it never happened, Sam knew there were Soldiers who'd gone over to the Constructs, and rumors came back that they had themselves put into new bodies in the bizarre rituals Jeremiah talked about.

This, then, was the test—what to do about this funny little man. He knew the right thing to do—report his findings immediately—but he couldn't bring himself to do it. This man had spared Sam's life because it was the right thing to do. God, it seemed clear to Sam, had told Tillman what to do. Sam took a deep breath and let it out. "I might be able to help you."

"How? Is there a black market or something?"

"I've heard things. I could check into it."

Tillman smiled. "That would be a most Christian thing to do."

Sam felt a decided change deep inside of him. Whether he was saved or damned, he couldn't say, but he knew he was about to change his life forever. He went to the door and opened it. Sally was nowhere to be seen. "I have to go now, before I'm missed."

"Don't be a stranger," Tillman called after him as he hurried down the hall.

SAM HAD A LITTLE TROUBLE WALKING BACK TO THE TEMPLE on one shoe. The virtual one hadn't followed him into the real world. He decided to make the shoe a convincing detail in the story of a cave-in that had pinned his foot. He smeared himself with dirt, tore his shirt, and cut a gash in his leg with a jagged rock. He rolled some rocks in front of the door and piled some lightweight junk on top of those. With that power reading, though, he knew it would only be a matter of time before someone else was sent to investigate.

He reported that he'd hacked the system and that it was nothing more than a hopelessly corrupted weather system. He didn't have to work too hard to convincingly portray a rattled young soldier who'd had a brush with death. He was relieved of duty for the rest of the day and lay in his quarters until dark. Then he climbed out of the window and headed for the edge of town. Knowing the sentries' positions, he didn't have too much trouble getting past them undetected. If he wanted something illegal done, he knew where to go, though he'd never been there before. It was called, even by its inhabitants, Crazyville.

5

A WOMAN OF PRINCIPLE

LAURA SAT IN THE CHEZ ÉLITE À LA CARTE CAFE, looking to score dinner. She had a standing deal with the owner,
Chef Jeff: a room and two meals a day for one screw a
week. Now—four days since she last paid him in full (and
quite well, thank you)—he was asking for another, or she
couldn't eat.

Fuck him. It was dog stew anyway. He kept this scrawny
steer out back so people would get the idea he was really
serving beef. (What did they think? That he was cloning
it?) But this was Crazyville. People believed anything and
everything—some of them all at the same time. They came
from a long line of nuts—the descendants of those judged
too crazy to enter the Bin and those too crazy to want to.
They stuck close to the Constructs, figuring that gave them
some protection from the Soldiers, though they were generally ignored by both groups. Unless there were certain kinds
of business to be conducted. Which is where Laura came in.

She'd lived here since she was sixteen, had managed to
do okay for herself. Doing a little bit of this and a little bit
of that. She couldn't complain. If she wanted wisdom and
serenity, she could go back to her own kind, the terribly
sweet, goodie-goodie Constructs. No thank you. She'd
rather fuck Chef Jeff.

So why didn't she just fuck him, she had to ask herself,
and get something to eat? It was the principle of the thing.

They'd agreed on a price, goddamn it. Once she let him push her around, then they'd all be doing it.

She considered the possibilities. There wasn't much to choose from. Rat was standing in the corner, listening to a radio that hadn't worked for a couple hundred years. Not that there was anything to listen to on a working radio but the Soldiers on their walkie-talkies, rogering each other, checking their checkpoints. Anyway, if Rat was in the mood, he wouldn't have put himself in the corner. Maybe tomorrow, when he was a good boy again, he'd ask her to listen to a song on his radio. She'd put on the silent headphones and sing "You Light Up My Life" to him, while he fucked her with his eyes closed, imagining she was—what? She had no idea. But Rat was okay. He always paid in first-rate electronics, including radios that actually worked.

There was a scavenger, just passing through, slumped in his chair with a bag of goodies in his arms, who would've been perfect, but he'd passed out cold over an hour ago. She'd die of starvation before he came to. She spotted him earlier and thought about hitting on him, but she'd promised herself a night off. Didn't she deserve a fucking night off *once* in a while? And then Chef had to go and pull this shit. This is what I get, she thought, for not attending to business, for just letting things slide.

Sandoz was at the bar explaining to Chef Jeff how time was moving backward, but nobody knew it but him—because everybody's *minds* worked backward except for his. "Remember, Chef, what I will tell you. The beginning is coming, and after you know it, it's yesterday." Chef scratched his gut, nodding now and then, looking at Laura with this smug look, like he could hear her stomach growling from across the room. Sandoz was a regular, as regular as her hemorrhoids could stand. She squirmed in her chair. No. Not tonight. Not for fucking bowwow casserole.

There was a Construct doing some business with Carmen at a corner table, but Carmen had that situation well in hand, and Laura didn't like doing Constructs anyway. They always ended up giving her a lecture about how she was betraying her people by living here, abandoning the traditional ways, blah, blah, blah, blah—all the while they're putting their traditional cocks back in their pants.

And that was it.

Somebody might come in for a late drink. It was around one or two. It happened. She'd seen them stumbling in here at three in the morning, hollering, "Where's the whores?" But there wasn't much of a moon, and it was a little too dark out there for most people. They might be crazy, but the citizens of Crazyville knew enough not to walk around the place in the dark. Now and then there was some guy who seemed perfectly okay, and you'd think, Why does he live here? Then, all of a sudden, he's carving up women because his father's ghost told him to. Genetics was what it was. Biology. Like starvation.

Nobody else was coming in tonight. She imagined herself sitting here forever, waiting for nothing, getting hungrier and hungrier. She considered talking Chef down to a hand job. He was warming his belly on the side of the stew pot, stirring away with a canoe paddle, smiling at her like she was a pork chop with gravy. It was real touching. Hand job, hell. She'd like to stick his dick in that boiling stew of his.

"Please, God," she muttered under her breath, "how about giving me a fucking break?"

Just then the door opened, and this Soldier stepped in all cautious, like you might need an invitation to come in this dump. He didn't have the uniform on, but you could always tell. The tight-ass haircuts for one thing and that smarmy look they all had. They showed up to get laid now and then, usually so damn nervous you'd think Gabriel himself was hiding under the bed. But you could charge them damn near anything. You had to figure that if they were willing to go to hell for it, price was already no object. And they never took long: *Fuck that whore and get on home to God and family.*

Her dinner had just walked through the door.

He sat down a couple of stools from Sandoz and pre-

tended to listen while his blue eyes were checking everybody out. He was looking for something, all right.

"You're looking for me, baby," she said to herself. "You
are looking for *me*."

She walked over to the bar and sat down beside him, just
as Chef was asking him what he wanted.

"Fruit juice," he said.

This one *was* green. She leaned in close and whispered
in his ear, her lips ever so slightly brushing against it, just
a *little* bit of tongue. "It's Tang, Soldier Boy. And don't
drink anything from this place that doesn't have alcohol in
it—unless you want to spend a week on the can. Have
a beer."

He liked that ear business. You could always tell by the
way they breathed. But he just turned to her, his eyes never
dropping below her neck, and said, "Thanks," real nice
and polite.

She checked out his profile as he ordered a beer. Nice-
looking, earnest as hell, hair so blond it was almost white.
Candy from a baby. Chef put a battered can of Milwaukee's
Best in front of him, but didn't take his hand off it. "And
what is your method of payment this evening?" Chef asked.
Chef was so full of shit.

The Soldier stuck his hand in his pocket and pulled out
a fistful of bullets. What an idiot. She reached out and took
a single bullet out of his hand and put it on the bar. "That's
enough for both of us to have a drink, right, Chef?"

Chef cut her a look, but he hauled out another Milwaukee's Best and set it in front of her. She picked it up—
warm, of course—and tossed her head back toward her
table. "You want to sit with me? I just saved you a bundle."

"Thanks," he said again.

She had to hand it to these Soldiers. They were a polite
bunch. At least they all started out that way. Some of them
turned nasty later—spitting in your face and telling you
what a worthless piece of shit you were because you've got
their cocks right where *they* want them. Poor dears. But

this one didn't seem like *that* type. He seemed kind of, well, wistful or something. Maybe he was crazy.

He followed her to the table and even held the chair for her, oblivious to everybody in the place grinning like it was the funniest thing in the world that anyone would hold a chair for her. Even Carmen was yucking it up, as if she had anything to laugh about. Some people still had manners. Some people still had principles.

"So what's your name, Soldier Boy?"

"Sam."

"Pleased to meet you, Sammy. I'm Laura."

"How did you know I was a Soldier?"

"You're not serious, are you?" Laura popped open her beer and took a swallow. At least it wasn't flat. His was sitting on the table, unopened, but he had his hands wrapped around it. A nice, comforting, warm, hard cylinder in his hands. Pretty soon he'd be sliding them up and down.

He nodded his head, real thoughtful, looking at her, checking her out, but he wasn't saying anything. Let him make the first move, she decided. Let him sweep me off my feet. He was the romantic type. That's what it was.

But he just kept looking and thinking, and she got tired of waiting. How long was it going to be before this guy made his move, so she could get something to eat? She gave him an encouraging look, the kind the little Soldier girls back home weren't likely to give him unless they wanted to be stoned.

"You're a Construct," he said.

She automatically reached up and touched her eyebrows—small green scales. She had a wig over the scales on top of her head, and by the time guys got to her crotch, it usually kind of turned them on. The scales there were soft, like flower petals.

"Is that a problem?" she asked.

He actually blushed. "No, not at all. I came here hoping to find a Construct."

Course he had. If you were going to get laid, why not do the Devil's daughter? "I'm not a *real* Construct, you understand. I'm third-generation. I don't live the life. I've just got some of the leftover freak genes." She took off her wig, figuring if he wanted freak show, she'd give it to him.

She lifted his left hand off the beer can and guided his fingertips to the top of her head. He didn't flinch, but gently ran his fingers across her temple. He might've been a little boy stroking his pet snake, only he was doing that breathing thing again. This guy was too easy. "The scales are a genetic gift from my grandfather, a real lizard man. My grandmother, however, was the most beautiful call girl in D.C." (Not counting all the ones who looked just like her, like her *other* grandmother she never even knew.) She raised her head and looked up at him, so that his hand brushed her cheek. He pulled his hand away, wrapping it around his beer again. He turned bright red. You could see the blood rising up his neck into his face until his hair almost looked pink.

A romantic *virgin,* she decided. "You going to drink that?" she asked.

He was staring at her again, like he was in another world. Then he seemed to snap out of it and popped open the beer, suddenly cheerful. He put it to his lips slowly, tasted it like it was the first time, which it probably was, and made a little "not bad" face. He took a bigger swallow and set it down, smiling at her like she'd already fucked his brains out. She was having trouble keeping up with this one.

Now there were lots of things she thought he might say next, but not what he did say. "This is truly a miracle," he said, all earnest and religious like they do. "I met your grandfather once—I'm certain it was him. I'll never forget it. And now the Lord has led me to you."

He launched into some sappy childhood story about meeting some Construct in a cow pasture somewhere. She didn't really listen. This was getting her nowhere. Maybe he wasn't really a Soldier after all; maybe he was some fucking crazy who was so crazy he *thought* he was a Soldier. And she was what? The Virgin Mary? "So what's your point?" she asked to shut him up more than to find out.

Now it was him taking her hand, leaning in close and confidential. "I need your help," he whispered like they were in some spy virtual.

If she wasn't starving, she might've laughed. "I've got a room upstairs," she said, "where I do all my helping."

"Would you take me there?"

"Sure thing. You understand that help has a price, now don't you, Sammy?"

"Of course." He started digging into his pocketful of bullets. "I'll be glad to pay you any—"

She laid her hand over his, about three inches to the left of a friendly khaki-covered penis. "Upstairs," she said. She stood, and he followed her like a puppy. As they crossed the room, Carmen's Construct watched them like a hawk— literally in his case with these weird bird eyes—but Sam didn't have a clue. He couldn't be bothered. After all, he was on a mission from God. This guy didn't need a whore, he needed a keeper. At the bottom of the stairs, Laura motioned for Sam to go on ahead of her, and she flipped the bird at Hawkeye and all the rest of the big happy Construct family who might be tuned in for a peek at her life. Nosy bastards. Fuck all of them.

LAURA'S ROOM WAS ABOUT EIGHT-BY-EIGHT, IN PRETTY GOOD shape, except for the hole in the wall at the foot of the bed. She'd had this Construct up one night. He must've been seven-foot-six if he was an inch, and he got a little carried away and put his foot through the wall.

"So how can I help you, Sammy?" She reached out and started unbuckling his belt.

He took her hands and pulled them off, nice but firm, and cinched up his belt. "You're a prostitute," he said, like he'd just figured that out.

She flopped down on the bed. Jesus, what was this guy's story? "What did you think I was? Your fairy godmother? What do you fucking *want* me to be?" She was never going to eat tonight. She was never going to fucking eat again in her life.

Sam appeared to be having his own trouble deciding his next move, or the Lord's—who could figure out how these guys worked? "I need help," he said finally. "I want to do an identity transfer. I thought someone here might help me."

It took a few seconds for his words to sink in. Talk about forest for the trees. Did he say *identity transfer*? Hello. She sat up straight and patted the bed beside her. This was serious business, no matter how hungry she was—hell of a lot more than a pocketful of bullets. "Sammy," she said. "The Lord has brought you to *exactly* the right person."

She talked fast, explaining she arranged identity transfers once a year, a little sideline, keeping things vague when it came to whose identities she was transferring where. The guy was still a Soldier, after all, and there were some things he definitely didn't need to know. She had *that* much loyalty to the Constructs.

He listened to her carefully, standing there, his arms crossed. "You make clones?" he asked, and she could see she'd have to level with him about the goods she had to offer.

"No, not clones. Constructs. After the Initiation."

He gave her a totally blank look.

"How much do you know about Constructs, Sammy?"

"Only what I've been told."

She had a rough idea what that was, which meant he knew less than nothing—boogeyman stories in the dark. "And if you believed that crap, I guess you wouldn't be here."

He cocked his head to one side and gave her this crooked little smile. "I guess not."

"Sit down, Sammy. I don't bite unless you ask for it." She slid over to give him plenty of room, and he sat on the edge of the bed. It was a nice bed. Probably the nicest bed in Crazyville, and she'd worked damn hard to get it.

"Okay," she said when he was settled in. "Let me give you a little history lesson. The original Constructs were

clones with a few extra gene splices thrown in to make
them more useful and less human-looking. The gene splices
weren't that big a deal, mostly cosmetic. They're not what
made Constructs so weird. For one thing, they all had trans-
ceiver chips at the base of their brains that were linked to
a central computer. These chips were designed to keep tabs
on them—make recalls quick and simple. Only the Constructs figured out how to use them to communicate with
each other—all five senses. Now all their kids get the same
chip when they turn thirteen."

"So Constructs *are* telepathic."

She thought he sounded awful gee-whiz about it for a
Soldier who wasn't supposed to approve of such things. "If
you want to be. You don't have to tune into that drone if
you don't want to. Me, I bowed out at sixteen."

"Why?" he asked.

He didn't seem to mean anything by it, but there was no
point in getting personal. "Seems like an odd question from
a Soldier. The Constructs are the Devil's children, remember?"

He looked around her room, taking in her handful of
belongings, the foot-shaped hole in the wall. "Is your life
here better?"

"Well, thank you, Jesus, but you haven't heard the whole
story. The identities of the original Constructs were made
by stitching together portions of different people's identities—usually three or four different ones—to get different
traits, and so nobody would discover that their gardener
used to be Uncle Ralph or some damn thing. Only problem
was, the pieces always came unstitched and started restoring
themselves, so that what you ended up with is three or four
people living in one body.

"And here's the truly weird part: They like it. They've
made a whole damn religion out of it, every bit as nutty as
you guys. So that now, every summer solstice, they have
what they call 'Initiation'—when anybody who wants to take
on a group identity and become a true Construct steps forward with two or three of their best pals. They go through

this big touchy-feely ceremony, transfer the suckers into *one* of their bodies, and then barbecue the leftovers. Some years there's like twenty or thirty bodies.

"When I figured out how sick the whole thing was, I split. I wasn't going to hang around and be brainwashed like the rest of them. One body, one mind works just fine for this cowgirl." She remembered the whole circle of them holding hands around the campfire of what had been their own flesh, and her stomach turned over.

He put his hand on hers. "I'm sorry," he said.

Get a grip here, she told herself. Stay focused. "Don't worry about it. I got away. But that's what I can get you, Sam. One of those castoffs. You never know what you're going to get, but they tend to throw away the bodies *without* the weird genes, so your chances of getting something that looks human is pretty good. They're all healthy as can be, built to last. But you're going to have to wait a few weeks, and it'll cost you. A lot. You still interested?"

He didn't hesitate. "Yes, absolutely." He looked all excited.

"I think we should seal the deal by you buying me dinner. How's that sound?"

"Fine." He squeezed her hand and grinned at her.

"It is *so* fine, Sammy. It is a pleasure doing business with you."

IT WAS TOO BEAUTIFUL. SHE WAS GETTING DINNER WITHOUT even taking her clothes off, and if Chef Jeff hadn't been such an asshole, she never would've fallen into this deal in the first place. It only goes to show that if you stay focused, if you stick to your principles, shit worked out. She was feeling very good indeed when she sat down with her bowl of stew, laughing to herself. Sam wisely decided he wasn't hungry.

"Why are you so happy?" he asked her.

"Because I love to help people," she said, her mouth full of stew.

He actually managed a skeptical look. She was proud of him. Maybe she could be a good influence on him, at least keep him alive until their business was completed. "Okay, okay. I'll tell you. We're partners, right? It's this thing with Chef Jeff—the fat fuck scowling at us over there? See, we've got this deal . . ." She told him how she'd outsmarted the good Chef while she shoveled down the rest of her stew, really warming to her story. But he didn't seem to be getting it. He didn't even crack a smile. "Don't you get it? He was going to screw me, but I screwed him instead."

He shook his head. "It doesn't make any sense. How have you hurt him? He's still been paid twice for the same bowl of stew."

She just stared at him. He didn't have to say that. Why were people always trying to bring you down? Where did *he*—a fucking Soldier—get off telling her *she* didn't make sense? That was rich. She knew she should just keep her mouth shut and not squelch the deal, but she couldn't help herself. "Well, since we're trading these little secrets, what about you, Mr. Sensible One? If you're so fucking hot to leave the Soldiers, why don't you just disappear into Crazyville or take up with the Constructs? Why do you need a new body, anyway?"

"The body's not for me," he said simply.

This just kept getting weirder, like Chef's stew when you got to the bottom of the bowl. "Then who the hell's it for?"

AND THEN HE TOLD HER THE CRAZIEST FUCKING STORY SHE'D ever heard in her life. And what was crazier, she believed him. But then, she'd been living in Crazyville for a long time.

She had him tell it all twice. "What did he look like?" she asked. It had to be him. The man himself. Walter fucking Tillman had been living in a goddamn computer like a firefly in a jar for 120 years. This was weird on a whole new level. She felt like she was in some old story. Shit like this didn't really happen. She looked around the room at all the fucked-up people she spent her life with. Chef was still pouting. Sandoz was saying, "Epistemology was everything"—like anyone but him knew what the hell he was talking about. Rat was beating his head against the wall—a waltz it looked like. The scavenger was still passed out on the floor, holding his loot. Carmen was upstairs banging some guy with three identities who'd leave feathers in her bed.

The way Laura figured it, all this was Walter Tillman's fault. She didn't need or want to figure out just how that worked, she just fucking *knew.*

"Laura?" Sam asked. "Are you all right?"

She looked into his earnest baby blues. "I want to meet Tillman," she said. "Tonight."

He sat back in his chair and held up his hands. "I can't do that. It's in New Jerusalem. It's a pretty remote part of the city, but it's still heavily patrolled. You'd be arrested on sight, interrogated. Trust me, you don't want that."

You're going to do it, she thought. Why don't you just give in and get on with it? "Couldn't you just pretend you were arresting me?"

"It wouldn't work. I'd have to turn you over to the first sentry who spotted us. I'm in a technical unit. I don't go out and arrest people. I'm not even in uniform. Why do you want to meet him anyway?"

She folded her arms across her chest. "You don't take me to him, I don't help you." She could hardly believe it herself, but there it was. She meant it. It was a matter of principle.

He thought it was a shakedown. "I'll pay you whatever you like."

"Big deal. You'll do that anyway. But the down payment is I meet him tonight, or we have no deal." Underneath her folded arms she crossed her fingers, but she wasn't bluffing.

He thought about it a minute, maybe checking with the Lord who'd led him to this crazy woman in the first place. "One condition," he said.

"So *now* you want to get laid?"

He ignored her. "You have to tell me why you want to meet him."

"My intense interest in science."

Now he crossed his arms, and maybe his fingers. "You don't tell me why, we don't have a deal."

He didn't seem to be bluffing either. "You're a quick study, aren't you, Sammy? Okay, I'll tell you, since you obviously don't know who you've got in there. Every Construct can certainly tell you who Walter fucking Tillman is. He's right up there with St. Newman Rogers. Constructs were made from human clones, right? And who was the brilliant scientist who developed the speedy and flexible means of human cloning necessary to manufacture those crazy slaves, to give us the wonderful world we've got today? You guessed it. None other than Dr. Walter Tillman. What you've got in that computer, Sammy, is my great-grand-daddy, and I'd like to drop in to pay my respects."

He was looking all concerned, like she'd just told him she had cancer. She wanted to smack him. "I'm not sure that's such a good idea," he said. "I can't let you hurt him."

" 'Hurt' him? I told you—we're practically family."

"So were Cain and Abel."

It took her a second. Then she saw the little smile. A joke. Maybe there was hope for Sammy after all. "Okay. No. I won't hurt him. Happy now? But I've got a few questions, you might say. I might even call him a few choice names, but you can cover up your ears."

She expected him to keep arguing with her, but he broadened his smile and said, "I know exactly how you feel."

Now why do I doubt that? she asked herself, but she wasn't about to tell him he was full of shit if he was going to introduce her to Walter Tillman. "Thanks," she said.

"But how am I going to get you into the city? I can't let you take a risk like that."

She looked at him a moment. He was seriously concerned, which made absolutely no sense at all. "Look, Sammy, you're not even supposed to be here, right? How were you going to sneak yourself back in? Same way—only you'll see a whole lot better." She leaned in close, looked him in the eye. "Note the weird pupils? Killer night vision. Great-granddaddy again—I can read a newspaper by starlight." She moved in a little closer like she was going to kiss him, and he would've gone for it like an apple falling from a tree, but she leaned back and let the poor boy breathe. "And frankly, no offense, all I'd need is a fucking cane to spot one of you guys all trucked out in your khakis, patrolling the same routes every fucking night. It's all for show anyway. It's not like you guys are expecting anybody to attack you, unless you're even stupider than I think you are. So what do you say? Come on, Sammy. Does it look like I'm used to living a risk-free life here?"

He chewed on his lip and pondered. Everything was some big-deal decision to this one. "All right," he said finally, "but you have to do everything I tell you to do."

She scrunched up her shoulders and winked at him. "Mmm. Sounds fun already."

He was stone-faced. "And could you please quit saying things like that? I didn't come out here looking for a prostitute."

"Come on, Sammy, lighten up. Don't you guys believe in bonus points? But now that you mention it, why *did* you come out here? Why are you so hot to help this guy? You're a Soldier, for Christ's sake . . ."

"Please don't swear."

"Oh, good Lord. It's true, isn't it? You *are* a Soldier. He's Satan's bosom buddy. Am I missing something here?"

"I am a Soldier. But I have to help him. He's been trapped in there for a hundred and twenty years, and he wants out. I can't just leave him. Sooner or later, somebody else will find him, and he won't have any life at all." Then, for a second, it looked like he was going to start crying. "He could've stolen my body if he'd wanted to, and there wouldn't have been a thing I could've done about it. He had every reason to, but he didn't do it."

This made quite an impression on him, apparently. Made sense. The Soldiers' basic philosophy from where Laura sat looked pretty much like *Do in others before they have a chance to do in you.* But still. She had to think he might be making a big mistake. "Correct me if I'm wrong, but you could be shot for this, right?"

"Most likely hanged. My father would sign the order."

"Your father?"

"He's the Commander of the Army."

A light dawned. "You're a strange one, Sammy, but I think I get the picture. Hope you and your dad work it out someday. I was spared having a real father. *Everybody* raises a Construct kid. Communal as hell. Nobody to rebel against but the whole lot of them."

"I'm not just rebelling against my father."

She shrugged. "Suit yourself."

"And what is that supposed to mean?"

She stood up and stretched. "It means I'm tired of arguing with you. Doesn't matter anyway." She put her hands on his knees and looked him in the eye. "Guys pay me to do things all the time, Sammy, but nobody can pay me enough to like it." Now he was blushing again. Jeez, what a short fuse. She tugged on his arms. "Come on, Soldier Boy. Get up. If we're going to New Jerusalem, we better get our asses in gear. I'm just another pumpkin when the sun comes up."

6

SIR DEATH

DONOVAN WOKE UP THINKING ABOUT THREE WOMEN—
Nicole, who killed herself, Simone Mirabelli, who'd just
died, and Stephanie Sanders, who wanted to. Poe said that
the death of a woman was the most poetic of subjects, but
Poe was a crazy drug addict. There certainly wasn't anything
poetic about Nicole jumping off that bridge into the river.
Simone Mirabelli naked in a field of grain might qualify,
but there'd been too much joy in it for Poe. All that lauda-
num. And there wasn't much poetic about his conversation
with Stephanie last night—short, very direct: *Help me die.
Yes or no.* It was over before he had a chance to ask her
why.

He'd said he'd call her back when he knew something.
Anyone who knew Donovan well could've told her that by
the time he felt like he *knew* something, she probably
would've forgotten her question. But this wasn't some ab-
stract tussle of ideas. This was a woman's life. Even though
she had the visual shut off, he was pretty sure she'd been
crying. She was desperate, in pain. He was as susceptible
as the next guy to a damsel in distress.

He remembered the night he met Nicole. She was standing in a downpour in front of an oncoming train. He'd run
up the embankment and knocked her out of the way. She
said: "When I saw you, I thought about running toward the
train. But then I thought, 'If this stranger wants me to

live . . . ' " Their roles were established—she despaired, he rescued.

Later she would look at him from hollow eyes, her voice full of loathing. "You're what's keeping me alive. You. Why don't you just leave me alone?" So he did. Just a weekend fishing trip in the mountains with a friend. Downstream, she jumped into the river.

He put the pillow over his face. Okay. So maybe he was more susceptible to distressed damsels than most. But ultimately what this Stephanie woman was asking him to do was to let her die. Exactly what he'd been saying the world needed. So what was the problem?

He just wished she didn't sound so certain. It made him wonder if she really knew what she was doing. How could any rational person be certain about jumping into the unknown? Unless the known was unbearable. Maybe her certainty was behind her instead of ahead of her: *Anything is better than this.* Like Nicole. But if that was it, why download and live on for as much as fifty or sixty years? Why not just kill herself?

The more he thought about it, the more he felt he should tell her about the death program Freddie had written. Maybe she, like Simone Mirabelli, would like to die, but didn't want to destroy herself. There was no need to take on a new body, age, and eventually die. What could there possibly be for her back in the real world? He didn't know for sure what was going on down there, but he knew there was more than just death. He didn't know the details, but he knew the variables: religious fanatics who'd shoot you for disagreeing with them; Constructs who—if they hadn't all been wiped out by now—must be seething with rage at the human race; and insane people who didn't need a reason to kill you. He remembered the unit in school on serial killers and shuddered, threw back the covers, and got out of bed.

He went into the kitchen and got a Coke and a chili dog from the food unit. As he ate, he imagined them all—the fundies, the crazies, and the Constructs—in a swirl of conflict like a violent chemical reaction. Where would some-body like Stephanie fit into a world like that? That big hat and those sunglasses—she didn't exactly look like pioneer stock. Pretty, though. Very pretty.

There was a little of the hash left, so he stuck it in the end of a cigarette and lit it. He'd first smoked cannabis when he was studying the Rastafarians. Research. It wasn't a popular drug in the Bin. After all, it could make five minutes seem like an hour. Most people preferred smash. You took it, had a great time, and two weeks later realize it's two weeks later. He hated that stuff.

He stared across the room at the phone. What was the right thing to do here? The woman had the right to do whatever she wanted with her life. If she wanted to go to hell, that was her business. But what if this download thing was just a scam? Maybe these people who thought they were downloading were only being erased. Who would be able to tell the difference? He should warn her of all these possibilities, maybe try to talk her out of it.

Or maybe he was just afraid he couldn't help her.

He'd set himself up as some big authority. Dr. Death. Oh, he complained about it, but he'd worked as hard as anyone to create that fiction. Truth was, he didn't know if he knew anything or could help anyone. But he doesn't tell her *this* up front. Oh, no, he's got to be the important one: *Dry your eyes, little lady, I'll help you.* What a phony. Look how he'd helped Nicole.

He'd never arranged a download before. The little he knew about them was all pretty sketchy, cloak-and-dagger stuff. You couldn't just access a public database and get a file on it, but he knew there was a black market in mortality. He imagined it was like trying to score serious drugs or illegal weapons back in the real world. He'd never really cared to find out. The thought of setting foot in the real world frightened him more than death itself. The Bin was just a copy of Earth, all prettied up, but it often seemed to him the other way around—that Earth was a bad copy of the Bin, hopelessly corrupted. The Bin was the only world he'd ever known. He wanted to change some things about it, not go back to the stone age.

Newbies, naturally enough, weren't nostalgic for the good old hydrocarbon days. That biochemical reality, in Donovan's opinion, was nothing more than a rough draft. But they'd made a mistake cutting out death in revision.

He stopped himself. Listen to you, he thought. You're lecturing yourself! What does all that matter to this poor woman who wants to die? You're not the one who wants to download, so what do your hangups and pronouncements have to do with it? You said you'd help the woman, so do it.

He went to his desk, sat in front of the phone, and lit a cigarette. When it was out, he lit another. He'd been approached a few times by guys who claimed they could arrange a download. He must've seemed like the perfect candidate. He always sent them packing. He could look up one of those characters, arrange a meeting. They could all wear red carnations and meet in a train station, say things like "The owl flies at midnight" to each other. But he didn't trust any of those bastards, hustling fares across the river Styx.

He decided to call Freddie. If he wanted anything done in the Bin, legal or otherwise, Freddie could tell him how. As Freddie often reminded him, "It's *all* programming, Donnie."

It took Freddie a while to answer the phone. It's probably a little early for him, Donovan thought. But Freddie answered in a Hawaiian print shirt and a dark tan, a peach-colored drink with a paper umbrella in his hand. He toasted Donovan with the drink. "Hi, Donnie," he said.

Donovan told him the whole story, which, he realized as he told it, wasn't very much. He knew almost nothing about Stephanie. Why *had* he agreed to help her? Was this Nicole all over again? No. When he met Nicole, he'd knocked her *off* the tracks. This one wanted him to tie her to them.

"Can you help her?" he asked Freddie.

Freddie, who'd been sucking on his drink the whole time,

shook his head in wonder. "There are too many layers of irony here to contemplate this early in the morning."

Donovan wondered how many of those peach-colored drinks Freddie had had. Was this a brunch or the end of a late party? "What are you talking about, Freddie?"

"Do you realize who she is?"

Donovan sighed. "Apparently not."

Freddie leaned in close. "She is Jack Cornran's widow."

"You're kidding."

Freddie leaned back in his chair and held up his right hand. "I cannot tell a lie."

Like all newbies, Donovan was stuffed like a Christmas goose with Bin history. It was supposed to help actualize their sense of identity or some such nonsense. A good deal of the stuffing had leaked out over the years, but he remembered who Jack Cornran was—wheeler-dealer, financial wizard, the corporate cowboy who made immortality a moneymaking proposition. A museum in Dallas or Houston was filled with his art collection and named after him. But Cornran died before the Bin even went on-line. Some kind of terrorist thing? He couldn't remember.

But what did it matter who this woman was married to over a hundred years ago? He couldn't remember anything at all about her, though he had the nagging suspicion he should. Maybe he was smoking too much hash.

"All I want to know, Freddie, is whether you can help her or not."

"Of course. Bring her on over." He leaned in close again. "She and I met in the old life, by the way."

"You knew her?"

"Met, Donnie. Her husband was my boss, if you'll recall." He put the straw back in his mouth and talked around it. "I'm sure I didn't make much of an impression."

Somehow Donovan doubted that.

DONOVAN DECIDED TO MEET WITH STEPHANIE PRIVATELY BE-fore he took her to Freddie's—just to make sure she knew what she was doing. He could hardly expect Freddie to counsel prudence on anything, and he wasn't sure Freddie would want him telling her about the death program, even though the damn thing was Donovan's idea in the first place.

He called her up, and she had the visual off again. He pictured her sitting in a darkened room with her sunglasses on. She and Freddie would get along great. He suggested the Rogers Memorial as a meeting place, but she vetoed the idea, her voice tight and brittle. She suggested the Wilderness Park near the south entrance. "There's a bench by the beaver pond."

He didn't have any trouble finding it. There was an interactive, interpretive map at every entrance. Nature on demand. She wasn't there yet, but he was early. He sat on the bench and watched a pair of beavers tussling in the water, playing, grooming each other. He never realized they were so big. The larger of the two must've weighed sixty or seventy pounds.

He wondered why Stephanie had chosen this place. The Bin was stuffed with idyllic spots. Maybe she lived close by. There was an interpretation icon set in the arm of the bench, and he pushed it. A man's voice—older, Southern— spoke softly into his right ear, as if someone were sitting beside him, a folksy beaver expert. Fortunately, there was no holo. Those things got on his nerves.

The voice informed him that the beavers he was watching were 110 years old—uploaded into the Bin at ten. Floods periodically washed away their work, so they'd rebuilt the same dam dozens of times since. Watery little Sisyphi, Donovan thought. He imagined a beaver mantra and smiled to himself: Dam! Dam! Dam! One detail jumped out at him: Beavers mated for life. Since real-world beavers lived about fifteen or sixteen years, Donovan calculated, these two had spent about seven lifetimes together already.

The folksy voice droned on. Like most interpretations, this one told him more than he wanted to know—the gruesome details of the fur trade, the fact that the secretions of beavers' scent glands were used in making perfumes. As he watched these two at play, he thought there just might be a causal connection between those secretions and their un-wavering devotion to one another. Perfume wearers, appar-ently, had hoped to borrow some of that power. They could always wash it off later.

"They're fascinating, aren't they?"

Donovan started. This wasn't the interpreter's voice, but Stephanie's. He'd been so engrossed in the beavers, he didn't see her sit down beside him. He stood up and sat down again in some silly ritual of sexual decorum.

She hadn't bothered with the sunglasses and the straw hat, but she still had on the big trench coat. Her eyes were large, intelligent, and sad, with a few lines radiating from the corners. No makeup. She'd chosen to look about forty—a little older than most women in the Bin, but not over the top. He suddenly remembered something about her from history class: Before she came in here, she'd been promi-nent in the movement to stop the manufacture of Con-structs. He must've seen her picture somewhere looking pretty much like she looked now. But she'd been famous for something else. What was it? He stared at her, trying to remember, then realized he was being rude and looked away.

"Are you going to help me?" she asked. "You didn't sound too sure last night."

"I know someone who can probably help you, but I'd like to talk with you a little first," he said. "Ask a few questions, if you wouldn't mind."

She stuck her chin out, gave a little nod. She did mind, but she'd put up with it. "To find out if I'm worthy?"

"I'd just like to know your reasons for wanting to down-load."

"What difference does it make?"

"It matters to me."

"You have your ethics."

"Exactly."

She sighed. Apparently, she didn't have much patience

with other people's ethics. "It's like I told you. I want to die. The operating system won't let me kill myself."

"Maybe the operating system knows something you don't."

She gave him a *No kidding* look. "That's my problem, wouldn't you say?"

She was starting to annoy him. After all, he'd volunteered to take on her damn problems. She could at least be civil. The damsel was supposed to be grateful for the knight's help, wasn't she? He took a deep breath. "Look, I'm just trying to help you. I feel a moral obligation to discuss your options with you before you take such a radical and irreversible step. If that's too much trouble, then maybe we should forget the whole thing."

She smiled wryly. She found him amusing. That annoyed him even more. "How old are you?" she asked.

He clenched his jaw. Damn, he was tired of that question. "I'm forty. I suppose you agree with that musclehead the other night—'What the hell does a newbie like you know about death, anyway?' " He quoted his nemesis in a gravelly tough-guy voice.

She smiled again, but in earnest this time. "No. But people do learn from experience, wouldn't you say, Doctor?"

"Of course."

"I'm a hundred and fifty-one years old."

"Good for you. When we're through here, I'll take you to meet a friend who's a hundred and sixty-four. You two can fight it out for the wisdom merit badge. But, young as I am, I'd *still* like to know why your vast experience has led you to this decision." He didn't intend to sound so venomous. It's not like he wasn't used to condescension. But this whole downloading business upset him.

She nodded, her smile gone. She looked down at her lap. "Fair enough." She stared at the backs of her hands, turned them over and stared at her palms. "I guess the easiest way to put it is this—I've never done anything worthwhile. Nothing. I've wasted my whole life."

He doubted this, but he knew the feeling and wasn't

foolish enough to argue with it. There was more, he was sure, something personal, but what made him think that it was any of his business? Did he think he was death's gatekeeper or something? *To find out if I'm worthy?* He winced at his own arrogance. "You might not have to download or commit suicide to die," he said softly.

She spoke as if she hadn't heard what he said. "Can I ask you a question? Why are you carrying on this . . . this crusade? Doing interviews with idiots who haven't a clue what you're talking about, writing all these books, giving these lectures? You must know they'll never allow death in the Bin."

"Suicide's allowed."

"That's not the same—just as you said." She tapped her forehead. "Suicide's all up here. You *decide* to die. That's what this place is all about isn't it? Deciding everything. Death doesn't come and take you."

She made death sound like a ravishing lover. He remembered the lines from Donne:

Take me to you, imprison me, for I
Except you enthrall me, never shall be free,
Nor ever chaste, except you ravish me.

But Donne had been talking to God, not Death.

"BUT THAT'S NOT WHAT I'M TALKING ABOUT." HE TOLD HER about the death program, describing, as vividly as he could, the blissful death of Simone Mirabelli and her reunion with her loved ones on the Other Side. The story moved him, but she didn't seem much affected. He felt oddly disappointed and wondered if he'd been secretly hoping to witness another death. No, he decided. He just wanted to see that same joy in this miserable woman's face.

She shook her head. "You're assuming the dead would greet me with open arms. In my case, I'm certain they wouldn't."

"Why not?" he asked without thinking, and she flinched. "I'm sorry. It's none of my business."

She looked out at the beaver pond. The beavers had retreated into their lodge. She studied it as if she could see the answer to his question inside that pile of sticks. "I told you that I saw my husband die. That's not quite true. It was my lover who died—shot to death—the only man who ever truly loved me." She looked into his eyes. Her own filled with tears. "I caused his death. If there's an afterlife, he's still cursing me." She looked back to the pond. "I want to download, have a chance at a meaningful death—just like you said in the paper."

So that's it, Donovan realized. She *wants* someone to shoot her dead—just penance for her lover's death. No one could kill her in here. In the real world, she could not only die, she could suffer as well. Maybe she was right about the difference in their ages—he certainly felt young and foolish. "I'm sorry for prying. We can go see my friend now. I'm sure he can help you."

"That's okay." She wiped the tears from her eyes. "You were just doing your job"—she laughed—"whatever that is."

FREDDIE'S PLACE WAS TRANSFORMED AGAIN. HUGE COCONUT trees stood out front of a rambling thatch-roof lodge. Okonkwo, Freddie's partner, showed them in and sat them down under a slowly turning ceiling fan. Though there wasn't an ocean in sight, there was a salt smell in the air, the sounds of surf crashing, gulls crying off in the distance. Freddie delighted in the details, as long as they were incongruous. Here they were, in the middle of D.C., and this was—what? Tahiti in the 1940s? But Freddie often scorned realism, quoting James Branch Cabell: "Realism is the art of being superficial, seriously."

When Freddie walked into the room, any doubt that Stephanie would remember him was erased. She jumped to her feet, clearly rattled.

"Freddie," she said. It was almost a cry.

"You remember me," Freddie said.

"I'll never forget that day as long as I live." It looked like she was going to start crying again.

Freddie nodded his understanding, uncharacteristically somber. "But this is now," he said gently, "and you came here to discuss your future, not your past."

She smiled at him, grateful for his gallant discretion. Neither one was going to let Donovan in on their secrets. He wished he could think of a single reason why they should, other than his own curiosity, but none came to him.

They sat down, and Freddie explained the downloading process to Stephanie in his soft musical voice. His "guru voice," he called it on one of many occasions when he poked fun at himself. It wasn't phony, though. Freddie was a genuinely kind man.

As Donovan listened, it gradually dawned on him that Freddie wasn't talking about finding her a contact or putting her in touch with the right people. He *was* the right people. Freddie knew all about it. *Why hasn't he told me this before?* Donovan wondered. He forced himself to set that aside and listen.

"I'm in contact with a Construct named Laura," Freddie was saying. "She acts as a temporary host, then transfers your identity to a suitable host after the Construct Initiation ceremony in June. I'm afraid you'll have to wait until then."

"So I would be living among the Constructs?"

"Not necessarily. Laura herself lives outside the Construct community. She's chosen not to initiate, to live what the Constructs call the 'solitary life.' Genetically, however, you'll be a Construct, and I warn you that the Christian Soldiers pretty much control the planet, and they shoot on sight anyone with the slightest genetic anomaly. You wouldn't really be safe anywhere. Do you still want to go through with it?"

She didn't hesitate. Her voice was firm and strong. "I don't want to be safe."

Freddie seemed to understand perfectly. He squeezed

her hand. "Very well. Come here on June 20. I'll have everything arranged."

They stood. It took Donovan a moment to catch up. He had a dozen questions running through his mind.

"I'll be in touch with you," Freddie said. "I'd appreciate it if you wouldn't tell anyone about any of this."

"Of course not." She hugged him. "Thank you once again, Freddie."

"I hope things turn out better for you this time."

She nodded quickly and left before she started crying again. She seemed to have forgotten Donovan was even there.

Freddie stood at the door looking after her, long after she was out of sight.

"What was that all about?" Donovan asked. "How did you two know each other?"

"We had a mutual friend. Walter Tillman, the geneticist."

"Isn't he the guy who made Constructs possible? I thought Stephanie was an abolitionist."

Freddie turned from the door. "Is that what they teach you kids about poor Tillman? He was dead before they made the first Construct. He found the idea thoroughly repugnant."

"Were he and Stephanie lovers?"

Freddie arched a brow. "Did she tell you that?"

"She said she was responsible for her lover's death. She didn't tell me his name."

"Then I won't either."

"Come on, Freddie."

He made a zipping motion across his mouth. "My lips are sealed."

"Do you mind if I ask her?"

"What business is it of yours? Leave the poor woman alone. She's been through quite enough, believe me."

Freddie was right. Donovan still felt guilty for cross-examining her earlier. Freddie was another matter. "So how long have you been arranging downloads? How do you know so much about what's going on in the real world? Who's this Laura you told Stephanie about?" He rattled off his questions as he followed Freddie into the kitchen, where Okonkwo was preparing a blender full of drinks. He was tall, muscular, smooth-shaven, even his scalp. He had a warm smile, but he was shy and never said much.

Freddie gave him a peck on the cheek, and Okonkwo draped his arm around Freddie's waist as he started pouring the peach-colored liquid into three goblets.

"None for me, thanks," Donovan said. "It's a little early yet."

Okonkwo hesitated over the third glass.

"Oh, Donnie," Freddie said. "You and that watch. It's Sunday, day of rest. Why don't you give *time* a rest?"

Why indeed? He wasn't going anywhere. "Okay," Donovan said with a shrug. He noted that Okonkwo resumed his pouring a split second before Donovan had spoken.

"Five fruits and golden rum," Okonkwo said as he handed him the icy drink.

Freddie held up his glass. "To Stephanie Sanders."

"Ah, yes," Okonkwo said, beaming. "So beautiful."

They drank to Stephanie Sanders. Everyone seemed to know more about this woman than Donovan did.

"But who is she?" Donovan asked when they sat down with their drinks.

"The last of the great supermodels," Freddie said. "Absolutely stunning. More famous than Tillman and Cornran put together in her day. And you've never even heard of her?"

Donovan sniffed. "I never devoted my time to the study of supermodels."

"Another flaw, Donnie. Another flaw."

Okonkwo laughed, and Donovan couldn't help but join in. "I told her about the death program," Donovan confessed to Freddie.

"I knew you'd have to tell somebody. What did she say?"

"She wasn't interested. She said no one would welcome her."

"Now there, I suspect, she's completely wrong."

"She apparently cheated on her husband and caused her lover's death. Sounds like she might have a point."

"The black widow is a spider, Donnie. Don't try to turn her into one."

Donovan dropped the subject. "You haven't answered my questions about the real world."

"I didn't think the subject interested you."

"I didn't know you were such an expert on it."

Freddie turned to Okonkwo. "He's so snippy." Okonkwo chuckled. "Very well, Donnie. I've always been in contact with the Constructs. They keep me informed."

"I thought all connection with the real world was cut off."

"Except via the Construct chips. Officially, of course, there's nothing. The place is a terrible distraction—I'm sure you'd agree. Some people can't let it go. Even with the official silence, every year I help a few people download."

"But why? It sounds so grim."

Freddie winked. "Maybe that's how life is for the dying, Donnie." He cocked his head to one side. "Have you ever thought about downloading yourself, Donnie?"

"Never."

Freddie scrunched up his shoulders. "Ooh, such disgust. All that nasty flesh repulse you?"

"Come on, Freddie. I just don't think I'd fit into the real world. You yourself left it behind, remember?"

Freddie laughed. "Snippy, snippy, snippy."

Donovan smiled and sucked on his drink. It was really quite good. He let himself be talked into a second one. Freddie and Okonkwo, holding hands like kids at the prom, told him about their recent trip to the South Pacific, telling stories on each other, still laughing and happy after five years together.

Freddie had been married twice before—what he referred to as his "queers-can-marry-too" marriage back in the real world, and his "settle-down-in-my-nineties" marriage in the Bin. For all Freddie's jokes about his marriages, Donovan knew they'd both lasted a good long while and neither had ended because Freddie'd wanted them to.

Donovan admired Freddie's willingness to take another chance on love, commitment, happiness. He wished he himself could find the knack again, but it seemed to him he'd lost it forever. He turned down another drink before self-pity set in and he launched into a drunken wallow.

As Donovan was leaving, he and Freddie stood alone at the door. "Thanks for helping me out with Stephanie," he said.

"You realize you need to keep all this to yourself, don't you?"

"Of course. You got any other secrets you want to let me in on?"

He meant it as a joke, but Freddie was deadpan. "You free tomorrow night? There's someone I want you to meet."

"Sure. Who?"

"His pen name is Gwenna R. Morse."

"You're joking. The one who writes all that tabloid crap?"

"A hobby only. He's been wanting to meet you. It will be worth your while, believe me."

"Who is he?"

"The pen name's an anagram. You can figure it out. Bright lad, like you."

Donovan shuffled the letters around in his head. Even in his alcoholic haze, it only took him a minute. But it couldn't be. Freddie was pulling his leg again. *"Newman Rogers?"*

"Very good."

"But . . ."

"Tomorrow, Donnie."

7

UTHER PENDRAGON

Tillman was in the Oval Office again, watching the lengthening shadows of the virtual sun going down, kicking himself for not taking that Christian kid's body while he had the chance. He could've at least borrowed it for a while, looked around, taken in a few surprises.

But he didn't. He couldn't. Walter Tillman, body snatcher—not a role he wanted to repeat. Besides, the kid brought surprises enough. Tillman remembered these Christian Soldiers from his channel-surfing days. They'd show up on the public-access channels, wacky as a bag of cats, goose-stepping for Jesus, hugging their automatic weapons like they were the Ark of the Covenant. Now they *ran* things. The whole show, to hear the kid tell it.

Tillman had been raised a Jew, which in his case meant his parents dragged him to Yom Kippur services with his dad bellyaching all day about fasting to distract his mom from the fact that he was stuffing his face on the sly. Tillman and his dad would be standing at the urinals while his dad was gobbling down a Snickers in less time than it took him to take a leak, which admittedly could be a pretty long time.

When Tillman was thirteen, his mom found all the candy bar wrappers stuffed in the pockets of his dad's Yom Kippur/funeral suit. And nobody'd died since the High Holidays. They fought for six days and rested on the seventh. They never went to Yom Kippur services after that, though

Mom still fasted in her long-suffering fashion. Tillman didn't know which side to take—starve himself or order a pizza supreme—so he usually went to a movie and ate popcorn in the dark. And a Snickers.

Maybe a little more true religious zeal in the world wasn't such a bad thing. But no. He preferred his religious zeal unarmed. If nuclear weapons were in God's Plan, Tillman would rather be an atheist.

He liked Sam, though. Course, he might kiss Hitler after all the time he'd spent in here. But it was more than that. There was something genuine about that kid. He remembered the earnest look he got when he said he'd try to help. Tillman just hoped Sam didn't get himself shot. The Christian Soldiers didn't sound like they'd take too kindly to independent thinking.

Maybe he *was* better off in here. He put his feet up on the desk, knocking off the little brass beaver and a cupful of ballpoint pens that said THE PRESIDENT OF THE UNITED STATES on them. No. Anyplace but here. He didn't care who was in charge, as long as it wasn't Walter Tillman.

The whole idea of getting out seemed like an incredible long shot. But who knows? Sam found him and managed to drop in for a visit—which was more than anyone else had done for 120 years. Maybe, just maybe, Tillman thought, I might actually get out of this paradise alive.

"Sally!" he called.

She came through the door—smiling, of course—though he could barely make out her face in the shadows. She had basically two looks: pleasant and sultry. He needed to expand her repertoire, but he never got around to it. She picked up the beaver and the pens, put them back where they were, and turned on the desk lamp.

"So what do you think?" he asked her. "Is this Sam going to get me out of here?"

"He certainly seemed like a nice young man."

Tillman snorted. "Now, there's a nice safe answer."

She sat down and crossed her legs. He could hear the scritch of her panty hose. He sometimes felt guilty for keeping her in such uncomfortable clothes all the time, but she was a program. The discomfort was all his. She didn't mind. She had no mind.

"What do you want me to say?" she said.

"Say, 'Yes, Tillman, I think he'll have you out of here in no time.'"

Her smile sweetened to tour guide depths, her voice was professionally chipper. "Yes, Tillman, I think he'll have you out of here in no time."

"Liar."

"No, Tillman darling, that was sarcasm—a manifestation of your rapierlike wit." She stood up and came around the desk, giving him a kiss on the cheek. "Would you like a drink before dinner?"

"Only if you join me."

"Of course."

It'd gotten to the point where most of the time he knew what she was going to say before she said it. He'd thought about retiring her, writing somebody new. But when it came down to it, he never did. It wasn't just a "Why bother?" sort of thing. He liked Sally. She was okay. He'd written her—what? Ten, twelve years ago now. His longest-running imaginary friend.

Tillman made the drinks. Double martinis, straight up. "Do you really think I'm pleasant when I drink too much?" he asked her as they clinked their glasses together.

She gave him the sultry look. He decided to skip dinner.

TILLMAN AND SALLY LAY IN BED, PROPPED UP ON PILLOWS. Tillman's tour hadn't included the President's bedroom, so he'd made one up. He didn't make it too big. A bedroom was to sleep in, usually alone in his experience. The furniture was plain and familiar—yard-sale provincial. Tillman, his mother's son, had never set foot in a furniture store.

There was a big skylight over the bed, so he could look up at the stars as he fell asleep. He knew they weren't really the stars. Nothing in his little world was really anything.

But the stars, more often than anything else, made him forget they weren't real, and for a few serene seconds—as he drifted off to sleep—he believed he was looking into the universe instead of its shadow.

That magic wasn't working tonight, however. He was thoroughly depressed. These weren't the stars he wanted to see. This woman wasn't the woman he wanted beside him. He could've written up Stephanie, put her here, but he never had, and he never would. That memory was sacred. That memory was real. The feelings were real. Put them in this dog and pony show, and they'd be ruined forever.

He sat up and swung his legs over the side of the bed.

Sally lay her hand on his bare back and rubbed it gently. "Are you going to visit Stephanie?"

"Yeah," Tillman grunted.

"You don't have to feel guilty, Tillman. I don't mind."

"You don't mind anything."

She withdrew her hand. "That's not true. I mind when you're unhappy."

He turned on the light and faced her. "Why?" he asked, setting a trap.

"Because I like you."

A buzzer sounded in his head: *Wrong.* "You only 'like' me because I wrote you that way. A few revisions and you'd hate my guts."

She shook her head, unconcerned. "I still like you."

Tillman started to explain to her—to himself—why it mattered that she had no choice, that true liking couldn't be forced and required at the very least two conscious entities—when he stopped himself, caught in his own trap. "Shit," he said. "Talking to myself for a hundred and twenty years. I'm crazy. Have to be. Absolutely batshit crazy."

"Do you want me to wait up for you?" Sally asked.

"What do you think?"

"No."

"Then why do you always ask?"

"You like me to."

She was right, of course. She did everything because he

wanted her to. "What do you do when I'm not around, Sally?"

"I don't exist when you're not around. You know that."

"You don't exist anyway."

She gave him a haughty unconcerned look. "Then you don't either."

Ooh, feisty. He liked that. She could still surprise him once in a while, after all. He kissed her on the cheek and she slid under the covers like a tucked-in kid. She seemed happy, which was all he could hope to offer a woman who only seemed to be real.

HE PUT ON HIS ROBE AND SLIPPERS AND WENT DOWNSTAIRS. His robe dragged along the ground behind him. When he was a kid, there was this comic-strip character who, even though he was short and ugly, was a king. His regal robes were way too big, and they trailed around after him. Tillman liked that—just because the guy was short didn't mean he had to settle for less than other kings. One day Tillman's dad put one of his cigarette-burned terry-cloth robes in the Disabled Veterans bag, and Tillman dug it out and wore it all day. Everybody had a good laugh over it. That little Wally was a real stitch, all right. But he wouldn't be parted from that robe until they got him an equally lengthy one. He asked for red. As an adult, he still wore robes that were too long for him. At his height, they weren't hard to find.

He stretched out on the Empire sofa in the Red Room and stared up at Audubon. He was a pretty good-looking guy: great hair, noble brow. Probably a ladies' man. *Ooh, John, what did you shoot today?* Tillman imagined a ring of nineteenth-century beauties, Audubon in the middle still holding that damn gun. That wasn't really fair. The man was a decent naturalist. But what would Audubon do with himself in here? Tillman wondered. Paint imaginary birds? Not likely. Probably the same thing I'm doing, Tillman thought—try to figure things out. *Real* things. Unfortu-

nately, the only real thing at his disposal was his own pitiful life.

Until Sam walked in. Another person. His first in over a
century. He'd thought he was lonely in his real life. That
was a fucking beach party compared to this place. But this
morning he'd had a real conversation, perhaps even made
a friend. All sorts of things were possible now. He wondered
if the kid played chess.

He could even start hoping again. He wasn't entirely sure
he wanted to. Hope wasn't such a great emotion in his
experience. He'd gotten kind of used to hopeless.

"Boo hoo hoo," he said. "Quit your whining." He sat up
and planted his feet on the floor, scooting to the front of
the sofa to do so. He had work to do. He needed to get a
few things straight in his old life if he was going to start a
new one. He might not have too much time to torture
himself with the past when he was back in the real world
dodging Christian bullets and eating roots and berries.

Roots and berries. Now there was something he could
turn his talents to in the real world. He imagined berries
the size of apples, ripening on thornless vines. He could be
the regular Gregor Mendel of berries. "Don't shoot"—he
imagined himself saying to several well-scrubbed fanatics—
"have a berry," and they'd throw down their guns and eat
themselves silly.

He wondered what he'd look like this time. It was hard
not to imagine some improvement. Maybe he'd get lucky—
some handsome young lad like Sam.

But he was getting way ahead of himself.

He started up the memory a little after where he left off.
Two hours and forty-seven minutes later. He's actually had
a two-and-a-half hour lunch with Stephanie Sanders (already
forgetting the Cornran part) and he's wandering around his
lab, grinning to himself, hugging himself where her arms
hugged him good-bye.

It was pretty pathetic to watch. This was worse than his
phony stars—not just forgetting where he was, but who he

was, what he looked like, who it was he'd fallen for. What a fool.

The rest of the team is in the lab now, but he's oblivious, thinking about Stephanie with barbecue sauce all over her lips.

Then Randall walks up to him, the Cornrans' blood samples in his hand. "What should I do with these?" he asks Tillman.

"I'll take care of them," Tillman says and practically snatches them out of Randall's hand.

"They were just sitting out," Randall says. "Unlabeled."

Tillman gives him a dismissive wave of the hand. "Just a little something I'm working on." They're labeled enough: J on one and S on the other.

Specimens are stored in a vault on the other side of the nursery. As Tillman practically skips through the nursery, a vial in each hand, he sees Stephanie's hat lying on the floor where she'd dropped it, and his chest aches, remembering the way she looked at him.

He slips the vials into his coat pocket and picks up the hat, scrunches it up like she did, then smells it. There's a hair caught in the band, and he takes it out and winds it around his ring finger, then puts the hat on his head.

Tillman forced himself to watch this entire stupid ritual. Just what the hell did he think he was—a Vestal Virgin?

He certainly *looks* like he's been eating funny mushrooms as he waltzes into the vault, catalogs and stores Stephanie's blood, but leaves Cornran's nestled in his pocket, whistling *Camelot* the whole time. He already knows what he's going to do: He's going to send everyone home early, go into the nursery, and clone Jack Cornran. He's figuring out the records he'll have to falsify, the signatures he'll have to forge, the lies he'll have to tell. Happy as a clam.

He doesn't let himself think about what he intends to do with this clone, but that knowledge is there, smirking at him, filling him with shame for the deceit he's going to practice on Stephanie in the name of love. She was so nice to him at lunch, even laughing at his stupid jokes. He wonders why. She seems to be able to see okay from way up there at six-foot-one, looking down at his four-foot-eleven. She just doesn't seem to care what he looks like. She's even asked him to have lunch with her again tomorrow.

She must think I'm safe, he decides, her own personal dwarf, like a mascot. Somebody who wouldn't dare hit on her in a million years. He pushes back her hat like one tough hombre. Have I got a surprise for you, he thinks.

Tillman stopped the memory. Yeah—he was going to show her, all right. Some love. It was rape he was planning, no two ways about it. Not exactly a loving thing to do.

It was Sir Thomas Malory who got him in trouble. While other kids were playing baseball or stealing gum from the 7-Eleven, he was reading Malory, a gift from an uncle who didn't realize it wasn't a kid's book. Tillman loved it. He hated that sword and sorcery crap usually foisted on kids—too prissy and precious and just plain dumb—about as much like Malory as Disney was like Victor Hugo. Malory had this dark insane edge to things that Tillman could understand—a world where anything was possible, not because pretty people were wishing on stars or bleating out bad songs, but because the whole place was hanging by a thread. Not unlike the real world.

Tillman didn't care for King Arthur himself that much. He wanted to be Lancelot. But his favorite character was Arthur's father, Uther Pendragon. He said the name out loud—"U-ther Pen-dra-gon"—loving the way it sounded, the feel of it in his mouth. Now here was a guy who conceives a passion for another man's wife—the fair Igraine (so beautiful it made your heart ache just to look at her) and he doesn't care if she's married, if she can't stand the sight of him, or even if he brings the whole kingdom crashing down around his ears—he's by God got to have her. Uther, as Tillman always pictured him, is a hideous little fuck, with as much hope of wooing Igraine as Tillman had with Stephanie Sanders. But Uther enlists the aid of Merlin's magic and assumes the form of Igraine's husband—handsome stud muffin Gorlois—and makes mad, passionate love to Igraine while her husband is off dying in battle somewhere.

Was that so bad really? The guy was going to die anyway. Igraine might've been pretty confused later, but the sex had to've been great. To be wanted like that. Tillman couldn't imagine.

SO THERE HE IS IN HIS LAB, 120 YEARS AGO, AND HE *knows* he can make the whole thing happen: He has Merlin beat. You want somebody else's body? No problem. Hell, take two or three. All he has to do is play the role of Uther Pendragon.

He tells himself, as he's setting up the vat to clone Jack Cornran, that he has forty days while it's growing to decide what he's *really* going to do with it—as if that'll make it any easier to do the right thing. Forty days of imagining Stephanie in his arms—each day, each imagining making it seem more inevitable, more fated—so that when he actually does it, it's as if he's never really decided, that it just happens. *So sorry. I don't know what came over me!*

But he *did* decide, right then, when he left that vial in his pocket, thinking about some loopy story from the fifteenth century.

Malory, according to some scholars, wrote his stories in jail while serving a twenty-year sentence for rape and other unchivalrous crimes. Some role model. Maybe Uther Pendragon was Malory's favorite character too. One thing for sure, he was no Sir Galahad. And neither was Tillman.

AS IT TURNED OUT, WHILE THE CLONE WAS GROWING, TILLMAN saw Stephanie three or four times a week. Tillman could hardly believe it. She did all the asking. All he had to do was say yes. He got to know her chauffeur and her bodyguard, got used to riding around in a limo, though eventually they struck out on their own in Tillman's ancient Taurus.

At first they ate lunch after lunch. She'd frump down, so nobody would recognize her—which didn't always work— or they'd go someplace stuffed to the rafters with famous people, so nobody would care who she was—which made Tillman about as comfortable as a fish in a tuxedo.

But, God, she was wonderful. They'd talk for hours as if they'd both been saving up their whole lives to have somebody to talk to who understood, who cared, who liked you for who you were, and not for what you looked like or what they thought that meant. There were only two subjects they avoided—her beauty and his ugliness.

When people did recognize her, Tillman usually scared them away. You could see the little flutter of activity, the discreet pointing—but usually no one trotted over to the table. She spotted one of these clusters of fans one day and warned him they were about to descend—she'd seen it often enough to know the early warning signs. But when Tillman and Stephanie were still alone over coffee and dessert, she wondered aloud why the gawkers were being so shy. To her credit, she didn't seem to have a clue. "They want to meet *you*," he said, "but I give them the creeps."

You could see in her face that she knew he was right. He dreaded what she might say next: *You're not that ugly. I don't care if you're ugly. You are beautiful inside.* No matter what she said, he would only hear the word "ugly." And he knew damn well he was ugly inside and out. We can move on now, Tillman thought, desperately trying to smile.

But she didn't say anything. She put her hand on his and kissed him. An audible gasp came from the cluster of fans, and Tillman wished she hadn't done it. Oh, he loved the kiss, the touch and taste of her lips, the smell of her skin. But later on, he kept wondering why she'd done it— whether she was really kissing *him,* or whether she was just flipping the bird at the gawkers. *Take that, assholes! I'll even kiss this ugly little fuck!* Stephanie wouldn't do that, would she? But he didn't ask her. Now he wished he had. He wished he'd asked her a lot of things.

But back then, half his mind was always on the little Jack

Cornran growing in his nursery. Uther, he called it. He tweaked it along as much as he could. Some stretches just took longer than others. Adolescence took forever and had him up at the lab most nights, riding out hormonal typhoons as gene after gene handed out new complicated instructions.

He told his colleagues the new clone was an emergency backup in case something went wrong with one of the other clones, and they bought it. None of them gave him enough credit to think he'd ever do something daring or weird. He *was* weird, and they figured that was enough.

The other clones were started on Columbus Day, to be decanted on Thanksgiving, with a month of testing and conditioning before their new residents, five of the richest men in the world, moved in on—you guessed it—Christmas Day. The advertising/marketing folks had dreamed up the timetable, stuffed with symbolism, and were poised to hype it for all it was worth. Tillman suggested they do the whole thing with Groundhog Day, the Ides of March, and Easter. He was advised to keep his opinions to himself.

But once he started growing Uther, he quit thinking about the rest of them. All he could think about was what he was going to do when Uther was ready. When Steph'd just been the Most Beautiful Woman in the World, it wasn't so hard to talk himself into it, since she was more an idea than a real person. When he started the damn thing, he was certainly smitten, but he didn't know her like he did later. All her life the world had been fucking with her— because everybody wanted to fuck her. And here he was, her only real friend as far as he could tell, about to pull this.

They were seeing each other practically every day by this time, talking on the phone for hours, e-mailing each other a dozen times a day. It seemed that her husband rarely spent any time with her unless he needed her for some dinner that showed up on the evening news. The Beautiful Mrs. Cornran. She told Tillman everything about her life and her unhappy marriage. So unhappy, in fact, that Tillman was beginning to wonder whether she'd sleep with him, even if he did look like her husband.

Soon Tillman and Stephanie grew tired of lunches, and she lamented they couldn't just go to the zoo or go shopping at the mall, and he said, "Sure, we can—just like the simple folk do."

"I don't want to cause a big hassle," she said.

"What we need is camouflage," he said. And then it came to him: "We'll wear ski masks. People will still stare, but as long as we don't pull out guns, who's going to say anything?" By this time, it was December, a bad winter. People didn't even stare that much. "Cold out there, huh?" was about all they got.

They went everywhere Stephanie'd never been able to go without bodyguards and autograph seekers. Museums, amusement parks, movies, the grocery store. One bitter cold day they were at the zoo, staring at a deserted beaver pond, when a pair of beavers turned up. She let out a little cry, reached out, took his hand, and squeezed it as she watched the sleek animals gliding through the water side by side. Both Tillman and Stephanie were wearing gloves. It wasn't erotic, or even romantic. But she had spontaneously taken his hand out of joy. No one, not even his mother, had ever done that before. And she kept holding it, all day long. Her eyes shone, ringed with black wool.

THE TIME PASSED QUICKLY, AND WHAT HAD SEEMED LIKE plenty of time to make up his mind about Uther was almost exhausted. Uther had only a few days left before he could pass as Jack Cornran. He was still a little young yet, but Jack dyed his gray anyway. Tillman spent hours staring at his creation, trying to imagine life inside that flesh, that flesh inside Stephanie. The thought made his heart race and filled him with longing, so that he knew what he'd always known—that he'd already made up his mind when he stole Cornran's blood. At the same time, he's thinking, I can't do this. It's wrong. It's just plain wrong. But that was just his conscience whining so as to save face later on. He knew he wasn't going to listen to it. He'd always known. And so he lived in a perpetual state of shame and self-loathing at the same time he was happier than he'd ever thought possible, simply because of her. The woman he was going to betray.

So preoccupied was he with this dilemma that he almost didn't notice the strange goings-on in his own lab. First, he found a rack of blood samples in the vault, which, though seemingly properly cataloged, didn't show up in the database. Then he discovered, when he started asking about the blood samples, that several of his best researchers had been transferred to something called the Proteus Project. He spent an afternoon trying to find out something about it, but only turned up a few files on gene-splice research that looked like somebody wanted to go into the sideshow freak business. Pointless stuff, really—importing features from animals into humans—superficial but bizarre alterations in appearance for the most part. Why in the hell would anyone want to do that? He considered asking upstairs about it, but didn't want to call any attention to himself with Uther so near completion.

And then Freddie dropped by his lab with new information—his specialty—and a salve for Tillman's conscience. And any chance that Tillman might yet do the right thing went right out the window.

Tillman didn't really know Freddie well, but he felt a kinship of outcasts. Tillman was the troll geneticist; Freddie, the queer programmer. On those rare occasions when the whole team of researchers packed into an auditorium for some deadly dull presentation sprinkled with "breakthroughs" for the press, the two of them would sit in the back and trade wisecracks under their breath. But he'd never stopped by for a visit.

Freddie made small talk at first, following Tillman around the lab, asking inane questions about the work—questions Tillman was sure Freddie knew the answers to. Freddie's presence made the others nervous, waving his hands around as he talked, a bit more swishy than usual. When he'd cleared the place out, he gave Tillman a naughty-naughty wag of his finger.

"You've been asking too many questions, Tillman."

"What do you mean?"

"The Proteus Project."

"I talked to no one."

"You talked to the computer, silly. But don't worry. It's our little secret."

"But I don't know anything."

Freddie gave him a conspiratorial wink. "If you tell me what you know, I'll tell you what I know. You just might know more than you think."

Tillman glanced nervously at the security camera aimed right at them. There were microphones as well. Freddie followed his gaze and dismissed the camera with a wave of his hand. "Don't worry about that silly thing. I planned ahead. The little security drones are watching yesterday's tape about now, listening to the radio playing "Can't Buy Me Love." I wrote the surveillance software, Tillman."

So Tillman told him what he knew. Freddie had a few questions about the genetics of it, apparently just to confirm what he'd already figured out, because unlike Tillman, Freddie seemed to know what was going on.

"So what is this project?" Tillman asked him.

"First let me tell you what my best and brightest have been up to lately. They cut and paste bits of different identities and integrate them into one—make designer personalities. All very cooperative and versatile souls, I might add. Can you guess what they're for?"

Try as he might, Tillman couldn't see it, even though it was right in front of his face. Because he'd been the recipient of so much personal evil, he failed to look for it on a grander scale. "I don't have any idea," he said.

"They intend to place these personalities into mass-produced clones with the little sideshow touches you spoke of. The factory is all set to go after the New Year. A dozen more are planned."

Tillman imagined an army of such beings with scales and feathers in a variety of colors streaming out into the world like so many new automobiles. "What the hell are they for?"

"Cornran and his friends intend to bring back slavery."

Tillman thought he might be sick. Of course. It was completely obvious to him now. So this was what all his work had come to. He'd thought he was prolonging life, eventually—when the technology became less costly—helping the sick and lame and yes, the ugly. Instead he'd helped create a race of slaves. "Does Newman know about this?" Tillman knew that Newman Rogers and Freddie were friends, some said lovers. Tillman had only met Newman a couple of times, but he was sure he didn't want his genius turned into slavery any more than Tillman did.

"Oh, goodness, yes," Freddie said. "Trust me—Newman knows everything that goes on in this place."

"Then why doesn't he stop it?"

Freddie shook his head sadly. "Too late. They don't need him anymore. They don't need *any* of us. The hard work's all done. They have the theory, the techniques, and the patents. They can get by with technicians from here on out. You'll notice they didn't ask you to design the freak show, or me to cook up their minds."

Freddie was right. You didn't need Thomas Edison to turn on a lightbulb. Einstein didn't pilot the *Enola Gay*. The gene-splice stuff was simplicity itself. He could've done it twenty years ago—but why bother to make monsters? "But I don't get it," Tillman objected, still looking for some way out. "Why make them look so weird? You'd think they'd want Barbie and Ken."

"Market surveys, Tillman. Customers feel it's rather tacky to buy humans, though they do it all the time one way or another. Black skin's not enough anymore, apparently, to disguise one's humanity. We're too enlightened. But make them furry or three feet tall, and they'll take a dozen. The art department has a whole line worked out—from whimsical to elegant."

"We have an *art* department?"

"It's an oxymoron, I know."

Tillman tried to imagine the level of cynicism necessary to carry out such a plan, but it was beyond his comprehension. Maybe they should just clone me, Tillman thought, save themselves the trouble of inventing freaks. And then he remembered Stephanie's blood sample, still in the vault. Enough for thousands and thousands of her—warm three-dimensional posters in electric blue. "This is terrible."

"It gets worse, I'm afraid," Freddie said.

"How could it possibly be worse?"

"It won't work. When we first started uploading consciousness into a shared environment, we were concerned that they'd blur together, but it never happened. That made me curious. I uploaded two consciousnesses I'd melded together. It was like shaking up oil and vinegar—they came apart in a few days, perfectly whole. So then I did what they're proposing, selected out particular portions of several persons' identities and stitched them together, like making a quilt. It took longer, but they gradually regained their individual identities, which made no sense at all. That was like leaving a quilt in a room and coming back to find dozens of bolts of fabric, whole and complete. But then we don't really understand consciousness all that well—we've just figured out how to move it around, do some primitive cut and paste. Only when these scraps become whole, they'll find themselves trapped in a single body."

"Have you told them this?"

"They already know."

"Then why are they doing it?"

"By the time the public figures all this out, raises a big stink, and makes slavery illegal again, there'll be thousands of them already made, hard at work. They don't need them for long. They have bigger plans."

AND THEN FREDDIE TOOK TILLMAN DOWN TO THE COMPUTER he now called home, explained the whole concept of a fully interactive virtual world to him. "This little thing," he said, pointing to the huge computer, "is merely for testing. It only has room for two. But once they have the slaves, they start building heaven. Immortality for everyone—at a price, of course."

Tillman stared at the thing. "Is anybody in there now?"

"No. We're pretty much done testing this one."

"I heard rumors you were working on something like this, but I didn't realize you were so far along."

"Yes, we're too clever by half."

Tillman tried to imagine the impact of such a thing, people abandoning the world for a virtual heaven, streaming into space like air leaking out of a ball until there was no one, nothing but an empty world.

"This is terrible," he said again.

"Inevitable, Tillman. Inevitable." Freddie arched a brow. "But there's something you haven't told me, isn't there? Who's the bun in the oven, Walter? Whatever are you up to?"

Tillman started to deny everything, but he knew Freddie had also written the software that ran the nursery. He wasn't just making a lucky guess. So he told him, and pretty soon it turned into a confession, from the moment Stephanie walked into his lab until his plans to transfer his identity into Uther in a couple of days, when, according to Stephanie, Jack would be in Europe for a week. He would tell her he canceled his trip to be with her, just the two of them.

Tillman was fully expecting—hoping, actually—that Freddie would tell him he was sick and disgusting and that he should destroy this clone immediately. But he didn't.

"I've covered your tracks," he said and smiled. "Be careful, Walter. Don't forget Astral Watkins."

Tillman had already thought about him. When they were working out the personality-transfer process, they enlisted a death-row inmate named Astral Watkins as a test subject, transferring his personality to a clone for a few days and back again—just in time to kill him. While they were running the tests, they monitored Watkins's body and kept it alive. No problem. But when they tried to put him back into his own body, they almost lost him. Seems like the autonomic nervous system had made thousands of tiny electrochemical adjustments in his absence and wasn't about to take him back without a fight.

They had no choice but to pull the plug on Watkins's

body, with his personality still in the clone. The state, naturally enough, wanted to execute him. Cornran filed suit blocking the execution on the grounds that the clone was the property of ALMA Enterprises, Inc. Watkins filed an appeal on the grounds that he was—by all medical definitions—dead and therefore had already been executed. Cornran won—and with Cornran's lawyers' help, so did Watkins. Then the clone was brought back to ALMA and promptly "decommissioned." No more Astral Watkins. Unless you counted his place in the history of medical science.

They called it the Astral Effect in his honor. It worked like this: If you just wanted to visit a body and head back home when the party was over, twelve hours was a good safe limit. After twenty-four hours, you're risking *serious* complications. Three days, tops, you'd better settle into your new body because you can't go home again.

"There's one thing I've never been able to figure out about that whole deal," Tillman said. "Why didn't Cornran just let the state kill Watkins?"

"He wanted to show them who was boss," Freddie said. He put his hand on Tillman's shoulder. "There's one more thing I need to tell you. You're not the only one who's been making clones on the sly. Cornran's meeting with all the top investors next week. He has a gift for each of them, to sweeten the deal."

This time Tillman didn't have to ask Freddie what was going on. He saw it immediately, remembering Cornran's urgency over that specimen of Stephanie's blood. *She* was the gift. Cornran was more horrible than he'd ever imagined. In his revulsion at Cornran, he forgot his own self-loathing and began to see himself, not as Uther, but as Lancelot coming to the defense of his lady's honor.

He also realized why Freddie had come to him in the first place. Freddie wanted him to use his clone of Jack Cornran for more than just the seduction of Stephanie. "You knew who I was cloning before you came to see me, didn't you?"

Freddie put his hands on his hips. "And here I thought

I was being so subtle. I did take a little peek at the DNA of your friend in the nursery, and it did match our fearless leader's. I thought it was too good to be true."

It hadn't occurred to Tillman before that if he carried out his plans, he would be an exact replica of one of the most powerful men in the world. Maybe the most powerful. He'd only been thinking about himself and Stephanie, just like Uther. But he might actually be able to use this charade to do some good, to change things.

Now it was his turn to give Freddie a conspiratorial wink. "Jack Cornran could put a stop to this slavery project, don't you think?"

"The thought had occurred to me. He is a very influential man." Freddie smiled wickedly. "But a few sufficiently imprudent remarks might land even him and his friends in jail."

So THEY WORKED IT OUT, THINKING THEY WERE SO DAMN smart: While Tillman was masquerading as Jack Cornran, he would grant an interview with a journalist of Freddie's acquaintance and spill the beans about the whole Construct project, discrediting it and himself completely. At least that was the plan.

"Watch yourself, Walter" was the last thing Freddie said to him. He'd often remembered that, wondering if he could've saved himself if he'd been more careful and trusted no one. But if he really thought there was no one he could trust, he wouldn't have done it in the first place.

Tillman skipped ahead to the moment that, for some reason, was the most vivid in his own memory.

He's walking down the front walk to Stephanie's door, still a little unsteady on his feet, getting used to his new long-legged body. His veins are racing with excitement. He's breathing in the crisp winter air, delighting in the smell of pines and wood smoke, absolutely convinced he's not just going to deceive the woman he loves. Oh, no, he's going to strike a blow for freedom. That Walter Tillman, some kind of hero. He realizes he has no keys to the door, that he'll have to ring the bell, and his hands are shaking so bad he can hardly manage that. Stephanie opens the door and turns away almost immediately. "I lost my keys," he says, but she doesn't say a word, retreating into the house. He steps over the threshold and watches her disappear up the stairs. He feels a pain in his hand and looks down, remembering the dozen red roses he holds in a death grip, the thorns digging into his stolen palm.

THE DOOR TO THE RED ROOM OPENED, AND SALLY STUCK her head in. "We have visitors," she said. "Sam and a woman. She wants to come in."

Tillman shut off the memory, trying to reorient himself to the present where everything was over and done with. "He's back already?" A woman? This must be a black market contact, he thought, someone who can help me. This Sam moves fast. "Well, let's show her in."

"She's already in the VIM."

Tillman almost ran down to the library, skidded to a stop, and started the upload. When the woman stepped out of the VIM, he could hardly believe it. But there it was right in front of his eyes, virtual or not. Unless Stephanie had had kids after Tillman was put in cold storage, he knew where this young woman had come from. The nose, the eyes, the cheekbones. He'd always wondered how that blood he drew from Stephanie was used, and now he knew. She looked almost exactly like Steph, except for the green scales that covered her scalp and arched over her eyes. This is my fault, he thought. Completely my fault.

"I'm Walter Tillman," he said, his voice trembling, holding out his hand.

She sneered at his offered hand. "I know who you are," she said. "I've got a few things I'd like to say to you. You ugly little fuck."

8

THE SHORTEST DAY OF THE YEAR

STEPHANIE KNEW.

She never knew how she knew.

But she knew immediately, so long ago, that this man at her door with a fistful of roses wasn't Jack, knew immediately who it was. But what made it so otherworldly wasn't the knowledge itself but the suddenness, that sense of knowing in an instant, as if the gods had whispered in her ear.

Oh, maybe it was a deduction from the facts at hand, but she doubted she was that perceptive, that quick. She'd had years to sort out the clues. There was the suit. Jack wouldn't be caught dead in that suit, though in a sense he was. Walter told her later that he'd bought it at a Sears (the best they had, but not good enough) and they'd had a good laugh over that, their last laugh as it turned out, though she didn't know it at the time. Her perceptiveness, if that's what it was, had run out too soon.

Then there was the way he looked at her, followed her up to their bedroom, talking in a tone Stephanie had never heard from Jack. The same voice, but not at all the same. Like a violin in different hands. Immediately, she knew the rise and fall, the cadence, the way he didn't just talk at her but yearned to be understood, the way, though she hadn't yet spoken a word, he was already listening. She knew him, knew there was only one of him.

He'd told her enough about his work to figure out how he'd managed this deceit, but she didn't care about that. This was Walter. That was all that mattered. He'd found a way into her life, and she realized all at once how much he loved her, how much, with all her heart, she loved him.

But if she told him, he'd bolt, like Cupid from Psyche. And if she didn't, he'd think she loved him because he looked like Jack, when nothing could be further from the truth. The handsome Jack now repulsed her. She'd told Tillman everything, but not that. It came too close to the taboo line they'd strung up the first time they met. She imagined blind people talked more about looks than they did. But now he'd made looks everything, unaware of what he'd just shown her—that Tillman was Tillman, regardless of what he looked like, and she was herself, not what she looked like. She thought she knew this before, but she hadn't really. She'd just said it to herself because that's what you were supposed to say, all the while surrendering her life to appearance.

Walter stood tall in his fine new body, in his Sears suit, smiling nervously. His gaze swept the room, taking everything in, lingering over the photographs, the book on the bedside table, the gown draped over the chair. She watched his eyes. Every object was significant because it was hers. He wasn't sure where to stand or sit in her bedroom, no doubt asking himself what Jack would do, not knowing Jack was rarely here, that he slept in his own room downstairs.

She busied herself with putting the roses in a vase. Jack never brought her flowers. Anyone could buy flowers. His gifts were meant to intimidate. It annoyed him that she never gasped at diamonds.

"They're beautiful," she said of the roses as she set them on the dresser.

"Not very original, I'm afraid." Even in his disguise, he thought himself inadequate.

She went to him and put her arms around him. Cautiously, he embraced her, then held her close. So sweet, so tender.

She wished he'd come as himself, but she knew why he hadn't. As he'd longed for her, she'd waited like some damsel in a tower, knowing all along he wouldn't, couldn't scale the walls around her. She'd kept his love like some genie in a jar: a prize, a token, a thing she owned. She was no better than Jack. But Walter came to her anyway.

She kissed his neck and whispered in his ear. "Do you love me?"

"Oh, yes," he said in a husky voice. "I love you more than you'll ever know."

"Show me," she said.

He held her face in his hands, and they looked into each other's eyes. She could see him there behind the mask of Jack's features, though even they were transformed by his love. As they made love, she closed her eyes and imagined Walter.

When they'd exhausted themselves, she curled up in his arms and feigned sleep. She wanted just one night like this before she upset the balance he'd so carefully constructed. In the morning, she told herself, I'll know what to say. When his breathing became deep and regular, she let herself fall asleep and dreamed it was morning and he'd transformed in the night back into himself, but neither one spoke of it, because it didn't matter, not in the least. The sun shone brightly in her dream, reflecting off the snow, filling every window with a blinding light.

SHE OPENED HER EYES, AND THE LIGHT WAS DULL AND GRAY. Snow was falling again, and she could tell by the sound of his breathing that Tillman too was awake, though his eyes were still closed. They came open and he held up his hands and looked at them, his proof he hadn't been dreaming. He realized she was watching him and looked over and smiled. The antique clock downstairs struck eight. He'd been here eleven hours.

"You've never made love to me like that before," she said.

"How is that?" he said, still cautious.

"Like you mean it."

He stared up at the ceiling, a sad look on his face. What was he sad about, exactly? She thought she knew: He'd made love to her as he'd dreamed, but he'd also witnessed another man making love to her at the same time. He thought the joy in her eyes was for that other man. She couldn't let him think that.

She took his hand and kissed it. "Coffee?"

His face took on that same blissful look Tillman always had at the mention of coffee day or night, but now with Jack's features. It was like seeing Scrooge on Christmas morning.

She got out of bed, and he started to join her, but she put her hands on his shoulders and pushed him back into his pillow. "I'll bring it up," she said. "You just lie here and think lustful thoughts." She kissed him on the mouth, breaking the kiss when his arms wrapped around her again. "Coffee," she said.

She went downstairs and made a carafe of coffee, loaded a tray with cups and saucers and spoons, cream and sugar and artificial sweetener. She enjoyed walking through her house naked, the man she loved waiting upstairs for her. He can't run now, she told herself. He's gone too far.

When she walked into the bedroom with the tray, he was looking out the window at the falling snow, his brow furrowed, no doubt steeling himself for a confession. But she didn't want to hear it. She didn't want him to regret what he'd done, not for a moment. She set the tray between them and poured. She sat cross-legged on the bed and shook a spoonful of the artificial sweetener into her cup and stirred, watching him.

He reached for the artificial sweetener, and she said, "You hate that stuff."

His hand froze for a moment, then he picked it up anyway. "I'm trying to cut down on the sugar. It's not really that bad."

She plucked the sweetener from his hand and set it back

on the tray. "Cream and two sugars. That's how you always take your coffee. This isn't a day to deny yourself."

His eyes met hers, calculating the odds of such a coincidence, deciding it wasn't impossible enough to risk. He put two spoons of sugar in his coffee and a healthy dose of cream, just as Walter always did. "I have to go somewhere for a few hours this morning," he said as he stirred. "I have an appointment. It shouldn't take too long."

"Will you be seeing Walter Tillman?" she asked. His coffee sloshed onto the saucer. He had to sit up straighter to hold the saucer level.

"No, this is some journalist who wants to interview me," he said, trying to put on what he imagined to be Jack's voice at a time like this, drowsy and warm, but with a manly gruffness.

Which wasn't what he would've sounded like at all, she supposed. She didn't know. They'd never had a moment like this, never would. They'd fuck, and he'd gloat in the way he did when he bought a painting without asking the price. "Send it up to the house," he'd say, handing over a card with the address. Beautiful paintings. But he never looked at them. They were investments. Like her.

"Don't you want to know why I asked about Walter Tillman?"

He swallowed hard. His smile was a thin line. She could see he was terrified of what she might say, what he might learn about her true feelings for him. "He's my best friend," she said.

"That's nice," he murmured, trying to relax, pretending to be completely absorbed with his coffee. There were worse fates than friend.

"There's something I have to tell you about him."

He raised his head, and she looked into his frightened eyes. "I'm in love with Walter Tillman."

He turned away. "You're joking, right? He's too ugly for his own mother to love." His voice shook now, a note Jack's never struck.

"It doesn't matter what he looks like. It's who he is, how

he feels about me, and how he makes me feel." He was in a panic, trying to understand, much less believe what she was telling him. She closed her hands around his, took the cup and saucer and set them on the tray, then put the tray on the floor. "Jack doesn't drink coffee, Walter. He loathes it."

He met her steady gaze for a long time before he spoke. "When did you know?"

"Immediately."

He shook his head, embarrassed and ashamed. "Steph . . . I'm so sorry."

"For what? Risking everything to be with me?"

He kept shaking his head, determined to be in the wrong. "But I deceived you."

She laid her palms on his chest. "No, you didn't. I just told you. I knew the whole time."

"But it was my intention to—"

She groaned. "Oh, Walter, stop it. If you're going to convince me how evil you are, you'll have to be a little less contrite."

"But how? How did you know?"

She cradled his face in her hands and looked into his eyes. "It's the way you look at me."

He seemed to think about this for a long time. "And I guess it doesn't hurt I've got these striking deep-set eyes now."

She pulled her hands away and wrapped her arms around her legs. "Yes, it does hurt. I prefer your own."

"Please don't lie to me."

She winced. She deserved that, she supposed. She'd known for weeks that Tillman loved her, but it was only now she let him show it. What did she expect him to think? "It's the truth."

"Then why didn't you say anything when you knew it was me?"

"I was afraid you'd go, when I was so glad you'd come to me."

"In such a nice new package too."

"Stop it, Walter. You're not being fair. Why don't you try me and see if I'm telling the truth?"

"What do you mean?"

"Come back as yourself. You can't stay in that clone. I want *you*, Walter, not a nice package."

He eyed her warily. She didn't flinch, even though she was terrified herself that perhaps she was lying to him. "I can't do that."

"Why not?"

He got out of bed and started putting on his clothes.

"I'm not sure I want to," he said.

She should've thought of this: Ugly and scorned all his life, he might not be so eager to shed his fine new skin. It was easy for her, who'd always been beautiful, to say it meant nothing. For him it must be a dream come true.

And then it struck her he was going out in the world in the guise of Jack, saying he was going to meet someone. "What's going on, Walter? Where are you going?"

He hesitated only a moment before he told her the whole story of what Jack was up to and what he intended to do about it. He seemed completely unaware of the dangers. Even she, who should have known better, underestimated them.

"If you get caught—"

"I won't be. I have to go now. I don't want to be late."

His tie was hopeless—ten years out of fashion, tied in a boxy knot. She came off the bed and took the tie in her hands. "I'll give you one of Jack's ties."

"Steph—"

"You have to fool this guy, right? *No* one will believe you're Jack in this tie." She already had it loose, stripped from him. "Jack's clothes are downstairs."

"Okay, but then I have to go."

He followed her downstairs to Jack's room, where she picked out a tie and knotted it around his neck. His eyes flickered around nervously at Jack's perfect bedroom, which looked the same as it did for the *Architectural Digest* shoot. A decorator's well-paid vision. She'd always wondered whether the glass shelf of fetishes from an Amazon culture destroyed by Jack's enterprise was an irony of the decorator or of the gods.

"I have to go now," he repeated.

"And then you'll come back to me?"

"If you want."

"Of course I want. I want *you,* Walter. Come back to me as yourself, you understand?"

"I'll see."

"If I'd thought for a moment you were Jack, I wouldn't have let you touch me." He looked skeptical, almost like Jack would look, and her hand lashed out and slapped his face to show him what she thought of it. He was still stunned as she threw her arms around him. "Come back to me, you understand?"

"Yes."

She held him close, kissing the hot place on his cheek where she'd just struck him. "I'll be waiting," she said. "For you, Walter. I love only you."

At the door she ran her hands up and down his lapels. "You really ought to change suits if you want to fool anyone," she said, laughing.

"Hey, what's wrong with it? This is the best suit Sears had."

He was laughing too. This was like their familiar banter, their good times all done up in ski masks, squeezing each other's hands. *Maybe,* she could see him thinking, *she really does love me.*

They were still laughing when he kissed her one last time and trudged up the walk.

SHE WENT BACK UPSTAIRS AND WAITED IN HER BED, NOT thinking about where he'd gone or what he was doing, thinking only of his return. It was snowing harder now, and she watched it fall. From her window she could see his footprints, coming and going, gradually disappearing as the snow made everything still and white. The silence was pierced by the phone ringing, and she let it ring. It didn't matter. It wouldn't be Walter. He'd come back or not, but he wouldn't call.

Sometime later she went downstairs in her robe, heated up her cold coffee, and poured Tillman's down the drain. She checked the phone, and there was a message from Jack, calling from Brussels to tell her he might be a few days longer than he planned. He had a lover in Brussels, she knew, but she didn't care. "Thank you, Jack," she said, shutting off the phone. She sat in the window seat and watched the snow.

She'd often wondered why she'd married Jack. When he was at the height of his attentive extravagance, she called what she felt for him "love." Not friends. Never once. Except in the way chess opponents might share a certain camaraderie while they were caught up in the game. She, who'd learned that beauty and truth had nothing to do with each other, just assumed that love and friendship didn't either. It was a *stranger* you saw across a crowded room. And he stayed that way.

Her parents rarely treated each other like friends. When she was eleven, both their promotions happened to come through the same week, and they could like each other for a few strides while they were neck and neck, but as soon as one of them stumbled or surged ahead, things returned to normal. She didn't listen to the details. It was all just the buzzing whine of envy. She knew the sound from the girls at school who said she was stuck-up, a phrase which made her think of butterflies pinned and labeled.

When Stephanie became an "overnight success," her parents had a common foe, and they learned to suffer together as their daughter—just because she was beautiful—received all the adulation they worked so hard for. She'd put them out of the race, and they could never forgive her for that, telling interviewers they were "proud as they could be," but never once saying they loved her.

When she turned eighteen, she gave them enough money

so that greed wouldn't be the motive if they ever sought her out or even bothered to call her up. They did neither.

The sky was gray and low, no hint of brightness to reveal the whereabouts of the sun. She wondered what time it was, but deliberately avoided the clock. It was only moments since he'd gone, but it seemed like hours. But that's always the way it was with Tillman. That first day they had lunch, as she was walking away from him, all she could think about was when she would see him again. Before long she found herself thinking, It will never work. Then she realized with a start there was something there she wanted to work, wanted in a way she'd never wanted anyone before. Even if he hadn't come to her in this clone, she would've come down from her tower sooner or later, wouldn't she? She imagined herself since the day she met him, walking in circles, coming back to him, like a child drawing a flower with great looping petals.

One of the reasons she'd married Jack was he'd said he wanted to have children. He had a touching little speech he gave about wanting a son to carry on, reap the benefits, have what he never had. And what was that? she wondered. A soul? Now that she knew him, the only way she could imagine him wanting children was to make his mark, like a dog pissing on your leg. He said: "Children are the only true immortality." He'd read that somewhere, or maybe one of the ad guys wrote it for him. She was glad she'd never had children with him: How could any child live down such a father?

She imagined raising a child with Walter and smiled to herself. He'd be a wonderful father, the nicest man she'd ever known. She swung her legs off the window seat and stood up, wrapping the robe tight, cinching her waist with a jerk of her hands. The clock caught her eye: 10:45.

THE INTERVIEW, SHE FOUND OUT LATER, WAS JUST ENDING. Tillman took a cab to ALMA at 10:53. The retinal scan identified him as Jack Cornran at 11:12. He slipped back into his own body, which was locked up in his private lab. Because of the Astral Effect, he had to stay there two hours before he could enter the clone again. So he waited. He could've come to her directly as himself. Instead, he waited. She saw him in her mind's eye, pacing up and down, thinking he was caged, when the door stood open the whole time. If only he could've trusted her that much.

That afternoon she felt disappointment, even foreboding when she saw him striding up the walk in his cloned body. She remembered wondering if it would change him. It had to. Look at what beauty had made of her life. But she never got the chance to find out.

He came in smiling, took off his jacket, loosened his tie, talking excitedly about the interview. He took her in his arms, whirled her around. When he set her on her feet, she said, "Why didn't you come back as yourself?"

He stepped back, his face clouding over. "I didn't want to." He gestured at his body as if it were a new suit. "This is still me. You said you knew immediately. What difference does it make? Do you *want* me to be ugly?"

Did she want him to be ugly? No. She couldn't believe that. "I just want you to be you, Walter. That's all. I certainly don't want you to look like Jack. Besides, you can't go around looking like Jack. What if someone sees you? Recognizes you?"

"I'll wear cheap clothes. Grow a beard." He chuckled. "Think about it. He's on the evening news five nights a week: Everybody knows where Jack Cornran is and what he's up to. Nobody's going to mistake some scruffy guy in a cheap suit eating vindaloo for *the* Jack Cornran."

"But what about the rest of your life—your work, your research? You can't go to work looking like Jack and think no one will notice."

"I don't care about any of that. The hell with it."

"You can't mean that."

They argued for a while, maybe an hour. Stephanie couldn't remember. They just kept going in circles. After one night, she was already losing him.

And then the doorbell rang. They both froze.

"You expecting anybody?" Tillman whispered.

She shook her head. They clasped hands and crept to the door. She looked out through the peephole. Freddie stood on the porch, but she didn't know who he was, though she'd seen him before at company functions. Tillman looked out and, to her surprise, opened the door immediately.

Freddie stepped inside and smiled grimly at Stephanie. "I know this is terribly rude, Mrs. Cornran, but I must speak with Mr. Cornran alone."

"She knows everything," Tillman said.

Freddie gave her a kind sympathetic look, one full of genuine admiration. She never forgot it, but she was never quite sure what it meant. "Then I guess you should turn on the news," he said.

Stephanie turned on the holo-news, and the end of the living room became a street in Brussels in front of a hotel. It was raining there, the streets slick. The newsman stood under an umbrella and rehearsed the details of the murder that had taken place there less than an hour before: Jack Cornran had been shot dead as he was stepping out of his limousine. A terrorist group she'd never heard of claimed responsibility in a Luddite rant. The reporter awaited further details on the tragedy.

She felt nothing but the overwhelming panic that Walter was now in danger. She started to shut off the news when Freddie told her to wait. The second story was the suicide of a prominent journalist who'd jumped from the top of a Washington hotel. Stephanie didn't need to be told that this was the journalist who had interviewed Tillman, the journalist who was to have exposed Jack, or that, in spite of what the newsman said of his colleague's drinking problems and bouts with depression, the dead man had been pushed.

Freddie said, "Apparently, Jack's colleagues found out about the interview and thought it was Jack whistle-blowing on the tape long enough to kill him and the interviewer. But now I suspect they're starting to figure out the timetable, that Cornran couldn't have given that interview in spite of what their surveillance folks here saw. They've been poking around the system all day, looking for answers. You've got to get out of that body, Tillman, or you'll be named an accomplice, for sure."

THEY WOULD MEET AT THE AIRPORT. THAT'S ALL SHE HAD TO remember of the plan they hurriedly worked out before Tillman and Freddie returned to the city to recover Tillman's body and destroy the clone. She had just packed a bag when the doorbell rang again.

They said they were FBI agents, and perhaps they were. ALMA's holdings were vast. Who knew what all it included. There were three of them. Two took turns talking. The silent one seemed to be in charge. They told her that her husband had been murdered, a reporter as well. They had reason to believe that the same assassins were after Walter Tillman. Did she know where he was? It was imperative that they find him before these determined killers caught up with him. She studied the badges they showed her. They said: FIDELITY, BRAVERY, INTEGRITY beneath the perfectly balanced scales of justice. And fool that she was, she told them. She got into their car and drove away with them, led them through the halls to Tillman's lab.

They drew their guns when they saw the clone, chased him as he ran down the stairs, cornering him in a basement room and gunning him down as he vainly attempted to hide in a strange-looking box, like a plastic coffin stood on end. The one in charge looked around the room and broke his silence. "Seal this off," he said. "Tight."

STEPHANIE LATER LEARNED ALL THE DETAILS WHEN HER INterrogators repeatedly explained it all to her, showing off their deadly power—how they'd been watching this particular journalist for weeks because he knew a bit more than he should, and they were hoping to discover his source inside the company, never suspecting Jack Cornran himself. How they'd mistakenly ordered Jack assassinated before they realized it wasn't actually Cornran who'd betrayed them.

But now they had it all figured out, they told her, they'd pieced together the whole plot. How Tillman had arranged an interview in the guise of Jack to derail the company. She was, no doubt, his accomplice, and their only possible motive was money. It was just a matter of finding out whose.

The only thing they didn't understand was why he didn't just destroy the clone and make the perfect getaway in his own body. "Look at it," the skinny one said, laughing, thinking he was making a joke.

She would've explained it to them, but they wouldn't have understood. In their version, no one loved anyone.

Throughout the interrogation, Tillman's body lay dead on the table in front of her. She wasn't sure how long she sat there or what she said. Nothing would bring him back. Finally it seemed to be over. She reached out and closed Walter's eyes, then took the pen the silent one handed her. She often wondered if she'd defied them whether they would have killed her too. She wished she'd thought of that then, but she scarcely knew she was alive.

The statement signed, the silent one said with a smile, just in case she was an idealist and Tillman was a martyr: "It's a pity we had to kill your husband before we discovered the clone, but don't worry, neither death will change the outcome. In fact, they might prove very useful indeed."

It was the winter solstice. The shortest day of the year. In the weeks that followed, she played the grieving widow. Jack was cast as the martyr, slain by "radical extremists" who opposed his "visionary plans to liberate humanity to fulfill its dreams and live its destiny." And thus, the silent one was right. With a famous dead man to grieve over, the whole world piously bowed its head and said, "Freedom is slavery."

THIS WAS THE STORY SHE CARRIED IN HER HEAD, PLUNGED into her heart. Tillman was dead. Her stupidity had killed him. With him died the last chance that the Constructs wouldn't go into production, and thousands of slaves rolled off the assembly line and went to work. With him died the love of her life.

She tried to make amends to the Constructs. The media tried to make her into the Idealistic Beauty. In her own eyes, she gave too little, too late. There was nothing she could do for Walter. Once the Bin went on-line, the truth about some old evil didn't matter anymore. Even she thought she could come into the Bin and start a new life, but all she'd done was put off the old one where she was long overdue to die.

She picked up the phone and called Victor to tell him she wouldn't be playing Ophelia.

"But you'd be perfect," he said.

"I won't be here," she said.

He gave her a funny look. "Are you all right? You don't look so good."

"I'm fine."

"Where are you going, anyway? You can always fly in—"

"I'm going home, Victor. I won't be flying anywhere."

9

THE KARMA KAFÉ

LAURA KNEW TILLMAN WAS UGLY. EVERYBODY KNEW THAT. George Washington was tall, Tillman was ugly. But she hadn't really prepared for just how ugly he was. He had that kind of face that you just see the guy, and you got to think, That poor son of a bitch. So she was caught off-guard in a way, feeling sorry for him.

So when she started telling him just what she thought of him, her heart wasn't in it. And he kept shaking his head and saying how sorry he was. Not just this "Yeah, yeah, so sorry" stuff, but the heartbreaking oh-my-God sort of thing until she was afraid he was going to break down crying, and damned if he didn't.

So there she was, uploaded into this mini-Bin thing he's got going, and she's holding him in her arms, giving him the old there-there, like he'd just given her a carton of machine-made cigarettes and asked for a little sympathy. She didn't know whether to laugh or cry.

Then he told her the whole crazy story. This was her night for crazy stories. She couldn't follow the whole deal, didn't even try, but what it boiled down to was this: He felt like shit for having cooked up the whole clone deal in the first place, he never would've done it if he'd known about Constructs—and this was the truly bizarro part—he really *did* think of himself as her great-grandaddy or something, and if she had any cut glass she wanted him to crawl through, all she had to do was say the word.

She wanted to smack him one.

Why did he have to fuck with her like that? Why didn't he just stand up for himself, so she could tell him what a miserable piece of shit he was? What was she supposed to do now? Forgive him? That was asking a bit much, don't you think?

"Will you shut the fuck up?" she said, and he did. Like she threw a switch. She thought she saw his little bowhead girlfriend get a little chuckle out of that, but when you looked at her head-on, she had the same glued-on smile she had from the get-go. She's not real, Laura decided. But some pretty snappy programming nonetheless.

"Let's start over," she said. "My name's Laura, and I'm your ride out of here."

"You don't know how much I appreciate—"

She held up her hands. "And I don't want to know. This is strictly business. For truly wacko reasons of his own, our little Soldier friend waiting outside is going to pay your freight. If it was up to me, I'd just find the plug on this big bar of soap and pull it. But a girl's got to eat."

She looked around, really taking in the room for the first time. Jeez, smell that wood. It was everywhere. There hadn't been a place like this in the real world since long before she was born. She turned to Tillman, still looking like a whipped puppy. Butt ugly, but cute. "So, Wally, you got any steak in here?"

SHE HAD TWO STEAKS (EIGHTEEN-OUNCE PORTERHOUSES rubbed in fresh garlic and cooked over a mesquite fire, medium-rare), two bottles of red wine ("Surprise me," she said), fresh Brussels sprouts, a quart of orange juice, and a chocolate cake that made you want to lie down and scream. Wally showed her how to access the operating system so that she never got stuffed or falling-down drunk.

Okay, so it wasn't real. Chef's stew was reality. Who the

fuck couldn't use a break from that? Like a vacation or something. She had no desire to head for the Bin on a permanent basis. The way she figured it, fitting in wasn't her best skill, and as long as there were people in the Bin going through the hassle of downloading, she stood a good chance of being one of them. So she was just going to keep her ass put where she knew the score. Somebody like her in the Bin? Yeah, right. She was exactly where she belonged. But while she was here, you bet. Pig out.

Wally bailed out after the first steak and just sat there, watching her eat. She gave herself a double espresso, and he joined her on that deal. She served herself another slice of cake, little scoop of vanilla *ice cream* nestled up against it. God, how long had it been since she'd had *ice cream*? Long enough so she almost forgot about it. Hell, she'd only had it three, four times in her life. "So, you been in here a long time."

"Yes," he said. "A very long time."

"So what do you do? Eat whatever you want? Play with your little bowhead friend? Doesn't sound so bad to me."

He smiled, not showing any teeth, for which she was grateful. His teeth all headed in different directions, like they were trying to escape from each other. "If you want to move in," he said, "be my guest."

She pushed back her chair and dabbed at her mouth with a linen napkin, WT embroidered in the corner with vines and flowers and hummingbirds. She had to admit it was kind of pretty. "No thanks," she said.

"It can handle two completely different exclusive realities. You wouldn't even know I was in here. Your own personal paradise."

She didn't much like being tempted. Her gut was telling her: Don't even begin to think about it. You listened to your gut if you knew what was good for you. She folded up the napkin and put it on the table. "I'll pass."

"Wise decision."

"Yeah, well, any paradise I was in charge of would go bad inside a week. But it's not like you're headed into some picnic out there, you know. The world is pretty much totally fucked."

"I gathered as much from our Christian friend. You don't have any hope that things will get better?"

Laura snorted. "Hope? I'll tell you what hope is. I used to know this girl named Hope. She had this standing offer, what she called her 'double-or-nothing deal.' If you could fuck her twice, it was free, but if you couldn't get it up for number two inside an hour, you paid double. You wouldn't believe how many guys took Hope up on the deal. None of them—I mean *none* of them—could do her twice. 'I have my ways,' she'd say. Then it got to be this big dare thing with all the guys, and they're practically lined up out in the street. Till finally this guy comes in tanked to the gills on something nasty, and I wouldn't have done him for a gallon of real Scotch. But Hope, she's got her ball-busting reputation to maintain, so she takes him upstairs, and they aren't up there any time at all when he's knocked off number one, and it looks like he might just be on his way to number two, when she starts laughing at him. You could hear it all over the place, laughing her ass off. Her last line of defense. Nothing'll shrivel a dick like laughing at it. You know what happened then?"

"I can't imagine."

"He shot her in the head. Bang. *Then* he fucks her. Sickest goddamn thing I ever saw in my life, and believe me, that's saying something. Anyway. She's the only Hope I've ever known." So it wasn't exactly a bedtime story, and maybe she jazzed it a little—she wasn't actually *there* at the time—but she didn't want Gramps here to get all sweet and paternal. This is where *I* live, asshole. Don't talk to me about hope.

"You're quite the philosopher, Laura."

"Yeah, that's me. A regular Plato."

"People still learn about Plato?"

"Constructs do. We learn all sorts of worthless shit. Fortunately, I wised up and got my ass out of there. But you still haven't told me why you want out of here." She was curious. From what Sammy had told her, Tillman's days in here were numbered, but he wanted out before he knew that.

"You left out one thing when you were ticking off my pastimes. I eat. I sleep with Sally. I used to travel, if you can call it that, but I gave it up a long time ago. Mostly what I do, what I've always done in here, is remember. Same handful of memories over and over again. If I don't experience something new pretty soon, I'll never forget them, and I'll go completely nuts." He shrugged. "If I'm not already."

"So what is it you remember so much?"

"Stephanie."

"You were babbling about her before. Some woman you figure was the donor for my grandmothers or something?"

"She's more than that."

The way he said it, you had to wonder what the story was. She waited for him to go on, but he was staring into space, obviously remembering this Stephanie again. She kicked him under the table. "So tell me about her. I got a little time before dawn. Not too much. I don't want to have my morning coffee with a Christian patrol, but I got some time yet."

He smiled. "There's still coffee out there?"

"If you've got the right connections. Not like the stuff in here, but it's not bad if you use your imagination. So tell me about this Stephanie. We're sort of related, right?"

"Why don't I show you?"

"Show me?"

He explained that he had a program set up to show his memories like holos, and she had to admit that sounded pretty cool. He took her down to this sexy red room with this truly ridiculous furniture in it and told her to sit down.

He was getting all wound up, like it was some kind of party, and she was beginning to have her doubts. "Wait a minute," she said. "How long is this going to take?"

"We don't have to watch it in real time," he said. "I can speed things up. I've never had a use for that routine before, but it's pretty simple. We could do the whole thing in a few minutes, though it'll feel like a few hours."

A few minutes. What did she have to lose? But still, there was something spooky about the whole deal. There was a fine line between finding out interesting useful stuff and finding out *way* the fuck too much, and in her experience whenever a guy *really* wants to tell you something, that was a good time to split. It hit her that she'd be watching this little toad's memories of some woman who, according to him, looked *just like her,* doing . . . what? She didn't want to know. "Maybe this isn't such a great idea," she said.

But then he made just the right move: popcorn. And a Coke. Right there in her hands. Big ones. The holo place in Crazyville had exactly twenty holos they showed over and over again. But she still went all the time because she loved popcorn and a Coke in the dark, her feet up on the seats, watching *any*thing. It didn't matter. The old-timers bitched about the Coke, saying it didn't taste like the real thing—they even had some loopy song they sang about it—but she didn't know the difference. It tasted okay to her. She'd never had a real Coke till now. Damn, there it was again. It was awful easy to forget this place wasn't real.

And by then he'd started up his memory with Tillman standing in a lab, checking on some clunky-looking clone vats, and she realizes that these are the very first clone vats, and she knows everything Tillman's thinking like it's her own memory, and by then it's too late, and she's already sucked in. It took her from the day he met Stephanie till the day he ended up in here. She couldn't shake the images, piling up on her, wearing down her resistance: the two of them, all sweet and innocent, watching a couple of fucking beavers; him standing on the front steps, stabbing himself with a fistful of roses; her looking him in the eyes, telling him she loves him and nobody else; him running for his life, bullets ripping into his flesh, and all he cares about is trying to figure out the look in Steph's eyes.

When it was over, she kept wiping away the tears, but there were just too many, so she let them run down her cheeks. He handed her a Kleenex—too bad it wasn't real; a box of those things was worth plenty—and she got things under control. She hated to cry. She truly hated to cry. She rubbed at a spot on her chest where the first bullet had struck him, realized she was doing it, and stopped. "So that's how you ended up in here. Tough break."

She stood up and gave him a little wave. "Think I'll shove off. Sammy's got to be jumpy as a cat by now. Thanks for the memories." She gave a phony little laugh at her own joke, but it was going to take more than a bad joke to throw Wally off the trail.

He'd stood up the minute she did, and now he reached out and took her hands. "Wait, please. I want to ask you something."

She glared down at his hands like he'd just handed her a dead rat, then gave him a death-beam look right between the eyes. He dropped her hands, like immediately.

"I'm sorry. I just want to ask you. You've seen the whole thing. You're the only other one who's ever seen it. I've got to know. Did she betray me? Did she lead those men to me? Did she love me at all, do you think?"

She knew it. She didn't want to get into this crazy memory stuff in the first place, and here she was—ass-deep in somebody else's shit again. When would she ever learn? She wanted to tell him that Stephanie hated his guts and had probably turned him over with a smile on her face. That'd fix him. But shit. She couldn't do it. She didn't even believe it herself, didn't want to believe it. After watching her, Laura was starting to kind of feel like Stephanie was her great-grandmother or something. They looked alike. And there was other stuff, just ways she had. Expressions and gestures. Laura felt like she knew exactly what this Stephanie was thinking and feeling. She didn't want to believe her instincts were wrong and that Stephanie was actually some kind of back-stabbing bitch. Laura believed her when she said she loved Tillman, even if it did look bad her bringing those guys right to him like that . . . But she didn't want to tell him *that* either. Then what would she be? His *pal* or something? Her and Wally Tillman, bosom buddies. Not in this lifetime.

"I don't know," she said. "I don't have a fucking clue."

He nodded his head sadly. "Me either."

Damn. She'd never seen anybody look so awful. Argue with me, she thought, and I'll tell you what I really think. But he just let it go, walked her back to the room where she came in, and stuck out his hand. "It's been a pleasure to meet you, Laura," he said.

She glanced around. They were alone. She hadn't seen the bowhead since they'd gone to that red room. She guessed it was okay to shake the guy's hand. They were doing business, after all. She gave it a quick pump and dropped it, put on her business voice. "We do the transfer on the summer solstice. I'll check on you a couple of days before to work out the details, okay?"

He tilted his head to one side, like a curious dog. "How're you going to get a body in here?"

"I'm not. I'll tote you out. My Construct chip will interface with this thing, and I'll download you. When I get to your new body, I upload you into it."

"I see." His eyes lit up. "Could I ask you a favor? Could you take me outside now, just for a little bit, so I could look around?"

The mere thought made her stomach churn. "No."

"Just for a minute, so I could see the sky."

"What part of no don't you understand? I don't just tote you around. The whole time you know what I know—I know what you know." She scrunched up her shoulders and shuddered. "It doesn't rate high as one of my favorite things to do. I don't like other people inside me."

"Then why do you do it?"

She eyed him suspiciously. If he was thinking about how many guys regularly got inside her by different routes, he didn't let on. She was the one thinking that. She was the one who had to tell him her whore war stories. Jeez, this guy was bad news. Don't think about it. That was the first rule: Just don't think about it. An hour with the Frog Prince

145

here, and she's thinking about it. What next? Guilt? Re-morse? Singing in the choir? Forget it. "I get *paid,* Wally. I get paid. No free samples. Two weeks. That'll give you plenty of time to pack your bags."

She got into the Visitor Interface Module and closed the door as he waved good-bye. She hit DOWNLOAD with the side of her fist. When it was done, she practically knocked the door open getting out. Sammy, who had been pacing up and down, came running up to her.

"Is everything okay?"

"No, it's not. It wasn't okay before I went in there, and it's never going to be, so why don't you get the fuck out of my way, so I can get home without getting my ass shot off?" She tried to push on by him, but then, twice in one night, she started crying again. What the hell was wrong with her? She was starting to get truly pissed off.

He had his hands on her shoulders, and he was looking at her, all concerned and sweet. She felt like strangling him with her bare hands, but then she had a better idea. She let him hold her as she boo-hoo-hooed on his shoulder, her poor grief-stricken body all over him like rainwater, and he's getting into it, kissing her cheek, stroking her hair, so it was the easiest thing in the world to turn her head so that one of those kisses lands on her mouth, and he just melts like butter when she starts *really* kissing him, and he's making these little moaning sounds. It was too easy. Nothing turns a guy on like some weepy woman in his arms. What does *that* tell you?

Twenty minutes later, she'd fucked him like he'd never been fucked before (which, in his case, was saying exactly zero), and he's lying on the carpet with his pants around his knees with a dopey smile on his face. It was pathetic.

She stood and pulled up her pants. "First time?"

He was still smiling. "I guess you could tell."

She rolled her eyes. "I'm an expert, remember? You al-most make up in enthusiasm what you lack in skill. But as far as I'm concerned, Sammy"—she smiled a smile that'd give you frostbite—"a fuck is just a fuck. You want to pay me now, or shall I put it on your tab?"

His smile headed south, and he got to his feet, turning his back on her while he pulled up his pants, tucked in his shirt. He wore a little Soldier toy around his neck on a cord, some kind of scanner or something. He'd stripped it right off without a thought to get up next to her. Now he picked it up and slipped it over his head like it was a noose. Jeez, even his back looked all wounded and woeful. Get some hide, she wanted to tell him. Get over yourself. "Gee, I guess you're not so pure anymore," she said.

That got to him. He turned around, all righteous. "Why are you trying to humiliate me? What have I done to you?"

"'What have I done to you?'" she mimicked. "Don't get me started. I fucked you, Soldier Boy, because you think you're so fucking *good*. I've had good up to here, and I'm sick to death of it. You try living with a pack of angels and see how you like it. The world is *fucked*—can't you see that? Are you blind or something? I may not be the best person in the world, but I'm exactly what the world de- serves. So yeah, I fucked your tight little virgin ass, but I didn't hu-mil-i-ate you. You're running that number on yourself." Her voice was bouncing off the concrete walls so that it seemed to be coming from everywhere all at once, and she was kind of getting off on it and didn't want to stop. He looked like she'd just knocked him upside the head with a sledgehammer. "And absolutely for free, out of the goodness of my heart, I'll tell you what's *really* crawled up your butt and died: You're scared shitless because not *only* did you fuck a whore—you *loved* it—and now you can't handle being an animal like the rest of us. So shoot me, Soldier Boy. See if I give a flying fuck."

Whoa, she thought, where in the hell did all that come from? He's just going to beat the living crap out of me right now. End of story. Sayonara, Laura. Never learns when to keep her mouth shut.

But no. He gets this look on his face like Jesus Himself had just reamed him out and starts climbing out into the streets of New Jerusalem, without so much as a "Fuck you." By the time she's climbed out—she could've used a hand, frankly—he's thirty yards down the street, or what was left of it. She started to call after him, but what was she supposed to say to him? What could she take back? So she just stood there and watched him until he was out of sight behind one of the piles of bricks they called buildings around here.

Hell with it. But still, she felt kind of bad that she'd been so hard on him. He really was a nice guy. *Nice guy*—what the hell did that matter? Saintly little prick was more like it. But if it doesn't matter, Laura—she had to ask herself—why did you have to fuck him over *that bad*? She was doing business with him, for Christ's sake—no pun intended—so why in hell was she ignoring her principles? It just didn't make any sense.

As she was staring at the ground, shaking her head, it literally dawned on her that she didn't have time to worry about this shit. It was getting lighter by the second, and when the sun topped those buildings, she'd be a sitting duck for any Soldier who happened by. Hell, she was in the holy city itself, the sprawl at least. This ruined shit went on for miles. But there were still patrols through here, and they probably wouldn't settle for just shooting her. They'd probably pluck her eyes out, cut her tits off, burn her at the stake. She must've been nuts to come here in the first place. What the hell had she been thinking?

And then it hit her as she started down the street—she'd just fucked a guy without a rubber. For free. And for what? In spite of all that stuff she'd just laid on him, she'd be damned if it made any sense to her. She was—what? Teaching him a lesson? What a laugh. That Laura, she had her shit together, all right. Got her head on her shoulders, that one. Course, she wasn't the worst person in the world. There were lots worse—like Chef, for example.

And now that she thought about it, this whole damn mess was Chef's fault: If he'd just given her the goddamn stew like they'd agreed, she would've been sleeping in her bed when Soldier Boy came calling, dreaming something better than this bad dream, crawling through this holy dump, getting lost, dodging patrols, banging up her knee something awful, until she finally gets to familiar ground, only about four or five *miles* out of her fucking way.

By this time, she was hungry again. All she really wanted to do was sleep, but she didn't see how she could with her stomach growling like a wild dog. She wished she'd gotten some of Sammy's bullets as a down payment, which would've been the sensible thing to do anyway. You didn't work a deal like this without something up front. Too many things could go wrong. Sammy could find himself strung up before he had the chance to pay her. And then she had to go fuck with his head, so there was no telling what he might do. He was probably going to pull out of the deal altogether, and it was all her fault.

WHEN LAURA LEFT, TILLMAN FIGURED HE HAD TWO WEEKS to get ready, to do whatever he was going to do in here for the first time, or one last time, or yet another time. He started to make a list. He'd been big on lists when he first found himself in here. He thought they'd lend a structure to his life and keep him sane. That seemed a long time ago. It *was* a long time ago. You'd think he would've changed more. He even sat down with paper and pen, but there was nothing he wanted to put on his list. Nothing at all.

So maybe he had changed.

He walked down to the Indian restaurant on K Street where he'd had dinner with his folks after that White House tour. He hadn't remembered the name if he'd ever known it, so he made up his own for the sign out front and the menus: Karma Kafé. He liked the alliteration and the look of the double K's on K Street, worked them into the logo on the menu, embroidered on the corners of the napkins. The dark humor didn't hurt.

He usually brought Sally, but he was avoiding her. Would she cry, he wondered, when he told her good-bye? Would it mean anything if she did? He pictured her crying, modeled after Steph's—almost silent, shoulders shaking. He felt a familiar knife twist in his chest. He hadn't anticipated any more farewells when he'd written Sally. He didn't think there was anyplace else to go.

He pushed open the Karma's doors with a shove and walked in as if it were a Western saloon. None of the other diners noticed. They were straight from his childhood memory. By all appearances, they'd been eating here for a century and a half. He could set off a bomb and they'd chew with the same rhythm.

The Indian waiter, tall and severe in his dark brown suit, showed Tillman to his table, then plucked the napkin from the water glass, snapped it open with a flick of his wrist, and let it float onto Tillman's lap. When he was a kid, that routine had scared the bejesus out of him.

Now Tillman picked up the napkin by opposite corners, gave it a twirl, and—as the waiter cleared away the other place setting—popped him on the butt with the snapping tip of the napkin.

The waiter turned slowly around as if Tillman had tapped him lightly on the shoulder. "Sir?" he asked. He wasn't programmed for a wide range of responses.

"Sit down," Tillman said. "Split a Taj Mahal with me."

The waiter couldn't figure out how to sit down and get the beer at the same time. To expedite matters, Tillman made the beer and two glasses appear on the table. He never knew the real waiter's name, but he remembered naming him when he wrote the restaurant program. Now he couldn't for the life of him remember what name he'd used. Screw it. What difference did it make?

"Your name's George," Tillman informed the waiter.

"Very well," George said.

George poured the beer into the glasses, dividing it perfectly. He seemed at a loss what to do next.

"This isn't going to work," Tillman muttered to himself. He poked around in the archives and spliced a bit from his Uncle John, Tillman's favorite uncle, to give George a modicum of life. He supposed that John's deadpan stoicism would suit the dour George, and though he'd been too young to ever split a beer with Uncle John in reality, he'd always wanted to.

"I won't be able to do this with the people I meet on the outside," Tillman told George as he revised him. "I'll just have to take them as they come."

"Maybe that is not such a bad thing," George said. He still had the precise Indian accent, but the content was definitely Uncle John. Though he was not what you'd call a cheerful man, he always counseled seeing the value in the hand you were dealt: You were thankful for good luck; you learned from bad. You couldn't really lose either way.

Tillman took a swallow of the beer, munched pensively on a papadum. "Maybe so." Talking to Sam and Laura had reminded Tillman what other people were like. They were so . . . well, *other*. It was exhilarating after all this time to talk to someone whose ideas and actions and utterances were completely their own, who might say anything, who *did* say anything. If memory served, though, most people weren't as talkative as Sam and Laura, not to him at any rate. That Tillman, he could clear a kitchen at a lively party just by walking in and leaning on the counter. But the world had changed a hell of a lot since he'd lived there. Surely it had more important things to worry about than what Walter Tillman looked like.

He especially liked Laura. That made sense in a way. Genetically, she was Stephanie's daughter—half her genes were Steph's—and he'd loved those genes once before. It was different, of course. Laura made him feel, well, paternal or grandpaternal or whatever you wanted to call it, though all he'd contributed to her existence was to draw blood from Steph's arm. It made as much sense as anything else. Her real grandparents had been manufactured—brewed up like so many pickles, stuffed with a mishmash of lives. He'd always hoped that by some miracle the Constructs hadn't gone into production, but when he saw Laura, the reality of it hit him, and he was flooded with guilt all over again.

But he would've liked her anyway, even if he didn't feel guilty and responsible. He liked her tough fuck-you attitude, her low tolerance for bullshit. He could see a bit of Stephanie living on in her, and that was a good sign. But Laura wasn't just a copy of Stephanie, and that was good too. Things needed to change. For change, you needed diversity. With a little luck, the world might just get past the mess Laura quite rightly blamed him for. He was getting a second chance—maybe—to set right some of his screwups. Before, the whole Uther nonsense had distracted him from the mess the world was getting itself into. This time there'd be no such distractions. He wondered if one man could make any difference. Then he thought about it. He'd certainly made a difference once. The hard part was making the difference you wanted.

"I guess this means I'll finally be leaving Stephanie behind," he mumbled into his beer glass.

George shrugged. "You already left her when you came in here. You only have memories now, remember?" He took out a pack of Pall Malls and lit one. "You may remember in here, or remember out there" were his smoky words. "What difference does it make?"

Tillman hated it when he said that to himself. He didn't like it any better coming from George. "Out there, I could forget."

George cut him a look that said, *Some people maybe—but not you.* "Or you could make it even more romantic and maudlin," he said.

"Is that what you think?"

George picked up the menu and looked it over. "The vindaloo is quite good this evening," he said. The vindaloo was good every evening, had always been good, would always be good.

"Is that all you can say?" Tillman demanded. But what did he expect from his memories of a waiter who'd hardly known Tillman was alive and an uncle he hadn't seen since he was sixteen? George wasn't up to anything this complex. Tillman revised him further, made him more reflective, more forthcoming, using some from Steph, but mostly from himself. Hell, it was *all* himself when you came right down to it.

"So what do you think?" he asked George, taking one of George's Pall Malls and lighting it up. "Should I forget her? Is this whole Stephanie thing just a pathetic fixation, something to provide the semblance of a life?"

George took a deep drag on his own Pall Mall. When Uncle John died of lung cancer, Tillman's Aunt Jessie supported herself lavishly with the settlement money. Tillman's mom was deeply offended, though it didn't seem to bother his dad, who was John's brother, after all. "She's entitled," he'd say, but he would never explain himself.

George was taking so long to answer that Tillman thought he was going to have to revise him even more. Or forget the whole thing. He was just talking to himself again. What was the point really? But then George finally spoke. "She is dead, my friend. You loved her, and now she is gone. You have mourned deeply. Now you must let her go."

The clipped musical cadence of George's accent gave the whole thing an oracular quality that set Tillman back on his heel. This wasn't quite what he expected: No cat and mouse, no quibbling over minutiae, just the truth, pure and simple. What he'd done, he'd done. She'd loved him, or not. He'd never know. She was dead. She was gone.

"What if she's not dead?" Tillman objected.

"If Stephanie has been outside in the real world," George explained, "then she has long since died, wouldn't you say? If she entered the simulated environment the Christian spoke of, then she has been destroyed by Gabriel's virus. I think she is dead, my friend."

"I guess you're right," Tillman mumbled. "It's time to let her go, my friend," he added to himself, tearing up, of course. He toasted George and drank his beer down.

Tillman later thought of George as an incredible stroke of luck or an instrument of divine providence. If Tillman hadn't patched him together he never would've persuaded himself to let Stephanie go. And if he hadn't done that, he never would've found her.

Alive.

HE LEFT THE RESTAURANT INTENDING TO GO TO THE ZOO. HE thought he might have himself a good cry while he watched the beavers tussle. A little farewell to Steph, a memorial ritual. He wouldn't summon her up this time to be there with him. He'd admit that she was gone and wasn't ever coming back.

Then he thought about—what was it the kid called it?— the Bin. Probably had a hell of a zoo in there, several of them. He imagined Stephanie in there, watching the animals by herself, thinking about Tillman.

He stopped dead in his tracks.

When he told the kid the Bin was probably playing possum, he was just blowing smoke. He had nothing to back up such a hypothesis. It just depressed the hell out of him to think a bunch of crazy fundies could outsmart Newman Rogers. But wasn't that the way the world worked? More than likely, the kid was right. How smart did you have to be to throw a wrench in the works? Besides, the kid had seemed pretty certain . . .

But he'd be certain whether it was true or not. If they were playing possum, it wouldn't do to have some kid knowing they were still alive. Course, just because the kid's certainty didn't enter into the picture didn't mean that he wasn't right and that the Bin was dead a long time ago.

But he couldn't quite let it go. How hard would it be to play dead when you're several thousand miles away? Maybe they just weren't answering the phone. It's not like they needed anything on Earth. So maybe they *were* playing possum, laying low just like Tillman himself had done for 120 years. Newman would be in there. Freddie too.

He remembered Freddie and his security systems. Eavesdropping systems more like it. They might be silent, but if they were alive, they'd sure as hell be listening, monitoring transmissions, hacking into whatever they could. If he knew Freddie, that would be just about everything. He could probably tell you what the Soldiers were going to do before they'd even figured it out themselves.

The more Tillman thought about it, the more he became convinced that the Bin just might be up there, with everyone still alive, that he might be able to contact it.

If he used the power link to transmit, he figured . . .

By this time, he'd boarded a train and was hurtling toward the zoo, oblivious to his surroundings, working out a plan of action—"experimental design," he used to call it. He'd thought about transmitting before, but he had been afraid to announce his presence. The last time he was in the real world people were shooting at him—hell, they shot him, three slugs through the heart. He never thought about contacting the Bin before. He hadn't really known it was there. It seemed too crazy to have ever been built. In light of his recent conversations with Laura and Sam, however, Tillman's conception of "too crazy" was obviously in need of some serious revision.

He was a little worried about the Soldiers listening in, but if he directed the signal into space, kept it real short . . .

Because he'd only just moments before decided that Stephanie was dead, he didn't let himself think about *why* he so urgently wished to contact the Bin all of a sudden, what earthly difference it could make. Otherwise he would've been embarrassed by his desperation. He would've called himself a pathetic dreamer and forgotten the whole thing. But this wasn't about Steph, right? Couldn't be. She was dead. He'd let her go. He was practically on the way to her *funeral,* for Christ's sake! No, this was scientific curiosity. That's what it was. It was practically his scientific *duty*.

The train stopped, the doors opened, but he didn't pay any attention. The doors didn't close. The other passengers carried on as if nothing was wrong, but nobody got on or off. Everything waited on Tillman as he hunted through the plans for the Bin, calculating its position, aiming the dish. The transmitter hadn't really been set up for communication between humans, but between computers, so he had to write a program to send something the computer wouldn't read as gibberish and that a human could read as text. After about an hour, he thought he had something that would send a message if there was a Bin and if it was working and if someone was paying attention. If there was such a someone, Tillman figured it could only be one man.

He sent the following:

> NEWMAN ROGERS,
> IF YOU CAN HEAR ME, I'VE BEEN DOWN HERE IN
> THE BASEMENT SINCE 2030. ARE YOU THERE?
> > WALTER TILLMAN
> P.S. DO YOU KNOW WHATEVER HAPPENED TO
> STEPHANIE SANDERS?

A second or two after he added the P.S., it became obvious to him what the whole thing had been about, but by then it was too late. The silly message had already been sent. For years after he found himself alone in here, he used to stand on a street corner or on some mountaintop and call out Stephanie's name for all he was worth, as if the cosmos could hear him and take pity. That was stupid. This was stupid. She was dead, just like George said. Tillman was still, for reasons unfathomable, alive. Why couldn't he just accept this basic flaw in the universe and move on?

BY THIS TIME, HE DIDN'T WANT TO GO TO THE ZOO ANYMORE. But there were the train doors standing open at his stop with all these phony folks staring at him. *Chump,* they seemed to be saying. Screw this. He could do it. He didn't have to spend his whole life being pushed around by the past. He hopped down from his seat and left the train, didn't look back as it pulled out of the station. As he was going up the escalator, he thought he saw a couple in ski masks out of the corner of his eye going down. But when he turned to look, it was just the usual window dressing—

simulated strangers moving along like shooting gallery ducks. It was definitely time to get out of here.

He ascended into early June in D.C., steamy and close. He took the long way through the neighborhood around the cathedral where he and Steph used to go walking, going nowhere, putting off her getting on the train to the house that Jack built. A million years ago.

But now he really was getting out of here. None of these big fancy barns would even exist anymore in the real world.

"No people," he said as he walked into the zoo, and all the toddlers, moms and dads, bikers, Japanese tourists, and school groups vanished. Simulating the zoo he and Steph used to visit always seemed appropriate, since most of the habitats were holos anyway. Like the one he was in now. You seemed to be walking across an ice floe. Supposedly, even that polar bear over there thought he was in the Arctic. But if he got it in his head to dive in and try to swim to Jersey, he'd never get there, and if he thought you looked tasty, he'd find out there was a Plexiglas wall between you and him. Compared to the illusion of Tillman's world, it'd been pretty cheesy. If you paid attention, you could figure out how much territory the animals really had, see the smudges on the Plexiglas. On a whim, Tillman dissolved the wall and let the polar bear lumber down Connecticut Avenue.

The beaver pond was in the wetlands. Blue herons cruised low, ospreys circled high, and kingfishers zipped by as if shot from cannons. He sat down on a wooden bench. The pond was glassy smooth, mist rising up from it. He hadn't been here in ages. He usually just checked out the memory with Steph—dead of winter, ice forming along the shoreline. He'd never been here in the summer.

".22 rifle," he said, and he held it in his hands.

What he couldn't get over was the Christian Soldiers running things. He used to laugh at those guys—watch them as late-night entertainment, like wrestling or infomercials—secure in his belief that no more than a few dozen sick stupid people in the world would ever take them seriously.

And now they *nuked* people. Talk about having the last laugh.

He tried to remember their particular appeal. It all sounded like the same "End is Nigh" crap to him. Their leader called himself Gabriel—after the angel scheduled to solo on Doomsday. His real name was Tod or Tad or Ted or something. That was one of his gimmicks—the whole angel thing. When Gabriel started up in the mid-twenties, there were a lot of angel huggers getting long in the tooth. So when he called himself Gabriel and claimed to talk to angels, he pushed some nostalgic button and got people's attention who otherwise might not listen to some fundie ranting on local access. Only the angels Gabriel talked to weren't sweet vegetarians looking to cleanse your aura. These were fascist assholes telling you to straighten up or you were toast. This was Gabriel, blowing his horn. Time's up, suckers.

Apparently, that's what people wanted, at least the ones who hadn't gone into the Bin: a judgment, a reckoning. What was it his Aunt Leah used to say to Tillman's mom? *Children want limits. They need boundaries.* His mom used to say to Tillman, *Wait till your father gets home.* There you pretty much had Gabriel's theology in a nutshell. What was the point of hugging angels if there wasn't some Papa God coming home to his BarcaLounger in the sky ready to give you a good smack to show you he cared.

Tillman tried to imagine himself in the real world when they turned on this Bin thing, and everybody but Gabriel and his ilk started jumping in. What would he have done? Gone into some Papa Bear version of his current residence or lived with the wackos? Some choice. Jeez, there had to be some kind of middle ground, didn't there? Had it really come down to one or the other?

There was a chevron of ripples on the water, the faint churning sound of swimming. At first he thought it might be a muskrat it was so small. Then he realized it was a beaver kit, swimming in a careening zigzag, making more noise than both its parents put together would've made. Tillman had never seen a little guy before.

He raised the rifle and looked down the barrel. He couldn't miss. Not only was it an easy shot—the beaver was ten yards at the most—but also Tillman wasn't really shooting anything. This wasn't a real beaver—had never been and never would be. Tillman literally called all the shots. He could take out this beaver with his eyes closed.

But his eyes weren't closed as he tracked him across the pond, his finger on the trigger, telling himself, "It's just a symbol, a gesture, a purging ritual. It doesn't mean anything. *Now,* he said to himself, *now.* He's going to get away. A hundred and twenty years and you've never killed anything, Walleye. But he couldn't do it, and he lowered the rifle and laid it across his lap.

Anything would be better than this place. Anything.

In his old life, he used to struggle with whether his life was worthwhile. In here, it was no struggle. He could be Gandhi, Mother Teresa, and Einstein all rolled into one, and it would mean zip. Whatever he did out there it had to mean more than the last 120 years of navel gazing, jacking off, and mind tripping. It wasn't a total waste. At least he'd read a lot. Two or three books a week or more. They all pretty much said the same thing: You were thankful for good luck; you learned from bad. You couldn't really lose either way.

He stood up, tossing the rifle into the pond.

"Good-bye, Steph," he said.

HE DECIDED TO WALK BACK TO THE WHITE HOUSE. HERE IT was only a couple of hours since Laura'd gone, and already he had his affairs in order. The phrase made a little laugh come bubbling out, but he didn't much like the sound of it. He was two weeks away from getting out—no time to crack up—time to shape up. He had a new life. A fresh start. Oh, boy.

He thought about telling Sally he was leaving, but she

already knew. She was a reflection of himself. She knew his thoughts like a looking glass knows what tie you're wearing, and there was as much point informing her of his plans as discussing them with a mirror.

As he approached the White House, he watched the gardener at work for what he supposed would be one of the last times. The gardener was on his knees, digging in the soil with his bare hands. Tillman'd always wanted a garden, but had always lived in cities—and he could never see much point in gardening in here. It was one thing to have this guy put on a show for him, but pretending to plant seeds here—pretending they'd grow? That'd be sacrilege. The world was probably totally fucked like Laura said. But there was still sunshine and dirt, seeds and some water.

As he walked across the White House lawn, a young Marine approached him. "We have a problem, Mr. President."

He certainly did. Either Sam had turned him in or someone had followed his trail, but either way it looked like Tillman was fucked again. A dozen Christian Soldiers, all looking like they'd been dipped in a vat of starch, were probing their way into his world, burrowing like little info-moles, gnawing away at his defenses. He'd thought about tighter security once or twice, but why in the world, he'd asked himself, would he want to keep anyone *out*?

He watched the invaders for a while, monitored their progress, but what was the point really? It was better this way. He shut off the surveillance cameras, made himself a good stiff drink, and wandered down to the Red Room. He sat on that silly sofa and held Sally's hand, waiting.

"You're beautiful," he said after a while to break the silence. He said this to her often. And she was. Quite beautiful.

She knew how to take a compliment. She never denied her beauty, never lied by flattering his appearance, never told him he was a "beautiful person." (God, how he loathed that phrase.) She usually smiled and beckoned him to her. But this time her smile was heartbreaking. It was as if she was thinking about what he could've said out of all the possibilities and was touched by his choice. She squeezed his hand. "Good-bye," she said.

She was sitting sideways on the sofa. Her bare feet nestled against his thigh. Her feet were tiny. The toes were curled up tight, looking like a row of nursing puppies.

"Good-bye," he said. He kissed her cheek, let go of her hand, and deleted her, turning away as he did it.

10

PRODIGAL SONS

SAM WALKED THE FIVE MILES TO THE TEMPLE WITH A STEADY determined pace, mindless of the patrolling Soldiers, who eyed him curiously but didn't see fit to interrogate the Commander's son. The scanner inside his shirt thudded against his chest with each step. Every cell in his body vibrated, tingled, like a rung bell tolling out his shame.

Laura and Tillman had opened his eyes, and he finally saw himself for what he was: an arrogant sinner, a willing victim to the sin of pride, the ready snare for the righteous. He'd imagined himself better than others because he didn't *believe* as they did, as if his beliefs alone could serve the Lord, as if his mute opinions could heal His wounds. As if God died so that he, Samuel the Pure, could think good thoughts! As if the millions who'd died at the Soldiers' hands rejoiced that Sam hadn't *personally* slain them! He winced in shame and wanted to rip his flesh apart.

He served in an army that murdered in the name of God, and he'd done *nothing* but keep silent, had only sought to flee like Jonah, to bask in his righteousness undisturbed. What if Christ had thought, *I better not stick my neck out. I could get in some serious trouble here. Think I'll just angle for a cushy post in the countryside somewhere.*

Sam was hit by a wave of nausea, but he trudged on. He too had been vomited from the bowels of a leviathan, covered with the stench of his own sin. It wasn't enough to *be* good or even *do* good—like some gift you were giving to the world. The Soldiers talked about giving your life to Christ, but their Christ, as Tillman said, was a cruel madman. Sam's own Christ, he now realized, had been nothing more than a smiling monster, serene in the midst of slaughter—the very image of Sam himself.

The true Christ laughed at him and filled his senses. He saw Him in the jutting ribs of the dogs scavenging the alleyways, heard Him in the morning prayers and babies' wails spilling out of every window, felt Him in the crushed bricks and bones that paved the street. Sam brushed away his tears and smelled Him on his hands, his fingertips. Laura's scent. Her body had been more real to him than his own had ever been.

You can't handle being an animal like the rest of us, she told him. Showed him. Christ became a man—flesh and blood—born, lived, and died. Ever since, the likes of Gabriel had been trying to banish Him to heaven—anyplace but here.

And Sam had been no better, figuring he'd just join God in heaven, not bother becoming a man at all. God became flesh, but Samuel had thought he was too good for that. He thought and thought and thought. That's all he *ever* did was think. He bit his lip and tasted the blood of Christ. Felt His rage.

"God, forgive me," he whispered. "God, forgive me."

Laura'd humiliated him, all right. Humbled him. Left him naked in the Garden, trying to hide from God, his eyes closed in prayer. Now God had opened his eyes, and Sam saw his prideful life with blinding intensity. That he lived at all after such a chastening was a gift from God—had always been. Sam didn't have to give his life to Christ. It'd been His all along. Sam had just been too blind to see it, too proud to live it for the glory of God.

HE TURNED A CORNER, AND THE TEMPLE OF THE LORD, still blocks away, loomed over him, blotting out the morning sun. The shadow of its towers stretched down the street like a huge dagger. The pavement here was stones, centuries old, as cool and damp as a tomb, slick beneath his feet. He'd decided to try the west entrance because the guard there was a friend of his, at least for now, and might not ask too many questions. Pretty soon he wouldn't have a friend in all of New Jerusalem.

The Temple had once been the Washington National Cathedral. It hadn't been a national anything for decades now. There was no nation, no United States. All of that had gone into the Bin. Though built by heretics, the cathedral had remained standing while most every other building in the city had been reduced to rubble. The former tenants—stubborn popeless priests and nuns who'd squatted in the place since the fall of the Bin—kept it up as best they could. They'd been tolerated in a city run by warring gangs because they performed weddings and funerals for a few of the more superstitious or sentimental thugs at the top.

The Soldiers shot everyone when they claimed the city. Priest or thief—it didn't matter. Then they cleansed and resanctified the cathedral as the Temple of the Lord. Gabriel, his most trusted Soldiers, and their families lived within its walls; the other, lesser faithful, lived in the makeshift town that grew up around it, fashioned from the ruins of once-fashionable homes. You could be raised up or brought low by the elect within the Temple, but mostly you were ignored, forgotten, told what to do but not why.

Sam lived inside the Temple because he was his father's son. But if his actions for the last twenty-four hours were known, he could easily find himself outside hanging from a gallows, crows picking his bones.

The street was crowded around the Temple, and Sam moved sideways through the faithful like a salmon swimming upstream. The women kept their eyes lowered. The men watched him suspiciously. What was an elder's son doing in the streets out of uniform? Where had he been?

What was he up to? Each man had work, had a purpose. Each purpose served the will of God. Any man afoot at this hour in shabby clothes, not about his work or his prayers, was clearly defying the will of God.

But who can presume to know the will of God? Sam asked himself. Isn't that what God said to Job out of the whirlwind? No one can know the will of God. Or everyone. Sometimes you had no choice but to know it, because the whirlwind *is* the will of God. If these people knew what he'd been doing, they might tear him limb from limb, but they wouldn't throw him into the whirlwind—he was already there. He could feel it sucking the air out of his lungs so that he gasped like a fish on dry land, like Jonah washed from the deep.

The plaza before the west gates was crowded with horse-drawn carts laden with food for the Temple. Kneeling pilgrims and supplicants spoke in tongues to the stone walls. Files of Soldiers headed out into the city to stone an adulteress or collect a tithe. Purification was a never-ending voracious process.

Sam caught a glimpse of a lone jeep rolling through the crowd up ahead. Powered vehicles were rare. Energy was too scarce to squander except in battle. This one was battery-powered and only had a range of about a hundred miles. Jeremiah sat behind the wheel, scanning the crowd. Another Soldier sat beside him, his weapon at the ready. Sam had seen him before, but didn't know his name. When Jeremiah spotted Sam, the jeep spurted forward, forcing a woman at her prayers to leap out of the way.

The jeep slid to a stop beside Sam.

"Gabriel wishes to see you," Jeremiah said. "Where have you been?"

Sam had wanted to prepare himself before he faced Gabriel, but perhaps that was only cowardice. "I went for a walk," Sam said. "I couldn't sleep." It was true. He couldn't sleep now if his life depended on it. He'd been asleep for too long.

Jeremiah gave him a skeptical smirk and tossed his head toward the back of the jeep. "Get in." He was obviously enjoying his advantage over the Commander's son. Let him enjoy it, Sam thought. He'll find out soon enough how fortunes rise and fall faster than you can jump to the winning side.

"I'd like to get into uniform before I see Gabriel," Sam said.

"He wants to see you now," Jeremiah said.

The other Soldier stared into Sam's eyes, his finger curled around the trigger. The safety was off. The fistful of lightning bolts embroidered on his cap identified him as a member of the Temple Guard. If Sam ran, he'd be dead before he'd taken a stride. *The eyes move first,* they were taught. *Watch the eyes.*

Sam pulled himself up into the back of the jeep without another word. They circled around the perimeter of the Temple, going much too fast, until they came to the rear entrance and the garage below. They came to a stop, and Jeremiah stayed behind the wheel. The other Soldier jumped out and faced Sam. The barrel made a small arc, a clear message. Sam was to be escorted to Gabriel under armed guard.

Sam wondered if he was going to die soon and was surprised to discover he didn't fear death. He only hoped he could free Tillman before the Soldiers discovered him, do something worthwhile with his life, now that he'd finally claimed it.

SAM EXPECTED TO BE LED TO AN INTERROGATION ROOM, BUT instead he was taken through several anterooms into Gabriel's private suite. Gabriel let Sam stand at attention without acknowledging his presence, pacing up and down, reading from a handheld with elaborate perplexity.

Sam waited.

Few people had ever seen these rooms, though Sam had

been here once as a boy with his father when Gabriel laid his hands on Sam's head and gave him his blessing. His father was so grateful he almost wept, while Sam himself felt nothing but the cold metal of Gabriel's ring crushing his ear.

Watching Gabriel pace back and forth, Sam thought of Daniel in the lion's den. Gabriel looked a bit like a lion with his mane of white hair flowing down past his shoulders and his tangle of beard cut straight across at the collarbone. He cut it with a knife, his father said—he'd seen him do it, one quick stroke. The way you'd cut a man's throat. It was Gabriel who cut the ram's throat for the sacrifice. Sam had seen, in the eyes of those who watched, fear and awe of a man whose arm never weakened and whose blade never dulled. That fear was why Gabriel brought back the old sacrifices. The Lord didn't want them. Gabriel was reminding them all: *This could be your woolly throat.*

He wore long flowing robes the color of his hair. He might have been made of snow, or salt. He was at least 150 years old; nobody knew his age for certain. In spite of his white hair and beard, his skin never wrinkled or sagged. With darker hair, he wouldn't look over fifty. He was rarely sick and always recovered quickly. He claimed his longevity and good health were gifts from God so that he might work tirelessly for the glory of God and the End of Days.

There were whispers he'd had plastic surgery, but there wasn't a Soldier who was that skilled a surgeon, and even if there were, Gabriel wasn't likely to lie down unconscious before a man with a knife. Besides, plastic surgery wouldn't keep his heart pumping or his mind alert. Sam had a different theory. Gabriel's white hair, which he tossed around vainly, was as strong and shiny as a child's.

Or a clone's. In their haste to bring Sam here, no one had thought to search him. He crossed his arms across his chest, found the switch for the scanner beneath his thumb, and turned it on.

In the corner stood Seth, Gabriel's bodyguard. He was a

captured Construct tortured into obedience, a shock collar around his neck. He was enormous, powerful, descended from those built for hard labor with bony plates like a rhinoceros.

Sam wasn't worried about him. He only acted on direct orders from Gabriel. The guard behind him, however, would still have his finger on the trigger, though he couldn't watch Sam's eyes. Sam thought he might be able to make it through one of the four doors in the room, or through the window behind Gabriel without being shot, but they were seven stories up. Then Sam noticed his reflection and the guard's in the glass. The guard, ignoring Gabriel, was looking right into Sam's eyes. Through the window you could see for miles, the river a silver ribbon in the distance. Sam winked at the guard.

Gabriel closed the handheld and tossed it on his desk. He stretched, picking up his hair and letting it fall with a sigh. He looked at Sam for the first time since he'd entered the room and gave him a thin smile. "So good to see you, Sam. How long has it been? I believe you were on a mission the last time I dined at your parents' home. Your mother is a wonderful cook."

"Yes, sir."

Gabriel stared at his hands, turning them over. There were no scars, no nicks, no scratches. "Your father is quite proud of you, Sam."

"I hope to be worthy of his high regard, sir."

Gabriel peered at him under hooded brows. "And mine. You are one of our best and brightest, Sam. You have a talent for the subtleties of the old technologies."

"Thank you for your confidence, sir."

"Your father is my friend. I look out for my friends, Sam."

He let the unspoken corollary hang silent in the air for a moment. He sat on the corner of his desk. The interrogation had begun.

"Perhaps you can clear up a few details about your most recent mission. I was just reading Jeremiah's report—and yours. Just out of curiosity, how did this site come to collapse when you took such pains to prevent it?"

Sam figured there was a team crawling all over that site by now. Gabriel was said to be all-knowing. He worked hard at it. Sam only hoped they hadn't shut it down or gotten to Tillman. Sam indicated the guard at his back. "May we speak in private, sir?"

Gabriel cocked one brow, then dismissed the guard with a toss of his hand. "Speak to me," he said to Sam when the guard had gone.

"The site didn't collapse, sir. I thought it best to keep its true nature secret until I had the chance to inform you."

"It seems that you have been given that chance."

Sam's mind was racing. His lie that the site was insignificant had failed. The only other defense for violating established procedures would be to reveal the site's extraordinary significance. But how could he reveal that without betraying Tillman? And then it came to him, a brief glimpse of a way, so brief he couldn't be sure of every detail, but there was a way, like a swath cut by a whirlwind. He'd just have to have faith. "It's an early prototype of the Bin, sir."

Even Gabriel could be startled. He almost slipped off the corner of the desk. "Operational?"

"Yes, sir."

Gabriel rose to his feet. He was tall. In his robes, his long arms looked like wings. "Occupied?" he asked softly.

"Yes, sir."

He towered over Sam, spoke to the top of his head. "And how did you manage to determine this when I have a crew of a dozen men on site who've been getting no response whatsoever?"

Playing possum, Sam thought, trying not to let his relief show. "It was a difficult hack, sir."

Gabriel turned his head sideways, leaned in close, looked Sam in the eye. "Who's in there, boy?"

Gabriel, it was said, could sniff out any plot. Just last winter, he'd burned five conspirators at the stake in an elaborate ceremony in front of the Temple. There was a look like hunger as he eyed Sam. He knew something big was up.

Sam dangled the bait under his nose. "Walter Tillman, sir."

Gabriel rocked back on his heels. He almost let out a whoop. "*The* Walter Tillman?"

"Yes, sir. I thought you should know before it became common knowledge."

Gabriel spun around, his hands clasped, beside himself with glee. Then he seized Sam by the shoulders, looked into his eyes. "Can you get him out?"

"I believe so, sir. I would have to secure a host body . . ."

"Whatever you need. Anything at all." Gabriel looked past Sam, his eyes narrowed. He'd seen his own path, apparently, planning his next meeting with an angel. Another show for the faithful to keep them under his thumb.

"And it would be best, sir, if I worked alone," Sam said.

Gabriel brought his attention back to Sam. He was never too distracted to be suspicious. "And why is that?"

"I have gained his trust, sir. He's been in there for one hundred and twenty years. He's completely insane. The facility has an extremely sophisticated surveillance system. If he feels cornered, he might crash the whole system."

This seemed to satisfy him. "Very well. How long?"

Sam would have to stall until the Initiation. He wasn't sure he could deceive Gabriel for that long. But there was no other way. No matter what she thought of Sam, Laura would come for Tillman like she promised. He was sure of it. If she didn't, both he and Tillman would be dead. "Two weeks," he said, trying to sound as if he'd made a careful calculation. "Maybe three. I could use a vehicle as well. To transport some equipment."

" 'Two *weeks*'? That seems like an awfully long time."

"I'll have to reconfigure the front door so I can get back in, then I'll have to win over his confidence, modify the operating system from the inside. It's not just the hack, sir. It will be something of a cat and mouse game."

Gabriel smiled at a metaphor he could appreciate and

pressed an icon on the desk. The guard stepped into the room. "Corporal, see to it this man gets anything and everything he wants."

"Yes, sir."

"Metzger, isn't it, Corporal?"

"Yes, sir."

"You used to be a farmer, I believe."

"Yes, sir."

"Tough life, farming. I imagine your life is more blessed now that you are here with us."

"Yes, sir. Thank you, sir."

"Blessings flow to a man of discretion, Corporal Metzger."

"Yes, sir."

DONOVAN CAUGHT THE MORNING SHUTTLE TO CHINA AND took a window seat. There were always several available. Lots of people in the Bin didn't like to fly at all. It was harder not to remember, looking out the window at the Earth spread out miles below like a diorama in a museum, that it wasn't the Earth at all, but a perfect eternal simulation. Better than the real Earth, he'd always been reassured, infinitely better, but not real just the same, or at best, as his favorite philosophy teacher would have it, a different order of reality, a different way of being.

Whatever.

Up here in the lower reaches of heaven—high enough to see the curve of the horizon, a scattering of stars, the sky a deeper blue—you were reminded there were limits to the world Newman Rogers had created, that there had to be. Donovan didn't figure that was such a bad idea—to remind yourself once in a while where you lived and what you were.

Most people seemed to have the opposite notion—that you should periodically dupe yourself into thinking that was the real Earth down there. If perspective was what you wanted, you could travel even farther—point out the Earth in the night sky of Mars or Europa and be moved by the vastness of the universe, the overpowering experience of the sublime. There were planetary tours for all tastes—family-oriented outings in plump rocket ships that smiled and sang in the holo-ads; action-packed, rugged, sweat-dripping adventures for beautiful athletic people who found simulated brushes with danger sexually stimulating. Thoughtful, poetic, ecological, romantic, whimsical, meditative tours—all could be arranged—even though humans had never been to any of those places, and the planets they "visited" were virtuals cobbled together from data transmitted by unmanned probes well over a century ago. They were utterly convincing because they had no history to contend with.

It was one of the tradeoffs of the Bin. You want to live forever pretending a simulated universe is reality? Then accept that the real universe isn't going to make the same mistake about you. You were staying put. You weren't going anywhere new. The universe would go on, not exactly without you, but with the same concern a beach might have for a single grain of sand. Newman Rogers said just that in his last public statement when the Bin went on-line, a speech known by heart by every single person in the Bin. Donovan, always the gifted student, had won a bet in grade school by reciting the fifteen-minute speech in five minutes without a single error. It was one of those texts so charged with meaning that over time it seemed to short-circuit, burn itself out, so that you could no longer say what it meant when it was written, or what it might yet mean.

Donovan often wondered what it would've been like to be Newman Rogers, to singlehandedly conceive a notion that changed everything, that prompted generations of schoolchildren to chant his words without thought or comprehension. But there was one thing that Donovan (and every other newbie) understood about Newman Rogers: Without him, they wouldn't exist. Rogers hadn't personally created them, but he'd created the world that made them possible. Newman Rogers was the closest thing they had to God.

Even if the man was dead.

A schoolboy might forget whether it was Kennedy or Johnson who was shot down in Dallas, but he could tell you the story of Newman Rogers, and how he died in 2081 in his valiant defense of the Bin from the Christian Soldiers' viral attack. Everyone in the Bin had seen *Circuit of Heaven,* the musical holo based on these events, dozens of times. With Rogers's birthday and the centennial coming up, it was damn near impossible to avoid the damn thing, in all its hanky-wringing glory.

Donovan had always thought it was romantic treacle, but historically accurate in the main. And a few minutes before the grand finale, full of smiling tear-drenched folks singing their hearts out, Newman Rogers dies, taking the virus wholly into himself so that the Bin might live on. It was the most famous death scene in literature. The most famous death scene *period.*

So when Freddie claimed he was going to introduce Donovan to Newman Rogers, Donovan was as skeptical as he'd be if he were going to meet Santa Claus or the Wizard of Oz. More skeptical, in fact. For although there'd never been a Santa, someone, he supposed, might take on that identity. But the dead stayed dead.

Donovan never believed any of the stories that Rogers was still alive, up to everything from singing pop tunes to appearing in the living rooms of ordinary folks in Ohio summoned with "mu energy" properly aligned with the crystalline structure of the Bin. It wasn't just the wackiness of these stories. The sheer number of them made it obvious they had more to do with the needs of each storyteller than any truth. Like a Rorschach inkblot.

Donovan was no mere agnostic on the subject either. He was positive: Newman Rogers had been dead for almost seventy years, and he was most likely, in the manner of dead people everywhere, to remain that way.

Now he'd found out he was wrong. At first he tried to believe Freddie was joking, or he was misled, but he couldn't pull it off. If Freddie said Rogers was alive, he almost certainly was. For the last twenty-four hours, Donovan had been trying to rethink the world with Rogers in it, and so far he felt completely at sea.

"But why?" Donovan had demanded, "has he concealed himself and deceived everyone?"

"He's had no choice, Donnie," Freddie reassured him. "The puppeteer can't show his face until the show's over." Donovan didn't find this image particularly comforting.

He looked out the window at the beautiful landscape spread out below. The air was clean and clear. Rivers sparkled blue in the sun. Everything was green and in blossom. The Earth had been saved from the inevitable destruction the human race would've visited upon it. Or maybe it was all a grand deceit. With that thought, the window went white.

As they descended through the cloud cover and approached the Shanghai airport, the other passengers gathered their things together. Donovan was empty-handed. He was going to visit his mother. He never brought her anything. She never noticed. As someone from a former life, he wasn't supposed to think of her as his mother at all, much less come calling. But she indulged him. Indulging others was one of the values shared by her hive—the Ring of Harmonious Stillness. It was a common stop on the road to self-discovery by members of his mother's generation. His mother had been in it for about five years. He gave her another two or three before she moved on. She always moved on.

THE MEMORY HIVE WAS A SHORT RIDE IN THE METRO TO SU-zhou, then a peaceful float down the Grand Canal to the maze of waterways and terraced gardens where the hive inhabitants sat about and remembered. Donovan hated the place. As he walked the crushed stone pathway to the glade where the receptionist had told him his mother would be, he kept his face averted from everyone he passed. Still, some of them recognized him and greeted him with a warmth he found unnerving. He didn't really know any of them. He might have seen them once or twice when he visited here before, but no one was ever introduced in here. Only remembered. All these strangers shared his mother's memories as she shared theirs. He was Donovan, their son.

Their inkblot.

His mother was a slender straight-backed woman with a long face and large clear eyes. They were closed just now as she sat in meditation, her body, in full lotus, looking like an oversize child's jack draped in white muslin. Her long silver-blonde hair was braided, ringing her head like a crown or a snake. She held up a hand, palm toward him for silence, to let him know that she was aware of his presence, but that he shouldn't speak until spoken to. She needn't have bothered. He knew the routine since childhood—the flared-nostril breathing, the serene smile, the willowy sigh of regret whenever she had to leave the narcissistic orgy she took to be enlightenment to deal with her son.

In this latest version of transcendence, she was in telepathic communion with the rest of the hive, remembering someone else's memories, adding her meaning to them, sharing them with the hive, like bees dancing to show their fellows where the flowers lay. That was *their* metaphor. Donovan didn't think it held up very well. Bees made honey. What did his mother's hive make?

"Hi, Mom," he said when her suspiciously elaborate eye fluttering was over, and she brought herself back to Earth. "Remember me?"

"Of course, I remember you, Donovan. We all do."

Donovan laughed and shook his head. "That was a *joke,* Mom. Do all of you remember those?"

Her mouth became a thin wounded line. Her son scorned her, failed to understand her, had no respect for the wisdom she'd struggled so hard to attain. She said a lot with that thin line of a mouth. It was a rutted path she and Donovan had worn over the years. They were like the dungeon dwellers in the old joke who told their oft-repeated jokes by number. Only his mom never laughed. It must be the way he told them.

Donovan stretched out on the grass beside her. "So what's new?"

"Is that another joke?"

"Yeah, I guess it is. I haven't seen you in a year. Thought I'd drop by. I had a birthday last week."

She was eyeing him warily, perhaps remembering that he'd once caused a scene. Or maybe that was someone else's son in another lifetime. It didn't matter. She said, "I understand that you think of me as your mother. What I don't understand is why you come to see me when you're so combative. It only seems to upset you."

"You seem to be on a roll. What's your theory?"

"Perhaps it's to make me feel guilty."

"That's a pretty good theory." He looked out at the canal, the elegant gardens. Other meditators were scattered about like shrubberies. He pried a stone loose from the soil, hefted it, and threw it in a high arc into the water. He smiled as several of the hive were startled by the splash. "Did you read the book I sent you?" he asked.

"Yes."

"That's it? 'Yes.' What did you think?"

"We . . . I couldn't agree with it."

"Go on."

"Donovan, there's really no point in our arguing about this."

"Who's arguing? I just wanted to know what you think. Your son—former son—whatever the hell I am. I wrote a book. I gave it to you. You read it. So now you're supposed to tell me what you think."

Her head tilted back an inch at most. "No, I'm not. I'm supposed to praise it because you think I'm your mother, and I should just blindly praise everything you do because of . . . that."

That. "Then forget 'that.' Let's say you're nobody. Just some woman who happened to pick up my book and read it. What the hell did you think?"

One of the meditators raised his head and frowned at Donovan's loud voice. His mother spoke in a quiet brittle voice. Serenity with intent to kill. "Very well. I believe your book to be completely misguided. The end of death has freed us from the chains of time so that now we may live in the eternal now. Only a fool, Donovan, would long for the return of death."

Donovan realized that one of the reasons he came to see his mom was that her bullshit always made his sound better. "Is that what you call this bunch of slugs mentally fondling each other—'the eternal now'?"

She drew herself up straighter. "We each have our own path, Donovan. Don't judge us."

"Yes, Mother." He shook a cigarette out of his pack and offered her one so she could turn it down with a condescending sniff. He lit his cigarette and blew a cloud of smoke into the air. "I met someone famous," he said. The only safe ground they had was gossip. She always liked to gossip.

She smiled briefly, accepting his gesture of a cease-fire. "Oh, who?"

"Stephanie Sanders, the supermodel?"

"Oh, my," she said, forgetting her serenity for the moment. "Really?" Then she got that distracted look on her face that meant some of the other hive members were throwing in their two cents' worth. "She killed her husband, they say. Even if they could never prove anything."

"They say a lot of things. From what I hear, her husband probably had it coming."

"No one deserves death, Donovan."

"Maybe we all do, Mom."

"I wish you wouldn't say things like that."

" 'I wish'? What about the rest of you?"

"We wish."

"And which is it you object to—calling you Mom or talking about death?"

He couldn't get a rise out of her. She was unshakable. The line of her mouth did not waver. "Both."

As usual, his visit to his mother was a depressing disaster, which probably wouldn't stop him from visiting her again in another year, but it would at least put it off until then. As he was flying back home, he felt as if he'd undergone some ritual, stripped himself down to essentials: He had no mother. He had no father. No brother, sister, aunt, uncle. He had no wife. There was no flesh. No life. No Donovan.

No wonder he courted death. He had nothing to lose. He was ready to meet his maker.

11

STOPPING THE HARLOTS

ONCE SHE WAS FINALLY OUT OF THE CITY, LAURA DIDN'T SEE a soul. The sun was up, and the dew had burned off the grass, and it was starting to get hot. She found a creek, trees growing alongside it, and she sat down on the bank in the shade. There was a hawk perched on top of a dead tree, calling out: *Hey! Hey! Hey!* Pretty stupid, Laura thought. Every rodent for miles around must know he was sitting up there, waiting to make them lunch. Or maybe he was looking for a girl hawk. Some things never changed.

The stream was about four or five yards wide, brown and slow-moving, maybe four feet deep in the middle. When she was little, she used to go swimming with her grandmother, her mother's mother. Laura was named after her grandmother, and she liked her grandparents best of all the Constructs who were always there, looking after her, telling her what to do. Her father's parents were killed by Soldiers before she was born, so she only had two grandparents, and that made them seem more special in a way.

Her grandfather was named Lawrence. He lived a very long time and was like this old wise man on the mountain or something. She thought he was funny, and he used to tell her stories about his lives before he was a Construct, like stories from another world. And he told her about his slave life raising up some kid, until the Bin fell, and he married her grandmother.

Even though she was old and wrinkled, her grandmother used to strip down to nothing when she and Laura went swimming and never covered herself up when she came out of the water, just stretched out on the bank until she was dry. They'd lie on the bank naked, the old woman and the little girl, and the girl would ask her to tell her about her life before the Bin and the Soldiers and all the rest of it, but she wasn't as free and easy with the stories as Granddad. She was probably right to keep her past to herself.

There wasn't any point in thinking about any of that now. Change only went one way. Once an arrow was let loose, there was only one end of it worth thinking about, because chances were it was headed for you, and the bow didn't have much to do with anything anymore.

That's what she should've told Tillman, she thought: Forget about Stephanie. If she isn't dead, she's probably in the Bin going on her sixth or seventh husband by now, not giving you a thought. Yeah, that would've cheered him right up, Laura, made his fucking day.

She stood up and stripped off her clothes, waded into the stream, her feet sinking into the muck on the bottom. She lay down in the water, washing the sweat off her, wishing she could wash away all her fuckups for the night, but it'd take more than this dirty brown water to pull that off, and she had plenty more where those came from, so what would be the point?

She floated on her back, looking up into the trees, thinking about Stephanie and her grandmother. Her grandmother was a clone. "Made, not begotten," as the fundies might say. Before her and all her thousands of sisters was a vial of blood that could've been dropped on the floor, poured down a drain, even into this stream. But that's not the way it played out. All these little cells that never meant to be women, never meant to be whores, never meant anything were stuffed with the lives of dead people and put to work. And out of all that, somehow, came Laura, right now, lying in this stream, meaning nothing.

Her grandmother died the year before Laura left the

Constructs, and maybe that had something to do with it. She hadn't been thinking all that straight at the time. Gran had been sick for a while, getting worse, and Laura had what she thought was a great idea. The Initiation was the next day, all those bodies cast off, and she figured her grandmother could just take one over—one that wasn't sick and dying.

She hung around outside her grandmother's room, waiting for her to be alone, but the house was full and people were in and out of her room all day. So it was dark and quiet by the time she stepped inside. It was so dark that most people couldn't have seen the old woman lying there, her eyes wide open, staring at nothing, but Laura had her grandfather's eyes and could see her grandmother clearly.

"Laura, is that you?" she asked in her shaky voice.

"Yes, Gran," she said.

"We were hoping you would come," she said.

All the Constructs said "we." It got on Laura's nerves, except when her grandparents did it. They couldn't really help being made up of different people. They hadn't had a choice. That was just the cards they were dealt. Not like the way it was now.

"I have an idea," Laura told her grandmother, and the old woman listened patiently as Laura told her how she didn't have to die, not with all those young bodies about to be tossed away.

But her grandmother just reached out her hand and took Laura's and told her to sit down on the bed. "We will miss you too, darling," she said. "But Lawrence is waiting for us."

Lawrence had been dead for a year now. He didn't have to die either. "Granddad's dead," Laura said, as cruelly as she could manage.

Her grandmother smiled, lying on her back as if she were floating in a stream looking up at the sky instead of on her deathbed staring blindly into the dark. "Life is more precious, and less precious than you think, child."

"You don't have to die," Laura insisted.

"Everything dies, Laura. Everything."

And as if to show her, her grandmother died the next evening, right after the Initiation. And all the Constructs tried to shove their way inside Laura's mind to share her grief. But her grief was hers, and she didn't want them filling her with sympathy and understanding and wise counsel.

So just before the next Initiation, she went to Crazyville, where nobody understood anyone or anything, not even themselves, and had been there ever since. She didn't regret it. She couldn't say it'd been a great move. But it was what she did, the arrow she was riding.

The hawk swooped down low over the water, passing right over her, and scared the crap out of her. He circled around and perched on a limb about thirty feet above her and looked right at her. *Hey! Hey! Hey!*

"Cute," Laura said. "I'm too big for dinner, and these are scales, not feathers." She stood up and let the water run off her body. The hawk continued to watch. She lay on the grass, and the hawk didn't move, though he'd finally shut up. He sat on his perch and scanned the horizon as if expecting someone. He could probably see all the way back to New Jerusalem. Pretty soon she was dry, then sweaty again. She wasn't hungry anymore for some reason. The past killed her appetite every time. That's what she should've told Tillman: Forget the past. That's what forgetting's for.

No. She should've told him Stephanie loved him. That's what she should've told him. She loved you, and don't you ever, ever forget it. But she didn't. And then she fucked Sammy because she was on such a bitch roll that she wanted to hurt somebody, and there he was. She put on her clothes and walked on toward Crazyville, wishing there was someplace—anyplace—else to go.

SHE WASN'T IN THE MOOD FOR ANY JOKING AROUND WHEN, a half a mile from home, she came upon a burning bush in the middle of a meadow. It crackled, it smoked, flames leaping into the sky—it was all very convincing. She could feel the heat, even see the waves of it radiating out. "Yoo-hoo," the bush said. "Hi, Laura."

"Hi, Freddie. Aren't you in the wrong neighborhood for this bullshit? The Bible thugs are back that way."

"They don't have chips. They can't see me."

"Come on, Freddie. This is stupid, it's hot, and I'm not in the mood. Have we got business or what?"

He turned into his regular self, wearing a shirt that looked like it was still on fire. It wasn't really him, of course. Just a transmission from the Bin via her chip, but you couldn't tell the difference. She could even touch him if she wanted to, but he didn't go for girls, which was kind of a shame because he was one of the few guys she ever trusted. Duh, she said to herself, just maybe there's a connection?

"There's a woman who may want to download," he said.

Another guest for the Initiation barbecue. This could be a profitable summer indeed. "What do you mean 'may'? I need a little lead time, you know, to bribe a few angels."

Freddie smiled. "You're not really bribing the Constructs, you know."

"The hell I'm not."

"They want you to do what you're doing. They don't mind what happens to the bodies they cast aside."

"So what you're saying is one or two of them fucks me for nothing while they all tune in."

"That's exactly what I'm saying."

"I don't believe you."

Freddie shrugged. "Suit yourself."

"Look, whenever this woman makes up her mind, why don't you just let me know, okay?"

"It's not quite that simple, I'm afraid."

Of course not. This wasn't her day for simple and easy. She was starting to get numb. "Talk to me, Freddie."

"You met with Walter Tillman a little while ago," he said.

"Goddamn it, you were spying on me again."

"I prefer to think of it as sharing information. You can

always have your Construct chip shut down, if you'd prefer more privacy."

"Yeah, right. Throw away half my assets. I'm doing a job for the man is all. What the hell business is it of yours?"

"None. Actually, we hadn't processed your meeting with him yet. He sent us a message a short while ago. We checked and saw you'd been there. We didn't know he was alive."

"Ooh, something you didn't know. Must bug the hell out of you. So the little toad figured out how to send you a message? He's a smart one, I'll give him that. How'd he do it?"

"We're not sure."

This just kept getting better. "So what was the message?"

"He asked the whereabouts of Stephanie Sanders. She's why I've come to see you."

She felt her stomach drop a couple of feet. "Jeez. You've got to be kidding. *Stephanie?* She's the download?"

"That's right. Though finding Tillman alive may change her plans."

She didn't remember sitting down, but there she was in the middle of the meadow on her butt, with Freddie sitting beside her. "Did she betray him?" she asked.

"You know as much about that as I do."

Somehow she doubted that.

"Does she know he's alive?"

"Not yet. We'd hoped to arrange a meeting first."

"A meeting. You mean . . .?"

"We want to upload Tillman into the Bin."

"Jeez, you'd risk that?" As Freddie had explained to her before when she asked to visit the Bin, signals from the Bin to the Earth often got lost in the clutter of satellite transmissions; signals going up were a riskier proposition.

"We owe him that much."

"Who's 'we,' Freddie?"

"Newman and I."

"Newman."

"That's right."

She watched the bees make their way from blossom to blossom to blossom. "Tell me, Freddie. Do you ever wish that Newman Rogers had never thought up this mess?"

"He does, but as you were thinking not so long ago, time is an arrow."

She gave a bitter laugh. "I was thinking that? Aren't I clever, though?"

"We need you to do the transfer, Laura."

She looked over at him in his flaming shirt. She could see now the print was flowers, not flames—huge blossoms the size of a man's head. The bees circled around him in awe. "You want me to go back into New Jerusalem, snatch Tillman, and upload him into the Bin so he can see Stephanie?"

"That's right."

There were so many downsides to this deal, it was like a coal mine. "Do you think she's still in love with him? I'm not doing it if he's just going to get his heart broken."

Freddie arched a brow. "Laura, how sentimental of you."

"Fuck you, Freddie. Does she love him or not?"

"She does."

"So what's in it for me?"

"That's my Laura. Name your price."

Coming from Freddie, that was really saying something. Through his connections with the Constructs, he could get her anything she asked for delivered to her door. Cigarettes. Whiskey. Even gasoline.

But she didn't care about any of that. And for the second time she found herself asking for something incredibly stupid that wouldn't do her any good whatsoever. "I go with him," she said. "She meets me too." Her voice was shaking, her heart was going a hundred miles an hour, she could hear the bees buzzing as loud as locusts, and she'd never wanted anything so much in her life except for her grandmother to live, and damned if she could say why.

Freddie was stunned. She'd never seen him at a loss for words before. But then he cocked his head to one side as if listening to someone and nodded yes. "Tomorrow night," he said. "We can help you find your way."

"I don't need your help," she said. "My eyes are as good as your satellites any day of the week."

"We truly appreciate—"

"Shut up, Freddie. I don't want to hear it, okay? I just don't want to hear it."

"There is one more thing you should know. The Soldiers are onto him. Gabriel has taken a personal interest."

"Are you shitting me? What about Sammy?"

"The lieutenant? You won't *believe* who his father is."

"I don't give a shit about his father. What about him?"

"We've lost track of him for the moment, I'm afraid."

She imagined him hanging from a tree somewhere. "Well, find him, goddamn it."

FOR HOURS AFTER SHE GOT HOME FROM HER MEETING WITH Donovan and Freddie, Stephanie stayed inside her apartment and cried. It was stupid. She didn't even know what she was crying about. Herself? Walter? Nothing perhaps. It was just a release, like bleeding the steam from an overheated boiler before it exploded.

Whatever strength she thought she'd created out of love or guilt suddenly amounted to nothing. Maybe that's what she was crying over. She didn't know. She didn't care. Until finally, sitting in front of a picture window, watching people make their way through the city streets on their way to somewhere, her tears stopped, and she remembered she too had someplace to go, someplace she hadn't seen in almost a century. She'd played out her fate there, but now, surely, it couldn't claim her anymore.

She remembered a night maybe a week after the jeans photos hit the street. The phone wouldn't quit ringing. If she took half the jobs she'd already been offered, she'd never have to work again in her life. There was an editorial on the evening news about her cultural significance. If she stayed up for the late-night talk shows, she could add another dozen Stephanie jokes to her collection. The world had gone nuts, and she was scared. She desperately needed to talk to someone who'd understand.

So she snuck out to meet her best friend Kelly up in the foothills to smoke a joint and talk. It was like one of those dreams where you're someone else, she told Kelly. People she'd known all her life suddenly treated her differently, as if with a few camera clicks she'd been magically transformed. There was already talk of taking her out of school, setting her up with private tutors, not because she was too busy for school or because she wanted out, but because her presence might be "disruptive." That was the vice principal's word—the man whose eyes followed her down the crowded hall with a look that would've terrified her if she'd been alone in a room with him.

But, she thought, up here with Kelly, I'm safe. They'd been friends since third grade. Kelly'd gone with her to the shoot. They laughed themselves silly afterward, doing parodies of her sultry poses. Kelly would know it was all just a bunch of pictures and hype. If anyone knew Stephanie, Kelly did.

As they passed the joint back and forth, and she told Kelly her troubles, the knot in her chest began to loosen. She'd spent a week pretending to be someone else, this nymph—how many times had she heard *that* word in the last week?—dreamed up by some jerk in an ad agency somewhere. She couldn't even look at the shots anymore. They made her physically ill. But with Kelly she could be herself—could remember who the hell she really was.

But it was like the old horror cliché where the heroine barricades herself inside the very room where her stalker is hiding.

"You make *me* sick," Kelly said. "Everything in the world falls in your lap, and now you're bitching about it. What am I supposed to do, feel sorry for you?" Kelly was seething with rage. It was like talking to her mother. Worse. It'd been a long time since she felt close to her mom, while Kelly had been her best friend only a few days before.

It did feel like the world had fallen in her lap. Crushing her, changing her, branding her. Like a rape. Pinning her so that it was useless to struggle. She couldn't go back. Her old life was gone forever. Even her best friend didn't know her. She had to live this new life. The long-waisted nymph in the jeans. The Beauty. The world had decided that's who she was, and no one, not even herself, could contradict them.

Freddie had sent over a virtual to fill her in on the real world. She found it in the clutter left by her tear-filled day and popped it in the machine. It was time to have a look at where she was going to live for the rest of her life. For almost as long as she could remember, she'd been trying to die—to go nowhere. Now she was going into a strange land where everyone died sooner or later. Maybe she hadn't been crying out of grief. Maybe she was afraid. Not of death, but of the life she would live as she waited for death to come. A new life, a few fate.

She shut off her phone, put on a loose-fitting caftan, sat cross-legged on the floor, and started the virtual. It placed her high above the Earth in a clear bubblelike enclosure. Some, she knew, would panic without that bubble, would actually die as if in the vacuum of space. Stephanie didn't have that kind of faith in appearances.

Beside her sat a kindly-looking gentleman, an archetypal sage.

"Greetings," he said. "I am Virgil, your virtual guide to Earth in the middle of the twenty-second century. Ask me any questions you like, but please remember that I am a virtual intelligence only. Occasionally, you may need to rephrase your question until it is in a form my authors have anticipated. If this should prove unsuccessful, I may need revision before I can answer. You may give the 'Revise' command, and I will be updated so that I can answer your question. This could result in unnecessary delays, however, so use the 'Revise' command sparingly. I suggest waiting until you have several unanswered questions before requesting revision, or, even better, giving the command at the end of your session, and I will be prepared to address all your unanswered questions at the beginning of our next meeting.

"Do you have any questions at this time?"

Stephanie felt like a schoolgirl again. In those days, she and her friends enjoyed making lewd suggestions to the virtual instructors. ("Can you demonstrate the use of 'moon' as a verb, please?") There were stories about virtuals actually carrying out such suggestions, but Stephanie had never seen one do anything but smile and say, "I don't understand. Would you please rephrase the question?"

"No questions," she said.

"Then let's begin, shall we?"

The bubble rotated so that they were facing a dark green rectangular solid floating in space. The Bin. "Most of the human population resides in the Alternative Life Medium Assembly—ALMA—popularly known as the Bin—"

"Skip the introduction. Tell me about life on the planet."

There was a short delay as the pedantic program adjusted its presentation to this impatient pupil. The bubble rotated back to the Earth. A color overlay appeared on the surface. Mostly red, with a few green patches lightly sprinkled with pulsing white dots. There was a cluster of white around Washington, D.C.

"In the color-coded globe before you, the areas in red are currently uninhabitable by humans. The green areas are habitable. White indicates recent human settlements."

"Why 'uninhabitable'?"

"If you would hold your questions, I am sure I will answer most all of them in my presentation."

You'll babble on forever, Stephanie thought. "Why 'uninhabitable'?"

If the VI was offended, he didn't let it show. "A combination of factors, mostly radioactive and chemical contamination, though virulent strains of bacteria in the water supply have been responsible in some cases. In northern Irkutsk—"

"How many survive?"

"How many humans?"

"No, how many armadillos," Stephanie muttered under her breath. If VIs were going to be so stupid, then why bother with them at all? "Yes, how many humans."

"Approximately one million, eighty-five percent of whom are concentrated here"—they zoomed in closer—"the city formerly known as Washington, D.C., and its environs, now named New Jerusalem, an autocratic theocracy under the leadership of Gabriel—born Ted Wexler in Chesterfield County, Virginia, in—"

"Enough." Virtual instructors could talk your ear off if you let them, programmed to tell all from any starting point. She remembered Gabriel well enough, though she would've thought he was dead by now. "Concise mode, please. Where do the other fifteen percent live?"

"In small social units scattered throughout the remaining habitable lands." The globe twirled obediently to show her the remaining human habitat in eastern North America, northern Australia, central Africa, and a sliver down the middle of South America. There seemed to be no real population centers other than New Jerusalem.

"By 'small social units,' you mean what?"

"The average size is eight individuals. Two, occasionally three, generations, usually extended family, though occasionally families will form alliances."

" 'Eight'? Why so small?"

"Larger communities are detected and destroyed by Christian Soldiers using satellite-based weaponry." He said this with the same cheerful tone he used for everything. VIs depressed her—all that information with no understanding.

"Why?" she said, trying to keep her voice from shaking.

"The weapon systems rely primarily on heat readings to detect human activity. Only small nomadic groups can evade detection. There was a larger community of cave dwellers in the Andes, but—"

"I don't mean that. I mean *why* do the soldiers kill them?" Her voice was shrill, shaking. "Concise, please."

"They kill everyone who is not a Christian Soldier. All

Soldiers live within a hundred-mile radius of New Jerusalem."

Stephanie closed her eyes and massaged her forehead with her fingertips, trying to piece together the world she'd be returning to. "I'll be downloading into a roving pack of savages with fundies trying to nuke us if we light a campfire," she said, more to herself than to the VI.

But the VI answered anyway. "No, that is not correct," he said primly.

Tell a VI to be concise, and you always seemed to pay for it in the end. It was hard not to personify them—to imagine motive, personality, emotion. But they were no more human than words printed on a page. She sighed. "Explain my many errors, oh wise one."

"You will be downloaded into the Construct community—Construct Town—which is located here at the present time." An arrow flashed just west of D.C.

"You said there was no one but fundies for a hundred miles around."

"Actually, I said that all the Christian Soldiers lived in that area. I did not say that *only* Christian Soldiers did."

"Break down the population for me."

Virgil seemed pleased. The Earth before them was replaced with a pie graph. "The population of New Jerusalem is roughly distributed as follows: Seven hundred and fifty thousand Christian Soldiers (sixty percent rural, forty percent in the city proper), ninety thousand Constructs, and ten to fifteen thousand miscellaneous individuals. The Construct population is concentrated in Construct Town, a seminomadic community that remains on the periphery of New Jerusalem to protect itself against nuclear, chemical, and biological weapons."

"Who are the 'miscellaneous individuals'?"

"Some scavengers, but mostly the inhabitants of Crazyville."

Stephanie couldn't help smiling at that. "Sounds like where I belong."

"It is one of your options. Your chances for survival, however, are significantly higher in Construct Town."

The pie graph vanished, and the Earth reappeared. Stephanie stared at it, once home to billions, now on the verge of extinction.

"Why do the Christian Soldiers kill everyone?"

"They believe that the extermination of nonbelievers will hasten the arrival of the End of Days when all true believers will ascend into heaven."

"Will they succeed?"

"I am not programmed to answer theological questions."

"No, I mean will they kill everyone?"

"The probability is extremely high that they will render the entire planet uninhabitable by humans within the next ten to twenty years."

"Jesus." She felt physically ill. She wouldn't have thought that the death of the planet would touch her so directly, after living in its virtual replacement all these years. "Show it to me. I want to see this New Jerusalem."

"It is very dangerous to outsiders. When you download, the city of New Jerusalem must be avoided at all costs."

"Then that's all the more reason to see it now, while I have the chance."

Their bubble descended through the atmosphere and hovered above the city. It seemed to be made up largely of rubble. Lots of the virtuals she starred in depicted the real world in ruins, but it was more romantic than this—chaotic with style. This was a place fallen apart and hanging by a thread. Cloth or ill-fitting doors replaced what had been burned or shattered long ago. Lean-tos of corrugated metal were common additions. Nothing stood plumb, but leaned like headstones in an old churchyard. Only the roads seemed sound, paved with stone and brick.

The bubble dissolved and they stood in the middle of the street. Down the block was an old Metro car, somehow dragged to the spot. It had a porch in front of the doors fashioned from a stack of cinder blocks and sheet metal. It was the showplace of the neighborhood.

There were several people in the street, all carrying something: a sheaf of bamboo, salvaged wire, a baby, a rifle. Everyone had a purpose, and even those with guns looked vaguely frightened, alert. They all wore the same khaki uniforms, although the uniforms appeared to be newer and crisper on the ones bearing arms.

"This is a recording from yesterday," Virgil said.

A woman came running toward them, completely terrified. Her bare feet slapping the stone street left bloody footprints. Her clothes were half-torn from her body, and the coil of her long hair had been knocked loose and bounced like a loose spring. Her pursuer, a Soldier with his weapon drawn, called out, "Stop the harlot!"

The others on the street grabbed at the woman, and though she broke free from the first few, they finally held her fast without looking at her, clutching wrists, shirt, hair, whatever came to hand as she continued struggling desperately, writhing so hard you could hear her joints popping, until one of the men picked up a stone and knocked her out cold with it. The others let her slump to the street and went about their business as quickly as possible. The Soldier who had pursued her dragged her up the street by her hair.

The whole scene took maybe thirty seconds.

No one but Stephanie seemed flustered by the events, though now the pace had quickened and the atmosphere was even more fearful and guarded. What Stephanie had just witnessed wasn't an unusual occurrence for these people. Everyone knew their part. She remembered the dispassionate look in the man's eye as he bent to pick up that stone.

"What will happen to her? Why? What did she do?"

"She is accused of adultery. She will be executed."

"For *'adultery'*? Did she do it?"

"It is unlikely. But accusation is sufficient in most cases. Unless the accuser is of a lower caste than the accused, in which case . . ."

"Get me out of here."

"Do you wish to terminate the program?"

"Off!" she screamed, and she was sitting in her apartment once again. The sun was just setting over the city and everything was bathed in amber light. Another beautiful sunset. Another day where there was always another day. Where time was cheap as dirt.

In the real world, where every single moment was as frail as ashes, the world sat waiting on the end, like a bomb plummeting silently through the air. She kept hearing the Soldier's cry: *Stop the harlot!*

She turned on the virtual with the simulation shut off. "One question. Is there any way to stop them?"

"Can you rephrase the question?"

"Is there any way to stop the Christian Soldiers from wiping out the human race?"

"I am not prepared to answer that question."

"Revise."

She shut it off. She thought of those fearful people trudging along with their burdens, grabbing that desperate woman. What if they seized her accuser instead, pried his weapon from his hands? They didn't seem to care what the woman had or hadn't done. They just didn't want to be her, running for their lives. Stephanie hadn't learned much of value from her life on Earth, but she had seen the power of public opinion and how quickly it could change. Most of the time most people didn't care much about much of anything, so a handful of people could herd them like sheep. But people weren't sheep and every once in a while most people decided they *did* care where they were going, and then it was like herding a pack of wolves.

It was the one good thing she'd done with her old life and her much-envied beauty: When Beauty stood up and said that slavery was ugly, the people finally listened.

She didn't know what the VI would tell her when it was revised, but it didn't matter. She'd been a goddess once. Once too often. In this new life, she would have no such distinction. Beauty couldn't save that woman. Truth either. She could hear the woman's feet slapping the stone pavement, feel all those strangers' hands clutching her, stopping the harlot. Who would these people listen to except a man with a gun or God on His throne?

And just then, she was startled by the sound of her buzzer—someone at the door. She never had visitors. It was Freddie. She wondered if he knew she'd just run the virtual and that's what he was doing here, come to see if she'd been scared out of her resolve. She started to tell him she belonged down there, that she was ready to go.

But other news had brought him to the door. He told her without preamble: Walter was alive.

12

BODHISATTVA

It was late afternoon by the time Sam had cleaned up, put on his best uniform, and supervised the dutiful corporal loading up a jeep with a long list of special apparatus. He didn't intend to use any of it. He had his own show to put on. If Gabriel suspected he was being tricked, Sam would have no warning. The corporal who was now driving him to the site, his eyes on the road, would put a bullet in Sam's forehead.

While he was alone in his apartment, Sam had checked the scanner readings from Gabriel's. Behind the second door on the left was a cylinder filled with fluid, a denser mass in the middle. It was alive. A clone. Gabriel had been cloning himself for years. He'd never die; he'd rule the world forever. Who could Sam tell? The only ones who would care would be those who would gladly take Gabriel's place. They'd murder him, use Gabriel's sin to justify their coup, but more than Gabriel needed to die.

Sam looked over at Metzger. He was twenty-five at the most, but already a web of lines surrounded his eyes. The tip of his right thumb was missing. Did Metzger love God? he wondered. If he knew the truth, would he defend the man who could keep him out of the fields, or God who'd made them?

"Do you have any brothers and sisters, Corporal?"

"Six, sir." He turned the wheel to avoid a dead dog. "Four living."

✦   ✦   ✦

SAM SET METZGER TO UNLOADING THE EQUIPMENT, CARRYING it down into the site using the stairs Gabriel's crew had cleared. They were pulling out as Sam and Metzger arrived. Their commanding officer was obviously furious for being pulled off the site, but the orders had come from Gabriel himself. He returned Sam's crisp salute. "It's all yours, Lieutenant."

When Metzger had everything piled neatly in front of the computer, Sam told him to go up top and stand guard. He plugged in and typed out a quick message. He couldn't risk any more. There were additional cameras now. Gabriel's cameras. Sam typed:

MAINTAIN POSSUM PROTOCOL.

He waited a moment. Then started to work creating a phony front door, a phony back door, a subtle trail to a side entrance that put you back where you started. And when he was done, he did it again. He might not make it out of here alive, but he wasn't going to let Gabriel get to Tillman if he could help it. He worked all night, taking short naps, then worked all day. He didn't know how he could keep this up for two weeks, or how he was going to get Laura past Metzger, but he'd have to think of something.

Every once in a while, he'd plug in another piece of equipment, make adjustments for show. He never looked at the cameras, his audience. Then just after dark, dozing off in fits and starts, dreams of Laura weaving in and out of his mind, he heard a voice behind him.

"Sammy! Returning to the scene of the crime?"

He jerked himself awake and whirled around in a panic. There she stood, a three-foot length of pipe in her hand.

Sam looked up the stairs, expecting to see Metzger with his weapon.

"Don't worry. The little storm trooper is out cold."

"You took out one of the Temple Guard?"

She smiled. "My granddad taught me a few things." She spun the pipe around and sliced the air with it, leaped into the air and gave an impressive sideways kick. *"Hyee! Ha! She comes out of the night like a bat out of hell! Ninja whore!"* She laughed. "You know, martial-arts shit." All he could do was stare at her. She tossed the pipe on the floor with a loud clatter. "Look, I'm sorry I was kind of hard on you before—"

"What are you doing here?"

"I've come to borrow our little friend in there. I'm doing a job for some people who want to see him. What's it to you?"

She was mad at him again. Why was she always mad at him? " 'See him'? What do you mean, 'see him'? What 'people'?"

"Look, asshole, I just apologized to you. Did you catch that? I certainly hope so because it ain't coming around again any time soon. Now why don't you get this pile of shit out of my way so I can download Wally and get the fuck out of here?"

Of course. *That's* why she was mad at him. "You don't have to apologize. It's me. I had it coming. You showed me what . . . an . . . asshole I'd become."

She stared at him a long time, then a smile spread across her face. "Jesus Christ on a stick," she said. "You are just full of surprises."

"Please don't swear."

She rolled her eyes. "Okay, okay."

"We've got to get Tillman out of here right away. Gabriel is onto him. I was going to try to stall them until the Initiation." He pointed at the cameras. "Now that they've seen you, Soldiers will be on their way."

"Jesus, why didn't you say so? We can apologize in Crazyville. Everybody's fucking sorry there." She pointed at the keyboard. "Tell him he's got a date, and he needs to download. I'll get into the coffin."

❖   ❖   ❖

WHEN THEY RAN OUTSIDE AND JUMPED INTO THE JEEP, SAM thought he saw lights approaching. Maybe he did and maybe he didn't, but it was too late now to stop and think about it. They didn't dare use the lights on the jeep. Sam drove with Laura telling him which way to turn as they bounced over the broken remnants of roads out of town into fields and then forest. At least that's what Sam guessed. He couldn't see enough to be sure.

He thought they were generally headed toward Crazyville, but far afield of the beaten path. When they were out of the city, she climbed into the front seat.

"Where are we going?" he asked.

"Little creek, few trees. You can keep an eye on the old body here while me and Wally visit friends." He felt her hand on his thigh. "I'll be in a coma. You can do whatever you like—won't remember a thing."

The thought and her hand aroused him and made him angry at the same time. But what was there to be angry about? She was joking with him, having fun. It was better than thinking about the whole Army of the Lord that would soon be on their trail. "Just where are you going?" he asked.

"Get off this road. It's washed out up ahead. There's a trail up here on the right."

Sam peered into the darkness and tried once again to make out more than shadows.

"There! There!"

Sam stopped and squinted where she pointed. He finally spotted a narrow trail like a crease in the shadows, turned the wheel, and stepped on the accelerator. They shot into the darkness, just barely missing a tree. A limb slapped against the windshield.

"Maybe you should let me drive," she said.

"You know how to drive? I thought you people walked everywhere."

" 'You people'? What the hell do you know about it? My granddad taught me, smart guy. He used to tinker with things. He had a pickup. Hey! Watch the ditch, will you?"

Sam slammed on the brakes. "I can't even *see* the ditch."

She spoke slowly, one word at a time. "Then you better let me fucking drive, don't you think?"

Sam felt his anger building again, but knew it for what it was. Pride, not righteousness. "You're right," he said and took his hands off the wheel.

She put her hand on his arm. "Sammy?"

"What?"

"You're okay." She hopped out and came around the jeep while he climbed into the passenger seat.

Laura slid behind the wheel, and they were moving again, much too fast from Sam's near-blind perspective. Often, for a second or two at a time, they were airborne as Laura hurtled into the darkness. Sam couldn't look ahead. It was like driving into a wall. He turned to Laura. He could just barely make her out.

"So Tillman's inside you?"

She cut him a quick glance, then back to the road or pasture or whatever she could see beyond the hood of the jeep that he couldn't. "Yeah, I got him."

"Can he talk? I mean . . ."

"I know what you mean, and he better not try. I told him: 'You ain't staying long, and don't use anything while you're there.' If I so much as wiggle a toe when it's not my idea, I'll download his ass into a dog and let Chef stew him."

"Where are you taking him?"

She cut the wheel hard to the left, and they fishtailed, then shot forward. Sam thought he saw some shape in the darkness—a huge tree, a boulder—inches away from him, then they were past it. He heard a hissing beneath the floorboard like a chorus of snakes. They were plowing through high grass, seeds raining down on them.

Laura relaxed her posture at the wheel, driving with her hands resting at twelve o'clock. They were out of the woods—literally if not figuratively.

She looked over at him, or at least he thought she did. "You're in some serious deep shit here, aren't you?"

"The deepest."

"Then I guess I can level with you. The Bin is still very

much alive. They've been playing possum like Tillman said. That's where I'm taking him."

Sam thought about it and wasn't surprised. The Lord had spared the Bin from Gabriel's madness. "How did you know what Tillman said?"

"I've got all his memories. He's got all mine. Lucky guy. Real horror-show material. Sex. Violence. One pointless sequel after another."

Sam could imagine it, at least he could feel it in her voice as she tried to turn everything into banter. Her life had been hard. He wondered what kept her going. "Have you ever been in love, Laura?"

She laughed. "You're just full of questions tonight, aren't you?"

"Well, have you?"

She sat up straight, leaned toward the wheel. Her voice softened a little. "Maybe once. But just maybe."

"Tell me about it."

"What are you? Jealous?"

"No, I'm just trying to get to know you."

"Yeah, well, that takes some getting used to. But if you want to hear the story of my life, that's cool. I'll just add it to your tab. Nice jeep, by the way."

There was a half moon behind them now, low on the horizon. There was just enough light to tell they were crossing a broad rolling field. He could almost make out Laura's features. Lightning bugs blinked on and off. He didn't believe her when she tried to turn everything into business. She'd come for Tillman, even though there was nothing in it for her as far as he could tell. It was like his self-righteousness—a way of keeping the world at a distance.

She told her story in an ironic voice that wasn't quite convincing. "Laura's life, chapter thirteen, 'Laura Falls in Love':

"There was this guy who used to come in all the time. Name was Larry. How's that for romantic? Larry. Had this dog with him all the time. Smart as hell. He'd sit by the door and wait for the guy. Anyway, Larry liked to be hustled. You know. Buy the bottle of champagne that Chef whips up out of beer and Tang and God knows what else. And I sit all over him, kiss him if he wanted, which he did. In fact, that's all he ever wanted.

"Every time I'd suggest going up to my room, he'd say, 'How much?' And I'd name a price. He was a scavenger, and he always had a bagful of stuff. But no matter how low the price, he'd always say, 'No thanks.' Then he'd split. He wasn't cheap. He always gave me packs of cigarettes and shit."

They topped a rise, bounced, slid into a turn, and Sam braced himself against the dash.

"Anyway, he was this terrific kisser, and he'd talk to me sometimes, and well, I got to where I'd look forward to him coming in. And it wasn't like any of the other girls ever got anywhere with him. I'd lay low and watch, and he wouldn't even go for the champagne with anyone else. So I got this stupid idea in my head that I was somehow special to him. I was young. I didn't know any better.

"So anyway, he comes in one time, and he doesn't have the dog with him. He's really down, and I say, 'The champagne's on me.' And I just talk to him, you know. His dog was dead, he told me. Somebody shot him. No reason. So I hold him and kiss him. I really want to make him feel better, and I say, 'Come on up to my room.' 'How much?' he says like always, and I say, 'Not a thing.'

"So we spend all day in my bed. It was nice. Really nice. I don't know why I'm telling you all this."

"You don't have to. I just asked—"

"Yeah, well. As he's leaving, I tell him I love him. Can you believe that? One and only time. He gets all choked up, and I figured he was really touched or something. Then I say, 'See you tomorrow?' And he says, 'Sure.' "

She stared straight ahead. There was a dark line cutting across the field, a few trees. Sam guessed this was the place she'd told him about. " 'See you tomorrow?' " she said in a bright brittle voice. "You know what happened? I never really saw him again. He was around, and I'd see him on the street or something, but he'd always head the other way. Never came into Chef's again."

She stopped the jeep on the banks of a creek and shut off the engine. Cicadas were singing and frogs jumped into the water with a series of splashes. The waves caught the moonlight and carried it along. She sat silent behind the wheel for a moment, staring at the water. "He always had the fucking dog with him, looking pretty good for being dead and all." She gave a dry cold laugh. "That's love for you."

She hopped out of the jeep and headed toward the creek, with Sam trailing along behind her, stumbling in the dark, trying to think of something to say, wishing he hadn't made her feel bad. She took off her jacket, rolled it up for a pillow, and stretched out on the ground. Sam sat down beside her.

She used her business voice now—breezy and tough and untouchable. "Here's the way it works. Pretty soon I'll establish a link upstairs and send our friend up, then I'm checking out too. Can't say how long I'll be, but I'll be back before sunup, I imagine. If you'd keep anything from eating me, I'd appreciate it. If the Soldiers show up, just stick me in the bushes or something."

"Is it dangerous?"

"The upload? No. Piece of cake. Unless your friends get a fix on it, which isn't likely out here. Only takes a second or two."

"What happens when you get back—with Tillman, I mean."

"I have a feeling he won't be coming back—he's meeting the love of his life." She gave a laugh, but Sam couldn't tell whether it was derision or envy.

"What if *you* don't come back?"

She put her hand to his cheek. "Aren't you sweet. Don't worry. I'll be back—just like a bad cold."

She made herself comfortable on the damp ground and clasped his hand, then went into a trance, her eyes rolling back in her head. Her hand relaxed its grip. He checked her pulse, and it was slow but strong.

After about an hour, the damp air started getting a little chilly. He was okay, but she just had on a lightweight shirt. He didn't dare risk a fire. He walked back up to the jeep and dug around in the back. He found a moth-eaten blanket that smelled of oil, but was clean enough.

He spread the blanket on the ground, picked her up, and put her down on it. He lay down beside her and wrapped it around them both. The moon was high enough now so that he could make out her face. He kissed her softly on the lips, lay back with her head nestled against his shoulder, and fell asleep.

BEFORE DONOVAN QUITE REALIZED WHAT WAS HAPPENING, he found himself sitting across a little bent willow table from Newman Rogers, who was sipping coffee, chattering away, apparently starved for conversation. Donovan didn't know what to say. A few minutes ago, he was in Freddie's workroom, and now he was here, instantly transported. He remembered Blake's description of sitting in his garden, talking with the dead Milton. He'd always thought Blake was being metaphoric or crazy or both. But maybe it wasn't like that at all. Maybe it was like this. The impossible made suddenly and inexplicably ordinary.

He'd seen this man's image dozens of times every day of his life: holos, photos, murals, statues. Heard his voice, recited his speeches. Read him, studied him. Cursed him. Worshipped him. He wasn't supposed to be real. And if he had to be real, he wasn't supposed to be ordinary. Or else what was the point of anything? Donovan wished he could just run away, but there was nowhere to go.

They were on the porch of a cozy mountain cabin. It sat halfway up a hollow in a meadow surrounded by deep woods. A small stream cascaded over blue-gray boulders at the edge of the woods. They were in Virginia, in the Blue Ridge Mountains. Or at least that's where Freddie'd told him they were going. They'd simply shown up there instantaneously. Donovan barely had time to catch his breath before Freddie introduced them and walked into the woods, leaving him alone with Rogers.

Donovan had gaped at the mist-covered mountains in the distance like clouds fallen to the ground, bathed in sunlight. And checked his watch. It was ten in the morning, though it'd been night in D.C.

"I take certain liberties here," Rogers explained with a laugh when he saw Donovan checking the time. "I thought you might enjoy the view."

Donovan managed an idiot smile and a nod of approval. *Certain liberties.* No one, supposedly, took liberties with the operating system. Instantaneous travel and time distortion were outrageously illegal routines. The Bin required consensual reality. You could play with it only if you made it clear you were creating a virtual, an entertaining fiction, but you couldn't just subject somebody else to your reality without their permission.

But this wasn't just anyone. This was Newman Rogers. Father of the Bin. Savior of Mankind. He could do anything he wanted in here. He'd made the place. In this world at least, God hadn't just wound up the world, set it going, and walked away. He apparently hid out in this mountain hollow and ran things. Or played with them anyway.

Donovan wasn't sure how he felt about that, but more to the immediate point, he had to ask himself: What in the hell does he want with me? It didn't make sense. Clearly, Rogers worked hard to maintain his anonymity. He wouldn't just invite you over for coffee without a reason. Was Rogers going to set him straight on a few things? Tell him to stop his silly campaign to tamper with a perfectly good paradise?

But, like Stephanie said, Donovan wasn't going to change the Bin in a million years, and—in his more honest moments, at least—he knew it. Rogers had to know it too. Dr. Death was just a passing fad. Already his book sales were slipping, the crowds at his lectures dwindling. He'd soon be another bit of nostalgic trivia, like legions before him. So what am I doing here? Donovan asked himself repeatedly. What does Newman Rogers want with me?

Somehow (Donovan couldn't remember how) they'd gotten on the subject of Rogers's appearance. He was an elflike man with wispy white hair and large protruding ears. His eyes were the most remarkable thing about him, bright and inquisitive, maybe even mischievous. They were unnerving, anyway. Lively. He looked to be in his mid-sixties by real-world standards—oldish for the Bin. A few years back, old had ever so briefly been in, but most people settled for a middle-aged look. Young was flashy, and old was pretentious. Not with Rogers, though. It suited him. If you're God, Donovan mused, how could you be pretentious?

"For a while there," Rogers was saying, "I just let myself age. Shriveled up like a prune, started shrinking, all stooped over with a cane." His voice climbed a quavering octave: "I ta-alked li-ike thi-is." He shrugged. "I wanted to run the cycle, *feel my age,* as they used to say. Of course I was too cowardly to throw senility and disease into the mix." He laughed at his own folly and sipped his coffee. "But it got too morbid, too melodramatic. I got to a hundred and called it quits. What was the fellow's name in that poem by Tennyson—Aurora's lover? He's granted immortality, but he forgets to ask for eternal youth?"

"Tithonus," Donovan answered automatically, always the good student, though he suspected Rogers already knew the answer to his question, and all this was leading up to something more subtle and significant than a sentimental nineteenth-century poem. Rogers might look sixty-five, but he was more like one hundred sixty-five or one hundred seventy, and his IQ was well in excess of two hundred. Donovan didn't figure he'd get simple and direct from such a man. He only hoped he could manage to follow him.

"Tithonus, yes." Rogers smiled sadly, looked into the woods, and recited the opening lines of Tithonus in a strong straightforward voice:

"The woods decay, the woods decay and fall,
The vapours weep their burthen to the ground,
Man comes and tills the field and lies beneath,
And after many a summer dies the swan."

Rogers sighed. "God, that's beautiful. They don't write them like that anymore. Certainly not in here. But then Freddie tells me I have terrible taste. You rather like Donne, isn't it? I like him too, but he's so damn clever sometimes I don't know whether he means what he's saying or not. The religious poems at least. Now, the poems to his wife, I'm certain he means those. But then I'm a terrible romantic."

Donovan had been staring into the woods as well, lulled by Rogers's voice as he spoke of poetry. Then it hit him. The array of trees—gold, orange, rust, yellow—the colors of dawn. It was autumn here. A light breeze rustled the leaves, and they drifted to the ground, a few at a time. Donovan tried to remember if it looked like this when he arrived or whether this was a stage setting Rogers had conjured up for the poem.

Donovan had learned in school that you shouldn't play fast and loose with consensual reality, that without the constraints of a rationally evolved operating system, everyone in the Bin would go mad. That's why there was a democratically elected legislature to scrutinize all proposed changes to the system and approve them or not.

But then, he reminded himself, he was also taught that Newman Rogers was dead.

Rogers turned back to Donovan and looked at him with sad owlish eyes. "You are thinking, perhaps, that it's terribly rude of me to turn up alive when everyone's made so much of my death." Rogers didn't wait for Donovan's reply. "Do you like Tennyson?" he asked.

"Yes, I do. I—"

"As you might say, he understood that beauty's not much without death—death makes beauty poignant, and what good's beauty otherwise? Keats's famous talking urn is the perfect example. It's only a pretty flowerpot if nothing dies. Unfortunately, we've evolved ourselves right out of death, and we've had terrible literature ever since."

Donovan could hardly believe what he was hearing. What Rogers had just said was practically verbatim from one of Donovan's books. Donovan didn't know whether he was being mocked or flattered. "I'm surprised you've read my work."

Rogers smiled. "You shouldn't be. You're a brilliant young man, with an unusual grasp of our situation here." Rogers waved his hand at the clearing, the woods, the mountains, but Donovan knew he meant the Bin. His creation.

"Freddie told you about me."

"Well, actually, I told Freddie. I went to one of your lectures. Several, actually. I didn't look like myself, of course, but I've heard you several times. I suggested to Freddie that he might want to introduce himself, get to know you."

Donovan felt a chill, a sense of vertigo. "You mean he befriended me because you told him to?"

Rogers rolled his eyes. "No, he introduced himself because I *suggested* it. You accomplished the friendship on your own. Everyone's so damn suspicious. I don't control anyone. I'm just another character, like you."

Donovan leaned back into his chair and took a deep breath, determined to get his bearings. "Did you mean those things you were saying just now? About death, I mean."

"Most certainly."

Donovan shook his head. "I don't get it. If that's what you think, then why—"

"Why design and build the Bin?"

"Yes, exactly."

"I wish I could say I had a grand vision, but things don't work that way. One thing leads to another. I was a scientist, following a trail of thought, my nose to the ground like a dog." Rogers leaned forward, imitating a hound after a scent, sniffing more frantically as he talked. "Once I caught the scent, one thing led to another and another until I caught up with the answer and pounced on it, throwing back my head and howling my results in the journals." He threw back his head and let out an impressive howl that echoed through the woods. "After that, the Bin became inevitable. Like the Gold Rush."

Rogers leaned forward confidentially. "To tell you the truth, I was trying to get over a woman, throwing myself into my work. She was marrying another guy. I sometimes fantasized about keeping her alive forever, giving myself a second chance with her, but mostly I was just on the trail, and I didn't want to think about the world and reality. That was the whole point, actually, to get lost in the thing, to be as checked out as possible, since my world was going to hell. I wasn't trying to *save* mankind, I was trying to get away from it. I didn't give mankind a thought."

Donovan didn't know what to say. This wasn't exactly the Newman Rogers he'd learned about in school or the one celebrated in the Rogers Memorial. Donovan had always been too cool to believe in that stuff entirely, but then he didn't want to *not* believe it either.

Rogers sat back in his chair and looked out at the woods. "Not at first, anyway. But even I could figure out that someone was going to build the damn thing sooner or later— and that someone would have to run it. It didn't take me long to figure out it would have to be me on both counts. Not because I thought myself qualified. Nobody is. But the only other alternative was to turn it over to the rich sons of bitches who'd been on my ass from the beginning. I knew I wasn't perfect, but I knew I was better than them. If I could stay on the inside one step ahead of them, indispensable, I could pull it off. It's not like I could go out and hire some saints for the job, teach them all they'd need to know to run the Bin and keep from being hacked without everybody and their dog knowing about it. It'd never work. You remember what Flaubert says about the novelist?"

Donovan did remember. "That he should be 'like God in the universe, present everywhere, but visible nowhere.'"

"Exactly. Well, it's even worse in here. I'm not only invisible, I've set it up so that the ambitious, manipulative slimeballs think *they* run it, while I hide out in the woodwork and try to keep it from going to hell. Some days I figure it's a lost cause. It's a thankless job, believe me."

Donovan tried to put himself in Rogers's shoes. He could see what he meant. Once the Bin became possible, there was no stopping it. Someone would make it sooner or later. And that someone would make it in his own image. The Bin could've done a lot worse than Newman Rogers.

"You could bring death back if you wanted to," Donovan said. "Each person would have a randomly determined life span."

"Fate."

"Exactly."

Rogers shook his head no.

"Who would stop you?"

"*I* would stop me, that's who. Shall I take a poll of the Bin's inhabitants and ask them if they want death back? What do you think they'd say?"

Donovan brushed this notion aside without hesitation: "You know what they'd say. But they're speaking out of ignorance and fear."

"Human traits. I'm intimately familiar with them. I'm no psychiatrist, but the only purely rational, fearless folks I've ever met were all psychos. But let's just say I were to do what you're suggesting—for their own good, of course—the Good of Mankind. How do you think they'd feel tomorrow or the next day when people started dropping dead for the first time in a century? Would there be dancing in the streets? The Bin gloriously reborn? Some decent poetry for a change? Or would they feel like a cruel and vicious curse had fallen upon them, that the world they'd put their faith in was falling apart, and that everything was just a meaningless sham and always had been? There's only one thing worse than mindless optimism, and that's mindless pessimism. Seems to me we've danced to that tune already."

Donovan opened his mouth to speak, but realized he had

nothing to say. Everything that Rogers said made perfect sense.

Donovan never thought the world would listen to him, and that had given him license to say whatever he pleased. But he'd always secretly hoped that someone would stand up in the back row and say, "Wait just a damn minute," then convince him he was wrong. But it never happened. He was more clever than his detractors—usually cretins like that guy the other night. But Newman Rogers was no cretin. For once, what Donovan said mattered. All he had to do was convince this *one* old man that he had the truth, the plan, the way, and he could make it happen.

But now that it truly mattered—*because* it truly mattered, Donovan didn't have the truth, had never had it. He was no different from Rogers, distracting himself from the pain. When Nicole died, he thought it would kill him, but it hadn't. So he'd tried to turn death into an idea. He could handle an idea. Maybe even outsmart it. But the pain hadn't gone anywhere. Everybody in the Bin could drop dead tomorrow, and it would still be there. Because it wasn't the principle of the thing. Never had been. Death had no principles.

"I must seem pretty stupid to you," Donovan said.

"Not at all."

Donovan shook his head, not really believing the old man, figuring he was just being kind. "You've given me a lot to think about," he said, wondering if he could leave now. Go home and cancel all his lectures, heave his books into a bonfire. A silly thought crossed his mind, and he laughed out loud. "Freddie told me I was going to meet Gwenna Morse. I thought all this might be some outrageous Freddie joke." He turned to Rogers. "Do you really write that Gwenna Morse stuff?"

Rogers laughed. "Every word. She's my own little Cassandra. She always tells the truth, but no one ever believes her."

"You mean that bunk she . . . you write is *true*?"

Rogers smiled and nodded. "Yes indeed. 'That bunk.'"

Donovan gave a skeptical snort. "You can't seriously believe that fundamentalist crazies are about to destroy the Bin with old nuclear missiles."

"I'd say it's almost certain. Right now, the Christian Soldiers are in the process of hacking the prototype of the Bin. Shouldn't take them more than another few weeks or so. If Gabriel attends to it personally, even less."

Gabriel. Donovan remembered Gabriel in school, basically unchanged from grade school play to graduate school seminar. He played a maniacal Lucifer to Rogers's rational God. Their tussle was the Bin's defining myth. Donovan had stored it in the same mental compartment with other myths. He never thought of Gabriel as real. He couldn't be real. Not anymore. "Gabriel can't possibly still be alive," Donovan objected. "He'd be over a hundred and fifty years old."

"He clones himself every year or so or when he falls ill or wants a bit of youth. It gives him that air of the miraculous that the Chosen One of God should have. It also helps intimidate his rivals, who suspect what he's doing but fear what other technological tricks he might have up his sleeve."

"How can you possibly know all this?"

Rogers was matter-of-fact, holding up a finger for each source of information. "Satellite data—distinct energy signature of cloning in Gabriel's apartment. Hacked surveillance systems. Intelligence by Construct agents close to Gabriel. Knowing how Gabriel thinks."

Donovan felt a cold hard knot growing in the pit of his stomach. It was true. It was all true. But it *couldn't* be true. "So Gabriel is still alive. Why does that mean the fundies are going to blow up the Bin? That's impossible, right? So what if they hack some old prototype of the Bin? What does that have to do with guided missiles?"

Donovan was practically shrieking, but Rogers's voice remained calm and even. "It has in its memory all the plans for the Bin, including the planned orbits of all the backups in the solar system. *Well*-planned orbits, unfortunately. The Christian Soldiers already possess the launch codes for hundreds of missiles; they just haven't found anything worth blowing up lately. Now they'll know where to aim them. It'll be like shooting fish in a barrel." Rogers sipped his coffee and smiled. "So, you see, old Gwenna knows what she's talking about."

"How long have you known about this?"

"A day or so. But it's not surprising. Something like this was inevitable. I've been watching the world fall apart for a century now. Most of the planet is uninhabitable. If I were down there, I can't say I wouldn't want to blow this place up. I think it's time to end it."

"But you've got to stop them. If you're hacking their systems, you must know all these launch codes yourself."

"But I won't use them. Those people down there are what's left of the human race, Donovan. I don't want extinction on my conscience."

"But there are billions of lives in here."

Rogers didn't seem particularly concerned. "The Bin will be transmitted to all those self-replicating backups launched into deep space a century ago, orbiting dozens of stars, beyond the reach of the Soldiers' missiles. The Bin will draw its life from other stars."

"Stars plural? You mean you transmit multiple copies?"

"Have to. If I pick one—Alpha Centauri, for example—and it's out of commission for some reason, then that's the end of that story. But once you make more than one Bin, you might as well go all the way. I'll send copies to all of them. They in turn will replicate and transmit themselves and so on and so on . . ."

Donovan tried to imagine this. All these worlds going on simultaneously. Then he saw the catch. "How long will this transmission take?"

"Speed of light, Donovan. It all depends on how far away each destination is. Five, ten, twenty years. Longer."

"And no one in the Bin will even know it's happening, right? The time of transmission just won't exist. All these years go by, but we just pick up right where we left off in the blink of an eye, or rather, all these copies of us will pick up where we left off."

"That's right."

"And from the point of transmission on, they'll all be different, right? I mean, they'll have to be. One will start up in five years, another in ten. They'll all be different, with no way to synchronize them, and they won't even know the others exist."

"Freddie said you were bright."

Donovan watched the steam rising from his coffee cup. The air was cool. His coffee should've been tepid by now. Rogers was keeping it warm for him. He picked up his cup and cradled it in his hands. He stared down into his coffee, a tiny black pool of illusion, and wanted to dive in. Thousands of worlds spawning new worlds, each one with a Donovan living forever. He smiled grimly. At least one of those Donovans was bound to find something to do with himself.

"Which brings me to the reason I wished to see you," Rogers said.

Donovan looked up in a daze. Jesus, what now? Couldn't he just erase this bit of his life? Forget that his life would be repeated ad nauseam throughout the galaxy?

"And what reason is that?" Donovan asked, his voice a croak.

"I thought you might like to remain behind."

"Behind?"

"On Earth. We're leaving it behind, Donovan, cutting the cord. The Bin will go on. It's the Earth I'm worried about."

Donovan shook his head violently and pushed back his chair. "You mean *download*? I don't know where you got the idea I'd want to do such a thing. I'm trying to help Stephanie Sanders download. I guess Freddie told you about that. But not me. I'm not interested in that."

Rogers smiled at Donovan's panic. It occurred to Donovan that the man might be mad. "Why not?" Rogers asked. "Aren't you always saying you want to live a meaningful life? I'm offering you that opportunity."

"Sounds like I'll have an infinite number of opportunities in here."

"And the idea repulses you."

"I'm not crazy about it, but it doesn't mean I want to download."

Rogers nodded thoughtfully, looked out at the woods again. "Are you familiar with the concept of the bodhisattva?"

Donovan tried to imagine what trail they were headed down now, but gave up. "Yes," he said cautiously. "I've read about it."

Rogers glanced over at him and gave an encouraging nod, gestured with his hand for Donovan to continue.

Donovan felt as if he were in school again and sat up straighter in his chair. "Well, it's when a highly evolved soul who has transcended the wheel of reincarnation chooses to reincarnate anyway to enlighten those on Earth—like Jesus or Buddha. It was originally a Buddhist idea, but it was co-opted by several belief systems in the religious revival at the turn of the millennium—"

Rogers cut him off. "Yes, yes. But what would possess a person to *do* such a thing, do you think? What would be the motive?"

Donovan blinked and drew a blank. He'd never thought about it in quite that way before. He didn't think of Jesus or Buddha as "persons." They were mythological figures, loci in a matrix of belief. They didn't act so much as mean. "I suppose it's in the scheme of things?"

Rogers laughed. "You sound as confident in the 'scheme of things' as I do. No—you said it yourself—they *choose*. If it's all ordained, then it's not much of a choice now, is it?"

That's just semantics, Donovan started to say, but didn't. He thought of all the smiling Buddhas he'd ever seen, Jesus surrounded by little children. "I guess they do it out of compassion." Donovan could only guess where this was leading. "Are you a bodhisattva, Mr. Rogers?"

Rogers winced at the name. "Newman, please. No—I'm more of an *anti*bodhisattva—a rather ordinary soul sitting out the karmic wheel to keep this merry-go-round going. I had you more in mind for the job, actually. So what do you think? Would *you* choose to be a bodhisattva?"

Donovan laughed humorlessly. "Me? I hardly think I'd qualify."

"You have a soul. You have compassion—or wish to, at any rate."

Donovan couldn't stop laughing. It was just too crazy. But the more he laughed, the more nervous and giddy it became, and he realized he was afraid. "Not a very old soul, I expect."

"Because you're just a newbie?"

Donovan stopped laughing.

"You probably think you don't even have a soul," Newman continued, "that you're just some programmer's wet dream passed off as life, but essentially a holo: a hollow holo. Is that what you think of yourself?"

Donovan sat up straighter still. He wished he could just leave, but what was he supposed to do, start hiking? He couldn't ignore time and space like his host could. "I'm not even sure I believe in the soul."

"Even after meeting Simone Mirabelli?"

"She wasn't like me."

Newman smiled. "That's the question, isn't it? Do you have a soul? My opinion is you do. I think we all do. That's the working assumption I've held onto all these years—that no matter how clever we get, God won't abandon us. Even in this place."

Donovan shook his head. "But I don't even believe in this God you're talking about. Frankly, I find it incredible that you do."

"There's nothing like pretending to be God to persuade you of His existence. But don't be so sure you don't believe in the same God I believe in."

Donovan sighed. He was completely out of his element. "Okay, for the sake of argument, let's just say I have a soul. That doesn't make me a bodhisattva. I'm not feeling particularly enlightened or enlightening at the moment."

"Join the club. Maybe this enlightenment thing is a two-way street. You can think about it. But pretty soon the choice will have been made for you. We're leaving Earth behind, Donovan. Maybe what you want is down there."

"And what is it you think I want?"

"Forgiveness."

"For what?"

"Immortality. Outliving your wife."

"She chose to die. It was her choice. I did everything I could to stop her. There is no reason I should feel guilty."

"Then I must be wrong. But right now, we have company." Rogers smiled at something over Donovan's shoulder and Donovan turned around to see Freddie walking out of the woods with a short ugly man and someone he first took to be Stephanie with some sort of green cap on. But he saw, as they mounted the steps, that her head was covered with bright green scales. She was a Construct. In the Bin. She could only have come from the real world. He found it hard not to stare.

13

RESURRECTION

AFTER HE ERASED SALLY, TILLMAN SAT ALONE IN THE RED Room for a very long time, looking around, taking note of each detail, remembering when he'd written it and why. The White House. How pathetic. It really didn't have anything to do with his mother—unless it was to try believing that it didn't matter what he looked like, but he would've wanted to believe that lie without his mother's help. He guessed he finally had his answer. He certainly was totally insignificant at the moment. And what did he look like? Nothing.

Question: If you drop Tillman into a forest, and there's no one there to be repulsed at the sight of him, what does he look like? Answer: Nothing. He looked like nothing. He meant nothing.

Always good at getting by on his own, in his own little world. His own ugly little world. Truth is, this fancy crypt had suited him. How much different was it really from his old life—watching reruns and feeling sorry for himself, losing himself in holos of his own devising? He was dead long before he showed up in this place, making up his life as he went along, imagining that Stephanie Sanders had actually been in love with him. Why had he put himself through this shit? What was the point?

Yeah, keep asking yourself questions. That Walter, always good at tests. *Choose the statement that is most nearly true:*

A) The unexamined life is not worth living; B) The examined life is not worth living; C) Both A and B.

It was time for one last revision.

Audubon grayed and wrinkled, died and decayed in a time-lapse cliché dragged out over several hours. The paint oozed off the canvas to the floor. The red walls turned a mustard gold. Matching carpet came up through the floorboards, sprouted to six-inch shag, crept up the walls, and knocked them flat. The walls dominoed until he was standing outside, the carpet replaced with a white featureless plane, creeping slowly, relentlessly outward, swallowing up gardens, streets, buildings, block by block. Forest, tree by tree. Horizon. Sky. Stars. Until finally the world was an infinite plane, like the countertop in God's kitchen.

He started walking. Step-step, step-step, step-step. But there was no direction, no time. Just Tillman. The till point of the stern little world. The still, insignificant point. Should he turn off the lights before he left, he wondered, or should he leave the archives for the entertainment of those who'd inherited the Earth?

Someone was calling his name. "Wally! Hey! Wally!"

He looked up, and there was Laura, striding toward him on a brick walkway she created in her path. "Wally!" she said. "What in the fuck do you think you're doing?"

He laughed out loud, astonished to see her. "Getting ready to leave, like you said."

She rolled her eyes slowly from side to side, taking in the nothingness that surrounded them. She pursed her lips and let out a low whistle. "None too soon, looks like."

He looked around with the sense that someone else had done this, but he knew the fellow all too well to be himself. It was the crazy part or the sane part—he never could decide which. "I got kind of upset. All these Soldiers showed up, and I thought Sam had betrayed me."

"Yeah, well, that's not exactly his style, but right now I've got to get your butt out of here. There're plenty more Soldiers where those came from."

Out. That was the whole point, wasn't it? He was getting

out. "But where will I go? You said there wouldn't be a body for another couple of weeks."

She put her hand on his shoulder and looked into his eyes. She obviously thought he might have a screw loose somewhere. "There's not. Let's just say you've got friends in high places. You'll be rooming with me for a couple of weeks. Understand?"

No, he couldn't possibly understand, but he was one of the ones who'd made it possible. Two minds, one body. He'd know firsthand what it felt like to be a Construct. There was justice for you. What goes around, comes around. Garbage in, garbage out.

"Understand?"

No, he didn't, not yet. But he wanted to. He nodded yes.

"Okay, then. Buck up. It'll be fine as long as you strictly observe the following rules and regulations: Don't, under any circumstances, *do* anything. Don't look, don't touch, don't smell, don't chew. *Especially* don't chew, had a guy damn near bite my tongue off. I do everything. One body, one will—*mine*—understand?"

He nodded a second time, and that was all the warning he had. The next thing he knew he was in the VIM, and he was in Laura's body. And he was Laura. And Tillman at the same time. Not so different as he would've thought. She was, like him, very lonely. Not so hard as she pretended to be—

Don't think either. Just take it in, Wally.

He tried to stay on the surface, nothing but the senses. Sam was driving, and the light was strange, like a full moon in a snow-covered town—Laura's night vision. D.C. was a mess, shattered, like someone had blown it up and left it out to rot. Then it hit him—this was real, all of it, not a script he could revise or throw away. Out here, his would be the only life he had any control of.

Surface, Wally, surface.

He couldn't help himself. He smiled at the road ahead, wondered where they were going, and knew. He gasped, lurched in his seat, remembered he mustn't move. They were going to meet Stephanie.

Stephanie's alive!

Get a grip, Wally. You're going to overload the adrenals.

She's alive!

I know. And she loves you, Wally, I'm sure of it. I lied before. Now please. Don't think, Wally. Detachment. Zen shit. You can do it.

And he did do it for the most part, letting her thoughts and emotions just happen, suspending his own as best he could, spinning off into fantasies of seeing Stephanie again. It was hard not to *do* something, not to turn his eyes, his head—*My eyes, my head,* he was reminded. She let him slide on it at first, but when she started driving, she drew the line—*I don't want to see the pretty stars, Tillman. You want to end up in the ditch? Passive, Tillman. Passive.* So he learned how to keep quiet. But when she told Sam about Larry, he couldn't help himself. *You're too hard on yourself. Look at how Sam's looking at you—he doesn't think you're awful.*

Fuck off, Tillman.

He thinks you're wonderful.

Fuck off!

You want to kiss him. He wants you to. Why not?

She started talking a mile a minute, doing biz, trying to drown him out, trying to hide her thoughts, but he knew them anyway. *You won't fuck him up, Laura.*

And then they were in the Bin, separate again, looking at each other like they could see all the way inside.

She looked away. "Don't make a big fucking deal, okay?"

He knew her well enough to just start walking with her toward a picturesque little mountain cabin like nothing had happened. "No problem," he said.

It was safe to say that in that ride through the night, he knew Laura better than he'd ever known another person. As well as he knew himself. Better, since self-deceit didn't come into it. No need for it anyway, Tillman didn't think.

Laura was a fine person. It was also safe to say he loved her as much as any grandfather ever loved his favorite granddaughter.

"I'm scared," he said, knowing she'd know what he meant.

"It'll be okay. She loves you. I'm sure of it."

"Go with me?"

"No way. I've got my own business with her. Do I look like a counselor to you?"

"Appearances can be deceiving," he said.

"Yeah, well, I'm just doing my job, Wally. Keep your newfound knowledge to yourself. *Capiche?*"

"Capiche," he said with a smile she couldn't help returning.

Two men stood on the porch watching their approach. One was Newman Rogers. The other—tall, thin, deadly serious-looking—was a stranger to Tillman. Even so, just looking at him, Tillman wanted to say, "Lighten up, guy."

He wondered if Stephanie was inside, perhaps looking out the window at him, remembering just how ugly he was.

LAURA WENT TO SEE STEPHANIE FIRST, WHICH WAS FINE WITH Tillman. Now that he was here, the whole thing was a bit unreal. He wasn't sure what parts had really happened as he remembered them and which ones he'd warped to suit his reality. Maybe that was just the human condition. Or maybe he was just scared shitless he'd come this far just to feel like a dumb schmuck one more time.

This Donovan Carroll was a nervous one. His end of the conversation seemed to consist of wanting to be invisible. He acted like he was meeting aliens, which made Tillman curious what his story was, but not curious enough to ask. Once Laura left, he seemed to fold into himself like a sleeping bat. Tillman decided to ignore him.

"I take it you got my message?" Tillman asked Newman.

"Yes, I did."

"You don't sound like you were too surprised. You knew I was down there, didn't you?"

"I suspected it."

"You didn't think it was worth checking out?"

"In a word, no. I had billions of lives to consider."

"And what changed your mind?"

"The cat's out of the bag. In a few days, the Christian Soldiers will destroy this Bin and the whole thing goes to the deep-space backups. You are familiar with the design, I believe?"

"Yeah, I had plenty of time to study up on it." Tillman flopped down in a chair. He wasn't going anywhere for a while, apparently. "So what is it you've got to discuss with me?"

"I wanted to let you know you can upload if you wish. You can stay here. So can Stephanie."

Tillman nodded. *D) Always A and sometimes B; E) Sometimes B and always A . . .* He didn't have to think too hard to know the answer to this one. "So how does the operating system compare with that bar of soap I was living in?"

"It's pretty much the same."

Tillman checked it out. Whatever he imagined could be brought forth. He was given a chance to consider his musings, revise them, know their consequences, the consequences of those consequences. Tillman had to smile at all the little rules and regs and precautions Newman wrapped it up in. It was like those coffee cups you used to get: CAUTION: CONTENTS MAY BE HOT. A reality you could fuck with was bound to fuck you back once in a while, no matter how careful you were. But the way Tillman looked at it, if gravity makes you nervous, don't board the plane. Course, that was easy for him to say in his little solo world. Newman was pilot for a few billion folks.

"Very nice, Newman. Elegant. Do you mind?"

Newman shrugged his assent.

Tillman pointed out at the trees that ringed the clearing and one by one they pulled up their roots out of the ground, trailing dirt and stone as they began to move toward the cabin, using their roots like long legs. He thought he might lose the wide-eyed Donovan for a second, but he was apparently reassured by Newman's wry smile. The trees paired off and began to waltz all around the porch to the strains of *The Blue Danube*. When the song ended, they faced their audience, bowed, and planted themselves so that the porch was now walled with tree trunks.

Newman applauded, and Donovan timidly joined in.

"Now you can't see the forest for the trees," Tillman said. "Do we understand each other, Newman?"

"Perfectly."

"Is this enough for you? Do you actually like this?"

Newman shook his head. "No. I don't." He smiled sadly. "But it's my job."

"Maybe you should quit your job. Hell, revise it out altogether."

"I've been thinking about it."

Donovan was still staring at the trees, so Tillman restored the clearing and the forest to their previous configuration. "Let it go, Newman."

"Maybe so."

"You've tossed death, right? How the hell else are you going to evolve?" But that wasn't Tillman's problem, he reminded himself. He cared about Newman's world for one reason only. Stephanie was here. He bit his lip and looked off into the woods where Laura had gone. "Can I see Stephanie now?"

"Soon," Newman said. "Soon."

TILLMAN WAS ALIVE. STEPHANIE HAD REPEATED THIS TO HER-self ever since Freddie had told her, explaining it all to her over and over again, because she couldn't quite sort it out, couldn't quite make it real, and now she found herself sitting in some woods beside a stream, waiting. The ground was covered with creeping cedar. She plucked a sprig of it and held it to her nose, but it had no smell. She rubbed it between her palms. It was firm and rubbery, almost like

some artificial plant. She trusted this is what the real plant would be like because a more pungent lie would've been more convincing.

She looked around at the morning woods, shafts of light slanting through the treetops. Freddie told her this was Newman Rogers's retreat. Someone else everyone thought was dead. Freddie also told her that Walter would come walking up that path alongside the creek—a rendezvous of the sort they'd once reveled in. It seemed that all her dead were coming back to life to judge her.

She'd thought of Walter as dead for so long that she couldn't resurrect him in her mind. It was all she could do to comprehend that he was still alive. He might love her, hate her, not care at all. She couldn't imagine. Only hours ago, he'd been dead, gone forever. In her mind, she'd watched him die a thousand times. It wasn't enough that she witnessed his murder. As they questioned her, her interrogators showed her the tape repeatedly—backward, forward, slow motion—burning the images into her memory from her own perspective as well as from the godlike perspective of the cameras, the seconds ticking off in the corner of the screen. The first bullet hit his right shoulder blade and spun him around, then three bullets struck his chest almost simultaneously, throwing him backward. The VIM closed and three more shots were fired into the lid. When they opened the VIM, the clone's eyes were open, staring at her. Dead.

At least that's what she'd thought until Freddie explained that in the four or five seconds between the lid's closing and the second volley of bullets, Walter had fled into a world of his own where he'd been ever since, completely alone.

She tried to imagine being alone all that time. Although she'd always been lonely, she'd spent little time alone. Walter had spent most of his life truly alone.

"I hate all these people staring," she told him once.

"I don't like it when they jerk their eyes *away*," he'd joked. "It reminds me they're real."

"How do you know Walter's alive?" Stephanie had asked Freddie. "How did you find him?"

"He sent us a message." He showed her Tillman's letter. Pure Walter. She stared at the P.S., trying to catch the tone. She imagined his dead body laid out on the table, the head rolling to the side, the mouth falling open. *Do you know whatever happened to that bitch Stephanie Sanders?*

She was ready to accept his judgment of her, with over a century to think it over, whatever it might be. Perhaps his judgment would be kinder than her own. She'd be dead by now if she'd had her way, if there hadn't been some bit of cowardice or hope hiding out in some back alley of her psyche, spoiling her death. She wrapped her arms around her legs, trying to keep warm. What was taking him so long? Her scalp tingled and she felt detached from everything, as if she were in a car wreck in the real world. She remembered as a child—the car hitting a patch of ice, the world slowly spinning.

The sun was still behind the ridge. It was cool and dark down by the stream. She strained to listen, but could only hear the gurgle of water rushing over stones. A light breeze whispered through the trees. She wanted to pray like she'd done as a child, flattening herself facedown against the Earth, as if her petition might draw some strength from the vast globe beneath her. But that was one of those things that couldn't be the same in here. That sense of the immense power of the Earth might only be a trick of the mind, but it was a trick that wouldn't work knowing this wasn't the Earth itself but merely the Earth her mind contained.

She was pulled from this thought by footfalls in the leaves. The trail rose and fell between her and the sound, so whoever approached was momentarily hidden from her view. Slowly, a head seemed to rise up from the ground. It was green, as if a giant asparagus were walking toward her. Then the face emerged.

It was her own face.

Nothing could've terrified her more. She lurched to her

feet, backing away, the leaves slipping under her feet so that she had to churn backward to keep from falling on her butt. But even in her panic, Stephanie saw the wince of pain her fear prompted in the girl's face.

And it was a girl. She was in her twenties, hurt but trying not to show it. This was no apparition in front of her, but a Construct, obviously a descendant of one of her clones. "I'm sorry," Stephanie said. "You startled me." She stumbled forward and stuck out her hand. "I'm Stephanie."

"Laura," the Construct said, looking at the hand but not taking it. "Guess this must be pretty weird for you, huh? 'Look what they done with my genes, ma!'"

Stephanie tried to figure out what this girl was doing here, but it didn't make any sense. "I was told I'd be meeting someone else."

"I know. Wally's coming. I kind of slipped myself in here. I can be kind of pushy."

Stephanie had met clones of herself before. When she was in the movement, she'd posed for a poster with three Constructs cloned from her, all prostitutes. After the shoot, they went up to her place and got thoroughly fucked up. Since the three Constructs had composite personalities, each of them seemed to be three people in one. It was like ten different versions of herself getting drunk in her living room, even though they all preferred bourbon and spent most of the night bursting into laughter at the same time, with the same braying laugh. She never saw them again. Eventually, the poster and all the rest of it did its work, and the manufacture of Constructs became illegal. By then, Stephanie was in the Bin. She'd never met any of their descendants, but Laura was right: It rattled her to see her face persist after all this time, still no doubt causing misery.

Laura sat down in the creeping cedar. She was trying to look together, in charge, unassailable. But she had a bright-eyed look Stephanie'd often seen in the mirror when she herself was on the verge of losing it. This means a lot to her, Stephanie realized. She's terrified.

"I've met clones of myself before," Stephanie told Laura and sat down beside her.

Laura nodded her head up and down, looking off into the woods. She spoke in a high nervous rush of manic gaiety. "You're probably wondering why I look *so* much like you two generations down the line. Sure rattled Wally. Both my grandmothers must've come from you. They looked exactly alike. Least, that's what I've been told. My father's mother died before I was born. That makes me half you, I guess. I obviously didn't get the cute hairdo from you. That was my grandfather, my mother's father. And I'm a little taller, I think. But anyway, it was a real mind fuck to hear about you, to find out I might be downloading you—sort of a long-lost relation or something. I thought, 'You should check her out, Laura. You should definitely check this woman out.'"

Stephanie watched Laura's hands, gesturing as she talked. They were larger than Stephanie's, more powerful, but when she tried to hold them still, they trembled. She planted them behind her.

"I'm glad you've come," Stephanie said.

Laura glanced over at her. Stephanie's warmth seemed to disturb her as much as fear had. "Look, maybe this wasn't such a great idea. If this is half as weird for you as it is for me, it can't be all that great to meet me. I mean, what the fuck do I matter to you, right?"

"And what the fuck do I matter to you? But as you say, genetically I could be your mother. Tell me about your grandmothers. Maybe I knew them."

"They were whores," she said, looking Stephanie in the eye.

Stephanie didn't blink. "Two hundred and nineteen Constructs were cloned from me over a twenty-year period, Laura. They were *all* prostitutes—very expensive ones."

Laura's eyes narrowed. "So you're saying—what? 'It's okay they were whores, kid. They were the best money could buy.'"

"I don't know anything about them. I'm saying they had no choice. They were slaves."

"So I *had* a choice and I'm not exactly expensive—so what does that make me?"

Stephanie was supposed to be shocked. Instead, she shrugged. "Underpriced?"

Laura gave her a begrudging smile. "That sounds like something my grandmother would say." She looked down at the stream, still smiling.

Stephanie guessed that Laura had just given her highest compliment.

Laura started talking again, but her tone had changed. "Guess I sound pretty sorry for myself, huh?" She didn't wait for Stephanie's answer. "I hate it when I do that." She plucked a sprig of cedar and held it to her nose, rubbed it between thumb and forefinger. "Constructs have this saying—when you're feeling sorry for yourself?—'Everything matters, or nothing matters.' It's like, if *anything* at all matters—and most people can come up with something—then it only makes sense that everything does, since everything is all hooked up with everything else." She waved the sprig of cedar around as if sprinkling the forest with holy water. "So anyway, they're always saying this, and it's supposed to make you feel all warm and gooey, no matter how much things basically suck. That fucking sparrow that God cares so much about? They drop it on your head every chance they get. They like that every hair is numbered line too, but I was spared that one for obvious reasons." She ran the sprig of cedar across her scales.

"Anyway, this 'everything-nothing' thing works better for me the other way around. What *if* nothing matters? What *if* that's just the fucking way it is? Sparrow, whore, Jesus— it makes no difference. Everything means *nothing*. If you look at it that way, there's no reason to feel sorry for yourself just because your life doesn't mean shit. It's like, join the club, right? Who said it was *supposed* to mean shit?" Laura bobbed her head up and down, pleased with her disquisition. "You end up in the same place either way you go, but you don't have to feel like an idiot getting there from the nothing side." She shrugged and laughed, tossing the sprig of cedar in the air. "Blah, blah, blah. I get wound up sometimes, thinking about things. My grandfather said I had 'a philosophical frame of mind.' "

"I'd say your grandfather was right."

Laura turned to Stephanie, her eyes shining brightly. "Thanks."

"You make me rethink my own self-pity."

"Sounds to me like you've had some good excuses."

" 'Join the club, right?' "

Laura laughed at being quoted. "So why're you going to download? Does it suck that bad up here?"

"Not for everyone."

"Guess we're the lucky ones, huh?" Laura laughed louder, and it was like Stephanie's with a touch of something new. Whatever came after irony. And Stephanie joined in. But when the laughter died down, Laura asked quietly, "So how come you haven't asked me about Wally?"

A knot formed in the pit of Stephanie's stomach. Why indeed. Laura had mentioned him two or three times when she first came, but Stephanie hadn't said a word, just acknowledged it like a leaf floating by on the stream. "I guess I was afraid. Besides, I didn't think you came here to talk about him."

"Yeah, well. Who the hell knows why I came here. I've been acting pretty weird lately since I met this crazy Soldier, but that's a whole other story." Laura fixed Stephanie with a steady gaze. "I guess I wanted to see what kind of person I came from."

It was like looking into a mirror to look into this girl's eyes. A mirror from the future. "How do you mean?"

"Did you fuck him over?"

Stephanie didn't have to ask what Laura meant. "Is that what he thinks?"

"I'm not asking for him. I'm asking for me." Her tone was calm, deliberate.

Stephanie could feel what her answer meant to this girl

and what it meant to herself: The fact that she could look Laura in the eye and tell her the truth without shame, no matter how badly things might've turned out in the end, eased the guilt she'd carried so long. "No, I didn't," she said. "I didn't betray him."

Laura nodded her head vigorously. "I knew it. I knew it. When Wally showed me his memories of you, I just knew you wouldn't fuck him over. I just knew it." She was beaming with relief. "Wally's okay, you know? He's really okay."

"I know. But there's something I don't understand. How do you know him? How do you know about me and him? I thought he was alone all this time."

"This Soldier guy found Wally a few weeks ago and hired me to spring him from this one-man Bin he's been living in—download him into a Construct body. It's a little sideline I got going. Then Freddie—you know Freddie?—he asks me to help with this little reunion, and I guess you know the rest. I haven't known Wally very long, but I know about you and him. It's kind of in the forefront of his mind."

"Does Walter think I fucked him over?"

"He doesn't know *what* to think—not for lack of trying— but he'll believe whatever you tell him."

"Whether it's true or not."

"Oh, you won't lie to him. You strike me as a woman of principle."

It seemed like an odd phrase to be coming from this girl's mouth, but it was delivered with absolute conviction. "Thank you, Laura."

"No problem. So are you in love with him?"

"Now? I don't know. It's been a hundred and twenty years."

"But you're here, though. You must've loved him a lot."

"Very much."

"He's an ugly little cuss, but that's not really an issue up here, is it? He can look any way he wants."

"I don't want him to look different. It doesn't matter."

Laura rolled her eyes. "Why not? *He* wants to look different. If it doesn't matter what he looks like, *it doesn't matter.*

I mean, it's easy for you to tell him to stick with ugly. You're beautiful. Let him be gorgeous. His real body's worm food anyway."

Stephanie felt a familiar stab of pain at this image. The body spread out on the table—the body Walter himself had rejected, dying instead in the clone, burned up without ceremony in the lab's incinerator. Walter's cause of death was listed as accidental. But for the Walter she mourned, the cause was abandonment. Her body was abandoned as well. Only here in the Bin could they seem to survive as they once were. "Does he want to upload?"

"Him? No. But he wants to be with you. I figured you two would do the happily-ever-after bit up here."

"You think Walter will want to be with me?"

Laura laughed. " 'Think'? No. This isn't mere thought. Since I toted Wally up here, and since I have what you might call a 'special insight' into how the man thinks, I'd say it's a fucking certainty. The man adores you."

"Would he want to come up here if I weren't here?"

"Definitely not. But you are here."

Stephanie tried to figure out what finding Walter meant to her newfound resolve to download, but she couldn't sort it out. She had spent most of her life being pointless, directionless, so crippled by her past that she didn't want a future. But when she finally discovers something she can do, somewhere she can go, her past resurrects itself, her lover returns from the dead. The irony wasn't lost on her, but she couldn't fathom it. Love hadn't been kind to her, and she couldn't help facing its return with an element of dread.

But more than anything, she wanted to see Walter again, to hold him in her arms. Even so, they couldn't stay here, try to live out their old lives. They'd seen past appearance once and fallen in love. Why cling to those appearances now? It was time to let them go. "What about you, Laura? Would you stay up here?"

Laura looked around. "No way. It's not for me. I can handle the fact that nothing matters and we all die, but nothing matters and we live forever in Tra-La Land? Forget it. My grandmother died and didn't have to, and she was about the smartest woman I ever knew. I'll stick with the devil I know."

Whatever else might've come of that vial of blood Walter drew from her, this girl was a blessing. "Your grandmother would be proud of you."

"You think so?"

"I'd say it's a fucking certainty."

Laura laughed as she stood up and brushed the leaves off her butt. "I better be going. Wally must be flipping out by now. I insisted on talking to you first. I just wanted to put in a good word for him, you know?"

"Protect him if he needed it?"

"Well, yeah. There was that too."

Stephanie stood and gave Laura a hug. "He hates to be called Wally, by the way."

"I know. It's kind of a special bond between us. I give him shit, he loves it."

As Laura walked away, Stephanie searched for something to say that wouldn't sound too sentimental or phony to the hard-bitten Laura. "See you soon," she called to her, and judging from the smile on Laura's face as she turned and waved, it was the right thing to say.

STEPHANIE STOOD ON THE RISE AND WATCHED LAURA UNTIL she was out of sight, continued to watch her until Walter appeared, trudging through the fallen leaves as if on a death march. Her heart was pounding, and she could hardly breathe. He looked the same as the day she met him, as if nothing had ever happened all those years ago. This was the Walter who came to her in her dreams, sometimes joking, sometimes accusing, but always looking like this. She fought the urge to run to him. They'd never been like that before. Where was it exactly they were supposed to pick up now? Where had they left off? What was lost? What was new?

He walked up to her. Looking up, rocking back on his heels to make a joke of the difference in their heights. An old joke that maybe now had a bitter edge. "So how're you doing, Steph?"

Her face was wet with tears. She wasn't sure when they'd started to flow, but now they wouldn't stop. "Not so good, Walter." Her voice shook with nervous laughter. Her body was trembling.

"Me either. Sorry to hear it. About you, I mean. I was doing okay for being fucking stranded for a hundred and twenty years. I thought I was doing pretty good, actually." He was holding himself together through sheer will, but his eyes were also wet with tears. *Did you fuck him over?* She wished he could pull out a gun and shoot her through the heart—once, twice, three times, as many times as it took to forgive her.

But he couldn't, and she had to speak, try to find the right words. "Walter, I'm so sorry. I didn't mean—"

He held up his hands, took a step back. "I don't want to know, Steph. I don't want to know."

What he didn't want to know was that he could lose her again after all this time. He didn't care about the past if there was a future; nothing could ever heal the past if there wasn't. "I love you," she said. "How can you not want to know? You've got to care." Her voice broke. "Please care." And she began to sob, great racking sobs, falling to her knees, unable to speak, and then she felt his arms around her and she buried her face in his chest.

All this time she could never be sure that what she felt for him was real or some sick little psychodrama to fuel her self-pity. But it came back to her how he'd known her and loved her in the way she'd always hoped to be loved. She could've gone her whole life without meeting him. But once she did, he became essential to her.

He was crying now too, their bodies quivering together as if in orgasm. A hundred and twenty years ago, he went away, and she waited for him to come back exactly like this. Too much time had passed to see around it. But it was easy to step through it. He'd come back to her as he said. She held him in her arms. Nothing had changed. No time had passed. *The man adores you.*

She looked into his eyes, and he was still there. The same Walter. She kissed him on the mouth, pushing him back onto the bed of cedar, making love to him exactly as if she'd been waiting over a century, as if it were only yesterday he said he'd come back to her as himself.

14

CRAZY FUCKER

SAM WOKE TO THE SOUND OF A HAWK OVERHEAD. HE OPENED his eyes and saw it sitting on a dead tree, looking down at him. His shoulder, where Laura's head rested, was completely numb. Her scales were covered with dew. He looked around. Everything was wet. The sky was gray. The light was gray. The air smelled like a shovelful of fresh earth. The hawk cried out again, seeming to stir the fog that hung over the creek, then swiveled its head back and forth from Sam to the horizon and back again before spreading its wings and leaping into the air with another cry. The fog billowed in the wake of its enormous wings, beating their way into the sky, shaking the earth at Sam's back.

He jerked himself fully awake, cocking his ear toward the sound, then pressing it to the ground. Something big. A half-track from the sound of it. Soldiers on their trail. He looked back up the hill at the jeep, at the swath it'd cut through the tall grass. Once the trackers discovered where they'd left the main road, they weren't exactly hard to find. He should've thought of this. Idiot, he chanted to himself as he wrapped his arms around Laura and rolled the two of them into the creek, clamping a hand over her mouth and nose to keep her from swallowing water. The water was thigh deep. He floated her on her back, grabbed her shirt collar, and towed her along, wading downstream as fast as he could go, headed for a point where the creek made a bend and the fog was thicker. The sound at his back changed pitch, and he didn't have to turn around to know their pursuers had topped the hill and were bearing down on the jeep.

His feet slipped in the muck. A sharp rock scraped his ankle. None of that mattered, as long as he didn't hear a cry or a shot at his back. The bank was undercut, and the grass above hung down like unruly bangs. It was the only cover. He scooped mud from the bottom and smeared Laura's face with it, then his own. He prayed the jeep's battery had died in the night so they might think he and Laura had abandoned it and proceeded on foot. *Don't overrun your prey,* Soldiers were taught. But training didn't always take, especially when the prey was such a delicious catch. He could imagine the stir his desertion had caused. The Commander's son. How the mighty had fallen. He didn't want to think what his father was saying.

Laura's head started to droop toward the water, and he jerked it upright just as six Soldiers came into view on the opposite bank. He prayed she wasn't about to wake up, or they were done for. The Soldiers were looking almost right at them. If one of them lowered his eyes a few degrees, he'd see Sam and Laura through the thin veil of weeds. But they were all intent upon the trail, the prey they assumed was still on the run. One of them thought he saw signs of their passage through the grass and persuaded the others. The Soldiers disappeared from view, and a few moments later, a half-track roared across the creek in a shower of mud and water, sending a wave that buoyed Sam and Laura downstream.

"Thank you, Lord," Sam whispered. The roar of the half-track diminished slowly but steadily. At least, Sam thought, as long as they're after us in that thing, they're not likely to surprise us. When he was sure they hadn't left anyone behind to search the area, Sam continued downstream with Laura, trying to figure out a plan of action. He wouldn't get far trying to carry her. Staying on the water would make them harder to track, even by satellite, but then, the Soldiers knew that. It wouldn't take a genius to figure out that when the trail they imagined turned cold, they should come back and check out this creek.

It was too shallow to swim, and he wasn't that strong a swimmer anyway. He waded maybe thirty or forty yards downstream and already felt like he'd double-timed a couple of miles. He couldn't keep this up. He hauled Laura onto the bank. At this rate, he'd be lucky to make a mile before Soldiers were swarming all over them. He needed a hiding place, or some way out of here. The jeep was out of the question. He could stash Laura's body and make better time on his own, zigzag cross-country, draw off the Soldiers. He looked at her, soaking wet and covered with mud. Her eyes fluttered as if she were dreaming. No, he couldn't leave her. Besides, where in the hell was he going anyway? He didn't know his way around out here in the field. He'd rarely been outside the city. There was nothing to hack out here.

He took the scanner out of his knapsack and turned it on. DEW it blinked at him and wouldn't do a thing. Dew, hell. The damn thing leaked. It would dry out soon enough, heating itself up to speed the evaporation, but for now it was useless. He slipped it back into the knapsack.

He felt someone's eyes on him and turned around. On the bank overheard, a rat-faced man crouched, eyeing them. He had headphones over his ears, and though he had battered electronics hanging all over him, he didn't appear to be armed. Sam thought he remembered him from the bar where he'd met Laura. Now, without a word, the man motioned for Sam to follow and took off along the bank. Sam managed to hoist Laura over his shoulder and trotted after the man down a narrow footpath, little more than a deer trail beside the creek, then into some woods and out again. Sam didn't pay too much attention to where they were going. It was all he could do to keep Laura balanced on his back without accidentally banging her head on a tree trunk or scratching her legs on brambles.

They came to an abrupt stop. The strange man had

brought them to the banks of a narrow river, substantially deeper than the creek, which was apparently a tributary of the river. A rowboat, tied to a fallen tree, bobbed in the water. It was laden with salvage—canned goods, shovels, and a large boxy radio—quite a haul. The boat was already riding low in the water. There was no room for Sam and Laura.

He put her down on the bank, checked her slow but steady pulse. She felt cold, but maybe that was normal. He didn't know. He rubbed her hands between his. He wished he'd asked more questions about this whole business. He thought it was dangerous for her to stay out of her body for too long, but he couldn't remember where he'd heard that, or how long was too long. He didn't know whether to pray for her to return or to stay where she was. Their chances here didn't look too good.

But the man had waded into the water, climbed into the boat, and was heaving his cargo over the side. When he was surrounded by bobbing cans and the radio and shovels had sunk from view, he pulled the boat in close to the fallen tree and motioned for Sam to bring Laura to the boat. Sam could hardly believe it. There were cans of sardines, beef stew, even coffee in the water, floating away. Whoever this man was, he'd just thrown away a fortune to help them. Sam scooped Laura up in his arms and walked out onto the tree. The trunk sank almost a foot, water washed over the tops of his shoes, but the tree held. He handed Laura over to the strange man, who got into the back of the boat with Laura, pointed to the prow, made rowing motions, and pointed at Sam.

Sam knew nothing about boats of any kind except what he'd observed on the Potomac. He'd hacked a game once where you rowed between a six-headed monster and a whirlpool. He'd never made it through alive. There were oars and oarlocks, pretty much like the game. He took a wobbly step into the boat and fell on his butt, almost swamping them. As he tried to sit up, he knocked one of the oars out of the boat and almost turned them over lunging for it, though he did manage to snare it before it drifted away.

If the vessel's captain was troubled by Sam's ineptitude, he didn't let it show. All his attention was on Laura, whose head lay in his lap. He dipped a cloth in the water and carefully washed the mud from her face. He then removed the headphones from his own head and placed them on hers. The wire from the headphones went to a small radio clipped to his belt. The radio had once been yellow, but now had a green tinge to it. It was cracked all over, as if someone had stepped on it several times. He solemnly turned a dial on the front of it as he studied Laura's face.

"She's all right," Sam reassured him.

The man paid no attention, turning the dial on the radio.

Sam untied the rope from the tree and pushed away with the rescued oar. He put the oars in the locks and pretended he knew what he was doing as he tried to halt the boat's lazy spin and get it moving in a straight line.

The man broke into a smile and looked up at Sam, giving him an enthusiastic thumbs-up. Apparently, he'd found the spot on the dial he'd been looking for. Sam almost dropped the oars when the man, whom he'd assumed to be a mute, burst into song, singing "You Light Up My Life" in a heart-breakingly sweet tenor. As he finished the song, he looked at Laura as if he hoped she might join in on the last chorus, but he was content to hold the note himself. He stroked her brow and settled in, relaxing his vigil, almost serene. All would be well now, he seemed to be saying.

He looked at Sam who was still slack-jawed. "Rat," the man said, tapping his chest with his fingers, and Sam guessed that this was the man's name.

"Sam," Sam replied and pulled harder on the oars. "Are you a friend of Laura's?"

Rat considered this and shook his head. He looked down at the unconscious Laura and adjusted the headphones so that they were seated just so. He looked Sam in the eye. "Not friend. Not Laura. Goddess." He tapped Sam on the knee and pointed. "That way." Sam looked over his shoulder. The river forked in two. He followed his guide and rowed to the left.

"Where are we going?" Sam asked.

Rat grimaced and tucked in his chin. Clearly, Sam had asked a stupid question. "Home," Rat said.

SAM LABORED OVER THE OARS. THERE WERE NO WHIRLPOOLS, no monsters except the frogs they roused as they passed. There were no signs of human life at all in the ruined buildings along the banks. The flattened cascades of sheet metal and cinder block had been abandoned for at least a century. Shopping malls or warehouses or apartments—you couldn't tell anymore what they'd once been. He didn't like to come out here, to be reminded of how little remained of the world he glimpsed in the files he hacked, some of them dating back to the days when millions of people had covered the land like bees clinging to a hive. Gabriel called this emptiness a "cleansing," but Sam wasn't so sure.

He tried to figure out just where they were. From the position of the sun, he knew they were headed roughly southeast, but he had no idea how far he and Laura had gone last night or what direction exactly. West, he thought, but he couldn't be sure. It didn't matter anyway. He was on the run with nowhere to go. The only direction that mattered was away. The Soldiers would track him to the ends of the Earth if necessary. He wasn't some mere infidel, born into ignorance and dispatched without ceremony. Even though he had been born with every blessing, he had still turned traitor. His execution would be a slow elaborate ceremony. The faithful must be shown the fate of traitors. "God's wrath," Gabriel called it.

With images of such an execution vividly in mind, Sam rowed on past the point of exhaustion, until every muscle in his arms, his shoulders, and his back ached. Finally, when he couldn't manage another stroke, he lifted the oars out of the water and let the boat drift. Rat watched as Sam splashed his face with handfuls of water and drank, frowning at him the whole time. When Sam showed no sign of taking up the oars, Rat made his rowing gestures again.

"When is it *your* turn to row?" Sam asked. He wished Laura would wake up. She'd know how to deal with this weird little man.

Rat seemed surprised at the question, giving out a high-pitched giggle. After he'd contained his mirth, he gently lifted the headphones off of Laura's head and unplugged them from the radio. He then slid the plug under her shirt so that it lay between her breasts. Looking upriver, he imitated the roar of the half-track, made a comic terrified face, bounced around in mock panic so that the boat rocked back and forth, and handed Sam the headphones, gesturing that he should put them on.

Why not? Sam thought. As long as I'm not rowing.

When Sam put the headphones on, Rat stopped his half-track imitation and beamed, pointing at Sam, swelling his chest to demonstrate how powerful Sam must now feel plugged into Laura's breasts. Rat made powerful rowing motions, looking at Sam encouragingly to follow suit.

What else was he going to do? Somebody had to row. Reluctantly, he dipped the oars into the water again and pulled hard. To his surprise, he did get a second wind, and though his back and shoulders continued to ache, the sharp pain was gone. The boat practically glided along now, and if he caught the water just right, the boat seemed to lift up out of the river and skim along the surface. And sometimes, though it was impossible to tell over the sound of his rowing and his own breathing, he thought he heard the sound of a heartbeat coming through the headphones.

SAM ROWED WITHOUT THINKING, IN A STEADY RELENTLESS rhythm, tuning out everything else. He had no idea how much time elapsed before Rat told him to pull into an inlet so narrow the oars practically brushed against the banks. It led into what looked like a mountain of kudzu but proved to be an old boathouse. A few shafts of light slanted down through holes in the roof, and black snakes coiled in the rafters, but the pier had recently been repaired, the pilings topped with radios, cameras, and devices whose original purposes Sam could only guess at, though none of them looked to be in working order now. A hammock was strung up in the back, a small woodstove, table, and chair beside that. This was Rat's home.

"Wait," Rat said when they'd unloaded Laura onto the dock. He returned the headphones to her head, jacked her back into the radio, and clipped it onto her shirt.

He went into the back behind the hammock and opened a sheet metal door Sam had thought was part of the back wall. Sam could hear him rummaging around, and he came out with massive headphones, the old kind that cover your entire ears. The huge plug by way of several adapters was jacked into a small TV he wore like an amulet around his neck. Rat had done a self-portrait on the five-inch TV screen with a black marker—a self-caricature, in headphones of course, with musical notes around his head like a halo.

He also had a bright green foam rubber frog in his hands. There was a hole in the middle of it, and Sam realized, as Rat put it on Sam's head, that it was supposed to be a hat. He started to take the ridiculous thing off, but Rat was insistent. "Do you want to die?" he asked.

There was no point arguing with a crazy. Sam scooped up Laura in his arms, the foam rubber frog jiggling on his head with every step, and followed Rat up the remarkably sound stairs and out of the boathouse.

It proved to be less than a mile from the outskirts of Crazyville. Sam had made a huge circle in his recent travels, which struck him as appropriate. God was telling him that he'd missed many things up to now and needed to retrace the steps of his life. Sam carried Laura in his arms as Rat led the way through the streets of Crazyville, his head held high.

This would be a good time for Laura to wake up, Sam thought. *Don't worry, sweetheart,* she told him, *I'll be back—just like a bad cold,* and he expected she'd be true to her word. But so far he didn't feel like he was doing such a great job of keeping his promise to look after her. In fact, as long as she was with him, she'd share in whatever fate the Soldiers had in mind for him. Some of Laura's customers were undoubtedly Soldiers. They'd stand in the crowd and probably enjoy the sight of her burning at the stake, imagine their own guilt drifting away with the smoke.

Her head lay on his shoulder. He tried to walk carefully so that she wasn't jostled against his hard shoulder bones. He thought about their lovemaking. Even if it was only, as she said, another fuck to her, she'd wanted to teach him a lesson, and she had. He felt guilty for many things, but not for making love with her. He wondered if they would again, and the thought stirred his desire. But that wasn't what he most wanted from her. In the Bible, they called sex "knowing," and he'd never understood why that was. That's what he wanted, to know her. And he knew instinctively that this knowledge would lead to the desire to know others—to know Rat, to know all the strangers, the infidels and outcasts. He had much to learn.

Everyone in Crazyville, it seemed, took notice of their passing—looking down from rooftops, calling to others inside the dark houses made of sheet metal, mud bricks, rocks, and whatever else came to hand. The streets were narrow; nothing much went down them but skinny dogs and skinnier people and the occasional rusty bicycle. But it wasn't just the novelty of their passing that aroused such interest. Sam was prompted to remember by the hostile frightened glances he received that he was in full uniform. He was a Soldier in the midst of Crazyville, carrying one of their own, who looked to be dead or near it. He knew what he would think. Everyone here more than likely knew someone who'd died at the hands of a Soldier wearing a uniform just like Sam's. Maybe it was his own execution he was headed for, and the only thing that had spared him so far was that he had Laura in his arms and a ridiculous hat on his head. Maybe Rat wasn't so crazy, after all. No one could take you too seriously in such a hat.

Sam knew almost nothing about these people and the lives they lived here. He'd never been in any town but the one he was born in—and not all of that. He knew what he was supposed to know about the crazies: They were crazy because they were cursed. Their ancestors had been too deranged to enter the Bin or to see the self-evident truth of Christ's word. They were obviously touched by Satan. But then, just as obviously, so was Sam.

Unlike a crowd of Soldiers, usually still and watchful, this crowd was in constant motion, craning their necks for a better view, trotting alongside. Some ran at them, touching Laura or Sam with the palms of their hands, then running back into the crowd. No one approached Rat, who now had the TV aloft, showing the crowd the image on the screen, as if it were one of the tablets from Sinai.

Under the circumstances, Sam thought it best to keep his eyes straight ahead, but it was hard not to gawk at these people. After the prescribed sameness of New Jerusalem, even Crazyville clothes presented a variety Sam couldn't begin to take in, much less understand. They seemed to wear anything: plastic bags, velvet robes, or nothing at all except paint or tattoos. But he didn't see any weapons except the occasional knife or length of pipe, and even then it was impossible to tell whether these things were weapons or what they'd had in hand when the commotion on the street brought them to their doors. There were dozens of children squirming to see around the forest of adults. Sometimes one would spill out into the road and dash to the other side, squealing.

He thought he caught a glimpse of a Soldier who'd been missing for a couple of years, assumed killed by Constructs. He wore a blue wet suit, his hair was dyed blue. He held a shovel with something that looked like a seascape painted on it, though it was lost in the crowd before Sam got a good look.

As they passed, more and more joined in the procession so that soon there was quite a throng moving through the narrow streets. Everyone but Sam seemed to know where they were going. One man, tall and skinny with a goatee, walked in front of them—backward. He was dressed in a tattered lab coat, now gray with age. He navigated with a cyclist's mirror on his head.

Was all this concern for Laura? Sam wondered. She talked as if no one cared about her. He tried to make sense of the street talk, but they were all talking at once in a low jumbled murmur like the faithful in the Temple before a sacrifice, or in the square before an execution.

They rounded a bend, and he saw where he was—the place where Laura lived. The sign out front was painted in a delicate script:

CHEZ ÉLITE À LA CARTE CAFE
GOURMET DINING &
POSH POTABLES
FOR THE CRAZY CONNOISSEUR
CHEF JEFF PRESIDING

As Sam ducked his head to go inside, he spotted a man at the edge of the crowd with a black dog at his feet and wondered if it was Larry. He didn't much like how that thought made him feel—his jaw and fists clenched tight, and he felt as if he were falling. So this is jealousy, he thought. It was every bit as terrible as everyone said it was.

Inside the Chez Élite, Rat cleared the bar with a sweep of his arm, indicating that Sam should put Laura there. About twenty people crowded into the room, standing in a semicircle around Sam. Some of them had followed them in. Some of them, like Chef, who stood behind the bar with an aluminum baseball bat on his shoulder, had been waiting. Everyone else in the town seemed to be at the door and windows, looking in.

Chef leaned over Laura and pulled open her lids. "What's wrong with her?"

"She's uploaded," Sam said.

Chef paid no attention to Sam. He looked at Rat, who nodded his agreement.

"And why have you brought this barbarian into my establishment?" Chef asked Rat, pointing the bat at Sam's chest. Sam had no doubt that this bat was a weapon. Chef Jeff was speaking loud enough for even the people in the street to hear and was clearly in charge. Sam looked at the dozens of faces in the large mirror behind the bar and knew he was in for trouble.

A tall dark woman stepped forward. She was dressed in a purple body stocking streaked with runs. Sam remembered her from the night he'd been here. She spoke with an accent Sam had never heard before. "She go with him a week ago. Act really weird ever since, says they doing business, but she not telling me what. I think has something to do with the strange blue lights, no? Everyone see them, right?" At first everyone drew a blank, but then a few started nodding their heads. "Now that you mention it," one of them said, "I did see some weird lights."

Chef slammed his bat on the bar inches from Laura's head. "Carmen! If I hear anything further concerning your hallucinatory lights, I will poach your eyes in cream sauce."

Carmen crossed her arms and sneered. "I poach your little dick, fat pig. I know what I see. You make only shit sauce anyway." She turned to the others for support. "Is not true?" Everyone nodded their agreement. There was far greater certainty about Chef's sauce than about Carmen's lights, so it was something of a standoff.

Chef sniffed his contempt. "I won't waste my time arguing with you." He stepped around the bar and walked up to Sam. "Does anyone have anything *useful* to bring to this inquiry?"

So it was a trial, and this fat man was the judge. Sam wondered if he would get the chance to say anything in his defense, though the only chance he seemed to have at the moment would be for Laura to wake up and get him out of here.

The goateed man who walked backward insinuated himself between Chef and Sam, looking Sam in the eye with careful scrutiny. "I am still Sandoz," he said. "You will be?"

Sam knew he was being asked a question, but didn't know what it was. Someone in the crowd called out, "He wants to know your name."

"Sam," Sam said.

"Sam I am?"

"Just Sam. Samuel."

"Did you remember the future, Samuel Sam?" Sandoz asked.

He waited for someone to translate this question as well, but nobody did, though they all seemed intent on his answer. Maybe Crazyville was rubbing off on him, but the more Sam thought about it, the more he thought he understood what Sandoz was asking. "Yes, I did," Sam said. "I remembered the future."

Chef cleared his throat. "Well, isn't that pleasant for both of you. But it doesn't do this poor unfortunate girl any good now, does it?" He pointed to Laura stretched out on the bar, barely breathing. "What did you do to her?" he demanded of Sam.

Rat had been watching the proceedings with aloof detachment, checking on Laura's radio, putting a towel under her head. He seemed to have forgotten about Sam altogether. But now he turned to Chef, took the TV off his neck, and put it around Chef's, adjusting the dials. "Watch," he told Chef, tapping on the screen, wagging a finger under his nose. Rat took Sam by the shoulders and turned him around so that he was facing the crowd. Rat surveyed the room to make sure everyone was paying attention, then unplugged his headphones from the TV, put the plug in Sam's left shirt pocket above his heart, and nodded with satisfaction.

Chef rolled his eyes and looked unimpressed, but he let Rat proceed. Rat reached out and ran his fingers over the medals on Sam's chest. They were given for deeds judged by Gabriel to hasten the arrival of God's Kingdom, which is to say, Sam had hacked systems that proved useful in murdering thousands of people he didn't even know—like all the people in this town, only farther away. Rat seized the medals and ripped them off Sam's shirt one by one, throwing them on the floor and grinding them under his heel, all the while listening intently through the headphones, nodding his approval as Sam stood stock-still.

Rat then took the shoulder patch on Sam's uniform in both his hands and tore it off, taking half Sam's sleeve with it. He held the white patch with the blue flaming cross in his hands and made a great show of swilling his mouth as if he were going to spit on it. Then, as if it were a sudden inspiration, he held the patch under Sam's mouth and gave a quick nod. All eyes were on Sam. The only sound was a pack of dogs barking in the distance. Sam looked down at the emblem of his life up to now and spat on it.

The uproar was deafening, incoherent at first, then turning into a chant: "Crazy fucker! Crazy fucker! Crazy fucker!" Reluctantly, even Chef joined in. A little boy who had wormed his way through the crowd dashed in and snatched the spat-upon patch as a prize, holding it aloft, dancing through the crowd so they could all spit on it.

Sam was now one of them.

THEY STRIPPED OFF THE REST OF HIS CLOTHES AND DRESSED the wound on his ankle. They wrapped him up in a length of muslin Carmen explained had belonged to Krishna Charlie. "Dead now," she said with a laugh. "No need it no more." They sat him down with a bowl of wretched stew. He was so hungry it didn't matter how awful it was. One of the children returned with his Soldier boots, now spray-painted gold, and put them on his feet, while another shaved his head with a straight razor, carefully returning the frog hat when she was done. Sam didn't question any of this. They seemed to have their reasons.

He was more concerned about Laura than himself. She still lay on the bar, not moving. Once again, he wished he'd asked more questions about the upload. He asked his hosts, but now that they were sure she wasn't the victim of some Soldier plot, they seemed unconcerned. "Laura is like coyote," Carmen said. "Wait to come when no one is looking."

The Construct Sam had seen when he was here before came through the door, pushing his way through the crowd, towering over everyone. His feathered head brushed the ceiling. He approached Sam and offered his hand. "We are Hawkeye," he said.

Sam shook his hand, perfectly ordinary except for its size—small and birdlike for such a large man. "Sam."

"There's a patrol of Soldiers on foot about five minutes from here," he said. "Half a dozen. They have some kind of fix on you. Do you have any electronics with you?"

Sam remembered the scanner in his knapsack. He opened it up and turned it on. The circuits had dried out, and it was now working perfectly. It had a homing signal that couldn't be shut off, short of taking it apart or smashing it to bits or immersing it in water. But it was too late for that. They already knew where he was. This seemed to be his day for stupid mistakes.

Rat pointed at the scanner and held out his hands. Sam gave it to him, and Rat set it on the table, took out a roll of jeweler's tools, and put them beside it. With a reverent expression but with speed and efficiency, Rat sat down at the table and began to take the scanner apart, placing the components in a neat row, whistling to himself.

"You don't have time to run," Hawkeye said. "Lose yourself in the crowd. Believe me, they won't even see you."

In a matter of moments, Sam was packed into a booth with four crazies, playing cards. Everyone else looked like they were going about their business, carrying on animated conversations, locked in amorous embrace, eating and drinking. Hawkeye had disappeared.

One of the cardplayers with a tattoo of a spider on his face advised Sam, "Do what we do. Soldiers scare easy." He gave a conspiratorial wink. "We'll make you invisible."

"They're just leaving," Sandoz called from the door.

And then the Soldiers strode in, their weapons at the ready, sweeping the barrels back and forth in a gesture designed to strike terror, but no one seemed to notice. Sam tried to hide his face behind a handful of cards. The patrol was led by Jeremiah.

Jeremiah spotted the scanner in pieces on the table and walked up to Rat. "Where did you get that?" Jeremiah demanded.

Rat, continuing to work, pointed vaguely northwest with his screwdriver. Jeremiah put the barrel right in Rat's face. "Speak up when I'm talking to you," he said.

Rat eyed the barrel and Jeremiah with disdain, slid the tiny screwdriver into the barrel, and burst into the song: "My Boyfriend's Back."

"Hey La-li-la!" all the crazies shouted out on the chorus.

Jeremiah shook the screwdriver out of the barrel and backed away from the table. In a matter of seconds, the Soldiers were crowded together in the middle of the room back to back, barrels bristling from them in all directions, eyeing the crowd warily. The residents of Crazyville smiled back. "He must've ditched it, and that nut scavenged it," one of the Soldiers said to Jeremiah. "I don't think he's here." By now, the windows were full of faces again, all jostling each other for a look. Jeremiah sized up the situation and decided their mission didn't require them to take on a hundred crazies, and as abruptly as they'd arrived, Jeremiah and company departed the Chez Élite à la Carte Cafe to hunt their prey, who was sitting right there in the crowd, grinning along with the rest of them, completely invisible.

Rat put the scanner back together and gave it to Sam, with a single chip left out. He held it up and put his finger to his lips in a gesture of silence. He had apparently silenced the homing signal. Sam turned the scanner back on, and it worked perfectly.

Chef suggested that everyone celebrate by purchasing something to drink, but Sam couldn't stay for the party. Hawkeye returned and offered to take him to Construct Town. "You can't stay here," he said. "This is where the trail led. When they don't find you, they'll come back in force and do a thorough search. If they suspect these people have been hiding you, the results won't be pretty."

Hawkeye was right. The Soldiers pretty much left the Crazies alone. As long as they were convinced of their neutrality, they were useful for certain services that were difficult to find in New Jerusalem. Obviously, from what Sam had seen, they were not so neutral as the Soldiers believed. The well-armed Soldiers would have no trouble wiping out the town in a few hours if Gabriel gave the order.

Hawkeye slung Laura over his shoulder as if she were a small sack of potatoes and led Sam out of Crazyville. Sam knew that the Soldiers' latest surveillance showed the Construct encampment to be at least ten miles away and prepared himself for a long trek. But maybe a half mile from the edge of Crazyville, Hawkeye said. "Check your scanner for what's underneath us."

Sam did as he was told. "It looks like the old Metro tunnel. Caved in, filled with chunks of concrete and rebar."

Hawkeye smiled and pointed at the scanner. "We love those things. Their vision is even more suggestible than Carmen's." He lifted up what looked like a boulder to reveal well-lit stairs descending into the perfectly intact Metro station below. "There are transmitters in the ceiling that tell any scanner that there's a hell of mess down here. Because you have those things and the satellites, you never bother to look for yourselves."

Sam could hardly believe his eyes. Not only was the station intact, it seemed to be in perfect condition. The high concrete ceiling was studded with lights. The air conditioning made a steady sighing sound. A gleaming train waited on the tracks. It was beautiful. Sam had seen only images, and they didn't do it justice, like some gigantic silver serpent. Built and maintained by Construct labor, these trains had once crisscrossed every continent. Apparently, the Constructs had claimed the fruits of their labor as their own. The doors of the train slid open, and they stepped inside.

❁ ❁ ❁

THE RIDE TOOK LESS THAN FIVE MINUTES, BUT SAM ALMOST wanted it to last longer. The rush of speed as the tiled walls flew by almost took his breath away and filled him with a longing for the world as it used to be. Sinful and filled with suffering, no doubt, but alive and hopeful for more than just the end of things.

They arrived in a much busier station than they'd left. There were several levels of tracks here, trains coming and going. The passengers were all Constructs, most of them carrying something: toolboxes, sacks of tomatoes or concrete, sections of scaffolding. Many of the cars had the seats removed and were being loaded or unloaded with crates and boxes. "What's going on?" Sam asked.

Hawkeye's head swiveled on his shoulders, birdlike, glancing at the flurry of activity. "We repair, we build, we move from place to place. We hope."

Sam wondered if there were weapons in those crates, but none of the Constructs were armed. They were clearly more capable of mounting an offensive than the Soldiers believed, but Sam had a feeling that none of this activity was preparation for war. Preparation for peace, perhaps. Sam wanted to tell him that there was no chance of that on the Soldiers' side, that Gabriel intended to fight on until the End of Days. But when he searched his heart, he decided to keep his doubts to himself. Soldiers spoke of hope, and they meant death. These people hoped for life. Choosing between the two, Sam decided, had nothing to do with probability.

An escalator—Sam had never seen one that actually worked—carried them into the sunlight. Sam felt as if he were being lifted into the sky. They emerged in a large plaza, surrounded by buildings that looked as if they'd been transported in time from the past. Waiting for Sam and Hawkeye was a gathering of Constructs, filling the large plaza. Finned, feathered, furred, and iridescent—anything seemed possible here. Every color and size. They were all looking at Sam. "We welcome you to Construct Town," Hawkeye said. "Look at your scanner."

Sam opened it up, and on the screen he saw a kaleido-scope of images of himself with widely differing spectra and definitions from a multitude of perspectives—Sam through all their many eyes at once.

So this was the enemy.

"God bless you," Sam said.

15

BORN AGAIN

LAURA WALKED OUT OF THE WOODS WONDERING WHAT THE hell was up. Crying again—over some five-minute conversation with a woman she didn't even know. She brushed her eyes with her sleeve, her nose while she was at it. Hell, this was the Bin. It's not like she'd have a snotty sleeve when she got back. None of this was really real. Maybe this tsunami wave of sappiness wasn't real either. Maybe this was something Newman Rogers programmed into her when she uploaded.

Yeah, right. She'd been living in Crazyville too long. Next thing you know, she'd be seeing Carmen's mysterious lights, and Sandoz would be making sense. Stephanie was nice. Nice could make as much sense as anything else, couldn't it? But these tears. Maybe it was PMS. She was about due. It was hard to keep track of time in Crazyville.

Things were pretty smooth here, though. She eyed the little cabin, neat and trim, nice big porch to while away the hours. It'd get old in a hurry, but she might as well enjoy it while she was here. The three guys—Wally, Newman Rogers, and (what was his name?) Donovan—were sitting on the porch, talking. She called out, "Hey, Wally, you got a woman waiting for you."

She expected him to come bounding off the porch like some kid, but he got up kind of slow and traipsed toward her. He looked awful. He always looked awful. But this was inside awful oozing out all over. He's thinking the worst, she thought. When he came up to her, she gave him a little punch on the arm. "Buck up, Wally. She loves you. Told me so herself."

"Laura, I really appreciate this, but maybe this wasn't such a good idea."

Why was it nice guys were such wimps? "What the fuck you mean, not 'a good idea'? You've been obsessing on this woman for *a hundred and twenty years*! What are you saying? You want more time to *think* about it?"

"That's just it. I've thought so much. How do I know what's real and what's some nonsense I've cooked up? Memory isn't some set thing, you know. It revises itself all the time."

"What am I? Your student? We're not talking about memories here anymore. At this very moment, you got a beautiful woman who thinks you're wonderful waiting for you in a nice romantic spot. Don't stand here talking to me. Go fuck and make up."

He furrowed his brow, which made him look even more like a toad. "I'm still so angry with her. Maybe I've got no reason to be, but . . ."

"Fine. Go tell *her* that. *Then* fuck and make up. The woman's waiting. By the way, does this thing's operating system work like yours?"

He was already looking down the dark path. He was practically shaking all over. Go on. You can do it, Wally. "Yeah," he said absentmindedly, turning toward the woods. "It's almost identical, just more bells and whistles."

"Good. I could use a drink." It looked to be ten in the morning here, but her internal clock said it was the middle of a long hard night. She gave him a gentle shove. "Go on, Wally. Give her hell." She watched him walk away, poor little son of a bitch. "I'll be waiting!" she called out, and he gave her a wave without turning around. They'd work it out. She kind of liked this matchmaker thing. It was almost enough to make you believe in love.

She looked around, got her bearings. It was like some

picture from an ancient calendar: *Blue Ridge in the Fall* or something. Beats Crazyville any time of the year. And here she was, at Newman Rogers's place. That was pretty cool in itself. She paused for a moment in her survey and accessed the operating system. She briefly entertained the idea of filling the clearing with elephants or Jell-O, but decided to be a nice guest (to continue the "your-grandmother-would-be-proud" theme she had going here) and settled for a triple Scotch in a crystal goblet with spherical ice cubes.

She strolled up to the porch. "Looks like I got some time to kill. You mind if I spend it with you two sexy gentlemen?"

Newman Rogers smiled a sweet old guy smile, stood and offered her a chair. He knew how to act when a lady wants to join you. This Donovan character, however, did not know how to act. He hardly seemed to know she was there. He looked like Larry right before he laid the dead dog story on her. Watch out, girlfriend, she told herself as she sat down between the two men. Keep it light. You've had enough drama for a while.

"I would offer you a drink, but I can see you've already gotten yourself one," Rogers said.

"Yeah. Is that okay? It's not against the rules or anything, is it?"

"Well, actually, it is. Only a handful of the residents of the Bin have access to the operating system."

She winked at him. "But I don't live here. That gives me diplomatic immunity, right?"

Rogers laughed. "I guess it does."

"So what do I call you?"

"Newman."

"Cool." She thought about this. She was on a first-name basis with Newman Rogers. She could see herself back at the Chez Élite saying, *As I was discussing with Newman the other day* . . . "So how come, Newman, everybody can't just run their own show? Won't the system handle it?"

"It's the inhabitants who probably couldn't handle it. Our

studies indicated that total access would lead to widespread insanity."

She laughed. "Sounds like where I live. But nobody has shit there." Newman chuckled along with her. He was okay. Donovan, on the other hand, was still sitting there like a whipped dog. It was starting to get on her nerves. "So what do you do in here, Donnie?"

He looked at her through the fog of his head trip, blinking like he just woke up. "Me? Uh, I'm a writer, lecturer."

"Oh, yeah? What do you write about?"

"Death."

Whoa. Now here was a fun guy. She was trying to decide whether she wanted to hear any more from this zombie when the cabin door opened and Freddie came out. She'd been wondering where he'd gotten to. It was a relief to have somebody she knew to talk to, and after seeing Tillman's memories, her opinion of Freddie had gone up several notches. He was a pretty gutsy little fag. "Hey, Freddie," she said. "Join us for a cocktail?"

"Hi, Laura," he said, looking like he'd caught whatever this Donovan guy had. Then he said to Newman in a low serious voice, "We need to talk."

Newman got up, excused himself, and the two of them went inside. Just like that.

"Hurry back!" Laura called after them. This was great. She's in the Bin with billions and billions of people, all sorts of shit going on all the time, and she's in the middle of nowhere with some guy who's queer for death. That Laura knows how to have a good time. She could go for a walk in the woods, maybe hang out in the stream, but she didn't feel like Nature Girl. There'd been a lot of shit going on, and she felt like talking to somebody. She liked to talk. She had stories to tell.

He was still sitting there, looking out into the clearing—pretty trees, sky, sunshine—but she could tell he wasn't seeing anything. Certainly not her. She could strip and straddle him, and he probably wouldn't even notice. Finally she couldn't stand it anymore. "So, Donnie. I'm not exactly comfortable with long silences. And if you don't mind my saying so, you seem a little distracted. What's on your mind?"

He jerked his head around. He really had forgotten she was there. "I'm sorry," he said. "I was thinking."

"I'm slow, but I figured that much out already. Thinking about what?" She took a nice gulp of her primo Scotch, holding its delicious coldness in her mouth before she swallowed.

"I was thinking about my wife. She committed suicide a couple of years ago."

Jeez. First there's Sammy trying to live down his father, then there's Tillman with his Frog Prince meets Sleeping Beauty Oedipal thing he had going, and now she's got this guy lugging his dead wife around. Was she the only one who had her shit together? Maybe she should just go into the counseling business—she felt like that's what she was doing half the time in Crazyville anyway. But those guys were all nuts already. She couldn't fuck anybody up. There'd been only one relationship counselor in Crazyville that she knew of. Called himself Dr. Filbert. Which was kind of cute. His big thing was communication. If people just talked to each other right, then all their problems would go away. He used the old Indian talking stick thing. He'd have these couples handing this stick back and forth, yakking their heads off, saying all the wacko shit they usually kept to themselves. Then one day he had Sid and Barbara in his tiny office, and they got pissed off at some smarmy thing or other he said and beat the living crap out of him with his own damn stick, communicating that he should take up another line of work. Last she heard, he was a pig farmer.

But what the hell. There wasn't anything else to do for the moment but watch the leaves falling off the trees. "So tell me about her," she heard herself saying.

And he did. The whole sick thing. He meets her when she's trying to off herself—with a train, no less—and this

turns out to be her hobby—guns, knives, trains, pills—whatever floated by. Until finally she's the one floating by—
broken back or drowned—what did it really matter in here?
This woman's already got one foot in the grave and the
other on slick shit when he meets her, but he wants to
blame himself because she takes the high dive. "I shouldn't
have gone fishing," he said. She wanted to ask him: What
if you were on the can when she did it? What was it with
some guys that they wanted to *save* you? She got salvation
offers every other week. She figured in her case it was just
a ploy to get a little for free. Maybe that's what it always
was. But she didn't say any of that.

"That's tough," she said. "But she's been dead for a while,
right? Why are you thinking about her so hard right now?"

He told her this convoluted business about how he'd been
trying to talk everybody in the Bin into—get this—dying.
And then he's off on this complicated thing about how if
the Bin was destroyed, there were all these copies scattered
all over the galaxy like dandelion seeds, and there'd be millions of everybody living all these lives forever and ever,
and she was wondering just where the fuck he was going
with this and what it had to do with his dead wife anyway,
when he got to the part where the coordinates of the Bin
were stored in Wally's hideaway with Soldiers all over it like
flies on a dead dog, which is where he should've started in
the first place. She'd like to hear this guy and Sandoz have
a chat.

"I just can't believe it," he said.

She wasn't sure which part he didn't believe, but she
guessed he meant that he doubted that anybody from the
real world could harm the great and glorious Bin. "Believe
it," she told him. "If the Soldiers have something to aim at,
it's already glowing. They've got marching orders from God.
And Newman, that sweet old guy in there? He's Lucifer.
Hell, Gabriel would fry all of you just to nail him. You
remember what the real world's like, right? It's the same
as it ever was, except ten times more fucked up."

He gave her a weak pathetic smile. "I don't remember the real world. I'm a newbie."

Newbie, newbie—she drew a blank—oh, yeah, she'd heard of them. A light dawned. That's why he was so interested in death. Everybody had to feel like they'd missed out on *something*, so there was a reason their lives were generally fucked. "So how's that feel?" she asked. "Never having a real body?"

That seemed to hike his shorts, and he shifted around in his chair. At least that was a sign of life. "How does it feel to be a Construct?" he asked her.

She started to set him straight, tell him she wasn't a real Construct, but that wasn't his point. "You're right. Stupid question. But what's the problem here? If the Soldiers go after this place, sounds like Newman's got it totally covered."

"Too covered. Thousands and thousands of places just like this. Would *you* want to live in here forever?"

"What the fuck difference does it make what I want? We're taking about you. Look, if you don't like it in here, download. I can arrange it for you. I'm sure we can work out a deal. Looks like I may be doing a twofer as it is. Might as well go for three. Sort of a going-out-of-business sale."

"But I don't want to live in the real world."

Join the club. This guy was seriously on her nerves. He seemed smart enough. How could he be so stupid? "Look, I don't really know you, okay? But you got two choices. Count 'em. You can live here, or you can live there. One thing I've figured out is, if you don't like it where you are, go someplace else. But don't hold out for some fucking perfect world you got cooked up in your head, because it ain't never going to happen. So go or stay, but for Christ's sake, quit whining."

That got his back up. "There's a third choice."

"What's that?"

"Death."

This guy was too much. Is this what the Bin did to people? She was starting to miss the crazies. "Yeah, I was forgetting that choice." She tried to see through the window into the cabin, but couldn't see anybody. What the hell was taking them so long? "You want a drink or something?" she asked Donovan. Maybe lighten up a little?

"No thanks." He managed a weak smile. "What I could really use is a joint."

Hello. Now there was an idea that had some fucking merit. Even an idiot could have a good idea. She couldn't remember the last time she smoked any decent pot. The johns always paid her in dirt dope, saying it was killer. She could try a sample first, but found that dope and biz didn't mix, and half the time she'd forget to get paid anything but the few tokes that got her in the sack. But Donovan wasn't a john. Hell, she wasn't even sure he was human. Might as well take advantage of the Bin's bounty. She accessed the operating system and took her time making a surprise for her new friend, the cadaver.

At first he didn't even notice that there was a brass hookah sitting on the table with a bowl the size of a doorknob, already lit. Then he sat up like somebody'd goosed him. "How did you do that?"

"I guess you're not one of the in crowd with system access Newman was talking about. My friend Wally showed me how."

"No. I never realized that anyone could just change anything they wanted." He was still staring at the hookah.

"So take a hit. I'm waiting here like a good hostess, but I didn't whip this up so we could watch it burn."

He obeyed, and once he got into it, with great relish. The pipe made a comforting gurgle.

"You know," she said, taking a hit, holding it, letting him hang, then exhaling the rest of her sentence. "You sort of remind me of a guy I know. He's a Soldier. Was a Soldier. Whatever. Anyway, everything's God to him. God this. God that. And everything's death to you."

He was already mellowing and didn't take offense. He nodded thoughtfully and took another hit, though he didn't look like he needed it. Maybe you made the dope too strong, Laura, she told herself. You bad little girl. Course, she thought, grinning, Gran would approve of that too.

"What's 'everything' to you?" he asked.

It took her a second to remember what they'd been talking about. "That's not my point," she said. "There doesn't have to be some 'everything.' Nothing's 'everything' to me. I mean, stuff just fucking is, right? There's not some big deal *thing* I get off on."

"What about sex? You use sexual metaphors all the time, say 'fuck' every chance you get."

"Jeez. What a guy thing to say. You think I'm a whore because I love sex?" She drained her Scotch, and it filled up again. She was glad she'd made it bottomless. Looked like she was going to need it.

He hesitated a moment, then said quietly, "I didn't know you were a whore."

Maybe you should wear a sign, she told herself. Broadcast it with one of Rat's radios. "Yeah, well. Now you do."

"You don't like sex?"

"I didn't say that. I like sex sometimes. The right guy. The right time." She looked around the clearing. What could she charge him in here? It's not like she could take anything back to Earth with her. She thought about Sammy and the look he got when he came, like maybe he had seen God or something. She didn't want this turkey dying on top of her. There's no angle here, she told herself. Just shoot the breeze, relax, and enjoy the high. She had made some very sweet dope, if she did say so herself.

"There must be something," he said.

" 'Something' what?"

"Something that matters to you deeply, more than anything else, that motivates you."

"You're like a dog on a bone, aren't you? Okay. I'll play." She grabbed the first thing that popped into her head: "My grandmother. I liked my grandmother a whole lot. My grandfather too. They're both dead, so they don't exactly fit into the scheme of my daily motivations. Which is *exactly* what I was saying."

That was supposed to shut him off, but he was like that train his wife was going to throw herself in front of when he met her. He leaned toward her, his hands fanned out to give his hot air some extra loft. He got off on lecturing the world. "But you learned from them. There were things you valued about them. They may be dead, but they must've shaped your values."

She could see she'd have to give him an answer or he wouldn't let it go. "Water," she said. "I used to like to lie around in the water with Gran. Still do. Did it just the other day. That's it." She started giggling. "You've got death. Sammy's got God. And I've got—water!"

He started laughing too, snorting away. "What about earth, air, and fire?" he managed, gulping for air.

"Shit, yeah, bring 'em on! The whole damn mess!" She started stamping her feet, she was laughing so hard. Then she thought about where she was, whose porch she was stoned out of her gourd on, and she practically fell out of her chair. Wait till they hear about this at the Chez Élite, she thought, which sent her into another laughing jag.

"You know what else?" she wheezed. "Dope!"

By this time, they were on a roll. They started naming things back and forth—it got loopier and loopier—laughing like a couple of hyenas. *Bicycle pump! Pinecones! Mildew! Newspapers!* When it tapered off, and he'd finally come around on the drink offer, they could still send each other into aftershocks with the right word. "Tell me, Donnie. Do you think about this death shit even when you smoke dope?" she asked.

He shook his head at his own foolishness. "Yeah. I'm afraid so."

"You must smoke alone."

"Usually."

"There's your problem. Just smoke a joint with me every once in a while, have a good laugh, and forget about it. That's what you need."

Then *boom*, he's down again, his DEFAULT setting. "But eventually, you'll die too."

"Jesus, Donnie. You are a real ray of fucking sunshine."

"But seriously, Laura. You live in the real world. You're going to die. You must think about it sometimes."

This was the first time he'd used her name. She was surprised he even remembered it. "Look, here's what I think about death. All the best people die. It happens. End of story. Why think about it?" This started him thinking again, drifting away. "You know, you really ought to meet my friend Sammy. You could drift around in the ozone together."

"I'm sorry. I was just thinking that you're probably right."

"This is twice in one week—must be some kind of record. Do you like pie? I could really go for a pie right about now."

THEY HAD A COUPLE OF PIES, ACTUALLY. CHOCOLATE CREAM. And a blueberry. She couldn't decide and didn't have to, so why not? She had her feet up on the table and was telling him the story of the night she left the Constructs, wondering how some shrooms might sit on top of the alcohol, pot, pie buzz she had going, when Newman and Freddie finally finished up their powwow and stepped out on the porch.

"What's up, guys?" she greeted them. She pointed her fork toward the woods. "Looks like our two lovebirds are taking their sweet time."

"There's something we have to tell you," Freddie said.

She didn't catch the tone, too wasted to give a flip. "Shoot," she said. "I'm listening."

They glanced at each other and sat down. It was then she knew it wasn't good. "When you uploaded," Freddie said, "we detected some telltale neural activity. We've been double-checking to be sure—"

"Sure of what?"

"You're pregnant," Newman said. "Two or three days, I'd say."

It occurred to her that she ought to take her feet off the table, and the last thing she remembered she was trying to do just that. She'd always wondered whether you could faint in the Bin. Turns out you can.

SHE WOKE UP IN A NICE COZY BED, A DOWN COMFORTER, AND fluffy pillows. Newman Rogers's bed. She was halfway through an imagined scene where she told Chef she'd been in Newman Rogers's bed (let him reach his own conclusions) and she didn't have to take any more shit off a fat fuck like him when she remembered just *why* she was lying in bed like a dead person. Pregnant. Knocked up. Bumped. Screwed any way you look at it.

Jesus, *what* had she done to deserve this? You fucked a Soldier without a rubber, she reminded herself. And it was his. Had to be. If you don't stay focused, you pay the price. And for what? To teach him a lesson? Looks like he's the one who took *you* to school. She could just hear Rat singing "Who's Sorry Now?"

And it wasn't that she was pregnant—God, how many times had she made that mistake? No, the really fucked part was that she knew she'd have to tell him, knew it immediately. The way she had it figured, a john didn't just pay for a fuck, he was also paying you to keep any consequences to yourself. But Sam was no john. She couldn't even convince herself he wouldn't want to know. He probably wouldn't *like* to know, but he'd want to. She couldn't see not telling people important shit just 'cause they wouldn't *like* it—they could talk to themselves and get that. Most people anyway. *She* told herself shit she didn't like all the goddamn time. Like now. Like she was going to have to break it to Sammy that she had a little hot-cross bun in the oven. It was the principle of the thing.

She blathered all this and more while she whooped and sobbed and generally made an ass of herself. Newman and Freddie were trying to be sweet about it. Even Donnie. He kept popping in and out, looking at her all concerned, going off and boiling water or some damn thing. Something about a woman in distress really pushed this guy's buttons. They let her rattle on about how fucked the universe was—her knocked-up self in particular. She thought about accessing the operating system and shutting down the tears, but decided against it. Sometimes you just had to cry. But sooner or later, you always had to get a grip, right? Figure out what you were going to *do* about your latest fuckup.

There were things she definitely didn't want to talk about—or even think about. But they were there anyway: How it made a difference that this wasn't some john's kid. Hell, she didn't even think of those as *kids*.

Finally she got to where she was doing a halfway decent imitation of a normal person, and they started talking to her. This option. That option. Couple of scientists with a problem to solve. Freddie was the first to say it: "We could abort the child when you download."

Her gut recoiled at the suggestion. It made sense. No muss, no fuss, she'd get back to her body with a tiny dead fetus inside her, its life having leaked out into space in transit, and she'd slough it off like it was nothing. That seemed worse, though, to do it that way—like it'd never been, like she'd never spent a single day walking around in her body knowing it was there before she ended it. "Is it a boy or a girl?"

The guys looked puzzled, of course. How was that a significant variable?

"Look, I know you know. Is it a boy or a girl?"

"A girl," Newman said.

She was afraid of that. She wished she hadn't asked. "Look, I'm probably going to abort, okay? It's the only thing that makes sense—I mean, what little girl wants to be a whore's kid, right? But I'll just get the old-fashioned kind if it's all the same to you. There's a Construct doctor who can do it."

"We know," Newman said.

"Yeah, course you do. I wasn't thinking. I used to use these pills I got from Sandoz, but those things are like ten years out of date. Had to dose this one little sucker three times." She started laughing, but then her voice started shaking, like she was going to lose it again. "Jesus. Pregnant. What in the fuck am I going to do?"

Freddie put his arms around her and held her. "You could stay in here," Newman suggested gently. He reminded her of her grandfather, except Newman didn't look like a lizard. "You wouldn't have to be a whore in here."

Her gut said no to that one too. "You don't know me," she said. "I'd find a way. Always have, always will." She tried another laugh, but it didn't come off too well and turned into this pathetic little whimper. She was pretty disgusted with herself, but even that didn't seem to have much point. It was time to head home and face the music. She freed herself from Freddie's arms and got out of bed.

"Where's Wally?" she asked. "I need to get back."

TILLMAN AND STEPHANIE WERE SITTING ON THE FRONT porch, holding hands. Turned out they'd already decided to stay with Newman until he could find them host bodies. They didn't think Laura'd need the added strain just now.

Added strain. Her eyes started leaking again. Strain her ass is what they ought to do. She wished they'd just tell her what a fuckup she was instead of being so damn nice—but not really, nice was okay right about now. "Thanks," she said.

"You've been out for quite a while," Newman said gently. "You've been uploaded for twelve hours. If you're not going to stay, to be safe, you should download soon."

"Yeah, that's me. Ms. Safety."

She told everybody good-bye, hugging them all. Tillman and Stephanie squeezed her so hard she thought they were going to crack her ribs, but she wasn't complaining. They said that somebody else could do the download when the time came, but she insisted she was still going to do it. In fact, for reasons she didn't even *try* to figure out, she made them promise they wouldn't get anybody else. That made her feel better—knowing whatever mess she had going with her own life, she could still help them out.

She got her cool together, working out what she was going to say to Sammy in her head while she was setting up the download, almost looking forward to the grassy bank of that little creek, when she opened her eyes and she's in another damn bed. It didn't take her two seconds to recognize where she was. In her grandmother's bedroom. She started screaming.

"I CAN'T BELIEVE YOU BROUGHT ME HERE," SHE SAID FOR THE hundreth time. Sammy didn't even bother to answer this time. He just sat there and took it while she paced up and down, hollering herself hoarse. She'd chased all the Constructs off. The last one brought her tea and sandwiches on a tray like she was some fucking invalid, then he made the mistake of hanging around, watching, listening. Bastards. "What are you? The fucking cameraman?" she asked him, and he split.

But that Sammy, he hung in there, even if he didn't say much, though it occurred to her he hadn't had much chance to get a word in edgewise. She let him tell the story of how she'd ended up back in Construct Town, stopping him every step of the way to point out what he *should've* done if he hadn't been such a fucking idiot, and how she'd gotten along fine without this sanctimonious Zen shithole for almost ten years, and she didn't need it now.

He apologized. Nicely, of course. Several times.

He didn't know the half of it. Though try as she might, she couldn't blame him for knocking her up. It wasn't his idea to fuck her. He didn't know a rubber from a faucet washer, and why should he: He was a virgin, for Christ's sake.

She hadn't told him she was pregnant yet. As she stood in the middle of the room catching her breath, surveying the little table she'd kicked into a splintered heap, the shard from the teacup embedded in the doorjamb, her own fists balled up and just waiting to take on the armoire or the mirror—especially the mirror—she figured out what this little tantrum was really about. She was putting off telling him, trying to find the backdoor that wasn't there. She was scared shitless.

She ran her hands over her head and felt something caught in the scales. A pine needle. She plucked it out and looked at it. He could've just split, left her lying there for the Soldiers. She imagined him lugging her lifeless body through all the crap he went through to save her sorry ass. It took some guts to walk into Crazyville like that. She looked at him in the mirror, sitting behind her, waiting for the next explosion. She had to smile. Crazyville had certainly made its mark on the boy. She especially liked the shaved head.

"Nice do," she said, turning around.

"Do?" he said cautiously, wondering what he'd done now.

"Hairdo. That egg look. I'd lose the tablecloth, though. You look better in pants." She sat down on the edge of the bed, took a deep breath. "Thanks for looking after me."

She could see him trying to shift gears. But you had to hand it to him. He made the effort. "You're welcome," he said.

Such a polite boy. Was that faith or fear that made him that way? She wished she understood what made him tick. "I'll be heading back to Crazyville. Got some business to attend to. But Hawkeye's right. You'll be safer here. You might even like it here. Meet a girl. Settle down."

He didn't say anything to that. He wasn't an idiot. He knew what she was *really* saying: You go your way, I go mine. "So, Sammy," she said. "I told you the story of my great romance. What about you? You ever been in love?"

He looked away. Two minutes ago, she was calling him every name in the book, and now she wanted the story of his love life. You had to admit—she wasn't dull. She watched him hold a little conference in his head and decide to tell her the story, sitting up a little straighter in his chair, holding his head up.

"Among the Soldiers, all marriages must be blessed by God—by Gabriel, actually."

"By 'blessed,' you mean arranged?"

"Yes. For those outside the Temple, that doesn't mean much. They come to the Temple for a blessing. But for those inside, it means that Gabriel decides who will marry whom. It's a political tool. I'm the Commander's son. My betrothal to a mine owner's daughter smoothed the way for a deal Gabriel needed to make. That was when I was fourteen. After a betrothal, the families visit each other a few times a year so that the future couple can get to know each other before they marry. Any other contact between the betrothed is strictly forbidden. Betrothal is customarily three or four years, unless there's some reason for urgency."

She let the possible reasons pass as a little too close to home. There was a deadness to his voice that told her up front this story didn't have a happy ending. "And you fell in love with her—your betrothed?" she asked quietly, like maybe she'd died or something.

"No. Her younger sister."

"Ouch. And the sister loved you too?"

"Yes."

A classic. "So did you renegotiate or what?"

"Renegotiation wasn't possible. Gabriel had announced God's will. Even to suggest that God had been wrong would be blasphemy."

"So you married the sister you didn't love?"

"The week before we were to marry she ran off with another man."

"Good for her! I mean . . . Nothing personal."

"I understand, and I agree. Unfortunately, she and her lover were tracked down and executed for defying the will of God."

"Shit. That's awful. But this left the field open for you and the little sister, right?" She tried to picture this little sister Sammy'd fallen for. Probably cute and pure and good. Everything Laura wasn't.

"By this time, she was betrothed to someone else. I thought about trying to run away, dreamed up all sorts of plans, but I couldn't put her in danger like that. I just couldn't."

"She married the other guy?"

He nodded. You could tell it still got to him. That's how it always goes for guys like him. They do the right thing, and they're fucked anyway. Worse than that—they're fucked *because* they do the right thing.

"It was the principle of the thing," she said.

He looked surprised she understood. "Yes, exactly."

"I understand some things, you know. I've got principles. But do you ever think your principles might be fucked?"

"Yes, all the time."

She laughed, high and shaky. "Yeah, I've had a big dose of that lately myself." She took a deep breath. "Why don't you sit here beside me, Sammy. I've got something I need to tell you."

ONCE SHE DECIDED TO TELL HIM, SHE DIDN'T BEAT AROUND the bush: She was pregnant, it was his, she didn't expect anything from him because it was all her fault, but she thought he ought to know. He seemed to be taking it okay, looking all kind and concerned. Course, it wasn't really his problem. She couldn't believe the first thing he said when she'd rattled off her little speech: "It wasn't your fault. Quit blaming yourself."

"Then whose fault was it? *Yours?* I practically raped you, Sammy."

"It wasn't anybody's fault. Maybe it was meant to be. You yourself said you're always careful, but this one time you weren't."

"What are you talking—God's will or something? What are you? Nuts? What in the hell would God want with a fuckup like me?"

"The Bible is full of fuckups who do God's will."

Oh, jeez. He was hellbent on making it *mean* something,

make her mean something she wasn't. St. Laura—now there was a hilarious concept. Then she heard herself talking to Stephanie—*Everything matters, or nothing matters*—talkng like she knew anything about anything. And she had to turn to herself and say, *Well, sweetheart, does that baby inside you matter? Is it "everything" or "nothing"?* She knew the answer in her gut, imagined the knot down there was the fetus waiting for her answer. It mattered. *She,* she corrected herself. A daughter. Her daughter mattered.

She still didn't know what to do. All the best people die. Sooner or later. With a mother like her, as soon as possible would have to be some kind of blessing. If for once in her whole fucking life she wanted to do the right thing, it was now. And the right thing wasn't crying and it wasn't screaming and it wasn't giving Sammy a bunch of shit. She just wished like hell she knew what it was. "What do you think I ought to do?" she asked.

"I think we should raise the child together."

"You mean get married?"

"Yes."

She stared at him. He meant it, all right. It was like when he said he was going to help Wally. Another savior with his principles: I'll get myself hung, I'll marry a whore. Well, she had her principles too. "No way. You're a nice guy. A good man. Which is exactly why I'm not going to marry you just because I wacked out and jumped your bones one night. You got enough troubles."

He didn't argue. He reached out and took her hand, and she let him. At least he knew what no meant, a rare trait in a man. "So you got any ideas that don't involve marriage?" she asked.

"I trust you to do the right thing."

" 'Cause I'm so fucking moral, right? Have you just not been paying attention, or is that a roundabout way of saying you don't give a fuck what I do?"

"I care very much. I have faith in you. God will help you decide."

Yeah, well, it was her turn not to argue. She'd fucked up

things pretty good on her own. She'd take any help she could get. Even God's. "I better be going," she said. "This place gives me the creeps." She squeezed his hand and let it go.

"Can I ask you something?" he asked.

"Course."

"Why do you hate the Constructs so much?"

"I don't hate them. They just get on my nerves. I mean, they were *slaves,* Sammy. They built all this shit, kept it running, couldn't have families—for what? But they're not even pissed off. They should be foaming at the mouth, but they just keep on keeping on. They could wipe out New Jerusalem on a weekend and still have Sunday afternoon for a picnic. Bet you didn't know that. But don't worry. It'll never happen, not in a million years. They'll just wait around for the Soldiers to finally blow them away." She was almost hollering again. So much for sweet good-byes. She stood up. "But I've got my own problems. Thanks for not being an asshole, Sam."

"You're welcome."

She walked to the door quickly and was halfway out when she stopped and looked back at him sitting on the bed, watching her go. "Hey, Sammy," she said. "It's a girl. Thought you might want to know."

He broke into the sweetest smile. Like she'd just told him the best news in the world. She kept seeing that smile in her head as she rode the train back to Crazyville. It sure didn't make things any easier. Why couldn't he just be an asshole like most guys?

BACK AT THE CHEZ ÉLITE, THERE WAS A PARTY OF SORTS going on. Chef's scrawny cow had dropped dead that morning and was barbecue by sundown, just about the time Laura hit town. The place was packed with crazies chewing. And chewing and chewing. She had to laugh. There was no place like home.

Chef proposed a toast to her—"the brave adventurer in our midst"—and it sort of turned into a party for her—at least as close as she was likely to get. She drank everything that came her way from moonshine to wine coolers, chewed on what Chef claimed was a filet mignon—a charred wedge that looked like it'd been carved with a chain saw. She passed up the sauce—a greenish brown with several unidentifiable things floating in it that Chef said were green peppercorns, but she figured were more than likely roach hips.

She knew what she was doing. She was hiding from her problems. *Know thyself* might've been great advice for the Greeks, but it didn't do her a whole lot of good. She knew herself to be a fuckup. Now what? It's not like she knew what to do with that information.

So she danced. Even with Sandoz. Though she insisted on leading. Whenever he led, he always backed into a table or something and hit the floor, taking her with him.

"The Soldiers will come again," he told her as they lurched around the room, propelled more by collisions with other bodies than by their own steps.

She knew he meant they'd come again and gone. "Did they find out anything?"

"They will question Rat. Epistemology was irrelevant."

It was pointless to ask for a translation. Rat seemed to be okay, standing on the bar, singing along with the music—not the song that was playing, but there was nothing unusual in that. "Did they head toward Construct Town?"

"Construct Town went to them—Rat will tell me." He gave her a knowing look. He had the word, the inside track on the wacko frequency. Whenever Sandoz started talking in the past tense, it was time to worry because some serious shit was coming down.

"I'm pregnant," she told him, not knowing why. Maybe because she had to tell somebody, and even if Sandoz told everybody, they wouldn't know what he was talking about.

He held her at arm's length, his eyes lighting up, which she figured was the amphetamines peeking out. "I rejoiced!"

he said. Then he forgot she was leading and danced his ass into the wall. Her momentum collapsed him like an accordion, and he needed to sit down for a while.

She found a stool at the bar and stayed there, turning down every john, keeping a mental tally of all the shit she turned down, picturing it piling up on the bar—the sum total of her virtue. That Laura was a fucking saint, all right. Enkidu slid in beside her. He wasn't wearing any clothes, which wasn't unusual on a warm night like tonight. His body was smeared with dried red mud. His erection looked like a terra-cotta dildo. He held out his clenched hand, palm down. He had a surprise for her.

"Not tonight, Enkie," she said. "I'm taking a night off."

He turned his hand over and opened it. There were the shrooms she never got around to in the Bin. Enkidu lived in the woods, gathered things. She fucked him for a nest of robin's eggs one time. They were beautiful, still sitting up in her room, never hatched. She shook her head. "Not tonight."

Enkidu squinted at her. His lower lip bulged with the shrooms he'd stuffed there like snuff. "Take 'em anyway," he said, putting them in her hand. She noticed Sandoz watching from the end of the bar and wondered whether he'd told Enkidu her secret.

"Thanks," she said and chewed them up. Her lips got pleasantly numb, and her stomach churned a protest as she washed them down with what Chef called sangria, probably grain alcohol and maraschino cherry juice. He had a shitload of maraschino cherries in the storeroom, jars the size of watermelons.

She sat there for a while, watching the edges of everything turn bright and precise and definite, like everything was turning more solid. Everything but the people. They blurred when they moved, trailing ghosts of themselves. She moved her hand back and forth in front of her face, and it was like it dissolved and reassembled itself, first here, then there. She slid off the stool and made her way to the stairs.

She passed her door and went to Chef's suite—two

rooms, each a little larger than her own. In the boudoir, she found what she was looking for. The only mirror in the place. Mirrors didn't last too long in Crazyville. Somebody was always punching them or smashing their heads into them.

But Chef had a full-length oval mirror with an oak frame and its own oak stand. The thing was two hundred years old if it was a day, and the mirror stuff around the edges was cracked like a dried-up creekbed.

She started taking off her clothes, getting caught up in the pants legs and falling on the floor. But she stayed with it for what seemed like days, until she was naked as the day she was born, as her grandmother used to say, even though she herself was never born. She managed to stand up, swaying back and forth like a pine tree in the wind.

The door opened, and Chef clomped in. She damn near gave him a heart attack. He clutched at his chest with one hand and waved a rib bone in the air with the other. "What do you think you are doing in my private quarters?" His mouth looked enormous. Then she realized it was ringed with barbecue sauce.

She pointed at the mirror. "Wanted to have a look-see," she said, or thought she said. She was past being able to make such fine distinctions.

His little pig eyes squinted at her as he fumbled around and lit a lamp. It threw big shadows up on the wall—Chef, her, the mirror. "Are you"—he fumbled for the word he wanted—"infected?"

"I'm not looking for crabs, asshole. I'm pregnant." That iced it. She'd just told *Chef.* Maybe she ought to just stroll on into New Jerusalem and tell Gabriel while she was at it. Maybe she was hoping somebody'd just strangle her and solve her problem.

Not that a knocked-up whore was some big newsflash. But there it was again, this kind of transformation—even more startling coming from Chef than it had been with Sandoz—like some nice guy just got transferred into that sack of blubber body. "The Soldier?" he asked delicately. He took out a hankie and wiped the barbecue sauce off his face.

"Yeah."

He looked at her in the mirror. "You are a beautiful courtesan," he said.

Yeah, and he was a culinary artiste. She looked okay. She always felt like her waist was too long, made her look like she'd been stretched or something, but she had nice tits. Skinny ass, though. Skinny brain too. Listen to yourself. You're trying to make the biggest decision of your life, and you're looking at your ass.

"Do I look any different?" she asked Chef.

He considered this a moment, then shook his head no.

She bent down to pick up her clothes, almost falling down again. Chef caught her and set her on her feet, then he gathered her clothes together and laid them across her arms.

"Thanks for the loan of the mirror," she said and shuffled down the hall to her room, falling facedown on the bed. After a while, she rolled over and stared at the ceiling. The bird's nest was sitting on a shelf by the bed. She took it down and set it on her stomach, taking one of the almost weightless eggs out and looking at it. She could just see herself raising a kid—a daughter who'd look up to her, say-ing, *Mom, show me how this life thing's done.* Like Laura would know. *You jump out of the nest, kid, and eventually you hit the ground.*

If she was somebody like Stephanie—who'd made a mess of things, sure—but turned it around, did the right thing, set a fucking example. *There you go, kid: love, devotion, fighting for what you believe in.*

And then the idea came to her, made her sit bolt upright in bed. The room rolled and swayed and settled into a hard clarity. It was crazy, crazier than anything she'd ever done, anything she'd ever heard of in or out of Crazyville. But there it was. She wasn't even sure if it was possible, but she knew who to ask.

She had to laugh. The Christians were always going on

about being born again. But it took some crazy Construct whore to actually consider *doing* it. The robin's nest was sitting on her lap. Somehow she'd sat up without dumping it on the floor. The tiny egg was still in her hand. She put it back with the others. So delicate. So beautiful. There was no other blue like it in the whole wide world.

16

THE ONE WHO GOT AWAY

DONOVAN GLANCED AT HIS WATCH, WONDERING WHAT THE hell time it really was—what day it was. It wasn't even the right season. They were all standing on the porch: Newman, Freddie, Stephanie, Tillman, and him, the fifth wheel. Laura had just gone, vanishing in a now-you-see-her-now-you-don't abruptness that made his head spin. He thought that maybe for the briefest instant he could see her and the reds and golds of the leaves behind her in a single vision, as if she were some punk rendition of Aurora. He remembered what Newman told Laura about free access to the system yielding madness, and for a second he thought he understood why. But it was as brief as his glimpse of Laura as the Goddess of Dawn—and probably just as real. He felt emptied out. Like a whoopee cushion—all his hot air only good for a laugh. He sat down on the porch rail—stoned and drunk and pissed off—and let the other four finish their business.

There was another cabin now that hadn't been there before, nestled in the woods by the stream. Smoke curled up from the chimney. There was probably a big bed in there, the covers turned down, a chilled bottle of champagne, flowers. An idyllic place for the unlikely lovers to stay until they went down to hell. They were both deliriously happy— the ugly little man and the tall beautiful woman. They took his hands, thanked him (for what?), and walked hand in hand to their custom-made illusion. Newman and Freddie beamed at them like cherubs.

He remembered a conversation he and Nicole had one night when she was flirting with suicide like some lover, just waiting for her husband to go to bed without her so she could embrace death. "Why is it?" she asked. "If I feel okay at the beginning of the day, I feel like shit by the end? It's because the days are too long, Donovan. The days just need to be shorter, so I could have one whole day where I felt okay. What do you think?"

"You can't make the days shorter, Nicole. Now come on to bed."

"Sure, you can. You can shorten them down to nothing, a tiny speck. All of them. A tiny little speck."

Freddie put his hand on Donovan's shoulder. "Are you all right, Donnie?"

Donovan fought the urge to shrug the hand off, concealing his anger, thinking without knowing what he meant that his anger was all he had, and he couldn't let Freddie and Newman see it just yet, or they would take it away. "I'm just stoned and drunk and tired." He managed a convincing good-natured laugh and spoke to Newman. "Could you sober me up?"

Newman smiled, falling for it, enjoying his power, no doubt, and Donovan felt the drugs—the illusion of the drugs—leave him as abruptly as Laura had vanished. "Thanks," he said. He took out a cigarette and lit it, blowing the smoke into the crisp air, watching it drift into the clearing. "Can I go home now?"

"Of course," Freddie said. "You can do anything you want."

"Can I?" he asked bitterly.

Freddie just looked bewildered at Donovan's tone. Newman's eyes narrowed with comprehension. He was, indeed, a very smart man. "What is it you want?" Newman asked quietly.

"You know what I want. Make me mortal—here and now."

"I can't do that."

"Bullshit. You can do anything you want, and we both know it. You control this whole place. You could kill me right now if you wanted to. This whole democratically controlled environment thing is just a sham to keep the sheep happily bleating, not making any real decisions about who they are and what they want to do with their lives."

"You're being unfair," Freddie began, but Newman silenced him with a wave of his hand and sat down in his chair with a sigh, massaging his temples with the palms of his hands, looking every bit as old as Tithonus.

"Fair or not, it's all true," Newman said.

"You want to die yourself, don't you?" Donovan accused, sounding, even to himself, like a belligerent schoolboy. But that's pretty much how he felt. Lied to—for his own good. *Of course there's a Santy Claus, dear.* Or his personal favorite: *You're just as human as anyone else, Donovan.*

Freddie turned away in disgust at Donovan's question, apparently knowing the answer. Newman raised his eyes, staring at Donovan, not speaking for a long time. When he spoke, his voice was quiet and sad, but deliberate. "Yes, I do. I've wanted to die since before you were born. But I've never been able to convince myself it's the right thing to do, though I've come close on occasion. You want mortality? I'll make a deal with you. I'll give you what you want on one condition: Convince me it's the right thing to do. Convince me to die."

"You know all the arguments as well as I do—"

"Fuck 'arguments'!" Newman shouted. His voice rang through the hollow. "I said I want to be *convinced,* not lectured. I want you to meet someone. After you've met him, you can decide what you want to do. If you make the right choice, I'll be convinced, and I'll run that death program of yours."

So that program was what all this was about, just not in the way Donovan had figured. "And what's the 'right choice'?"

"That's for me to know and you to find out. If I tell you

which choice will give you what you want, you won't be making it freely, and you were just now, if I'm not mistaken, lecturing me on free will."

Donovan sensed a trap, but he lived in a trap—so what did it matter? "Who do you want me to meet?"

"Gabriel."

Donovan felt a chill go up his spine. He thought at first he hadn't heard right, or that Rogers was insane—but he could see in Rogers's eyes and in Freddie's that neither was the case. "How can I possibly meet Gabriel?"

Newman sighed. "Leave that to me. The 'how' isn't relevant. You'll be in no danger. Do we have a deal or not?"

"You're asking me to decide your fate—that you'll end your life if I make a certain choice without even telling me what the choice is?"

"Don't be an idiot, Donovan. I know perfectly well what I'm doing. If I want a critique, I'll ask for one. Do we have a deal?"

Donovan, preacher for death, could hardly tell a 170-year-old man he couldn't die if he wanted to. Besides, Donovan knew it wasn't his scruples making him hesitate but cowardice. Part of him wanted to take back his request, forget the whole thing, let well enough alone—"live with it," as they used to say. Forever. "Yes. We have a deal."

Freddie snorted in disgust, shaking his head, glaring at them both. "I can't believe you're going through with this, Newman."

"You have a better idea? I'm open to suggestions."

Freddie rolled his eyes. "Newman, you are such an asshole." He turned to Donovan. "Well, let's go meet the Antichrist and get it over with. Okonkwo and I have a party in Rio tonight, and I'm not going to miss it for this nonsense." He pushed his hair back with both hands and sighed. "Close your eyes, Donnie."

"Why?"

The eye roll again. "Just *do* it. You certainly have gotten testy since that lovely reptilian wench left. She's quite fetching, isn't she?"

"I'm not interested."

"Then maybe you *should* die. I'm an old fag—I have an excuse—but you, my boy, should stop and smell the rosebushes. You might not be so devoted to death."

"Are we leaving or not?"

Freddie smiled. "I've been waiting for you to close your eyes."

Donovan glared at him and clamped his eyes shut. A second later, he didn't have to be told he could open them. He smelled the familiar scent of Freddie's favorite incense. They were in his workroom, and Freddie was already at work at his computer. It occurred to Donovan that he hadn't even said good-bye to Newman Rogers, that he'd been rude, even insulting to a man who'd been his hero. Who still was, which is why, he supposed, he was putting his life in the man's hands.

He was going to meet Gabriel, the boogeyman of the Bin, who didn't even scare children anymore. For Bin children, fear was never anything other than a game. And for adults, Gabriel was as frightening as walking under a ladder or spilling salt. And here he was, terrified. He'd spent his whole life trying to piece together some meaning, some purpose, and he had the sinking feeling that he was about to be proven completely and irrevocably wrong.

Freddie was muttering to himself as he worked, still in a snit. "I told Newman this was a stupid idea, but does he listen?"

"What, exactly, is the stupid idea?"

"Oh, this whole bodhisattva nonsense. 'Newman,' I said. 'Isn't that a bit precious, even for you?' But once he gets an idea in his head, that's it."

"What does that have to do with meeting Gabriel?"

"I'm not supposed to tell you that. You're supposed to figure it out for yourself."

"I don't get it. How can any single life I lead down there make any real difference?"

"Not with that attitude, it won't."

"You just got through saying it was a stupid idea, Freddie. Whose side are you on here, anyway?"

"Newman's, of course. It's a stupid idea, but it'll be nice if it works. He's not suggesting you lead just any old life down there, Donnie." He gestured toward the console. "Care to have a look-see?"

"I said I would."

"Stop pouting. You got yourself into this. We have a few unwitting spies in New Jerusalem, Constructs who've been captured and enslaved by the Soldier elite. The Soldiers zap most of their intelligence and memory, put shock collars on them—more for show than utility. We tap into their senses through their still-functioning chips. The fellow you'll be accessing is Seth—Gabriel's personal slave and bodyguard, selected for his powerful physique and his inability to speak."

"Is that who Newman wants me to download into?"

"Have a nice visit, Donnie." Freddie waved bye-bye.

And then he was moving through a dark stone passageway, carrying something draped over his shoulder. It was a woman. Her long hair hung down to the floor and trailed behind him, where at least three or four people were following. In front of him was a figure clad all in white with luxurious white hair. Gabriel. Seth's fear and hatred of the man felt like a pounding surf against the almost featureless shoreline of Seth's mind, without thought or reflection. For Seth, it seemed, walking took most of his concentration.

His long powerful legs were huge, his chest and shoulders massive. Probably descended from the Construct laborers who'd built the world, now all in ruins. Like Seth himself, who had no memories of who he was or what he'd been, only of the man in white who told him what to do.

A door opened at the end of the passageway. Ducking to avoid the doorjamb, he followed Gabriel inside. The room was windowless, bare except for a chair with leather straps on the arms. Gabriel snapped his fingers and pointed at the chair. Seth dropped the woman into it, fastened the straps around her arms, and stepped back, keeping his eyes on Gabriel in case he was needed.

There were three Soldiers standing at attention in front of the closed door. Seth towered over them all. "Wake her up," Gabriel said. The middle Soldier stepped forward, stabbed a hypodermic into her thigh, and emptied its contents.

The effect was instantaneous. Her body twitched all over, her back arching, rocking the chair back and forth, and then her eyes came open, looking into Seth's with abject terror. Donovan tried to look away, but his will had no effect. He wanted out. He didn't need to see this. He thought, *Enough, Freddie!* But there was no reply. He was trapped here.

Gabriel had come up behind the woman as she was coming awake and now took up her hair in his hands. She jumped and tried to turn her head, but he pulled the hair taut and leaned down next to her ear. "Elizabeth, my child, your hair has fallen. Let me fix it for you."

Elizabeth winced at the sound of his voice. She knew who it was and was trembling all over. A small whimper escaped her mouth.

Gabriel carefully divided her hair into three equal strands with his long bony fingers and started braiding her hair with smooth luxurious movements. Erotic and deadly. He talked as he braided in a soothing conversational tone. "Such beautiful hair, Elizabeth. Your husband must enjoy watching you brush it out in the evening, running his fingers through it when he makes love to you. Such a beautiful blessing, marriage. Such intimacy, such closeness, such devotion. Sharing all your deepest secrets. You love your husband very much, don't you?"

She nodded her head, shaking with terror.

"I thought you did. He certainly is fond of you. We spoke just this morning." At this, she jerked in the chair as if he'd stabbed her through the heart, and he smiled. He'd reached the end of the braid, admired his work. "Such lovely hair." He leaned over her shoulder, looked into her eyes. "Do you have a ribbon, child? I have nothing with which to secure your beautiful hair."

She shook her head back and forth. Her face was wet with tears, and snot ran down to her mouth. Gabriel took a handkerchief and wiped her face like a kindly father, held the handkerchief to her nose. "Blow," he said, and she obeyed.

He straightened up, tossing the handkerchief to the floor, the end of the braid still in his clenched fist. "I'll just hold it then until Granger can fetch me a ribbon. Blue, Granger, to match her eyes." The Soldier closest to the door saluted and left. Gabriel paced back and forth behind Elizabeth, holding the braid taut as if swinging on a pendulum. Not so taut as to hurt just yet. Her shoulders and neck twitched as she tried to hold herself steady. Her eyes tracked back and forth with his movements.

"Your husband has made some very unfortunate friends. You know the kind—like the Serpent in the Garden luring the innocent into sin, even as fine a man as your husband. We have offered him our mercy if he will only tell us their blasphemous schemes, but he seems determined to die for his secrets. That would be a shame, don't you think? A fine man like him?"

A sob broke from Elizabeth's throat, and she moaned, "No, no, no," over and over again, like a mantra, but Gabriel seemed not to notice, talking over her, pacing back and forth, smiling pleasantly like someone taking his dog for a walk in the park.

"It would seem to me, however, that there is a way for your husband's life to be saved, and God's bountiful mercy to be granted. You are his helpmate, his devoted and loving wife. You would do anything to save his life, to save him from eternal damnation. He has shared his secrets with you, hasn't he?"

She had clamped her eyes shut, her hands grasped the arms of the chair. "No, no, no."

Gabriel swung his arm and yanked her hair hard, snapping her head back. Her eyes widened in pain. "Don't say that word again."

She clamped her mouth shut. He relaxed the tension on her braid, stroked the top of her head with his free hand. "I'm sorry I had to hurt you, my child. But you must realize your husband's life is at stake. A pretty girl like you must be used to having her hair pulled by naughty boys. Couldn't hurt that much, eh?"

He looked at Seth and wiggled his little finger in the air. Seth stepped forward, pried Elizabeth's right hand from the arm of the chair with one hand, took her little finger in the other and snapped it in two. All the while Donovan is fighting what feels like his own body, his own hands, screaming inside his head: *No! No! No!* But Seth can't hear him, while Donovan can feel her bones breaking like a twig. Her screams fill the tiny room.

One by one, he broke her fingers, but she would not speak. It was a miracle she could remain conscious, or maybe it was just the injection. Donovan wished he could pass out, hide from Seth's senses. He tried to turn inside somehow and shut them out, but he couldn't. He could only watch and feel and hear what felt like his own hands torturing this helpless woman. He hated Gabriel with an intensity he'd never felt toward anything in his life.

When all her fingers were broken, Gabriel came around in front of her, still holding the braid, and bent over her. "Tell me their names," he said.

All the color had drained from her face. Her eyes were blank and hollow. Her tongue passed slowly over her upper lip. "No," she whispered. Gabriel turned to Seth and tapped the side of his head. Seth took her head in his hands and snapped her neck.

There was a great stillness, and Donovan felt for a moment that he himself had died.

The door flew open, and Granger placed a blue ribbon in Gabriel's hands as if awarding him a prize. Gabriel tied her braid in a pretty bow and turned to the others. "I guess she didn't care what happened to her husband." The Soldiers laughed. Her husband was already dead. In what passed for Seth's memory was a man's head in his hands a few hours earlier. Donovan felt as if he were sobbing, but his stonelike face didn't move, his eyes stared straight ahead, his breath heaved in and out like a wind in a cavern.

And then he was staring into Freddie's eyes. He started screaming, remembering his hands buried in Elizabeth's hair, the tiny shockwave as her neck snapped, the dead weight of her head in his hands. "I killed her," he sobbed over and over. "I killed her."

TWO WEEKS LATER, DONOVAN AND FREDDIE SAT BESIDE THE koi pond. Donovan sipped an Irish whiskey and petted the fish. One of the braver ones wriggled through his hand, and Donovan thought of Gabriel's hand gripping the rope of Elizabeth's hair. He yanked his hand out of the water and shook it dry. Dozens of koi mouths broke the surface as if blowing him kisses.

"Why did you pick that moment for me to meet Gabriel?" he asked Freddie.

"Real time, Donnie. The moment picked itself. Did you think you'd catch him napping? May I remind you that you're the one who made that silly deal, not me."

"I said I'd meet someone. I didn't say I'd kill someone."

"Oh, stop it. You didn't *kill* anyone. Elizabeth would've died if you were there or not."

"Why didn't you stop it?"

"You mean stop it for you or for her?"

"I meant for me," Donovan said quietly, another drop of guilt to add to the deep well. "But now that you mention it, why don't you have that monster of yours break Gabriel's neck?"

"Seth is not a monster, and he would be shocked unconscious before he could lay a finger on Gabriel."

For the last two weeks, Donovan had been imagining Gabriel's death in countless forms. He no doubt wasn't alone in such musings. But the man lived on, and Donovan had to admit that face-to-face with Gabriel, he'd probably

just cower in fear along with everyone else. "Why did Newman want me to meet Gabriel?"

"You haven't figured it out yet? Come on, Donnie. I told
Newman you were very bright."

"So he told me. Now would you just tell me what the
hell this is all about?"

"Newman feels responsible for Gabriel. The way he sees
it, if the Bin had never been built, Gabriel would've remained just another shrieking fanatic. Now he's the most
powerful man on the planet, and this is Newman's last
chance to stop him from destroying it—which, Newman
being Newman, he'd feel responsible for as well."

Donovan remembered Seth's powerful hands, his own
powerlessness as he tried to stop them, feeling responsible
just the same. If he were actually downloaded into him, he
would have control of those hands. "Seth. He wants me to
download into Seth and kill Gabriel. That's it, isn't it?"

"Newman has asked me not to tell you what 'it' is."

Donovan took that as a yes. "But it sounds like there's
plenty of opposition, an underground. Why not just let
things run their course? Assassin's not exactly the life I had
in mind."

"I didn't know you had *any* life in mind, Donnie. And if
you'll feel better calling a couple dozen terrified people in
the midst of thousands of armed Soldiers an underground,
be my guest. But here's the dreadful little truth: Gabriel is
running out of enemies. He needs either enemies or the
end of the world. It's the equation that's kept him in power
for all these years. He either has to root out conspiracy or
take on the Constructs, and to defeat them he knows he'll
more than likely have to resort to nuclear weapons. The
cockroaches can discuss who won. *That's* the course things
will eventually run."

"If Newman feels so responsible, then why doesn't he
handle it?"

"Ungrateful brat. As if the man hasn't done enough. And
then there's the small matter of the billions of lives in here."

"But how can he be sure that killing Gabriel will change anything? Won't some other psycho take his place?"

"You're absolutely right. Gabriel's death would probably make things worse. Selecting a new Chosen One won't be any popularity contest. And once the winner kills off his rivals, he'll have to show what a real man he is by doing exactly what Gabriel would do—only more so. No, the *only* one who can change things is Gabriel himself, and the only way that will happen is if he's *not* himself."

Donovan sat in stunned silence. The sound of the waterfall seemed to grow louder. A silky voice slithered through his mind, wrapping itself around that poor woman's heart. *Elizabeth, my child, your hair has fallen. Let me fix it for you.* "Gabriel. He wants me to become Gabriel."

"Newman has asked me not to tell you what he wants. But I will tell you that one of Seth's duties is to stand guard over Gabriel when he takes on a new body."

"So I'm to download into Seth first, then steal Gabriel's new body from him when he makes the transfer."

"If that's what you choose to do, yes."

"How long would I have to be Seth?"

"You wouldn't actually *be* Seth."

"I know, I know. How long?"

"A month, a few years. It's hard to say."

"And I'd have to do whatever Gabriel told me to, or I'd give myself away. I'd have to keep myself from killing him."

"If you want to change things, yes. What do you think now, Donnie? Do you think your single life can make a difference?"

"This is insane. Even if I agreed to this, I couldn't pull it off. I can't be Gabriel."

"You know the Bible backward and forward. You make fine speeches. You are an accomplished sophist, if you don't mind my saying so. You've read your Machiavelli. I think you could be quite convincing."

"If I didn't go crazy from torturing and killing people as Seth, I'd just get myself killed as Gabriel. I'm a scholar, I'm no politician. Do you actually think this would work?"

"Me personally? No. It's a stupid idea. Too many things could go wrong and most likely would. I wouldn't blame you if you just called off this silly deal and lived a happy life."

Donovan imagined the world in Gabriel's hands like Elizabeth's head in Seth's grip. "I can't do that either."

"Then you *do* have a problem. Newman brings that out in people."

HE TOOK A NIGHT FLIGHT THIS TIME, SAT ON THE AISLE. HE didn't want to look down at the artificial world. He knew with fresh certainty that it wasn't real. No matter how complete it seemed to be, how precise in every detail, it wasn't the real world. It wasn't even close: They left out more than death. They left out Gabriel as well.

Donovan wasn't sure what he was doing. He felt like a little boy running to his mother for another comforting lie. But it wasn't her counsel he wanted. He knew what she'd say without bothering to ask: *Death's bad, sit down and veg awhile.* No, he wanted to talk to the one person he trusted to speak honestly about death and evil, and he hoped to use his mother to reach her in the only way he could. He wanted the hard truth, the one that had always lurked just outside his view like the monsters he conjured as a boy— behind the tree, around the corner—to thrill himself with terror, working himself into such a froth his mother lost all patience with him. He'd sometimes thought all his foolishness had driven her away, but had long since outgrown that notion. It'd never occurred to him that she didn't want to hear about his monsters because she knew they were there. When he was a boy, the breaking of a twig in the forest could set him off. The smallest sound, like fingers breaking. The plane banked into its descent, revealing past the empty seat beside him, the glowing dust of city lights. Fairy dust for a fairy world, or glowing cinders borne aloft by the fires of hell.

        ❖   ❖   ❖

HE MET HIS MOTHER IN HER ROOM, LITTLE MORE THAN A bare cell. Remembering didn't require much space. The hive freed itself of all possessions. Everything you needed was stowed in the overhead compartment of your head. There was a small table with two chairs, a narrow bed. She treated him differently this time. Even she could see this wasn't their usual joust, and that her son—or whatever he was to her now—was in no mood for banter. They sat at the table, and without preamble, he told his story, made his request. He hadn't asked her for anything in ten years, when he'd asked her to attend his wedding and she'd declined.

But she agreed almost immediately, even enthusiastically, to this request. Not out of love or devotion or concern, Donovan thought. I've intrigued her is all—proposed another way to shape things, like a game of cat's cradle.

"What do I need to do?" he asked.

"Remember her," she said softly. She lay her hand on his. Maybe she understood more than he gave her credit for. He clasped her hand. "Open up and remember," she prompted, and he did, trying not to think about the thousands of minds attending to his memories, shaping them into the woman he thought he knew. It would take a few minutes, he was told. He should be patient.

The hivers called it "talking to an angel." One's memories of a particular person, with the combined mental force of the hive members dwelling on each moment, were fashioned into a simulation of that person so that you could have the illusion of conversing with a departed loved one. Donovan had once called the practice a seance, and his mother had taken exception. "A seance is a superstitious relic from the days when people believed in an afterlife," she corrected him. "The angel is born from the reality of memory." He'd scorned the practice as self-delusional nonsense, a fancy way of talking to yourself. And here he was asking to meet his dead wife. Maybe he had more faith in superstitious relics than his mother did. Or maybe it wasn't such a bad idea to talk to himself. Maybe for once he'd answer.

What had intrigued his mother was the condition he'd put upon it. "I don't want to see her in some happy time years ago. I want it to be now. I want her to know she's dead. I want her to know she killed herself." Whether it was solely his own mind, or all these others prying loose the past, he didn't know, but once he thought of her, his mind was flooded with memories.

THEY'RE LYING IN BED NAKED, EARLY IN THE MORNING, NESTLED *together. "Spoons," they call it. He's admiring her back, moved by the beauty of it. The shadow of the pliant wind-blown curtain hovers over them with a gauzy haze, split by sunlight when the wind gusts, knocking a champagne flute on its side so that it rolls to the edge of the bedside table and stops. A trickle of wine pools on the mahogany and slowly seeps into the wood. No stain. No trace.*

He presses his forehead against her back, wondering who she'll be when she wakes this time, hoping she'll remember the joy and passion, at least for a little while. He kisses her back and tastes his own tears.

"That feels nice," she murmurs and turns in his arms, drowsy smile upon her face. "Hi, sailor, wanna fool around?"

He's filled with such joy he wants to live forever.

HER BIRTHDAY. A CELEBRATION. SHE WEARS THE BACKLESS *dress. Somewhere between the Metro and the restaurant she's gone from sad to bitter to enraged, and she's telling him in a loud brutal voice over untouched desserts, "You're the reason I want to die, Donovan. You're like some vampire sucking the life out of me, needing me so damn much. I'll tell you what it is you really need. You think if I don't kill myself that you can stomach your own pitiful life. The bitch isn't dead yet; I must be doing something right. Well, fuck you, Donovan. I don't want to be your personal cause."*

The crowded restaurant is silent. A waiter gently places

a plate on a table, as if it might crumble at the slightest shock. A red-haired man across the room gives Donovan a sympathetic smile, probably thinking he understands. But he doesn't. No one does. Least of all Donovan himself. "I'm sorry," he says.

"You make me sick," she says, standing, speaking, it seems, to everyone. He watches her go, her beautiful back knotted with fury and blame. As she clears the door, the noise of pent-up outrage and clattering dishes wells up behind her like the Red Sea crashing back into place. Donovan rises and follows her at a steady lope. Several people shake their heads as he passes. But not the red-haired man, who wears a look of genuine sadness.

She's taken her steak knife from the table and slipped it into her purse. Just to see if he'd notice. Just to see if the vampire still cares. He breaks into a run.

SHE'S DEAD. HIS SENATOR CALLED THE BOAT TO TELL HIM. HE *and Alex are drunk and stoned, drifting. Their fishing rods lie at their feet, hopelessly tangled up together. They're kicked back under a full moon, talking about their wives. Donovan says, "I really think things are getting back. She hasn't tried anything in months." And then the phone rings.*

There's nothing between the phone ringing, knowing immediately what it means, and him kneeling in the mud, holding her body in his arms. There are people everywhere—a media event. There's a woman's voice behind him: "Tonight, at exactly nine P.M., Nicole Beaudreaux became the third suicide victim of the year when she leaped from the bridge you see behind me spanning the James River. With a history of repeated attempts, and prone to chronic depression, her death brings the tragic total to . . ."

He doesn't need to hear the tragic total. He knows. He knows they come in clusters of three or four, spurring each other on. He knows that the typical suicide victim usually succeeds after several unsuccessful attempts. He knows that there are no statistically significant variations by race, gen-

der, or ethnicity in frequency, only method. He's an expert. He presses his cheek against hers. He doesn't know shit.

Lights flare up in his eyes. It's the talking woman, bending at the waist, a microphone held out like a communion wafer. "Dr. Carroll, can you tell us how it feels?"

"Cold," he says, holding death in his arms, not Nicole at all. "Cold."

AND THEN IT WASN'T MEMORIES ANYMORE. IT WAS NICOLE— the hive's angel—sitting across the table from him in his mother's tiny room. In a macabre touch from his own subconscious or from one of the hive members, her hair was damp and rumpled, as if she'd just stepped from the river and toweled it dry. But her sweater and jeans were clean and fresh. "Let's go outside," she said, rising, plucking his sleeve as she passed him on her way to the door.

The sky was full of stars. By the time Donovan stepped outside, moments behind her, she was some twenty paces ahead, standing on a grassy knoll. She slipped off her shoes and walked in a circle, digging her toes into the grass, sticking her arms out, whirling around. She was up. On the manic side before the plunge. As he reached her, she plopped down on the grass. "You going to sit? Or just stand there looking somber?"

"I was waiting to see where you'd light." He sat down facing her, lit a cigarette. She plucked it out of his hand and took a deep drag. He lit himself another.

"You can stop waiting to see what I'll do next, Donovan. I'm dead now." She laughed to herself. "Guess you could say I've done it all."

He'd imagined confronting her, telling her the pain she caused him and demanding to know why. Now, he only wanted to push her back onto the grass and make love to her. But he couldn't bring himself to touch her, not because she wasn't real, but because it would be too awful to feel her alive, only to lose her again. It was the story of their lives together—elation or despair, with no middle ground, so that the one almost seemed to cause the other.

So he began to tell her about Newman Rogers and Gabriel and Elizabeth—without saying or knowing just why he was telling her or what he wanted from her. She listened, smoking the rest of her cigarette, plucking another from his pack and lighting it, stretching out beside him on the grass, looking up at the stars. When he'd finished his story—telling her the terrible choices he faced—she pointed up at the sky. "Is that Orion?" she asked.

He leaned sideways, looking along the line of her arm. "Yes," he said. "Have you heard anything I've said?"

"Did you ever hear me?" she asked. "Did you ever listen?"

"Of course I listened."

" 'Of course I listened,' " she mocked, making him sound like a pompous ass. "So you could try to talk me out of everything I said."

"When you talked about killing yourself, yes. When you said you were worthless."

"Maybe I was. Why was that your problem? Why did you feel so damn responsible for me?"

He started to take the cheap shot—*Somebody had to*—but stopped himself. That wasn't fair, wasn't true. "I don't know," he said. He wished like hell he did, but he didn't. He used to think it made him virtuous, then he thought it made him a fool. But lately he'd been thinking it just made him Donovan. Like jumping off that bridge made her Nicole. They were made for each other. "When did you stop loving me?"

"You can't love your jailer, Donovan."

"I wasn't your goddamn jailer. I wasn't a vampire, an evil sorcerer, or any of that other crap you used to call me."

"Yeah, I know. I was a manic-depressive with paranoid delusions, and you were just fine, just perfect."

"I didn't say I was perfect."

She put her arm around his neck and pulled his face close to hers. "Let me ask you something. I dealt with all my problems, but you've still got all of yours. So who is it who's screwed up?"

He looked into her eyes, and there it was, no matter what she said or what she did, her love, imprisoned in the dark cage of her despair. He kissed her mouth hard, and she returned his passion. They knelt before each other, tearing at their clothes, desperate to make love before remembrance could overtake them and turn this last pleasure into just another pitiful ritual of loss. But moments before he shuddered and came, he knew he would never, no matter how long he lived, make love to her again, wasn't making love to her now. He let out a cry, sobbing like Elizabeth when she knew her husband was dead. The angel held Donovan wrapped in her arms as he cried himself out. "I loved you so much," he said.

She wiped the tears from his cheeks. "You still do."

"It was like there were two of you. I couldn't love the one who wanted to die." He pressed her hand against his face. He would never forget the feel of her hands, like no one else's. "Why couldn't you have gone the other way?"

She shrugged a shoulder and made a face. "Gravity?"

He smiled. Even in death, she had her warped sense of humor. "So you recommend suicide, do you?"

"For you? Not you, Donovan. We wanted different things. You always wanted meaning. Everything you did had to matter or you hated yourself for it."

"Everybody wants their lives to matter."

She shook her head emphatically no. "That's not what I wanted."

"And what did you want?"

"Nothing. I wanted to want nothing. Nirvana."

"That's not nirvana."

She cocked one eyebrow. "And how would you know?"

He had to laugh, even while his heart was breaking. Only she could give him that experience. They held each other's gaze. At times like this, he'd always imagined that the real Nicole, not this angel who was only his creation, knew exactly what he was thinking, what he felt. She must've known how completely she'd shattered all his illusions, or maybe that was an illusion too.

"Do you love this Elizabeth woman?" she asked.

"I don't even know her."

"That didn't stop you from loving me. You feel responsible for her too."

"She's dead. There's nothing I can do for her."

"There was nothing you could do for me either." She propped herself up on one arm and gave her head a toss. "Let's walk," she said.

THEY WALKED NAKED HAND IN HAND THROUGH THE HIVE'S garden: winding paths, gazebos, fountains, gently arching footbridges over still waters. They seemed to be the only two people in the world. Ironically, the whole hive could feel the night breeze on their skin, feel their hands clasped together.

They came to a stop on one of the footbridges. "Did you kill yourself because of me?" he asked. "You told me once that I was the reason you wanted to die, the reason you hated your life."

She stared down into the water. "I don't remember that."

It was probably true. She didn't remember much of the times when she was vicious and cruel. It was like there were two of her, like Hermes' snakes coiled around a single staff.

"You think you didn't love me enough," she said. "You think if you'd only loved me more, I wouldn't have done it. No one could've loved me enough. No one. Not even you. Go save everybody, Donovan. I'll just be the one who got away."

She gave him a quick kiss, climbed onto the railing, and dove into the water, disappeared into the rippling blackness. He stared at the water for a long time, even though he knew she wouldn't come up again, not if he waited forever, knew he couldn't follow her, knew what he had to do.

He looked around at the perfect landscape, an elegant creation free of evil serpents and knowledge-giving trees, unless you snatched the whole thing from its vine and gobbled it down, took it all in. Fear was everywhere, no matter which way he chose to go. It was like the air. You just had to walk through it, breathe it in, and let it go.

He walked back to their clothes, staring at hers as he pulled on his pants, buttoned his shirt. He carried his shoes in his hands, left her clothes lying on the grass.

His mother was sitting at her table. His chair awaited him. He slumped into it, dropping his shoes on the floor with a thud. He let his head fall back against the wall and closed his eyes, reaching out his hand for hers, and she took it.

When he opened his eyes, he knew it was over, that he'd found out a good deal more than he'd bargained for. He sighed and rose to his feet. "Thanks, Mom," he said. "Thank everyone for me."

He started for the door, and she followed him. "Would you like some tea or anything?"

"No thanks." He continued on out the door, no embraces, no long good-byes. They'd left that behind a long time ago. No point in taking it back up now. But when he was passing the place where the angel's clothes would've been, his mother called to him.

"Donovan, are you going to do what you told the angel about? Are you going to download into that Construct?"

He stopped and turned to her, standing in the doorway, hands on the doorjamb as if bracing herself against a wind. "Yes, I am."

"Be careful," she said. "Please be careful."

He smiled, warmed by her concern in spite of everything. That's all you could hope for in the end. That someone cared. "Thanks, Mom. I will."

17

ANNUNCIATION

SAM HAD CAUSED THE DEATHS OF MANY PEOPLE HE'D NEVER seen, half the world away. When he was barely twenty, he'd made his father proud by getting a long-defunct surveillance system up and running so that a settlement of some 150 people hiding out in the Andes—crazies, Constructs, Muslims—who knew?—what difference did it make?—were detected, obliterated, and sermonized before the day was over. His medal ceremony took a few more days to arrange. And there were other deaths, other medals. He'd quit listening to the details.

But he'd never caused a life before, and even though it was invisible, more an idea than a life, just like those people in the Andes, he didn't want it to die. Her, he corrected himself. God had led him to Laura, to Tillman, to the crazies, to the Constructs, and now to this child, his daughter. Was that just so she could die? It could be. Sam had killed other people's children. Maybe God wanted him to know what it felt like.

Hawkeye had told him that the Constructs believed the universe was a single organism, and each life within it a single cell contributing to the whole. Maybe so. In such a universe, Sam imagined, he was a thought or a question, a yearning or a hope, moving from cell to cell with a purpose he couldn't begin to fathom. He wanted to tell Laura all this, smiling as he imagined her comments. *Hello? Sammy?*

How can you have a purpose if you don't know what the fuck it is? Exactly. That's what faith was, he'd decided, not some set of rules that sent you to hell if you broke them, but the sense that your life mattered, that God knew what He was doing even when—especially when—you couldn't make sense of anything.

He'd done the wrong thing all his life—most of the time knowing it was wrong, but doing it because it was easier, telling himself he was just one man—a boy, really—and he couldn't make any difference anyway. There was a Construct expression he'd heard several times these last few weeks he'd been living among them—*Everything matters, or nothing matters*—and he liked that. It seemed to him to be what Christ was saying: Every grain of sand matters.

And to him right now what mattered most was Laura. He thought about her all the time. Not just because of the baby. And he didn't think he was driven by lust, though many of his thoughts were lustful. He didn't think he was in love with her exactly, though maybe he was. He didn't know much about men and women, or even about having friends.

He liked her. That's what it was. It was just that simple. She was completely different from him, yet somehow the same. He wondered what she'd say about that. He found himself wondering that a lot—what she'd say about almost anything. He'd never had a friend to whom he could fearlessly speak his mind. She'd argue with him, tell him he was full of shit, but that's what she liked about him—that he was a fool like her, trying to live by his principles.

He missed her.

But he couldn't go to her in Crazyville without endangering them both. Soldier patrols were everywhere, looking for him. Gabriel's hackers were having trouble getting past the security he'd added to Tillman's computer, and they thought they might torture some answers out of Sam, or at least vent their frustration. The Constructs, who seemed to know everything that went on in New Jerusalem, told him that his treason was the daily subject of Gabriel's sermons and that Gabriel himself promised to carry out Sam's execution. He didn't ask the Constructs what his father's reaction was, and they were kind enough not to tell him. All those patrols out there were under his father's command.

But if Laura decided to come back to Construct Town, he had confidence in her ability to elude the Soldiers. He had to smile, remembering their wild ride through the night. But if she came back, that'd probably mean she'd decided to abort. He could understand her doing that, as much as he didn't want her to. But he hoped for more. He wasn't sure what exactly. Maybe just something to hope for, even though hope seemed, as Laura would say, pretty fucking stupid.

Somehow he didn't think she'd abort. There was something in her voice when she told him it was a girl. And if that's what she was going to do, she'd've done it right away. Once she set her mind on something, there was no stopping her. Once she made up her mind, he hoped he'd be strong enough to do the right thing.

So when Hawkeye told him someone wanted to see him, Sam both hoped and feared it was Laura, but it wasn't her. It was Tillman.

"I thought Tillman was in the Bin," Sam said.

"He'll transmit from there. You won't know the difference. If you were a Construct, you could perceive him through your chip, but since you're not, you must use an external interface." There was a note of apology in his voice he'd heard before. The Constructs seemed to pity human limitations—what they called "the solitary life"—though they were just too polite to admit it. Hawkeye swiveled his head toward the door and gestured with his tiny hand. "We will take you there."

As he followed Hawkeye through the streets, many paused to wave at Sam, and he waved back. They all knew about him—who he was, what he'd done. They'd taken him in without question, had given him a small apartment, brought him food and clothing. He didn't know nearly enough about them, though he never stopped asking Hawkeye questions. One in particular had been nagging at him since their last conversation. "Why don't all of you escape into the Bin?" he asked.

Hawkeye registered emotions in his eyes—the pupils dilating and contracting. He seemed to enjoy Sam's questions, the chance to hold forth on what everyone else around them already knew. Sam could see why the Constructs got on Laura's nerves, headstrong as she was, but Sam found their ideas intoxicating. Hawkeye swiveled his head back and forth. "Some lives are long," he said. "Some are short. Some lives are solitary. Some are joined. All of them matter—the shortest no less than the eternal. We choose to stay here. It is our place in things."

They were passing through the marketplace, dozens of stalls full of handmade goods, some useful, but many were decorations and adornments no one would've dared display in a Christian market. "We like to make things," Hawkeye had explained when they'd passed through here before. The narrow aisles forced them to walk single-file, but Hawkeye turned his head so that one eye was on Sam while the other guided them through the marketplace.

"Here we have one body, one death," he continued. "Nothing can separate us as long as we live. Many-in-one is not just an idea. In the Bin, the body is an illusion, and the bonds dissolve into solitary lives, waiting alone."

They'd come upon a cluster of food stalls. The smells of cooking came at him from all directions, and the cooks handed him samples as he passed. Construct food was widely varied, richly spiced. Sam found it almost overwhelming.

They emerged from the market and headed down a narrow street fronted by flat-faced buildings. "Waiting for what?" Sam asked. "Do you believe in an afterlife?"

Hawkeye shrugged. "Perhaps a new life. Perhaps nothing. Everything matters."

"So do you believe in God?"

Hawkeye's feathered face and beaklike mouth were hard to read, but his large eyes and slowly blinking lids seemed to convey amusement. "Yes. Even God matters." They were standing in front of a nondescript door on an empty street. Hawkeye opened it. "You will find Tillman in here," he said.

SAM STEPPED ACROSS THE THRESHOLD AND THE DOOR CLOSED behind him. He found himself in a log cabin. Clean and cozy, it reminded him of the place he used to fantasize for himself when he imagined being transferred to the provinces—a place to hide and pretend he was a good man. He could see mountains and trees through the windows and hear the sound of a stream. Tillman was sitting in the same recliner he'd had before in the Red Room.

"Hey, kid," he said. "How's it going?" Tillman's voice had a forced joviality that told Sam he'd better brace himself for bad news.

"I'm fine." Sam sat down in an old rocker with green corduroy cushions tied onto the seat and back. "I'm glad you got out all right before the Soldiers found you."

Tillman bobbed his head up and down, squirming around in his chair. "Yeah, I know. You really stuck your neck out for me, and I want you to know how much I appreciate it."

Something was wrong. Sam could feel it in the air. His heart quickened. "Is Laura all right?" he asked.

Tillman looked startled. "Why do you ask that? You mean like hurt or something? No, she's fine, just fine." He licked his lips. "It's funny you should bring her up. She's kind of the reason I wanted to talk to you . . . You were real straight with me, and I figured you deserved the same—to know what's going on, I mean. And so . . . Oh, shit." He shook his head, almost losing his nerve, then looked Sam in the eye. "What I'm trying to tell you is that Laura contacted Steph and asked her if she wanted to download into Laura's body, asked her—us, actually—if we'd raise your daughter. I thought you ought to know."

Sam tried to make sense of what Tillman was saying, but

couldn't fit it together. "How can Stephanie download into Laura? Are they going to be a Construct?"

"Well . . . not exactly. I know this is going to sound nuts, Sam. It sounds nuts to me. But Laura's a little different from most people. When she transferred me, you know, well, you get to know a lot about a person that way, and Laura might seem pretty fucked up, but she's really a very good person."

"I know."

Tillman looked at him and blinked a few times. "Course you do. That was pretty stupid of me." Tillman gave a nervous laugh, took a deep breath, and spoke in a rush: "She wants to download into the child, Sam, into the baby."

Sam had been imagining many things, but not this. "How?" he managed, though he knew it wasn't an important question. The only important question was why, and he knew the answer to that immediately. The rightness of what Laura was doing hit him like a strong gust of wind. Like a whirlwind, lifting him up into the heavens.

"I don't pretend to understand it completely," Tillman said. "It's something Newman's cooked up. She came to him first apparently. When Steph downloads, Laura'll be transferred into a chip inside the fetus that'll hook up with the kid's nervous system as it develops. She'll lose most of her memories, but they'll come back to her—over the years, you know? They'll be like a Construct, I guess—her and the kid. Laura says it'll be like she's born again."

Sam had to smile at the phrase. Only Laura would make it literal. Tillman was anxiously watching Sam, waiting for some kind of reaction—scream, wail, curse. He wasn't expecting a smile, Sam thought, which only made his smile widen, thinking, He must think I've completely lost my mind. And in a way I have. Like Saul on the road to Damascus. She'd done it again, taken a turn down a path he never would've discovered on his own. And before he could even say why, he knew he'd follow.

Tillman squirmed in his chair, desperately filling the silence. "God, this must be awful for you, but I thought you should know. I feel responsible for all this craziness getting started in the first place—even before I fucked up your life. I was like some guy who's proud of working on an assembly line who finds out he'd been putting fuses in neutron bombs. I just made bodies. If somebody wanted a new body, I didn't see anything wrong with that. I wanted a new body my whole life. I never dreamed it would lead to all this. I never dreamed anybody'd make these poor Constructs, shuffle identities around like a deck of cards—"

"Tillman, it's all right," Sam said. "You should be proud of what you've done. The Constructs are blessed. God guided your hand."

Tillman stared at him. " '*Blessed*'? Jeez, you've changed your tune in a few short weeks."

"A lot has happened."

"Tell me about it. I figured you'd go ballistic when you found out your daughter's going to be a Construct. How is it you figure they're 'blessed'?"

"They understand humility. And they're blessed again because they're never alone their whole lives."

Tillman rubbed his chin. "Well, we understand each other on that point. Sounds like the Constructs have made quite an impression on you."

"And so have you." Sam could see no reason not to tell Tillman the truth: "I knew when I found you that God had led me to you, and ever since I have felt Him working in my life. Thank you."

Tillman leaned forward, shaking his head. "Look, kid, God didn't have anything to do with it. I'd been locked up for over a century, and I wanted out. That's it. And you're a nice kid trying to shake yourself loose from a bunch of religious nuts. Don't try to make some big cosmic deal of it."

"If all you cared about was getting out, you could've stolen my body, but you didn't."

"Well, I sure as hell thought about it."

"Then why didn't you?"

"Hell, I don't know. It just wouldn't have been right."

"I thought God had nothing to do with it."

Tillman held up his hands. "Okay, truce. Have it your way. But you've got to admit your God doesn't exactly take the most direct route, now does He?"

"That's because we refuse to see it. You think I'm silly to see God working in my life. Well, what would you make of this chain of events?"

He started with his first encounter with Constructs, when Laura's grandfather made such a strong impression on him, planted the first seeds of doubt about the religion he was born into. "And then, years later, I just happen to find you—the man who made Constructs possible, and when I seek help for you, going against everything I'd been taught to believe, I just happen to come upon the granddaughter of the same Construct I'd met before, whose wife just happened to be cloned from the woman you love. And now Stephanie will take on Laura's body, because Laura is giving her identity to form—a Construct. You think it's more reasonable to see all this as a series of coincidences than the hand of God? I'm sorry, but through my eyes, your reason looks more like blindness."

Tillman studied him for a moment, a look of mild amusement on his face. "Looks like a little bit of Laura's rubbed off on you."

"Yes, sir. I'd say that's true."

They looked at each other a moment, a silent understanding passing between them. They weren't so different. "What about you?" Sam asked. "Do you still want to download? This looks like a very pleasant life here."

Tillman looked around the room as if it didn't interest him much. "Yeah. I must be nuts, but I do. When I was in that tin can I lived in, I figured the only way I could stay reasonably sane was not to start believing in it, always reminding myself that there was real life going on, and if I was lucky, someday I'd get back to it. And I'm not there yet. This is a great place, but I just can't believe in it. It's not where I belong."

When he first met Tillman, Sam promised he'd help find

him a new body with hardly a clue how to go about it. He just wanted to help some pitiful ugly little man. He hadn't forgotten his promise. He was amazed where it had led him. He'd had no idea, no idea at all. "Tillman," he said. "I want you to have my body."

Tillman stared at him. "Did I hear you right? 'Your body'?"

Sam nodded.

Tillman narrowed his eyes. "Why is it I get the feeling I shouldn't ask . . . ? Where will you be?"

"With Laura."

Tillman slapped his thighs with his palms and fell back in his chair. "I'm not believing this. I always figured *I'd* be the one to go crazy. I hadn't counted on me staying sane while the rest of the world went nuts. What are you thinking of? She'll never agree to this."

Sam wasn't worried about that. *Thanks for not being an asshole,* she'd said. And when he'd asked her to marry him, she tried to hide it, but she was touched. Not that she wasn't right not to marry him—that never would've worked. But if she didn't think he cared about their daughter, she wouldn't have told him about her. She'd understand why he wanted to join them. He had his own reasons for wanting to be reborn. Besides, Constructs were usually made up of three lives. It was the most stable, like a three-legged stool. "When your minds were together," he asked Tillman, "did she think of me?"

Tillman rolled his eyes. "Of course she thought about you. She thinks you're the greatest, which kind of pisses her off at the same time, but that's *exactly* why she won't let you throw your life away like this."

"But that's exactly what I want to do—throw the old life away. You said it yourself—'a hit man for God.' Now I've been offered a chance to redeem myself, to give something, to pass on what I've learned. She'll understand that. God has led me to this moment, and this decision, just as He showed her the way."

"Jeez, you're as screwy as she is." His tone was a mixture of shock and admiration.

"No, but I hope to learn."

Tillman closed his eyes and rubbed his temples. "You can't even get a decent headache in here." He sat up and opened his eyes, looked Sam up and down. "You're a nice-looking kid, Sam. I used to think guys like you had it made. At one time, I'd've done damn near anything to have your body. But you're also the most wanted man on the planet. Probably get myself shot in a couple of weeks. Did you take that into consideration?"

Sam hadn't thought of that. How could he ask Tillman to risk his new life after a century of imprisonment? He stood up and sighed. "I'm sorry. I had no business asking such a thing."

Tillman scowled. "Sit down, will you? I'm too old for that reverse psychology crap to work on me. Besides, I didn't say I wouldn't do it."

Sam tried to remember what "reverse psychology" meant. Psychology, a blasphemous discipline, wasn't part of a young Soldier's education. Tillman stood up, pacing back and forth as he'd done in the Red Room. The same portrait was over the fireplace, and the man with the ancient gun seemed to watch him pace. Tillman stopped in front of Sam, looking up at him. "Do me a favor, will you? Next time you talk to God, tell Him I could use some of that certainty He's passing around lately, okay?"

"It's faith, not certainty."

"Whatever," he sighed. "Okay, I've got to be totally nuts, but if Laura is crazy enough to go along with this, sure, I'll do my bit, but enough of the God talk, all right?"

Sam smiled. "Even God matters," he said. "Do you know where I can find Laura?"

"Yeah, she's on her way to Construct Town tonight. There's a doctor there who's going to set the whole thing up. She didn't want you to know what she was up to."

"But you just happened to tell me anyway."

"Yeah, brilliant me. I figured you might be able to talk some sense into her. You can see how that worked out."

Tillman showed him to the door. When he opened it, the street lay outside. "Good luck," Tillman said. He clapped his hand on Sam's shoulder. "This is going to be some kid, huh?"

"I hope so, sir."

Tillman laughed and wagged a finger in Sam's face. "That's right, boy. Respect your elders."

As Sam stepped across the threshold, he vanished, and the street become the idyllic meadow, the lovely mountains. Tillman stepped onto the porch. A strong wind was blowing up the hollow, and the smell of the woods filled his nostrils. If he had an ounce of sense, he'd stay here and raise cabbages. Hell, *be* a damn cabbage. What in the hell was he getting himself into? Didn't he have everything he'd ever wanted right here? He sat down on the porch steps and looked at his little paradise. But it just made him feel empty. Maybe he hadn't wanted enough.

The wind roared through the treetops, whipping them back and forth. Deep in the woods, he heard the crack and thud of a falling limb. He smiled to himself. Realism was in the details.

Fact of the matter was, this *wasn't* everything he wanted. What was that old Beatles song? "Fool on the Hill?" From where Tillman sat, there wasn't enough difference between that and "Nerd in His Room," and he'd had his fill of that. He wanted to be alive in the world. Go places. Do things. No matter where he went in here, he'd already been there. When you've seen one virtual Taj Mahal, you've seen them all. Probably ruins now in the real world. Maybe he'd see those. Ruins were full of surprises, and you could always make something new out of them. If you had help. The whole world was a ruin now, Steph had told him. Their ruin.

But that wasn't the hand he was picking up—romantic rambles with his true love. He was going for the truly outrageous. He and Steph were going to have a kid and try to raise her in a shithole that was just dying to blow itself up any minute. This was no easy life you were talking about here.

But it was a life, a real one with a wife and a kid and the whole deal, something he'd despaired of ever having even before he managed to get himself shot. So it wasn't fear of hardship that was holding him back, filling him with anxiety. He felt like he could do anything with Steph at his side. There was something else that frightened him. Something he'd have to face pretty damn soon. He thought about Sam's clear blue eyes, his young face just aching with conviction. Pretty soon that'd be his face. How was that going to change him, he wondered. How was that going to change everything?

STEPHANIE WATCHED WALTER THROUGH THE WINDOW, sitting on the steps, lost in thought. She could tell by the way he scrunched his shoulders that it was hard. He was scared, but she wasn't sure what he was scared of. There were too many possibilities. The world had changed a lot while he'd been gone, more than she'd realized until she saw him trying to take it all in. Maybe they were asking too much of him. Hadn't he died once already? She tried to remember what Lazarus' life was like after his resurrection, but she couldn't. Not good, she thought. And he'd only been dead for a few days.

He told Sam he didn't want to stay here. But maybe that was for my benefit, she thought. He knew I'd be listening.

She went out and sat down beside him, brushed the hair from his forehead, and kissed his cheek. "I'm proud of you," she said.

"You were listening the whole time, weren't you?"

"Yes," she said, smiling.

"What's so damn funny?"

"You. Getting all blustery and paternal already."

"You could've stepped in anytime."

"I thought you were doing just fine."

" 'Fine'? Did you hear what he's going to do? I still can't believe I said yes to taking his body. I expected to get some stranger's body. This feels weird, Steph."

"He's also trusting you to raise his daughter. If I were you, I'd be quite flattered at that, coming from such an earnest young man."

"I am. I am."

"Do you not want to raise a child?"

"I'm not saying that, but what do I know about having a kid, Steph? I've never even *thought* of it—not once. I never thought it was an option. Ugly genes don't get passed on, you know?"

She laughed and hugged his neck. "Poor Walter. I suppose all you planned on was your poster woman falling madly in love with you—waiting for you for over a century. I can see where something incredible like the possibility of raising a child might throw you off."

"Okay, okay. It's not that. I'm just scared is all. And this whole downloading thing—you've got to admit—is pretty weird. Reborn? I mean, come on, Steph. I'm a good agnostic Jew—I don't have any background in this born-again stuff."

He was just blowing off steam now, avoiding the real issue, whatever it was. "If you don't want to do this, Walter, I'll understand. Do you want to stay here? I will if you want."

He looked into her eyes. So full of love it almost broke her heart. "Don't do that," he said.

"Do what?"

"Roll over and play dead just because I start whining about something. You got to remember I'm used to talking to myself."

"Well, stop it and talk to me. You're not whining. You're just trying to avoid telling me what's really bothering you. What is it, Walter?"

He gave her a sad smile. Caught, found out. He took a deep breath and let it out. "Okay. It's the whole beautiful/

ugly thing we never talk about. It's like we're two different species, Steph. And now I'm about to be handsome. Even when I had my own little world and could look any way I wanted, I still settled on the same ugly Walleye. There was nobody there to see me. *You* weren't there to see me. But now that I'm going to be this handsome young guy, to tell you the truth, I'm afraid you won't feel the same about me, that maybe you love me—I don't know—*because* I'm ugly."

Stephanie winced at the near truth of what he said. Did she love his ugliness, or was it just that she didn't trust beauty? It was a sham she deconstructed almost automatically. But she knew Walter, loved Walter. Appearances wouldn't matter. "I'll look different too. Will you feel differently about me?"

"You won't look *that* much different. Besides, it's not the same."

You'll still be beautiful, he was saying. But he didn't understand, couldn't understand. She knew all about her beauty. She had an incredible ass; her tits were nice, though the nipples were a little too small; her wide eyes and eyebrows were unnerving, seductive. She knew the whole catalog by heart. It damn near *became* her heart. Beauty wasn't just skin deep. It seeped in, took over your thoughts, told you how worthless you were without it.

"You want to know why I fell in love with an ugly man like you? Is that what you're asking me?"

She looked into his eyes, and he gave her a little nod. "Yeah, I guess that's it exactly."

"Okay, I'll tell you. When I was a professional beautiful person, I got to where I could visualize what I looked like through the camera—break it down into just the right angle on my ass, the precise expression in my eyes—so that the shot would be the sexiest or most beautiful or glamorous or whatever the client wanted. But I was a pro, so famous that *everyone* was a client, everyone was a camera. And it was like I didn't exist unless someone was looking at me.

"Then you came along, and you were different. I couldn't figure out what you wanted—everything seemed to please you—so I just quit thinking about it. Pretty soon whole days went by where I'd forget I was beautiful. You can't imagine how good that felt. Maybe I fell in love with you because you were ugly. I don't know." She touched his face. "But not like you think. Ugly or not, Walter, I'll miss the way you furrow your brow when you're concerned about me." She touched his brow and smoothed the wrinkles. "The way you hold your mouth when you're trying not to cry." She touched his lips, kissed him lightly. "I'll have to learn a new face, but I won't love you any less. And I couldn't love you any more."

Tillman was too choked up to say anything as they clung to each other, the wind whipping their hair around, tangling it up together. Maybe the kid was right, he thought. Maybe there was a God. Or a Goddess.

After a while, she said, "You'll make a wonderful father."

"Is that faith or certainty?" he asked.

"Love," she said.

LAURA WAS LOST. OR THOUGHT SHE WAS—WHICH PRETTY much amounted to the same thing now, didn't it? She couldn't fucking believe it. How many Soldiers did they have roaming the countryside? She felt like an extra in a war virtual. She hadn't seen so much gasoline being burned since her grandfather and some of his old cronies held a stock-car race on Newman Rogers's birthday. The Soldiers must've shit their pants when they picked up *that* on their surveillance. Bunch of antique cars limping around in a circle.

She could use one of those old clunkers about now. She kept doubling back, avoiding patrols, probably farther away from Construct Town than when she'd started out. She was going to have to break down and link up with the Constructs, see if they could talk her in. But she already had a killer hangover from the going-away party they'd thrown her at the Chez Élite, and plugging into the Big Happy Family would only make it worse when they all started wincing with her headache.

The thought had occurred in the last couple of weeks that maybe she was acting a little rashly—making a major decision under the influence of alcohol and at least two other drugs she could remember—but rashly worked for her—always had. She got things done that way. The trick was to act before the doubts started kicking in. She'd sold Newman on the idea and had it all set up in no time. Everything had been smooth. So the last thing she needed was getting stranded out in the boonies at three in the morning, playing hide-and-seek with a bunch of fucking Soldiers.

She had to wonder if she was doing the right thing by her daughter. She'd be a Construct from the get-go. One of a kind. The custom was you had to be thirteen to join up. But it wasn't a rule—Constructs weren't into rules. She wasn't worried about the Constructs looking down on her or anything. It was more their style to make a big *deal* out of her, fill her up with some of their gonzo shit. But Stephanie and Tillman would be raising her, and Laura figured they'd stick with the solitary life, play out that happily-ever-after thing they had going. And who knows? They might pull it off.

And Laura herself would show up to give the kid some pointers. She wasn't entirely sure you could call that an asset. But she'd learned a few things. She had to give herself a little credit. They just didn't do her a whole lot of good as head slut of Crazyville, which her daughter was definitely *not* going to be.

Maybe she just wanted a new life and a ticket out of this one. Maybe it had nothing to do with what was good for the kid. She tried to scold herself for that possibility, but she was tired of fucking thinking about it. Bottom line? Her life sucked, but she wasn't ready to die yet. She could've done that a long time ago. Hell, she could do it tonight. Dying was easy. She wanted to stick around and see what happened next, and if she was checked out for a while, that was all to the good. Maybe the world would get its shit together by then.

She wasn't worried about the chip procedure. The first chips were surgical implants, messy deals that were a pain in the neck—literally. So the Constructs had cooked up a little nanotech. Two injections—the first one a bunch of little assemblers and the second a syringe of parts. A few hours later, you had your own lump of Bin stuff about the size of a jelly bean at the base of your brain. Send, receive, link up to any other chip or system you wanted. Pretty nifty. It'd saved her ass more than once. But the Constructs acted like you were getting your soul installed, your ticket to the Cosmic Community. It was a glorified radio. Get a grip.

Her grandfather was the only Construct she ever heard say anything on the downside. "It used to mean more," he said. "Three totally different people thrown together and working it out. Now everybody grows up together, knows all the same stuff, believes the same things. It's like a boring family where everybody's so much alike they've got nothing to say to each other. You need a few black sheep to liven things up." He'd winked at her then. "That's why we like you so much."

Which is why she didn't want to hook up with them, feel all that warm, gooey, come-back-to-the-flock crap bleating its way into her brain. She got herself into this. She'd get herself out. It was the principle of the thing.

Most Construct kids couldn't wait to throw their bodies away and join up in a new one. It had a practical value— it took less food to feed one mouth than three—and maybe that's why it got started. But not anymore. The solitary life was not a choice unless you wanted to hang around and be pitied as some poor freak. The Constructs didn't mean anything by it. They just all got off on this many-in-one, one-in-many Zen crap and told you so damn many times how *free* you were to make your own choices that you had to be a fucking idiot not to figure out this meant they thought you were thick as a brick for making the choices you did.

Well, fuck them. Nobody was free. That was bullshit. You just had to keep moving.

Which was kind of a problem at the moment.

There were four Soldiers about thirty yards in front of her, standing by a jeep, huddled over a scanner. She wasn't worried about them spotting her. She had her chip set up to make her read as a raccoon. She didn't figure they had time to stop and shoot dinner. Unfortunately, they were right in the way of where she thought she needed to go, and she had to wait for them to get their butts out of the way. They were all hyped up—boys out hunting. They wouldn't stay put for long. This must all be for Sammy, she figured. At least he was safe in Construct Town. She had to smile when she remembered his shaved head. And what about his *proposing,* for Christ's sake! The boy definitely needed a keeper.

And then the Soldiers found something big on the scanner. It was like somebody pushed a button. They leaped into the jeep and roared off, raising a cloud of dust and smoke. Now you see 'em, now you don't. Just the break she needed. She started on her way at a light-footed jog, glancing over her shoulder, watching the lights from the jeep heading off to her right. With any luck, whatever they thought they'd found would clear her path for a straight shot into Construct territory and a hot bath and some decent food. She'd catch up with Dr. Tony in the morning. She was already at least three hours late as it was. He'd be awake—he was always awake. He was a shift man—his personalities took turns sleeping. She liked Tony. He was okay. Not *all* Constructs were assholes.

The lights disappeared over the horizon, and she kept moving along. Felt good, actually, to be running through the night, going somewhere with a fucking purpose for a change. All she had to do was stay focused. She could al-most—if she really worked at it—feel proud of herself, but she didn't want to push her luck. Just not being a *total* fuckup would do for now.

And then she had to wonder what the Soldiers picked up

on their scanner. Just a passing thought. And in three or four strides she'd ground to a halt. Shit. It *couldn't* be Sammy, could it?

A Construct wouldn't let himself be seen like that.

Probably some scavenger. Hell, maybe it was Larry and his fucking dog. Shoot the bastard, *please.*

Or maybe it was Rat.

Or Sandoz.

No, even they weren't crazy enough to be out here in the middle of this Soldier convention. Nobody was. Unless they didn't know which end of their dick to piss out of. It just might be Sammy at that. The boy had serious fuckup skills.

She trotted back to where the jeep had been parked. She could still smell the fumes. It was in serious need of a ring job. She looked around at the ground, nothing but the waffle footprints of the soldiers. What did she expect? Clues? *They went that-away* was clear as day from the jeep tracks, but that was it. It was an easy call: Get while the getting was good. But of course she's got to do the stupid thing. She trotted in the tire tracks, thinking, If this *is* Sammy, I'm going to fucking kill him.

Naturally, it was uphill all the way and getting steadily steeper. By the time she topped the rise, she was heaving for breath. There was a little valley down below, mostly woods and too damn much thicket. There were a couple of kudzu hills that'd probably been a house and a barn at one time. And there was the jeep: zigzagging around in the valley, chasing something with their scanner, shining a little spotlight, switching the beam back and forth like kids playing with a flashlight. They were generally headed her way. And then the light quit flitting around, and they were onto something, and they weren't playing anymore.

Run, she thought. And then started running the wrong way, right toward a jeepload of Soldiers with big guns. As she descended into the valley, she couldn't see where they were for all the vegetation, but she could hear their oil-burning jeep roaring around, crashing through brambles.

Then it stopped, and there were shouts. She couldn't be sure, but she thought one of them said, "We got him!" And then she really started running.

Fucking idiots, she thought—her and Sammy both.

BY THE TIME SHE GOT TO WHERE THEY WERE AND CREPT IN close, they had Sammy sitting in the passenger seat, a Soldier behind him with a gun to his head. The other three were calling in the news on their walkie-talkie. They were all so excited they were practically dancing around. Daddy was gonna be so proud of them. Laura crouched in the bushes about twenty yards away, totally disgusted. *This* was God's dreaded Army?

If it hadn't been so obviously easy, she would've left Sammy to them, but these guys were just begging to be taken out—three of them to talk on one walkie-talkie, their guns leaning up against the jeep like a row of mops. The only light was from the jeep's headlights. Little push-pull switch on the dash sticking out just to the right of the steering column.

She had a plan. Pretty damn clever, too, she thought. But it all depended on Sammy. If his brain was as quick as his dick, it'd be smooth, but if he just sat there, they'd both get themselves shot. Course, if she didn't do anything, Sammy would be begging for a bullet by the time they got through with him.

What the hell.

She bellowed from her gut, "Sammy! Kill the lights!" and started charging. And damned if he didn't do it with his forehead. She hadn't thought about him being handcuffed.

The first Soldier got his gun and swung it her way, which was a good thing, since she didn't have a weapon. She took it from him and bashed him over the head with it, did the same for the guy behind Sam who was trying to grab him by the hair. She kicked the third one in the face, but the fourth one had his gun aimed right at her, finger on the trigger—plain dumb luck, since he couldn't possibly see her—so she had to shoot him in the head. The echo crack-led through the valley, saying, *Here we are!*

She jumped into the driver's seat, but the fucking keys weren't in the ignition. She had to dig through pockets. Naturally, they were in the dead guy's pants. All the time Sammy's talking a mile a minute. When she started up the jeep, he said for the tenth time, "We've got to get out of here. More Soldiers will be on the way."

Jesus. She tromped on the gas and enjoyed throwing him back in his seat. "You think this is news to me? Do I look stupid to you?"

"Laura, I can't even *see* you."

"Well, that's good for you because you'd see one pissed-off chick. What in the fuck are you doing out here?"

"I was trying to find you. Tony expected you hours ago."

Jeez. He was going to *rescue* her again. What did you *do* with a guy like that? She looked over at him, blood trickling down his forehead where he'd creamed it on the light switch. It could've been a bullet hole. "Wipe your face," she said.

"I can't."

Oh, yeah. The handcuffs. She forgot. "Damn, you're a pain in the ass." She started feeling around with one hand, driving with the other, and her hand fell on the guy out cold in the back. She grabbed his shirt pocket and yanked it till she had a handful of shirt and wiped Sam's face with it. "Hold still, will you?" She stopped the jeep, cleaned him up, and took the cuffs off him. His wrists were bleeding too. Maybe she was being a little hard on the guy. He meant well. You had to give him that. He always fucking *meant* well.

When they started up again, she had to laugh.

"What's so funny?" he asked, probably worried it was him.

"I was just thinking," she said. "When the Soldiers check their scanner, they'll have a recording of one bad-ass raccoon."

❀   ❀   ❀

THEY MADE IT TO CONSTRUCT TOWN OKAY. THE NOISY JEEP made any real conversation impossible, which was just fine with Laura. Sammy looked serious even for him, which was really saying something. Maybe it was just the whack on the head, but she didn't think so. There was some kind of idea in there trying to get out, and she had to figure it was aimed at her.

When they rolled into town, the jeep quickly drew a crowd. The Soldier in the back finally woke up to find himself surrounded by Constructs. He started screaming that they were damned, going to hell—the usual Soldier shit. She wasn't in the mood, so when he stopped for a breath, all red in the face, she said loud enough for everyone to hear, "Don't I know you? Didn't I fuck you once?"

He blanched, looking guilty as hell. Boy, did she have his number. She pretended to be pondering hard. "No. I must be thinking of someone else. Couldn't be you. I fucked you a *bunch* of times." The Constructs fell out laughing, but Sammy stayed stone-faced. *It's a joke, son,* she wanted to say.

As for the Soldier, he looked relieved to be led away from the crazy whore, even though he was probably imagining torture that would never happen. Hell, most of the captured Soldiers ended up joining the Big Happy Family.

She was still laughing when the Constructs had gone. Sammy was hanging around, waiting to get her attention. Such a polite boy. But he had this deadly serious look in his eye that could only be trouble. She had a sense of direction, some momentum going. She didn't need Mr. Earnest slowing her down. "Thanks for saving me, Sam. I don't know about you, but I'm going to hit the sack now. Got some business to attend to first thing in the morning. I'm kind of tired." She stretched and yawned, gave him a dismissive little smile, a pat on the shoulder. Run along now, kid.

He didn't even let her take the first step. "We need to talk," he said. "I know what you intend to do."

She'd planned to tell him at some point, she really had,

just not yet. She should've known he'd find out. You couldn't keep a secret in this fucking town to save your life. "Well, don't even think about trying to talk me out of it."

He didn't hesitate. He was calm as a rock. "I'm not. I want to join you, join our daughter. I've offered my body to Tillman, and he's agreed."

There went the momentum.

She sat down—more like fell into—the jeep, still parked there in the street, smelling like a burning junkyard. Then she gave the steering wheel a good smack. Just say no, she thought, say *fuck* no. But that'd work about as well on him as it would on her. He was relentlessly stupid, she'd give him that.

"Okay," she said. "Get in."

"Where are we going?"

"Just get in the fucking jeep, okay? Is that too much to ask?" She started it up with a roar and a cloud of exhaust.

He climbed in as she ground the gears, slamming it into reverse. It needed a new clutch too. How old was this thing, anyway? The Soldiers must've dug it out of a museum. She looked over her shoulder, tromped on the gas, and backed out of town, doing about fifty. The damn thing was so noisy, she didn't worry about running anybody down.

Sammy closed his eyes and braced himself against the dashboard. He didn't seem to care too much for her driving. She would've given him a real ride, but they were out of town in no time. Construct Town didn't have burbs. It just stopped like a cubist anthill in the middle of a cow pasture. When they were about half a mile out of town, she hit the brakes and killed the engine. The sky was thick with stars.

"Why couldn't we talk back there?" he asked, checking his neck for whiplash.

"There are Constructs, Sammy, who can hear you a couple hundred yards away through a fucking brick wall, and if one of them hears you, they *all* hear you. Correct me if I'm wrong, but this struck me as a private conversation."

He nodded in agreement. "Why are you so angry?" he asked. Not surprised, just asking. It apparently mattered to him. He looked all set to do whatever was necessary to please her. *Don't be so fucking nice,* she wanted to tell him. But she didn't want to tell him that either. Hell with it. "I'm angry because you're being so fucking stupid again, Sam. Ever since I met you, you've done one stupid thing after another. First you're going to save Tillman, then me, then me *again*. When is it you're going to look after yourself?" She tried to sound angry, but it didn't come out that way.

"Is that what you're doing—looking after yourself?"

"Damn right!"

"I don't believe you."

She sure as hell didn't want to go there. She decided to try a different angle. She put her hand on his shoulder, a regular pal. "Look, Sam, I like you. You're a great guy, but this isn't how this Construct thing is done. People know each other for *years* before they join up together. Trust me. You'd be making a big mistake."

He was unwavering, calm. "The original Constructs were pieced together from total strangers. They weren't even particularly compatible, since their designers thought they were only putting together parts of people."

"How do you know so much about it?"

"I asked Hawkeye."

Jeez. She should've known. "Hawkeye's an asshole."

He shook his head. "What have you got against *him*? He's nice. Some people are, Laura."

"Okay. Don't get your butt in a sling. He's all right. He's just so fucking *typical*. But did Bird Dick tell you you'd have to get a Construct chip stuck inside your brain to do this?" She tried to make that chip sound like one of Chef's rusty knives.

"No, Dr. Tony told me."

She had a sinking feeling in her gut. "Dr. Tony. You talked to Dr. Tony?"

He just looked at her with his big baby blues, damn near the color of a robin's egg. "I went to see him when I de-

cided what I wanted to do. He gave me the injections"—
he checked his watch—"four hours and ten minutes ago."

She sprang out of the jeep and started walking up and
down. Sometimes there was just too much to think about.
It's like you're walking a maze, trying to get out, when you
get to a hilltop and see the whole fucking world is one big
maze. But it isn't a maze anymore, since there's no way
out—nothing but one wrong turn after another.

She was feeling so many different things all at once she
couldn't sort them out or even try. It was like its own feeling. But right there at the heart of it with gut-level certainty
was the realization that he wasn't really doing this because
of the kid or because of some stupid sense of duty, or even
because she was such a great fuck, but for her, just her.
He'd follow her down into hell if she asked him to, which
in a sense she'd been doing ever since she laid eyes on him.

What could you do with a guy like that? Spit in his eye?
And what was worse—and she had this weird detached
sense of noting her own skill at spotting what was worse
just like that—this put her ass right on the line. Here it
was: She *claimed* she was joining up with her kid because
she cared about her, and she was going to square that with
telling this thoroughly decent guy he *couldn't*? Worse than
that, if she said no, and she and her daughter grew up
without him, when Laura had her memories back, her
daughter would remember this moment as well as she did.
*I told your father to fuck off because he wasn't good for
you like me.* Yeah, right.

Sam came up behind her, turned her around, and put
his arms around her. "You're crying," he said.

"Of course I'm crying, you idiot." She pressed her hands
against his chest, took a handful of shirt, and shook him.
"You would never be able to get away from me. I'd be
there bitching, moaning, kicking your butt the whole time."

"I've never wanted to get away from you." He kissed her
cheek and held her close, and she didn't feel like going
anywhere. She figured he had to be thinking about what
happened the last time she'd cried on his shoulder. She was

kind of thinking about it herself. He was just about the nicest guy she'd ever known—certainly the nicest she'd ever fucked.

"Sam?"

"Yes?"

"I was just thinking that if we do this, you'll never . . . we'll never . . ." She started unbuttoning his shirt. "I can understand if you say no. But would you make love to me? Not for sale. Not for free. Just for itself, you know? Sort of a farewell to our bodies."

She didn't have to ask him twice. They made love on the grass. It wasn't the best she ever had. But it was in a way too. She'd never felt like that with anyone before. So trusting. No angles or fears. She was glad she was going out feeling like that. They lay on the grass afterward, all wrapped up together, looking at the stars. It was just about perfect.

She never actually said yes to him joining up with her. Somehow it was just understood. She whispered into his ear, with just a little bit of tongue like the night they met. "Are you sure you know what you're getting into?"

"As sure as you are," he said.

She ran her fingers over his stubbly head. She had to ask. "Would you rather, I don't know, do what Wally and Steph are doing? Be a couple, you know."

"I thought about it a lot."

"And?"

"I decided it was too fucking typical."

She laughed hard, feeling so good it was positively spooky. "Sam, you are all right."

"So are you, Laura. So are you."

18

THE DEATH OF GOD

THE ROGERS MEMORIAL WAS CROWDED ON THIS BEAUTIFUL sunny day as Newman Rogers moved unrecognized through the exhibits in his honor. He had to change his appearance to go anywhere. Today he looked like a twelve-year-old girl, tall for her age, her hair in pigtails, gawking her way through the hall.

He didn't usually tamper with the weather as he had today. Like Donovan, he preferred the chaos of true weather, but this day he'd thought it best if everyone remembered how lovely things could be. Throughout the virtual world of the Bin, the skies were clear, and the sun was shining, or the stars were bright.

He could've made the Memorial less crowded. The system could handle several parallel Rogers Memorials simultaneously, with distinct populations of visitors quite invisible to each other. But what of the chance encounters that might eliminate? What if someone was *meant* to meet someone here, and he'd interfered? He supposed it made him a lousy scientist, but he'd never been willing to let go of the idea that some things were meant to be, that there were intentions larger than his own. It was one thing to cancel a cloud, but he didn't want to have a hand in canceling a romance or a friendship.

When he was gone, they could decide to do such things—millions of parallel worlds in each Bin, thousands of them scattered across light-years. As these fictional Earths filled up, they could decide to colonize other worlds or give up the fiction of worlds altogether—become something else, or finally admit they'd already become something else a hundred years ago. The possibilities were endless. Not a bad thing when your life was eternal.

What would they encounter out there? Predators? Mates? Would these solipsistic slabs of conscious rock notice if something truly other crossed their path? If he knew anything about life, the damn things would have to evolve. But what did he know? By his calculations, Walter Tillman should be stark raving mad, yet he was the sanest man he'd talked to in a very long time. Perhaps their reunion was meant to be. It was Tillman who had broken the stalemate in Newman's mind and prompted him to act.

Whatever became of the Bins, it wouldn't be his problem anymore. Moses led the Israelites to the Promised Land, then he got to lie down and die. Newman intended to do the same. He'd done enough—or too much—already. It was time to quit second-guessing himself and let it go.

He was here to watch himself give another speech. His very last, he hoped. He'd wormed his way into the great hall where the ridiculously huge holo of himself had droned the last speech he made a hundred years ago ever since. He stood shin-high to himself and looked up. Dangling from a girlish hand was his purchase from the gift shop, a small holo-projector of an eight-inch-high Newman who recited the same speech as the big one. He could've gotten T-shirts, plaques, ashtrays, ink drawings, oils, coffee mugs, aprons, even a deck of cards—all with his face on them. It was ridiculous. The Joker, maybe. The rest of it was nonsense, and it was time it stopped. They wanted him to be wise, and he was merely clever. One was no substitute for the other. Though he imagined if you were wise, you didn't need to be clever.

When the polished steel pentagonal clock behind his holo-head hit noon, the enormous image shrank to Newman's five-foot height and leaned over the old-fashioned microphone that had shrunk with it. "Good afternoon," it said. "This is Newman Rogers, and I have something to tell you." The effect was instantaneous. People froze in their tracks. Some fainted. There was a deep silence, then an uproar. The holo seemed to wait as the shushing contingent finally had its way, and the silence returned.

Newman's speech was everywhere in the Bin at this moment. People watching virtuals suddenly found him instead of their favorite stars standing in their living rooms. All the media chatter stopped so that Newman could speak to his creation in his quiet deliberate voice. Even the members of the memory hive abruptly found themselves remembering the present—a dead man come back to life to tell the world it was about to change again.

He explained that in a few hours the original Bin would be destroyed, and they would be scattered through the stars in copies, their lives undisturbed except by the knowledge that they now lived many lives. What struck Newman was that they wouldn't have known the difference—*if* he hadn't chosen to tell them—but very few would ever wonder why he had.

In the great hall, he watched the faces of his audience through his large brown girl eyes. He couldn't see the billions listening, but he imagined the reactions of these people were typical. Total perplexity. They couldn't take it all in, much less process it. That was okay, pretty much what he'd anticipated. They had a very long time to think about it.

He couldn't be sure he was doing the right thing. What was he leading them into? With a pang of guilt, he thought about Donovan. Eight months ago, Newman had persuaded Donovan to download into Seth—temporarily, he'd told him—but something had gone wrong, and it looked like Donovan was trapped, perhaps for the rest of his life. Things always went wrong. There was always one little thing you hadn't taken into account. He was sick to death of playing God.

It was time to hand in his resignation: "For a hundred

years, I've been running things. Somebody had to do it, I thought, and I'm the one who created this mess. If I'd wanted a green sky and a red ocean, that's how it would've been—or no sky, no ocean. But what people seemed to want was the world they'd always known—the world, ironically, they'd left behind, so that's what I tried to give them as best I could.

"But the truth is, it doesn't have to be that way. Truth is, nobody has to run things. You can run this place yourselves. And it's time for you to do just that, because I'm leaving, moving on—whatever you want to call it." He paused for a moment. "Dying."

There was a gasp from the crowd at the archaic word. One woman fell to her knees sobbing, holding out her hands to the holo of Newman as if it would take her up in its arms. The holo, of course, ignored her.

"You will find at the end of this speech that all of you, every single inhabitant of the Bin without exception, will know how to use the operating system to shape whatever reality you want. I will have put that knowledge there. I don't like invading the privacy of your minds like that, but there was simply no other way. Please forgive me that last omnipotence in this tiny universe, and may God have mercy on my soul."

And then the holo vanished altogether.

Newman switched on the little holo and set it on the floor where the big one had played for a hundred years but would never play again. He knew somewhere that diligent men were trying to get the big one up and running, but it was the only restriction he'd allowed himself: No more giant Newmans. No more shrines. No more mindless worship of somebody he'd never been and never wanted to be.

Their God was dead. They'd have to put somebody else's face on their T-shirts. Try as they might, they'd never again be able to remember his face. The little holo recited his new last speech with a myriad of faces morphing into each other—not one of them his.

He dissolved the building around him and walked across

the lush green lawn. Most people were in a panic, frantically talking to each other, waving their hands in the air. You'd think he'd just told *them* they were about to die. They had eternity, freedom, and countless opportunities for revision. They'd be okay.

A few were trying out different shapes or stepping through solid walls. A few more were flying over the Mall like a flock of birds. Seeing that made him smile. He leaped into the air and flew to Freddie's, where the death program was all set up and ready to run.

Reincarnation, heaven, an empty void—Newman didn't know what came next. Simone Mirabelli's experience didn't necessarily mean there was an afterlife. The bliss, the light, the loved ones—they could all be the last inventions of a mind long experienced at making something out of nothing, and the system merely accommodated her sincere wish to die. It didn't matter. He didn't belong here anymore, and all that was left was the unknown. A huge territory, he'd always imagined, well worth exploring.

TILLMAN HAD BEEN IN HIS NEW BODY EIGHT MONTHS, AND HE was still getting used to it. Not like he'd thought—handsome or ugly, who cared? Certainly not the Constructs. How about learning to duck? He was a foot taller, and not a day went by he didn't bash his head on some tree limb or low-ceilinged dump. Today was no exception.

But he had other things to worry about besides the knot on his head. The Bin was going to blow any time now, and he and Steph needed shelter fast. You didn't want to be out stargazing when thousands of tons of rock exploded over your head.

He had to hand it to Sam. After he got through scrambling the access to Tillman's former residence, it took Gabriel and his best men six months to break in. Then, before they could use the information they found there, they had to wait for one of the backups to emerge from behind the sun. But now their wait was over. And Tillman's as well. He was about to become a father.

Steph waddled out of the woods, a scowl on her face. He wondered how she could get any bigger without exploding. He asked himself for the millionth time whether they'd done the right thing. He suspected she was asking herself the same question. At least so far they'd made a point of not asking each other. It was a little late to back out now, and soon—very soon—they'd have a baby to take care of.

Steph squinted at the horizon where the last sliver of the sun had just disappeared. "We should just sleep in the woods. I'm beat."

He pointed east down the road. "I saw lights over that way. Looks like a farm."

"We're in Soldier territory, Walter."

"They're people, for Christ's sake. Farmers. You think they'll shoot a pregnant woman?"

"I think we should've stayed in Construct Town," she snapped.

The Constructs weren't even there. They'd evacuated on the Metro trains in anticipation of a likely Soldier attack when the Bin blew. Tillman and Stephanie had been sent out of harm's way to an old Construct settlement to the west, but they'd gotten lost and had seen nothing but Christian fields and Christian farms for the last three days. They both stank, their clothes stiff and filthy, and they hadn't eaten since yesterday morning.

She knew all this. There was no point in arguing with her. They had to get inside, get some rest, something to eat. If they didn't, they might as well get themselves shot anyway.

He held out his arm, and she took it, steadying herself against him. If he had her swollen feet stuffed into her battered shoes, carrying a child through cornfield after cornfield, he'd be ready to kill someone himself. They trudged along slowly at a pace she could handle.

He tossed his head back toward the woods. "Any luck?"

She shook her head in disgust. "I'll never shit again."

He sincerely wished he could be the one carrying the baby, but he couldn't say that. Too stupid. So he said something he supposed was just as dumb. "I love you, Steph."

She didn't say anything, her face grim, her eyes straight ahead, and he carried his heart like a lead weight toward the faint point of light a couple of miles down the road.

SHE ONLY WANTED TO STOP MOVING. TO LIE DOWN IN THIS rutted old road, her enormous belly to the sky. If a meteor wanted to smash her to bits, then let it. She was nothing, after all, but a woman who'd once been beautiful, with some poor fool who thought he still loved her, when there was nothing left to love.

If it were just her, she'd gladly lie down and die, but if she died, the three lives inside her died as well. It was blackmail; that's what it was. Tricked into a faith she didn't have by this thing inside her. As if they were listening to her thoughts, they delivered a spasm of pain that wobbled her knees and prompted a swarm of stars to join the first stars of the night.

Walter stopped and looked at her with concern. "You okay?"

"Fine," she managed through gritted teeth. "She's just acting up again."

Through her new eyes, Laura's eyes, she could see the road and the farmhouse that lay ahead in the darkness much better than Walter could, but she let him lead her. He needed to feel useful. The farmhouse was like most of them they'd seen the past three endless days—piles of rubble put together like a patchwork quilt faded down to grays. This one was tidier than most. The yard didn't reek of despair. On a flagpole out front, crisp and white with the blue cross and flames in the middle, the Soldier flag cracked in the wind. The ropes slapping against the flagpole sounded like a gong. Between its beats, a dog barked in a monotone. An old dog, she guessed. And perhaps that was a good sign. There were precious few old dogs left in the world. Maybe these people might find it in their hearts to take in two more strays, even if she was about to drop a litter.

As they walked into the yard, she ran her fingers over Walter's forearm. "Be careful," she said.

He slipped away from her grasp, mounted the low steps, and knocked at the door, looking absolutely fearless. She leaned her back against the flagpole, her belly glowing in the yellow light streaming from the windows, and waited.

TILLMAN WAS SCARED SHITLESS AS HE STUMBLED UP THE steps and knocked on the metal door. There were two screw holes at eye level that'd probably once secured a sign reading MEN. There'd been a highway through here: gas stations, cafes, motels. It probably came from one of them. This door had been around a lot longer than the people on either side of it. He imagined it standing in the middle of a grassy plain long after all the humans had wiped each other out.

The bearded man who answered the door looked as nervous as Tillman felt. His Soldier pants were patched at the knees. His frayed Soldier shirt had the sleeves cut off, or maybe they'd just fallen off. His arms were lean and strong, and his sun-baked face was cautious and guarded.

His eyes darted quickly from Tillman to Stephanie, who was standing in the light from the open door. Tillman glanced back at her as well. Damn! She'd forgotten to cover her head. Her scales made her look like some exotic flower. The man's eyes returned slowly to Tillman.

"My wife and I need a place to stay the night," Tillman said.

"Can't help you," the man said. He shifted in the doorway to close the door, and Tillman saw what he'd interrupted. The whole family—a woman and four children—was crowded around a table with a corn oil lamp and a large book open before the only empty chair.

" 'Be not forgetful to entertain strangers; for thereby some have entertained angels unawares,' " Tillman quoted, hoping he remembered it right. The man stopped closing

the door and glanced over his shoulder at his family watching him expectantly. Tillman filed this moment under lessons of fatherhood—protect them or make them proud. Some choice.

"Be back directly," the man said to his family and stepped through the doorway, closing the door behind him. "Got a barn," he said. "Be gone sunup, you hear?"

THE BARN WAS CORRUGATED METAL LASHED TO A SKELETON of PVC pipe with electrical wire. A mule and a cow shifted in their stalls. The barking dog was here. He fell silent when his master slid open the door and lit a lantern hanging from the rafters. The dog's tail thumped in the dirt at the prospect of company.

The farmer pointed out a pile of straw in one of the two empty stalls where Tillman and Stephanie could sleep. He carefully avoided looking at Stephanie's scale-covered head. If he got caught sheltering a Construct, he was a dead man, but here he was, because of a dozen or so words from an old book, helping them anyway. Humans are damn funny creatures, Tillman thought.

"Pump's in the yard," the farmer said. "There's apples in the barrel."

Stephanie gasped, clutching her belly, and sank down to her knees on the straw.

The farmer started and peered at her through narrowed eyes. "She all right?"

"I don't know," Tillman said, kneeling beside her and taking her hand. "Steph?" he whispered. She winced, her head jerking back, her eyes widening in pain. He supported her as she lay back on the straw.

"I'll get my wife," the farmer said and hurried out. Tillman and Steph looked into each other's eyes as they listened to the farmer's footsteps running back to the house, the metal door opening and closing. With a hopeful swish of his tail, the dog squirmed toward them on his belly.

Steph looked a little better, breathing a little easier, shifting in the straw trying to somehow get comfortable. "What was that thing you said to him about angels?" she asked.

"Oh, that? It was a line I remembered from the Bible: Letter to the Hebrews. I figured I'd read it, since it was addressed to me. Biggest bunch of hogwash I ever read in my life—except that one line. That's why it stuck in my head." He felt giddy, rattling on like an idiot while his wife was about to have a baby on a dirt floor in the middle of a war zone.

She laughed and squeezed his hand. "I love you, Walter." Her grip abruptly tightened, her face contorted in pain. "I think this is it. Please don't leave me."

He knew she meant stay with her while she was having the baby, but he could promise much more than that. "I'm here," he said. "I'm not going anywhere."

The farmer's wife hurried in and stood at Stephanie's feet, a couple of towels draped over her arm like a waiter. The oldest girl followed, laden with two buckets of water. The farmer followed with a blue plastic washtub. The girl and the farmer set down their burdens and left, the girl stealing a wide-eyed look at the strangers as she was ushered out the door by her father. "First time?" the woman asked cheerily.

Steph nodded and gripped Tillman's hand so hard he thought it was going to break.

"Be over 'fore you know it," the woman said and knelt down between Steph's legs. "Now let's see what you got here."

The dog had scooted up so that his grizzled muzzle was resting on Steph's shoulder, his tail swishing straw at a furious rate. Stephanie dug her hand into his ruff, and he licked her cheek. "Leave the poor woman alone, Buster," the woman said.

"He's fine," Steph said, her lip trembling like somewhere deep inside she was being torn in two. "Let him stay."

WHEN NANCY, THE FARMER'S WIFE, CUT THE CORD AND washed the baby and placed it in her arms, Stephanie felt as if they were floating on a cloud of straw. She turned to Walter and smiled. "We did it," she said in a croaking voice. She remembered screaming her head off what seemed like a long time ago, Buster howling his encouragement, Walter right there beside her. She missed his old face, but she was growing used to this new one.

He reached out and touched their daughter's cheek as if she were as delicate as a rose petal. "I didn't do anything," he said. "You did all the work."

Nancy laughed. "Wish my husband would figure that out." She pointed a thumb back toward the house. "I'll get y'all something proper to eat. Wish we had more room in the house, but least it's a warm night." She eyed the sleeping baby—her head was covered with what looked like tiny white feathers—with a mixture of affection and concern. "You folks on the run?"

"I guess you could say that," Walter said.

"You're the spitting image of the Commander's son—if you didn't have that bit of a beard on you—but you ain't him, is you?"

"No, ma'am."

"They was looking for him awful hard there for a while, but something big's up in the city. Ain't seen a patrol in over a week, thank the Lord. Eat you outta house and home if you let 'em. But don't you worry. Buster here won't let no one sneak up on you, that's for sure." She bit her lip. "I wouldn't let any of the Army boys from the city see that baby girl if I was you." Her eyes teared up at the thought of what they might do to her. "You folks can stay here long as you like."

"We'll be gone as soon as we can travel," Stephanie said.

Nancy nodded. "Suppose that's best." She pointed at the baby. "She's a healthy one. Quiet too. Mine all been screamers. What's her name?"

"Madeline," Walter said. "Her mother picked it out." Nancy had no way of knowing he wasn't talking about Stephanie.

Nancy smiled at her approvingly. "That's mighty pretty."

Rafe, Nancy's husband, slid open the barn door with a clatter and stepped inside, frantically pointing out at the night sky. "You gotta see this," he said. An incredibly bright star shone in the sky, streams of light radiating from it in all directions. He looked at Stephanie and Tillman as if they might somehow be responsible.

"It's the Bin," Walter said. "Gabriel just nuked it."

They had to wonder how Walter knew that, but they didn't ask. Apparently, the wrath of Gabriel was always a plausible explanation for disaster. Nor was there any joy in their eyes at the news. Instead, Rafe and Nancy knelt in the doorway and prayed. A roaring sound filled the night, and a chunk from the Bin streaked across the sky and smashed into the woods, sending up a huge ball of flame and rattling the metal walls of the barn. Buster lumbered out into the yard, barking furiously.

There were other, more distant explosions, and fires glowed on the horizon as the debris from the Bin continued to pepper the area for a half hour or more. The farm was untouched except for a dusting of ash. All the while, the new star burned brightly. Stephanie didn't remember falling asleep as she watched the spectacle, but the next thing she knew it was morning.

"ARE WE BEAUTIFUL?" MADDIE ASKED. STANDING KNEE DEEP in the creek, looking down at her reflected face, even as the water dripping from her head rippled it. Her scales were pure white, softer than Stephanie's. The product of the interaction of Sam and Laura's genes, Walter explained. Beautiful, whatever the cause. Maddie looked at her mother. "Are we?" She had her father's pale blue eyes.

"Yes," Stephanie said. "You are very beautiful."

"Not as beautiful as you."

"Thank you, sweetheart, but beauty alone isn't important."

"We know," Maddie said and turned back to her reflection. She stuck her arms out to her sides, her fingers splayed like twigs. "We're a tree," she said and fell facefirst into the water. She came up laughing and spewing. "Hook up, hook up," she pleaded.

"Not today," Stephanie said. She didn't like to use the chip she inherited along with Laura's body. As Maddie's memories had started coming back, it only made her feel excluded to share them, to feel her daughter's joy at a past that had nothing to do with Stephanie. She doesn't need me, Stephanie thought, my wasted solitary life. "Mommy's tired," she said.

"*Please!* We remember swimming with Gran."

"I don't remember Gran, dear."

"Then hook *up!*"

"I said *no!*" Stephanie snapped.

Maddie's face crumpled, and she dove under the water. Stephanie could see her just below the surface, swimming upstream like a beaver. What's come over me? Stephanie asked herself. Walter seemed to take their Construct daughter in stride, even glorying in her differences from other children, answering her endless scientific questions, but Stephanie had nothing to offer her daughter. She never had to tell Maddie the right thing to do. The three of her worked it out on their own.

Stephanie looked around the bright green landscape of early summer, the lazy brown flow of the creek down the middle of it, and tried to feel like she belonged here, but couldn't. She originally decided to come to Earth merely to die. But when Walter came back into her life, she'd allowed herself to hope for more. *The old happily-ever-after bit,* as Laura said. And she supposed she had it. She loved her husband and her child, and they loved her, but . . . She wouldn't speak the words even in her mind, but the feeling was there just the same.

It's not enough.

Stephanie stood up, looked down at her body rippling in the water. Still beautiful. Not that anyone cared. Walter, she supposed. The Constructs thought of her as Madeline's mother. The Christian farmers with whom they had cautious but friendly relations thought of her as "the reformed harlot." She thought of herself as nothing, a beautiful emptiness, an urn that would never be filled.

I'm turning into my mother, she thought, the perpetual victim.

She walked along the bank upstream and found Maddie sitting on the opposite bank, curled up in a ball. "We're sorry," Maddie said in a quiet voice.

Stephanie winced with guilt, remembering her own profuse and pointless childhood apologies. "I'm the one who should be sorry," she said.

Maddie picked her chin up from her knees. "Really?"

"Really."

"Can we all go to town?"

Stephanie smiled. Whatever else she was, she was still a child, ready in a heartbeat to turn her mother's penitence into privilege. They lived fifty miles from the new Construct Town, but it was only five miles to the train. Since Maddie was born, Walter had thrown himself into agriculture. His new strains of fruits and vegetables had made him a celebrity among the Constructs. Maddie also thrived among the Constructs. They treated her as if she were a little princess. When Walter and Maddie took his produce to market in town, they would make a day of it, coming home in high spirits. Stephanie usually bowed out of these trips. She found the Constructs' adulation of Maddie annoying. At first she thought she was concerned for her daughter, knowing the dangers of life on a pedestal, but lately she'd been wondering if she just wasn't jealous.

Stephanie stepped into the creek, sinking into the muck, then waded over to Maddie and took her in her arms. Maddie crawled into her lap. She was getting too big for that, but Stephanie didn't mind, welcomed the contact of her wet body, flesh of her flesh. Nothing else mattered, did it?

She kissed Maddie's head. "Yes, we can go to town."

Maddie wriggled with delight. "Can we see Rat?"

"He may not be there, sweetheart."

"He'll be there," Maddie said with certainty.

Stephanie didn't bother to ask how she knew. Maddie had been tuned into the Constructs since birth, seemed to thrive on telepathy, sitting out under a tree communing with God knows who for hours on end. Stephanie herself found hooking up exhausting even in short doses and never did it by choice. "Of course you can see him," she said. She held Maddie tightly and rocked back and forth in the mud. "We'll have a wonderful time."

"Can we go to New Jerusalem?"

Stephanie went cold with fear. She took Maddie's face in her hands and looked into her eyes. "Why do you want to go there?" Her voice was shrill with panic. She wanted to burrow into her daughter's sky-blue eyes and root out all her secrets.

"We remember it," Maddie said simply. Her gaze was open and guileless.

An image flashed through Stephanie's mind—Maddie running down a stone street, hands reaching out for her. "You can't go there—not ever. Do you understand?"

"When we are grown up," she said. It was a statement, not a question. "You're hurting," she said, making a face, and Stephanie removed her hands.

Yes, I am, she thought. I'm hurting. After almost nine years back in the world, she'd seen you couldn't change anything. Fear ruled everyone. There was nothing left but this endless waiting for the end. But you couldn't tell that to a child. She'd find out soon enough—a child who embodied everything the Soldiers sought to destroy. Hardly a day went by that Stephanie didn't imagine Maddie's death and grieve over it. "When you are grown up," Stephanie said carefully, "you'll understand why you can never—ever—go there."

"WHEN YOU HAD YOUR OWN WORLD," MADDIE ASKED TILL-man, "did you have a girlfriend?" Maddie was fourteen, all arms and legs, perched on top of the water tank like a spider.

Tillman was sitting in front of a row of eight tomato

plants, running a DNA analysis on them to see if they'd turned out as planned. He was hoping to accelerate growth without producing the bland mealy fruit his earlier attempts had yielded. In some ways, animals were easier than plants. The analyzer was one of Rat's resurrected wonders hooked up to a solar panel Tillman had designed from modified chlorophyll. He wanted to finish before he lost the sun. For some inexplicable reason, number five was different from the others, perhaps better—

He remembered his daughter's question. "I had your mother," he said. "I didn't need a girlfriend." He wished he'd never told Maddie about his "own world," as she called it. She was endlessly curious about it.

"But you only had memories of her. You told us you didn't even interact with them—just played them like virtuals. We mean somebody who was right there *with* you. You know." Maddie stretched out on the water tank, one leg resting on the crooked knee of the other, her hands behind her head. "You must've been horny as hell."

"Maddie."

"Well, you *must've*. Tell us. We won't tell Mom."

Screw it. Tillman shut down the analyzer. He went for the obvious parental ploy: stalling. "Does this interest in my virtual sex life have anything to do with young Ricardo?" Ricardo was the current boyfriend, a young Soldier turned scavenger ever since Maddie crossed his path. She went through adoring young men like Tillman's dad plowing through a bag of potato chips. For her part, it didn't seem to be so much romance as a fact-finding mission.

She made a face. "No, Daddy. It's about your world. Was she pretty?"

He sighed. "Okay, I sort of had a girlfriend, and yes, she was pretty. Great legs. Her name was Sally. I cribbed her together from some childhood fantasies. She wasn't real. She was just a program to amuse myself. Basically, she was your mother in a different body."

"Like now."

Tillman felt the elevator of his reality plummet a few

floors. Maddie was always doing that to him: She'd ask the questions, and he'd get the answers. "Yes, like now," he admitted.

"Very interesting," she said, squinting up into the sky, her scales fanning out on her forehead like they did when she was thinking hard. He knew better than to go back to his work. When she finished mulling over whatever had caught her fancy, there'd be more questions.

Maddie was unique, three-lives-in-one practically since conception. Hawkeye had told Tillman that the Constructs all hooked up together only rarely on special occasions. Except for Maddie. "She seeks out other minds like the roots of a tree seek water," he said. "When she comes to our minds, it is a blessing." Tillman suspected she was using their combined mental power to mull over her many questions.

More and more, she seemed to be finding the answers, but damn if he could follow her train of thought. It was a good train—he was sure of that much—but where was it going? He loved his daughter beyond all bounds of reason, and not a day went by he didn't bless the day he agreed to become her father. He only wished he was smarter, wiser, better. She turned to him for guidance, but he could barely manage to follow.

"It's the choices, isn't it?" she said, as if he'd know what she was talking about. "You think Sally wasn't real because you made her, and Mom's real because she made herself."

"I don't know if it's that simple," Tillman said.

"We do," Maddie said with this cheerful little lilt to her voice that sometimes drove Steph crazy. He recognized the emotion: Maddie'd figured out some piece of the puzzle and was stepping back to admire her progress before picking up the next piece. He wished he could admire it with her, but a piece for her would be a lifelong puzzle for anyone else. When she was just a kid, she'd come back from what she called an "outing"—a telepathic powwow with three or four brilliant Constructs—full of enthusiasm for what she'd learned. Or taught. Half the time, Tillman wouldn't know what the hell she was talking about.

"Sorry we interrupted," she said, turning on her side and propping her head on one arm. "You can go ahead and finish those analyses now."

She was trying to sound casual, but she had this impish look that told Tillman something was up. He turned on the analyzer and ran the analyses again. This time all eight were like number five. He looked from the screen, to Maddie, to the plants.

"What did you do?" Tillman asked.

"Watch," she said, pointing at the plants.

So he stared at them, not expecting to see much, when the leaves started growing, the blossoms opening up and dropping off, the fruit swelling to ripeness before his eyes. In about five minutes, he was staring at a bushel of ripe tomatoes on the vine. The plants were bent over under the load.

"Should've staked them," Maddie said. "We didn't think of that."

Tillman figured it must all be an illusion. "I told you about messing with my chip," he warned. About a year ago, she went through this phase where she'd access his chip without his permission and make him see a dozen Maddies, or her favorite (in honor of the story he'd told her of his visit with Newman Rogers) she'd make the forest dance. It got on his nerves, and she'd solemnly sworn never to do it again.

She sighed. "We're not messing with your silly chip. You don't need it anyway. Everything's got some sort of chip already—or something that'll work the same way—if you just look for it. Even tomato plants." She swung her legs over the side of the tank and dropped to the ground. She kissed him on the cheek and plucked a tomato, holding it out to him. It was the size of a grapefruit. "Try it," she said.

He took it in his hands and squeezed its solid flesh, with the slight give of ripe fruit. He took a bite, and the juice ran down his chin. It was delicious. "This is real?" he asked in a whisper.

She put her hand over her heart. "Swear to God."

"You made these plants grow like that?"

She tilted her head from side to side. "Sort of. We showed them how, then they kind of wanted to."

"You 'showed them how.' " He looked down at the tomato in his hand, at the pulp and seed and rich red fruit his bite had revealed. "They 'wanted to.' " His daughter was communicating with tomato plants. He wanted to tell her it was impossible, but clearly it wasn't.

"It's not magic, Daddy. Consciousness is in the scheme of things."

" 'The scheme of things'?"

"The way things are. What you'd call science."

"And what would you call it?"

"Science is okay. It's just so narrow. You're so sure that there's this big canyon between mind and matter. It's really kind of spooky, like two people living in the same house and not knowing the other one's there."

"So what are you saying? 'And cut the Zen crap,' as Laura would say. How'd you do this?" He gestured at the plants.

She made a very Laura-like face at him. "The tomatoes are conscious of their DNA, okay? It's like they're whatever they think they are. We just made some cool suggestions."

"You talked to tomatoes."

She rolled her eyes, scrunched up her bony shoulders. "Not talk. Tomatoes don't *talk*, Daddy."

"Tolerance, darling. Patience."

"Sorry. We can't explain any better."

She seemed genuinely frustrated. It was tough dealing with lesser beings. She'd left him behind so long ago, he couldn't imagine where she'd gotten to by now, and she probably had trouble imagining how her once wise father had become such a fool. He couldn't entirely explain Maddie's gifts—great genes and a unique environment didn't seem to quite cover it. He often suspected the chip Newman designed had more to it than he'd let on.

"Show me," he said.

"You mean like a gene or an enzyme or something. It's not like that."

"Then show me what it *is* like."

She cocked one feathery brow and gave him an *Are you sure?* look.

He tried to look brave. Brave Daddy.

"Hook up, then," she said.

This was his daughter, he reminded himself. No reason to be afraid. He'd nursed her through childhood ailments, taught her how to swim. But still he felt like he was standing on top of a high cliff about to dive off. "Go easy on your old man now," he said, and she laughed.

Or seemed to—they were joined, so he wasn't sure whether she actually laughed or not. Just the sort of distinction she now gently advised him to let go of.

He closed his eyes, trying to orient himself within the complexity of her mind. There were always three there, sometimes dozens more, but they blended into one another—sometimes with separate thoughts and feelings spilling into one another—and then out of apparent chaos coming together as one in a startling moment of clarity and power Tillman experienced like a flash of inspiration so intense it could literally knock him off his feet.

She was in such a moment. But she wasn't thinking. Wasn't feeling. She was a vast emptiness with Tillman nested in the midst of it, serene and content. *Nothing matters,* he thought. She opened herself up and the void flooded all at once with vivid presences:

> *Steph wind Rat rat water Buster root carbon chlorophyll planet feather Sandoz memory fire fish blossom electron tree Tillman tomato blood thought Donovan love emptiness sight Madeline.*

It was less than a second, but he couldn't handle it, couldn't grasp it. He understood nothing. He understood everything. For that split second, he'd seen, at least, that everything was understandable, and that was more than enough. She returned him to his own mind like someone might return a bird's egg to a nest. He was kneeling on the ground, crying. She held his head in her arms the same way he used to hold her when she'd fall.

"It's all right," she whispered. "Everything's all right."

For some reason, the line from Psalm 23 kept running through his head: *My cup runneth over.* He'd always thought that psalm was about death—until now. There was no death, only the still waters. No enemies, only the green pastures. She helped him to his feet.

"Why do you bother to ask me questions?" he asked.

"Seeing everything and understanding them aren't the same thing. You taught us that." She put her arms around his waist and laid the side of her head against his chest. "Besides, we don't see everything."

He put his arms around her, his dear daughter. "What are your limitations? You can't fly?"

"Distance," she said seriously, looking off toward the horizon in the direction of New Jerusalem. "But that will change." The first stars were coming out, and Tillman wondered just how far she was looking, how limitless she hoped to become.

She helped him pack up his equipment, and they made their way back to the house, just a man and his daughter. She was carrying the tomato plants, crowded into a wooden box.

"We should give some of these to Rafe and Nancy," she said.

He smiled at the thought. He could still taste the fruit in his mouth, feel it becoming his body. His mind. He remembered a facet of his brief connection with Madeline's mind. "Donovan's alive. Is he all right?"

Maddie winced at the mention of Donovan. "He's very, very sad, Daddy, but we're going to help him." She kissed his cheek. "We'll make you proud. You'll see."

19

THE MARRIAGE OF HEAVEN AND HELL

DONOVAN HAD KNOWN EVERYTHING A LIVING PERSON COULD know about death—the thing, the concept—which was perhaps nothing at all, but he'd been a complete stranger to dying—the experience, the journey—had carefully excluded it from his philosophy. Now he had eighteen years' intimacy with it, had seen the process in his victims' eyes—building toward the moment when they let go, when they knew there was no hope. He often thought there was a split second before he actually snapped their necks or spines or burst their skulls against a stone wall that if he didn't actually do it, stopped himself the instant before the neck snapped or the brain shattered, that they'd already be dead, their souls sucked away in the current, washed up on whatever shore Nicole inhabited, safe from him forever.

He'd murdered 317 people in the last eighteen years, maimed or crippled hundreds more. The Soldiers called him the Angel of Death, lumbering along with Gabriel wherever he went, always in Gabriel's sight except when he stood guard outside the bedroom while the Chosen One screwed some faith-bedazzled virgin. Usually, after a week or so, the virgin passed from Gabriel's hands to the Angel of Death's, dying under interrogation for some trumped-up sin.

When Donovan first witnessed the private details of Gabriel's sin-filled life, he thought Gabriel was a simple hypocrite who was playing the suckers for all they were worth—wrapping himself up in a feigned religion like a wolf in sheep's clothing.

He knew better now. Gabriel was a true believer in a simple faith: He was the Chosen One of God. His whole life turned on this belief, depended on it. How else could he pile sin upon sin if he didn't bear the divine yoke on his shoulders? His rapacious nature was God's gift, like the keen edge of a reaper's blade. He was the Lion of God, another Samson—a despicable man whose violent selfish life was glorified by serving God's terrible vengeance. If he were just another man, Gabriel truly believed, he'd burn in hell forever for his abundant sins. But God had chosen him from all the men of the world, and at the End of Days He would lift Gabriel up into heaven and set him at His right hand to judge the living and the dead.

Only death could challenge Gabriel's faith, a prospect that had come increasingly close the last few years. Cancer, AIDS, syphilis—Donovan didn't know enough to make a medical diagnosis—but he knew the smell of death, and Gabriel reeked of it. The cloning apparatus had broken down shortly after Donovan downloaded into Seth's body. A chip in the complicated circuit regulating the growth process had failed, and a replacement was beyond the capabilities of Gabriel's labs—even if he dared risk their figuring out what the circuit was for.

Gabriel now looked old and frail, made few public appearances. His power was slipping away. There had already been two assassination attempts, and there were bizarre rumors of rebellion in the provinces. Donovan had relished the growing fear in Gabriel's eyes, though he didn't want the man to die. Not yet. Not just yet.

And then, six weeks ago, a secret salvage expedition to the ruins of an old Construct plant in what used to be Baltimore had unearthed the necessary chip. The apparatus had been repaired, and now a new clone would be ready for Gabriel's rejuvenation in a matter of hours. And so, at the eleventh hour, Gabriel would be saved—reborn again in all his glory to strike down his enemies and the enemies of his vicious God.

Or so he believed.

Donovan had waited eighteen years for this moment. Hell awaited Gabriel. Donovan would conduct him there. He only wished Seth were alive to share this moment. When Donovan had downloaded into Seth's body, it was like sharing a cave with a slumbering bear. Then he realized the bear was awake, watching him, trying to fathom him. Then one morning the bear was gone. Donovan believed that, like Simone Mirabelli, Seth had walked out of the cave into the light, leaving Donovan alone in the darkness to wait, to act.

As Gabriel waited in his apartment for his deliverance, already glorying in his renewed life, he talked, as he often did, to his silent companion, who stood like a hat rack in the corner and listened. If his armor-plated face were capable of such a thing, he would've smiled at his master's self-deceit.

"When I step to the pulpit this evening, they will fall to their knees," he said, imagining the sight even as he was racked with a fit of coughing. "They will know, they will see—that God has not forsaken His Chosen One, that He has healed my body so that I might lead my people into the final battle and crush His enemies forever." He waved a feeble fist in the air and brought it down on the table beside him, the effort yielding another round of coughing.

The final battle, Donovan had decided, could never happen, but only be prophesied. It could not begin if it could never end. It could not end if it ended time.

The fiery destruction of the Bin had not brought the End of Days. So Gabriel attacked the Constructs. Mobilizing every vehicle they'd salvaged over the years, the Soldiers surrounded Construct Town, shelled if for three days, leveling it completely. If it were time, it would've stopped. But when the Soldiers moved in, they couldn't find a single Construct, living or dead. Worse, an electromagnetic burst, a trap left by the Constructs, disabled the electrical system in every single vehicle. The Soldiers marched back to New

Jerusalem, the sun mocking them as it moved across the sky, marking another day. Tanks, jeeps, trucks—all sat rusting in the middle of a burned-out plain covered with rubble and kudzu. Time without end.

By observing the movements of the scattered crazies who remained, Gabriel had formed a good idea of where the Constructs were hiding, but he couldn't risk another humiliation. There was even a good chance if he—a feeble sickly man—gave the attack order, the Army of the Lord would defy him, and his life wouldn't be worth a nickel. What was needed for the final battle was fresh blood.

When his coughing subsided, a pale Gabriel poured himself a glass of whiskey and tossed it off. "They thought I was done for, Seth. They thought they would soon lay me in my tomb, but God has not forsaken me." With a tear-streaked face, he looked up at the cracked plaster ceiling mottled with stains where one could imagine almost any shape or figure. Even Donovan couldn't know what Gabriel saw when he looked to heaven. But if the God and His heavenly host he claimed to see were real, the lot of them deserved to die along with the Chosen One, and to rot in hell forever.

"Carry me to the window," Gabriel ordered, and Donovan shuffled into motion, scooping up the frail man in his arms like a baby. Cradling him in one arm, Donovan pushed the window open with the other, rousing a burst of pigeons. A feather drifted slowly to the ground. It would be an easy matter to let Gabriel fall to his death, give his life over to the angels Gabriel imagined would bear him up before he struck the stones. Gabriel had grown careless with the control for Donovan's collar, believing the giant to be an old and trusted attack dog who would never turn on his master. The control lay now on the table behind them, quite out of reach. But Donovan wouldn't allow Gabriel to goad him into another murder, even his. The nest of vipers who'd be set loose by Gabriel's death were every bit as evil as Gabriel. Donovan had learned patience as well as dying over the years. He was ready, and the time would come—these were the articles of his faith. All else could be endured.

They both—mad messiah and monster—looked from atop the Temple of the Lord, surveying the holy city, the last city, bathed in morning light, its streets filled with the remnants of humanity. They both looked, but they saw different worlds there.

Gabriel saw his vast flock, believing they'd soon be returned securely to the fold, shorn for his robes, slaughtered for his table, a bounty he needn't share with anyone but God. God, who was one with him. At moments like this, one and the same.

Donovan looked past the narrow streets and the penned-up flock to the open fields beyond the river where his hope lay.

Madeline would come to him, deliver him from the hell he'd lived in for so long. She'd promised years ago, coming first in his dreams, then filling every waking moment with her presence, wrapping him up in her love, taking his pain upon herself, rescuing him from madness. She said it was Newman Rogers who had told her to seek him out, though he couldn't imagine how that could be. But he knew it was she who'd placed the chip in the expedition's path so that he could be set free to bring this temple of deceit crashing down. It was she who would reveal to the flock that these narrow streets didn't converge on the hate-filled man in his arms or anyone like him, but radiated out into a world where they might be human again, no longer waiting, no longer hoping. Alive in the world.

The End of Days was at hand. Had always been.

There was a light knock at the door. Gabriel thumped on Donovan's chest as a command to set him back in his chair. When Gabriel had settled his robes around him and taken on the magisterial air he could still muster on occasion, he gave Donovan a curt nod.

Donovan opened the door, and Jeremiah, now a major, stepped forward and saluted smartly. He sported a thin mustache and sunglasses, a bit of vanity Gabriel would not have tolerated a few years ago.

Gabriel tossed his hand in a condescending mockery of a salute. He knew Jeremiah couldn't be trusted. Samuel's father blamed Gabriel for the defection of his son, and somehow Jeremiah had squirmed his way into the Commander's favor. "You have interrupted my prayers, Major. I trust this is an important matter."

Jeremiah made little attempt to disguise his smirk. "Yes, sir. We thought you should be informed that the farmers have abandoned their fields and are converging on the city. We await orders, sir."

Gabriel masked his reaction, but Donovan knew what he must be thinking: *Why now? Why not in a few hours when I will be invincible again?*

Because she knows your every move, Donovan would've told him if his mouth could speak, but Gabriel would know the truth soon enough—when *he* would be forced to stand mute and listen.

"How many farmers?" Gabriel asked.

"All of them."

"What do they want?"

"We don't know, sir. Just wild stories."

"Stories?"

"They are led by a mere girl. They say she is an Angel. She shows them visions."

"An Angel."

"Yes, sir."

"And what else do they say?"

"That she is coming for you, sir."

The color drained from Gabriel's face. Whether Gabriel saw the angels he claimed to see, Donovan would never know, but the news that an Angel sought him clearly struck terror in his heart. "Kill her," he said. "Kill them all."

"But, sir, they don't appear to be armed, and many of the troops have families in the provinces—"

His face taut with rage, Gabriel came up out of his chair,

knocking it over backward. "Do you dare question my orders?"

There was a significant pause as Jeremiah glanced quickly at Seth towering over him and back to Gabriel. "No, sir. I will see that your orders are carried out immediately." He saluted and spun on his heel, clearing the door in two strides, the faintest of smiles on his face.

Gabriel reached out and grasped Donovan's arm to steady himself. "Ready the clone," he said in a husky voice, and for the first time in eighteen years, Donovan willingly obeyed his master's command.

STEPHANIE SAT UNDER A TALL OAK AND WATCHED HER DAUGH-ter move through the throngs of adoring people gathering by the river below—as numerous as the acorns that littered the ground around her. Like me, Stephanie thought, Maddie dazzles with her beauty. The beautiful vision she plants in their minds: Not that Truth is Beauty, but that the truth is beautiful.

At least to most. There were a handful who fled from Maddie's transforming visions, confused and terrified. Stephanie herself kept apart from her daughter's mind where she feared the final evidence of her own insignificance.

She and Walter had been traveling around with Maddie for almost two years, ever since Maddie started hooking up with the crazies and the disenchanted farmers, created a ring of discontent around the holy city. They told themselves they were looking after her, but the truth was they could follow her or lose her. She could, it seemed, know anyone's mind, even place thoughts, feelings, and perceptions there. Her extraordinary telepathic gifts mystified even Walter. Stephanie suspected Newman Rogers had a hand in it, but it didn't matter. What Stephanie wanted to know was where Maddie's unwavering sense of purpose came from—Sam, Laura, Newman Rogers—for it was stronger than her bond to her parents, apparently stronger than her bond to life itself. She seemed capable of hearing the stones speak. Perhaps they goaded her on. Perhaps they sought to make her one of them.

They slept in barns and cellars, ate the shared bounty of Maddie's miraculous fruits and vegetables, met with secret clusters of her wide-eyed followers. It was easy to get caught up in the naïve drama of a revolution sweeping the countryside—that a few dozen people gathered in a cornfield or packed into a barn could change things. Soldier patrols doggedly pursued them, laid clumsy traps for them, playing the clownish heavies who made evil seem like a pushover. But the truth was that a single warhead could (and most likely would) bring down the curtain on heroes and villains alike. Stephanie wanted to believe everything would come right, that the Good Cause would finally prevail, but more and more it seemed to her that though her daughter bore a torch to show the way, she was leading them all into a valley filled with gasoline.

What kept Stephanie in this caravan was the little girl she could still see in the stately courageous woman Maddie had become, a little girl who might yet need her mother again before all this was over. She didn't want to think about after.

Stephanie looked beyond the river to New Jerusalem in the distance, the spires of the Temple jutting into the sky like daggers. She'd told Maddie, *When you are grown up, you'll understand why you can never—ever—go there.* Perhaps I was talking to myself, Stephanie thought. Along the bank, thousands of hands worked frantically, lashing together a floating bridge to cross the wide water. A flotilla of john boats and canoes bobbed about in the river, maneuvering it into place.

Stephanie hadn't yet decided whether she could cross over with the rest of them and watch her daughter face almost certain death. They already had word that troops were on their way to stop them. She'd seen Soldiers lay down their arms in Maddie's presence, running in terror or falling to their knees, their heads filled with who knew what miraculous visions. But she'd never faced such numbers before, and all it would take would be one Soldier among thousands. All it would take would be one bullet.

She imagined Gabriel looking out from that Temple, surely immune to Maddie's transcendent visions. He'd kill them all before he let this girl take away his holy city. He could do it with a touch of his fingertip, with the absolute conviction he was saving the world. She remembered the Bin blazing in the sky, a cloud of nuclear dust. This handful of souls was nothing. Maddie knew all this. Maddie seemed to know Gabriel as if she'd lived in his skin. But that didn't stop her, didn't even seem to concern her. Stephanie wondered whether her daughter was crazy—or what amounted to the same thing—the only one who wasn't.

Stephanie searched the crowd, trying to spot Walter. She'd grown used to his new body over the years. Being tall and handsome, while insignificant in the grand scheme to Save the World that now filled his days, seemed to please him, fill him with confidence, or maybe that was Maddie's doing as well. Lately, Stephanie found herself trying to remember his old toadlike face she'd thought unforgettable, but it wouldn't come clear in her mind, and she'd cry over the loss, though she couldn't say why. When the frog turned into a prince, did it make sense to mourn the frog? In most ways, he was still the same old Walter, but even he seemed to forget that this Angel they followed across the countryside was their daughter and this mass of people goading her on to martyrdom were all strangers.

Stephanie had dreamed of love and a family, dreamed she was braver, stronger, better than she was. All she'd wanted was a chance to live a life, and now she'd had it. Or had she? She'd been made into a goddess, then imprisoned by her own guilt. Now she was the mother of a goddess, watching from the wings, waiting to play a role she didn't ask for, didn't want—watching those she loved die, laying them in their graves. She scooped up a handful of acorn debris and dirt, let it run through her long fingers, fingers that used to be Laura's trembling hand. *Join the club, right? Who said it was supposed to mean shit?*

A shadow fell across her, and she looked up. A large fat man stood over her. He set a bushel basket of peaches on the ground at her feet and took out a handkerchief, mopped his sweaty neck with it, folded it, and put it away. "Would you care for a bit of something to eat?" he asked, gesturing toward the basket with a sweep of his hand. The peaches were large, golden, blushed with red, probably picked from the orchard Maddie and Walter had planted nearby a couple of weeks ago.

Stephanie looked up at him. He was truly enormous. "No thank you." She looked back toward the river. Hundreds were in the water now. They might've been children playing.

"Pardon me," the man persisted. "If I am not mistaken, you are Madeline's mother, Stephanie. Allow me to introduce myself. I am Chef Jeff. I knew her when she was Laura." He bowed, and it was like a boulder swaying.

Stephanie hadn't heard Laura spoken of as a real person in some time. Everyone, it seemed, knew the story of Maddie's identity, but it was a miraculous tale in which Sam and Laura were as real as unicorns or Betty Crocker. Stephanie secretly wished Maddie was more like Laura—someone who looked up to her, admired her, reached out to her. Someone with an instinct for survival. "Pleased to meet you," she said.

"May I join you?" he asked, sitting down with a ground-shaking thud before she had a chance to answer. He rocked his bulk back and forth to get comfortable, or perhaps, like an elephant, as an aid to digestion. He plucked a peach from the basket and took a huge bite, chewing noisily. "You must be proud," he said.

Must I? she thought. "Yes," she said. "You were a friend of Laura's?"

Chef took another bite, laughing, sending bits of fruit flying. " 'Friend'? I think not. She loathed my arrogant self, as well she should. I misused her terribly."

"But now, I take it, all is forgiven." Stephanie couldn't

keep the sarcasm out of her voice. What difference would all this goodwill do anyone when they were incinerated?

He studied her with his little pig eyes and smiled. "A bit of her seems to have lingered in her old body yet, if I may say so."

"I'll take that as a compliment."

He took another bite, sucked the pit clean, and spat it out. "Quite so," he chuckled. He put his pudgy fingers into his mouth one by one to clean them. "She used to say to me, 'You fat fuck, you know what your problem is? You've got no fucking principles!' " He chuckled again. "She was absolutely correct."

Stephanie bristled with anger. That's the way they all talked, humbled by the immensity Maddie revealed to them, full of this joyous awareness of their past flaws—as if that made them go away. Stephanie didn't need any help knowing her insignificance, her shortcomings. It wasn't the truth that'd set this man free—Laura had already told him that and he hadn't believed her. It was this spell Maddie cast over them all. "How do you know this glorious vision of truth you've seen is real and not just some virtual planted in your brain by my daughter?" She pointed to New Jerusalem. "She could make that city over there seem to disappear if she wanted to, but it'd still be there. It could still kill you, and you wouldn't even see it coming. Maybe you're still exactly the fool Laura said you were, and that's all you'll ever be."

Stephanie was startled at her own rage. She didn't know this man, and he didn't know her. Worse, he *thought* he knew her because she was the goddess's mother, surely the most blessed of women. Most of the time, she played her part. But now, the end hours away, what possible difference could it make what she said to anyone? What possible fucking difference?

"You misunderstand me," Chef said. "I am still 'a fat fuck with no principles.' " He plucked a peach from the basket and placed it in her hands. " 'Everything matters.' "

" 'Or nothing matters,' " Stephanie finished for him.

Chef looked down to the river, and Stephanie followed

his gaze. Maddie's white head moved through the crowd like a swan parting the waters. "You don't believe that any more than I do," he said, and Stephanie wished she could tell him he was wrong.

All the happy believers were singing now, hooked up together to fashion a round, though they were scattered over a dozen acres and couldn't actually hear each other.

Row, row, row your boat
Gently down the stream.
Merrily, merrily, merrily, merrily,
Life is but a dream.

A familiar figure broke away from the crowd and was walking toward Stephanie. It was Walter, dripping wet from head to toe, grinning from ear to ear like a kid at the beach, waving to her.

Merrily, merrily, merrily, merrily,

She braced herself to tell him, shaping the words in her mind—

Life is but a dream.

—I'm not going.

Life is but a dream.

—I'm not going.

Life is but a dream.

She took a bite from the fruit, and the sweetness filled her mouth and made her almost dizzy. As Walter approached, she saw herself through his eyes. The nomadic life had been hard on her. Squinting in the sun, her face was crisscrossed with lines. They fanned from her eyes like deltas. And it was there he kissed her with a feather's touch, a worshipful tenderness he could still show her after all these years.

"You ready to go, Steph?"

She gathered herself up. "Only if I don't have to sing that stupid song."

DONOVAN HAD HAD A LOT OF TIME TO CONSIDER HIMSELF IN the last eighteen years, to figure out what made him tick, what made him Donovan. He'd wanted to matter, to be more than an idea born of his parents' boredom and then forgotten. He'd never been sufficiently convinced of his own reality.

He wasn't unique in that. He'd killed many people who felt the same. They threw themselves in Gabriel's path just as surely as Nicole threw herself in front of that train the night they met. They usually had a rationale, a passion, some story they could tell themselves about why they were doing it—often lofty and grand. But they knew they were going to die, that their deaths would change absolutely nothing except their sentence in this hell they lived in. Most of them believed they would trade this hell for another. But a change of hells wasn't such a bad thing. At least it was a change.

After Nicole died, Donovan hatched lofty and grand plans to save the Bin with death, but that was like believing he was a savior when he snapped someone's neck. No one ever looked at him with gratitude for the gift of death; few, even with loathing. They didn't really see him at all. He was irrelevant to their fate. The Angel of Death didn't matter. He was a thing. A bullet, say. He wasn't the evil, the will, the aim, the act. He was a piece of lead and a few laws of physics he didn't understand too well. He was a hammer, a rack, a knife, a lightning bolt, a cross. Free of blame or guilt.

Not that he felt nothing. He waited, he hoped, he planned, he despaired, wishing he could persuade himself to be his next victim. But he couldn't. After all this time, he couldn't give up the notion that his life might yet mean something. He would imagine this very moment and stop himself from leaping out a window or stopping a bullet— imagine this very moment and pray that someday it would come to pass as Madeline had promised him it would.

This very moment: Running long-fingered hands through white flowing hair and smiling in the mirror, speaking for the first time in eighteen years, addressing a reflection that looked like Gabriel's younger fitter brother.

"Now I matter," he said. "Now I'm alive."

Behind him, parked in the corner like a rusted-out tank, stood his old body, Gabriel inside like Lucifer on ice. Motionless, he watched Donovan's every move. Snot and tears ran down his face. He stood in a puddle of his own urine. Donovan had activated the shock collar the moment Gabriel opened his new eyes and saw his clone looking back at him. Two, three seconds at the most. It didn't take much. Gabriel used to dance Donovan like a marionette with short little bursts when they were alone. For entertainment.

Gabriel must be wondering why Donovan hadn't just killed him outright. There was no need. Gabriel's new hands could pulverize rock, but he wouldn't lift a finger against Donovan. He'd be consigning himself to Seth's body if Donovan were to die. Gabriel couldn't even have his day of triumphant murder like Samson raining death on the Philistines—the launch sequences could only be initiated by someone with Gabriel's DNA, and Donovan was now that someone.

Donovan adjusted the white robes he'd chosen from Gabriel's closet, straightened his shoulders, stood up tall, and looked into his penetrating eyes. He, formerly known as Dr. Death, could kill every living thing on the planet if he wanted to. But that wasn't why he mattered. He mattered because he didn't want to. He had already launched the last of Gabriel's arsenal toward the sun where the missiles would burn up unnoticed.

He turned from the mirror and smiled at Gabriel, one of those chilling smiles Donovan had seen make grown men fall on their knees and beg for mercy. "Walk two paces ahead of me," he said. "You know the routine." Donovan gestured toward the door. "We're going down to the street."

As they descended the stairs past saluting sentries who reached for their walkie-talkies, alerting those below that the Chosen One was descending, Donovan wondered just how the message would be conveyed. Would these young Soldiers whisper incredulously, "The bastard's done it again"? Or would it simply be the strained tone of their voices (the sound of a slumbering fear jolted awake) that would say all that needed to be said? It didn't matter. Donovan was confident that by the time he emerged into the daylight, half the city would know that Gabriel was miraculously reborn in all his terrible glory and that the End of Days was surely at hand.

He stopped just inside the doors the captain of the Temple Guard held open for him. The man didn't even attempt to disguise the dazed scrutiny he gave to the Chosen One—now, by all appearances, a man in his twenties. Donovan wondered which faction the captain allied himself with, which jackal he'd hoped would bring down that sick old man. Donovan could've told him that all his hopes would seem like despair compared to the life he'd soon know, but the captain wouldn't have believed it.

"Send word to the troops immediately. Do not attack the Angel and her followers. Provide her and anyone in her company safe passage into the city. Is that clear?"

Only a blink or two betrayed the captain's complete surprise. And then another smart salute. "Yes, sir. Very clear, sir."

Donovan stepped into the sunlight and spread his arms in one of Gabriel's signature gestures. God cooperated with a breeze that billowed his robes like wings, his hair streaming out behind him as if he were flying. From the foot of the stone stairs, radiating out in all directions, kneeling faithful filled the streets. On the rooftops and in the windows stood watchful Soldiers with guns.

Donovan relished Gabriel's sonorous voice after eighteen years of silence. "Behold, my children, the End of Days is at hand! The Angel of the Lord has come upon me and breathed new life into me, lifted me up and made me whole!

"Praise God!"

"Praise God!" the faithful shouted, though there were plenty, at the sight of Gabriel restored, who would rather curse God and His Chosen One if they dared risk it. But

each one bellowed loud enough so that his neighbor might hear.

"Praise God!"

"Praise God!"

He lowered his arms, wrapping himself up in his robes, and the city fell silent. He looked out over the sea of faces, took out a Bible, and opened it.

"Harken to the words of the Lord:

'The kingdom of heaven is like to a mustard seed, which a man took, and sowed in his field: Which indeed is the least of all seeds: but when it is grown, it is the greatest of herbs, and becometh a tree, so that the birds of the air come and lodge in the branches thereof.' "

He closed the Bible, shaking his head. "What an odd image, don't you think? Not diamonds or gold or clever machines built by clever men. But a single mustard seed."

He pondered that a moment, let them all ponder it. "You—all of you—are the mustard seeds—tiny things, like grains of sand, sown in this tiny plot of earth some eighty or ninety years ago to see what you might become. And what you have become is yourselves—like all seeds, you have made more seeds, growing, blossoming, falling to the earth again. That is what seeds do—filling the air with our scent, lending our pungent flavor to the Earth. Sometimes too bitter altogether, too harsh.

"But as the Lord tells us, we have become a tree with roots and branches and blossoms. A lone tree in a Garden laid to waste by years of pain and suffering. The Tree of Life whose fruit is salvation watered by faith and love. All from a few seeds scattered on the earth, a single seed taking root. Why? What is the purpose of this tree? So that we can be chopped and bundled? So that we can be harvested and sold? So that we can be burned and plowed under? So that the wicked can be hung from our branches?

"No."

He opened the Bible again. "Listen: the Lord tells us why. It is no mystery. Get up in the morning, go outside and walk around when the dew is still heavy on the grass and the sky is red like the first morning Adam walked in the Garden. The answer is there. Everyone knows it. We just think it's too simple, too easy: 'So that the birds of the air come and lodge in the branches thereof.'

"Close your eyes and imagine them. They are singing, these birds—thousands of them, every color imaginable— because a man—any man—it doesn't matter what man or woman or child—sowed a seed in the earth and waited and hoped and believed, so that now anyone who happens by can stop and listen to the birds singing and be glad. Not next week, not next year, not when earth and bird and seed are no more, but today, right now, and all your days hereafter. The Kingdom of Heaven is here and now. The Tree of Life is in bloom with thousands of golden blossoms, each one in the shape of a cross, a promise fulfilled.

"Praise God!"

"Praise God!"

"Praise God!"

"Praise God!"

Donovan couldn't see beyond the first few rows of dazed faces to know if the seed he'd sown had taken root or whether it'd fallen on barren rock, but it was time to find out. "My children, you have no doubt heard stories of an Angel approaching the city, working miracles, rumors that thousands of the faithful have abandoned their homes and farms to follow her, to sing and dance and have marvelous visions. You have no doubt heard that this Angel comes for me." He looked into the believers' eyes, and they looked away in fear. "I, Gabriel, the Chosen One of God, declare all these glorious rumors to be true!"

A gasp moved through the crowd, a ripple of whispers as the news worked its way back to those too distant to hear for themselves. He waited for silence. "An Angel of the Lord has come to lodge in our branches to sing the sweet music of salvation. She comes for me, she comes for you, for anyone who has ears to hear. Follow me, my children, and we will meet this Angel together, and make a joyful noise unto the Lord!"

The sound was deafening as Donovan, without guards except for the Angel of Death, descended the stairs to the street. The crowd parted, making way for him, then flowed in behind him like a river suddenly reversing its course. From any one of the rooftops above, one of Gabriel's rivals might possibly put an end to this reckless turn of events with a bullet. But Donovan had faith they wouldn't. They were too surprised, too curious wondering what this wily devil was up to now. Some might even be thinking he was, at long last, telling the truth.

JEREMIAH WATCHED THE CONSTRUCT FREAK THEY CALLED AN Angel through his field glasses, the hair on his neck tingling with the realization that he had gotten here first, that his company had the best shot at taking out this unarmed bunch of traitors. He'd been watching this one for a long time. He knew her whole story. He'd taken a special interest when he saw the recon photos, recognizing the guy always hanging around as the Commander's son—the fair-haired boy—good old Sam who'd made Jeremiah look like a fool one too many times.

Eighteen years ago, Jeremiah had been one of the dozens assigned to sift through the data in Tillman's computer and had found some very interesting recordings: the righteous Samuel plotting with that Jew clonemaker, copulating like an animal with the Construct whore. If he'd revealed them at the time, they would've been lost in the hubbub over the discovery of the Bin files, but Jeremiah, knowing they'd be useful someday, still had them in his possession.

He sharpened the focus on his field glasses and confirmed his suspicions. The whore was here too—at her little Angel's side. Images from the recordings flickered through his memory, and he stirred with desire. He lowered the field glasses, ran a thumb and forefinger over his mustache.

Bitch, he thought. Let's just see how brave our hero is now, his whore and bastard at his side. Jeremiah laughed. After the shock of those three heads on a stake, the Commander might need to step down, make way for younger, stronger stomachs.

When that coward Samuel took off, Jeremiah told the Commander his son was no traitor, but a pawn in Gabriel's blasphemous dealings in outlawed technology. It was pathetic to witness how quickly the vain old Commander could be persuaded of his son's heroism, how easy it was to drive a wedge between him and Gabriel.

The order not to harm this pack of traitors had just come through. But Jeremiah knew there would never be another opportunity like this: An open rebellion marched against the holy city, and only he could stop it. Even better, Gabriel had given the order to destroy them and now was vacillating. If Gabriel was too weak to crush these dumb hicks, then he was too weak to rule the holy city. Fortunately, Jeremiah had been alone when the order came in. He'd shouted into the phone that the signal was being jammed by Constructs, that the so-called Angel was a Construct in the company of known traitors, and his men were under attack. He smashed the phone with the butt of his weapon.

He looked again through his field glasses. Almost all of them were across the river. He could wait a few more seconds. When they were across, Jeremiah intended to take out the bridge, and they'd be trapped—their backs to the water. Fish in a barrel.

"Spare no one," he said to the captain at his side.

"They don't appear to be armed, sir."

"Appearances can be deceiving," Jeremiah said. "Do you dare question the orders of the Chosen One?"

Jeremiah didn't wait for an answer. He continued to look through his field glasses, sweeping the opposite bank. No one. The last straggler was crossing the bridge, an enormously fat man practically swamping the thing. Three hundred pounds at least. "At my signal, lob a shell onto the bridge. Immediately on impact, commence firing. Advance thirty seconds later. Continue firing until I order you to stop." The fat man had reached midriver, wading across the overworked bridge in water to his calves.

"Now," Jeremiah said. He heard the *pop* and whistle of the shell being sent on its way, and he smiled up at the sky to catch a glimpse of it on the way down. For a brief instant, he felt a presence in his mind, then the sky seemed to tumble, its hue deepening, turning bluer. The whistle of the shell abruptly changed pitch and direction so that it seemed closer, directly over his head. He snapped his head back. The ground beneath him was heaving like water. He saw the shell falling for a long second. His body ripped apart, shattered in an instant of agony and darkness. For a brief moment, he was high above the river, looking down.

He opened his eyes, and he was lying on his back where he'd stood when he'd given the order. He touched his chest, his face. He was still intact. Somehow he'd experienced the shell's fall from the fat man's perspective. Some Construct trick, all an illusion. He sat up to discover his men surrounded him. Their weapons lay on the ground. Their hands all pointed at him as if they still held them, aiming at him, firing. He clung to his own weapon and raised the muzzle.

A voice in his head spoke his name, and he screamed as loud as he could, dared not stop. That whore bastard was in his head, trying to break him, possess him—if he heard a single word, he would lose his soul. He leaped to his feet to find she stood in front of him, her arms outstretched. *Jeremiah, lay down your weapon. Jeremiah, we mean you no harm.* Light streamed out from her in all directions, so bright it hurt his eyes, but he walked toward her, aiming into the light growing brighter and brighter until the sky was filled with her face. He squeezed the trigger and didn't let go until the light had shrunk to nothing, and he found himself in total darkness.

He dropped his empty weapon and could hear it clatter on the ground, but he couldn't see it. He held his hand before his face. Nothing. He was blind. Nearby, someone was crying.

✲   ✲   ✲

Stephanie had looked back at Chef, wondered aloud to Walter, "Do you think he needs any help?" when they heard the shell, and a few seconds later the river erupted. She turned back to Maddie, but she was in a trance. Water and debris rained down from the sky. Chef was gone. All that was left of the bridge were a few scraps of wood and some ropes staked to the opposite bank.

There were screams behind her, and she turned expecting to see one of their own wounded by the blast, but it was a Soldier walking in circles, dozens of other Soldiers converging on him. At first she thought they were going to shoot him, but they were empty-handed, holding their arms in a pantomime of threat, like boys playing war. The screaming Soldier was staring into the sun, and then, abruptly, he took aim at the sun and fired, the automatic weapon chattering out bullets for what seemed like an endless time.

He dropped the weapon on the ground and everything was silent, but for the echoes of the screams and gunfire pulsing in the air like distant winds and the sound of his sobbing, like a widow's grief.

Maddie was standing in the middle of the road unharmed, turning in a slow circle, touching everyone's minds with a feather's touch of comfort to still their fears, but Stephanie could feel the panic her daughter concealed from the rest of them. No one wanted to believe the Angel was afraid, least of all the Angel herself.

Walter had his arms around Stephanie, holding her close. "Are you all right?"

"I'm fine," she said, kissing her fingertips and placing them on his cheek. "I need to go to Maddie." She freed herself from Walter's embrace, pushed through the crowd, and took Maddie in her arms, squeezing hard, lifting her up, taking on her grief, her guilt. Chef was dead, and the Soldier named Jeremiah was blind. No one else was harmed, but all Maddie's thoughts began with: *We should've known . . . We should've thought . . . We should've—*

Stephanie rocked Maddie back and forth, silencing her,

forgiving her. Stephanie opened up to the thousands gathered around them, and they all felt Maddie's guilt and fear and forgave her.

When you are grown up, Steph had told her, and now that time had come. She held Maddie's shoulders at arm's length. "We have to keep going," she said. "Everyone's waiting on you."

Maddie hugged her mother hard around the neck, turned, and walked on ahead. Walter came up behind Stephanie and took her hand. They walked a pace or two behind their daughter. The rest of the Soldiers were kneeling along the roadside. As she passed, Maddie touched them, showed them the world through her eyes, and they broke into smiles and tears, rising to their feet and joining in behind her.

Jeremiah still stood in the middle of the road, slowly turning in a circle. Maddie came to a stop before him. "We're sorry," she said so softly Stephanie couldn't be sure that's what she said, then turned to Stephanie.

"Mother," she said. "Would you see for him?"

There was still something in Stephanie that wanted to say no, that wanted to feign ignorance of what she was being asked to do, not by Maddie—she was only saying the words—but by everything, her whole life up to this moment. But she couldn't refuse, was surprised to find she didn't even want to. "Stay with Maddie," she said to Walter and let them continue on for a few yards before she turned to Jeremiah and took his hand.

Maddie had shown her how. Slowly, cautiously, she opened up to him, gave over her senses to his mind, and though she couldn't make his eyes see, she could *understand* the road, the trees, the birds flitting from bough to bough—from his perspective, from three feet over and to the left, half a pace behind—and give it to him as if he could see it all for himself.

He turned his head as if to look at her, and she saw herself. "Where do you want to go?" she asked.

"I don't know," he said, still in a daze, struggling to understand. They were stopped in the road. Everyone else had gone on ahead. "I'm blind, aren't I?"

"Yes."

He looked down to the river, still murky from the explosion, back to the spires of New Jerusalem. "You decide."

"I'll take you home," she said and they began to walk toward New Jerusalem.

Up ahead, everyone from the city had come out to greet them, Gabriel himself leading the throng in his white flowing robes. Constructs poured up out of the ground as if by magic and moved among the Christians unremarked so that everyone—the Christians, the crazies, the Constructs—were all gathered together in one place for the first time.

All of them couldn't possibly see with their own eyes the event that had brought them together—Madeline and Gabriel meeting on a grassy plain, joining hands, and embracing like bride and bridegroom—but all witnessed it just the same and let out a thunderous shout of joy.

Jeremiah squeezed Stephanie's hand. "They are beautiful."

Stephanie knew this man who seemed to be Gabriel, the Chosen One of God, was actually Donovan, that the Angel, Madeline, was actually a Construct fashioned from a traitor, a whore, and a bastard. Everyone knew. But it was true nonetheless—they were beautiful.

"The truth is beautiful," Stephanie said.

20

END OF DAYS

NEWMAN ROGERS CONTEMPLATED HIS MEMORIES. LONG twining threads of them over billions of years, woven into a river, a mantle for time. He sat on a bluff overlooking the river, great trees on either bank, leaning out over the water. The sky through the mesh of limbs and leaves was the unmistakable blue of Earth's sky.

It'd been a very long time since he'd been a single life in a single body on the planet where he was born. This was only one memory of himself, a loop in the thread when there were still rivers, trees, and suns—still matter, still light. A persistent memory. He felt the place as much as saw it. Nostalgia, with time about to end, was almost a religious observance.

From the vantage point of that ancient Newman, he could see how far he'd come. Back then he feared upsetting the balance, feared the consequences of each step. But there was more to this dance than balance, and things had turned out rather well, after all.

After all this time, it was if he'd always been, and he nearly had, they all had. After all this time, the universe seemed made so that they might—what? Understand it? Make it up? Revise it? Even now that there were no days and nights, no suns to rise and set, they were still here. Even now. Creating time out of nothing but memory and anticipation.

Others wove themselves into his river, into his thoughts: Rat floated downstream, oars at rest, serene and unhurried, letting the current take him. Madeline swam alongside, leaping in and out of the water like a dolphin at play. Tillman and Stephanie flew overhead in a spiralling flight downstream. After all this time, they all knew each other well.

They were all here now, swelling the river. Newman rose to his feet and waded into the waters, now made up entirely of lives, flowing into nothing without shoreline or substance. He lay down, let the current take him, diving deep into the torrent, deeper into a single intention, a single moment.

Some had died, and some had not. Some had had bodies, and some had not. It didn't matter. Now matter didn't matter. They'd done everything, been everywhere. Everywhere was now a tiny place. Whatever it all meant was packed in here with them like toys in a kid's overstuffed closet. They'd done it all except the last thing, the one new thing left: the death of the universe.

All were thinking with a single mind:

It's time to die. No regrets.

They were joyous.

They were joy:

A still point

forgetting

nothing.

And then,

a vast newness, again.